Magnolia Falls

By Alessandro Rede

Magnolia Falls
Copyright © 2025 by Alessandro Rede

ISBN (Paperback): 979-8-9940903-0-5
ISBN (Hardcover): 979-8-9940903-1-2

Published by Alessandro Rede

Cover Design by Alessandro Rede & Thomas Beckford
Interior Design by Alessandro Rede
Edited by Halley Sutton

Printed in the United States of America
First Edition

PROLOGUE

My body shook in nothingness as I slowly came into consciousness. My eyes refused to open but another shaking of my body forced them to unwillingly blink me awake.

It took some time for the darkness to take shape. First the lamp, then the nightstand, eventually the stars and moon outside the window became visible.

Still, I laid still, hoping that I'd soon fall back asleep. However, a small hand on the back of my shoulder once again shook my body awake.

"Mom," my child's voice called, "Mooooooom!"

Finally, I turned in my bed to face him. Nothing could ever prepare me for the most beautiful sight my eyes ever saw. My boy, the most precious, beautiful, thing I'd ever seen. I tried, every time I saw him, to be less dumbstruck with the awe of my boy.

He looked so much like his daddy. Even in the darkness, I could see his dark brown hair curling all over his head. His freckles mimicked the stars outside.

"What's wrong?" I asked in the softest tone I could.

He paused; not sure he should answer me. I felt a lot of frustration at his silence, despite his willingness to wake me. The possibilities became too heavy in my head.

Did he pee on the bed? Did he break something sneaking around the house?

I slowly sat up, my patience getting smaller the quieter he stayed.

When his eyes met mine, I cured myself of ever feeling frustrated with this boy. However, the call to sleep within me made sure the frustration never fully left my body.

"I...I think there's someone outside?" he finally said.

Those words would get any parent to jump up and take action. But not me.

He had done this at least once a week for the past month. Still, I wasn't stupid, much less careless. I'd patrolled the area outside my house many times since he'd first woken me up, all those weeks ago. I found nothing. I even had my best friend, Terry, look all over the place. He found nothing.

My bare feet froze when it hit the cold floor tile. To my despair, my hand instinctively slid along the silk bed sheet, finding nothing.

I hated that every time I woke up in this bed, my hand did that. I hated the habit I developed when I was with Luis. I would always wake up and reach out to feel him. But now that he was gone, I felt nothing. And it hurt every time.

It didn't help that Mateo looked just like him. Every day, there were more and more reminders of his absence.

Looking at my son and the worried face he made, I got myself out of bed, slipped on my slippers, and began to make my way outside.

I told Mateo to sit on the couch and wait. He did so with his wide eyes never breaking contact with me. I refrained from taking any of my weapons with me this time. It was just a waste of effort. Still, I'd never walk out there unprepared, so I did hold my mace tightly out of view of my son. He almost caught me plucking the small keychain out of the key bowl.

Opening the front door, the cold wind immediately made me groan in annoyance of being here once again. I took a couple steps outside, closing the door behind me.

Once again, there was no one out here but it was pretty windy; the cornfields were dancing all in unison, making the song of silence a little less apparent.

Soon grasshoppers started singing and the occasional coyote started howling again.

I made my way to the barn. When I flipped on the light, I was surprised to see the horses were a bit spooked. Raccoons back at it again; they always come back to see what's in here no matter how often I chase them away. I scanned the interior, finding no trace of those trash seekers. Only the small gaps along the wall left any hint of their presence. Regardless, they weren't here now.

I shut the light off and walked back to my house. Entering, I found Mateo waiting right at the door, wide-eyed. Once he saw me enter, he relaxed.

"Nothing," I reported.

His face grew delighted. "Nothing?"

"Nothing," I repeated.

"What if he comes back?"

"Baby," I said, taking a knee, "I just looked outside. There's no one out there."

His eyes darted towards the front window expectantly. He was still very afraid.

I sighed, knowing that he wasn't going to sleep tonight. Which meant that neither was I. I walked over to the TV and slumped down on the couch. I felt around for the remote until my fingers wrapped around it, and I switched the TV on.

I called for my son, who stared at me confused. "Go find a movie."

He smiled but it soon faded when he stared off into the dark hallway where a large cabinet held our collection of DVDs. He looked back at me with a visibly scared expression.

I began the motion of getting up, threatening him that we could also just go back to sleep. At my words, he practically sprinted and disappeared into the darkness and soon emerged holding out the movie *Bambi*.

I smiled. That was Luis's favorite movie as well. I frowned at the thought of Luis, but I rejected those sad thoughts.

I didn't even have to give Mateo directions. He turned on the DVD player and slipped in the movie. He crawled up onto me and soon we were watching the movie. Mateo didn't make it through half of the movie before he was asleep again. I caressed his face, admiring the beauty of my son.

I wanted to turn off the movie; the heavy emphasis of the father figure bothered me a lot. But I didn't want to risk waking up Mateo. It was a shame he'd never truly know his father. I wondered how different things would be if Luis were here.

One day, I'd tell him about his father. Eventually he'd start asking questions, and I'd have to answer. I'd have to tell him why his father wasn't around like the other kids' dads.

Soon the movie credits rolled, and Mateo was well past the point of no return when it came to slumber.

Soon the screen went silent, and it became unbearably clear how alone I was in my home.

It was strange and new, not having Gabby and Miguel here. Even now, the thought of their rooms being empty filled me with dread.

Mateo shifted in my arms. I couldn't imagine how hard it'd been on him. He was just as alone as I was.

I carried him with me as I walked to his bed. I laid him down and gave him a couple more kisses on the cheek.

Staring down at my son, I let a tear flow down my face. The many thoughts of so many people missing in my life in such a short amount of time. The thoughts swelled in my head, pushing more tears out.

I rushed out of Mateo's room and gently closed the door before my cries became verbal and loud. I resisted and successfully only produced a mild sniffle. With that, I pushed down those thoughts and managed to let out a sigh of relief. Other than those tears, I wouldn't be crying tonight.

I could practically hear my bed calling me from downstairs. As quietly as I could, I searched the living room for the TV remote. Once I found it, hiding under the couch no less, I felt around with my fingers looking for the off button. That's when something weird happened.

Standing in the living room, I couldn't help but suddenly face the window. My eyes searched outside, looking for anything that could've caused my sudden alarm and urge to look outside. But I found nothing.

Keeping my eyes on the window, I turned the TV off. The sudden silence chilled me.

Just as I felt the weird feeling, it dissipated.

"There's nothing out there," I said out loud. "Nothing."

CHAPTER 1

"How many of us are there gonna be?" I asked.

My mom let out a tired sigh before saying, "You asked me that question as if you don't know the answer already. Why bother asking?"

"I was just asking," I tried.

"While you're there," she said, holding up a finger, "please say nothing stupid."

I crossed my arms and slumped in my seat like a kid.

I immediately corrected myself when I felt my mom's glare burning through my skull. She was right. I knew who'd be there: my long-time-no-see family, whom I hadn't seen in many years. I was practically going to spend my summer with strangers, and for some reason, my attitude was something in need of correction.

"You're sixteen, Miguel. Act like it," she ordered.

I stared out the window of our red SUV and took in all the empty fields. After a while, I couldn't hold in my urge to correct her.

"I'm seventeen, turning eighteen," I pouted at her.

"Even worse," she answered.

I again crossed my arms and slumped in my seat, and I again corrected myself when I felt Mom glaring at me.

"Please, son, I know it's weird, you haven't seen your cousin in years, and it must feel like you are going to a stranger's house. But you and Mateo used to be like brothers."

So she did understand. Yet she still forced me to spend my summer there. I cursed her out in my thoughts. Although those thoughts soon made me feel guilty and I silently took back every negative thought I had of her.

She was still horrible for this. I hadn't thought about Mateo in a long time. We used to spend all our time together, up until I turned seven, and my mom and I moved to the city. But before then, I remembered times where we'd spend the day playing in the fields and running around in my tía's house, who was the mother of Mateo.

My tía was super cool from what I remembered. She let Mateo and I get away with anything and would even warn us whenever my mom or our grandma was on their way. That was what I remembered of her; she let us be kids.

For the first time in a long time, I thought of my grandmother. I could see her old face with a youthful look in her eyes. Even with my mind conjuring up her image, I had a hard time remembering exactly how she looked. It was like looking at an uncompleted puzzle.

5

A slight bump in the road returned my mind to my current predicament. Of course we were kids and only knew each other at the time. It was stupid for them to think things would be just like that after all this time of pretty much no contact.

Truthfully, however, I was actually excited to see my tía again. My mom was pretty strict; don't get me wrong, I appreciated it. I honestly believed that it made me a better person sometimes. But I couldn't read certain books or play certain video games, at least not when she was around. The worst was that I couldn't date a girl without her approval, which was never. She would act a certain way when she didn't like someone I brought around. And she made it obvious, which wasn't popular with the ladies.

My brow got sore, and I realized just how negative my thoughts were. Even worse, many of them were aimed toward my mom. I relaxed my upper face and faced her. I almost apologized for words I never actually said to her. Still, I felt horrible for how I thought of her just now.

I loved my mom. She was really doing her best. She went out of her way to make what I wanted for dinner whenever she could. She also helped a lot with schoolwork and was my biggest fan whenever I was on the football field.

But if I was being honest, it would've been nice to be off the hook for a while. Relax and get all the stress out of my body. I was sure my mom wouldn't mind not having to worry about an asshole walking around, so I guess it wasn't all bad.

It was just my cousin Mateo—we were practically strangers. It had been years.

From what I remembered about Mateo, he was always sort of the star of the show. He was the one who came up with all those scenarios that we kids would find ourselves in, whether it be battling rogue robots or pretending we were pirates escaping from cursed skeleton-filled ships. He was also always the one to venture further than what was our limit. But that aside, he was also a huge freaking idiot. I recalled times we'd be sneaking around the house for whatever reason, when we were supposed to be in bed. He would always find a way to get caught. He also argued with the adults all the time. I knew when to step back and take the ass-chewing and occasional ass-whooping. Mateo never did. He always fought back. He probably became a troubled child after we left.

But then again, I couldn't have been any better, being that I was always up for whatever he wanted to do.

Another speed bump knocked me outta my thoughts, bringing me back to the harsh realization that we had turned into some kinda path through thick and tall cornfields. I was able to see what looked like endless fields of corn. In the distance, I could see the sun, daring to drop below the Earth. Minutes passed, and up ahead I could see a large all-metal ranch gate. The name "Magnolia Falls" was engraved through the metal.

As we drove through the gateless gate, even more memories ambushed my head, keeping me from noticing our arrival to the house.

The house itself was exactly how I remembered it, big and old. But they had clearly done some work with it, adding double doors and a patio, along with a fresh coat of paint, making the house look more modern than what it truly was. The patio had a couple picnic tables with umbrellas stabbing right through the center. The old barn also looked to be touched up.

My mother and I exchanged a look of quiet impressment. Evidently, we expected the place to be exactly how we remembered it. I almost couldn't believe we never came to visit since we left.

We parked, and my mother told me to start unloading my bags. I did so but before I did, I found myself staring into the cornfields. They stretched so far out; you could get so lost in there. I wondered if it was even possible to start walking from one point and end up at the other. I even noticed how eventually there was a section of wheat fields far off in the distance. Probably belonging to someone else. I remember being forbidden to venture that far when I was a kid.

"It's not ours," she'd say commandingly.

I shook my gaze off of the fields and began to unpack my bags from the car. I had turned to face the house, then hesitated. I really would have rather gone back home. I made a crap-ton of excuses to get out of this and being right outside their house didn't stop me. I planned to beg my mom to let me go home. I'd lie and tell her about a school project that I needed to work on and couldn't work on while I was here. She would, of course, see right through me. I was ready to double down on the lie. Unfortunately, I knew nothing would get her to budge. Mom would never allow it. It was a hopeless dream. So I decided to man up and just get in there.

However, before I could I even take my first step, I heard my name being called by a familiar voice. The front doors swung open and out stepped my tía and cousin.

CHAPTER 2

"Hey dude, it's been a looong while hasn't it?" Mateo greeted me, shaking my hand.

"Sure has, how've you been?" I replied politely.

"It's been good, life's been good. Staying busy, I guess."

"I'm glad to hear that."

After we both sensed the handshake going on for too long, we awkwardly snatched our hands away from one another's.

"How've you been, dude? Anything special or interesting?" I asked. I bit my tongue for repeating the same greeting a second time.

"I'm getting my license soon," he answered enthusiastically. "I'm excited for that."

Mateo beamed a smile at me with pride.

This was undoubtedly Mateo. He had the exact same hair, curly with a middle part. His freckles covered his big cheeks and gently connected along his nose. I didn't know what I was expecting. For some reason, I thought he'd look different from when he was a kid. I thought I wouldn't recognize him, but I immediately did.

Then my tía came in with no warning and just straight up bear-hugged me. I couldn't really resist since she was my aunt and my mom was there. So I took it with a forced yet genuine smile. I was actually quite relieved at her sudden hug; Mateo and I were just about to go in circles greeting each other. My tía's hug became tighter, and I became aware of her surprising strength.

"You're so tall!" she said gleefully. Her voice bounced around in my head, lighting up parts of my brain that had been dark for so long. Her voice was soft and motherly. Yet at the same time, it was high-pitched. When she released me, she pointed at the house.

"Inside," she said, her hand on my shoulder gently pushing me towards the house. I instinctively reached for my luggage, which I dropped on the floor after the bear-hug ambush. However, my tía waved her hand at it and said, "Mateo can help you with the bags and show you to your room later. Please, let's sit and chat first."

I was sorta taken aback by her appearance. She had visibly aged, but she still seemed so youthful. Her hair was bunched up in a messy ponytail, and while her eyes carried a tired weight in them, like most parents, they still sparkled with excitement. Her smile revealed a row of perfect white teeth. From a distance, she could easily be mistaken for someone in her early twenties. Seeing her face brought back so many memories.

I glanced at my mom who had already scooped up Mateo in her arms. Her big giant smile revealed her own youthful features. Of course, her choice of glasses weren't doing her any favors. But she suddenly seemed so full of life. My mom had always just looked like my mom to me. I'd forgotten that she was also a young lady who was still full of life.

"Actually," my mom interrupted, putting Mateo down, "he needs to unpack now. I can't stay long."

The two sisters exchanged a look of sad understanding. My tía turned to her son and gestured for him to help.

I was sorta expecting an exaggeration of a welcome. Like how your grandma treats you when it's been a long time.

"You're not staying?" Mateo asked.

My mom shook her head sadly before explaining, "I have to be back at work by Monday morning. But in two weeks, I'll be back. I'll have some time off to be here with all of you."

Once again, the two sisters exchanged a quiet look of emotion.

My mom had fought so hard to be here. I didn't really understand it then, but it must've been hard to see your sister after so many years—just for it to be a moment.

I could see many emotions on my tía's face. Most of all, I could see on her face how happy she was to have me and my mother back home. She'd always been like this, very relaxed and calm. Maybe it was why she wasn't making a big deal about my mom's short "hi" and "bye." I guess sorta like a cool uncle.

But male figures weren't exactly always in the picture. I never knew my dad, and Mateo never knew his. Either it was cowardly men not wanting to deal with a family, or bad luck.

For example, me and Mateo never met our grandpa. But according to our moms and the little time they knew him, he was a good man. Mom said he was a saint on Earth. Unlike my dad, who left my mom before she even knew she was pregnant.

We entered the house, and I was again surprised by how large it was. I had thought that since it'd been a couple years, it would feel smaller. But it didn't; it felt big. What made this even more strange was how much of the same furniture remained in the home. What was still here seemed to have shrunken. Maybe that was why the house looked bigger. It was as if the walls expanded. Regardless of the familiar furniture, there was equally a large number of modern pieces of furniture, mainly the technology kind. Everything was all up to date, yet, still held that classy vibe to it.

The two main doors led right into the living room that housed a sofa and a La-Z-Boy. And sitting on top of the fireplace was a nice, flat, sleek-looking TV. Made me wonder what model it was. Must've been one of the newer ones.

There was a hallway that seemed to lead into the kitchen and along with that, another hallway that seemed to lead into another part of the house. My memory returned to me, and I immediately knew where it led. It led to the master bedroom and had the laundry room along the way. Other memories flooded my head which led me to take note of how much things had changed. Some of the bigger pieces of furniture from my childhood remained, like an old rocking chair, an ottoman, and a very old China cabinet. But almost everything else had been replaced.

My mom and Tía were chatting, catching up. They made their way into the kitchen where I could hear small laughter. They were so happy to see each other, it honestly made me smile. My mom wasn't a grumpy woman; she was far from it. I made her laugh, and on movie night she often laughed a little too hard at cheesy jokes. She rarely acted like this, though, so playful and giddy, like a fan meeting a celebrity.

I felt a tug on my shirt, after Mateo pulled my attention away from the house and the sisters. He gestured me upstairs. A loud silent awkwardness formed between us.

I followed Mateo up the stairs that were located along the left side of the living room. Once we were up the stairs, I saw again the largeness of the house, a huge living space that also housed a large TV and sofa.

"This is the game room. I play Xbox mostly, but I also got a Wii somewhere if you prefer," Mateo explained to me.

"That's pretty cool. I play Xbox, too. But on a much smaller screen," I said.

"Oh yeah? What do you play?" he asked.

"Mostly shooters and online competitively." After a long awkward pause, I added, "I play other games, too."

"Oh cool." He nodded. "I play shooters too, but not nearly as much as RPGs."

Again, another wave of nostalgia washed over me. I remembered playing games with Mateo till like three in the morning all the time when we were younger. He was always into the more story-driven games, while I loved to compete in the PvP modes. After he finished talking, I once again had nothing to say, leading to more awkward silence. Thankfully, Mateo spun away from me to face the other direction and led the rest of the way to my old room.

That just comes to show how you don't really change interest in things. You just get new ones.

We turned into a hallway that had two room doors across from each other. He turned to the one on the left, opened the door, and entered. I followed him in.

It was almost exactly like my old room. Well, it was my old room. However, things did feel a little smaller, given the bed was no longer a small twin but a queen with additional pillows. Other than that, it was almost exactly the same.

"Y'all didn't do anything to the room?" I asked, setting my bags down.

Mateo shrugged. "Mom always kept it as a guest room." He laid the bag he took from me on the bed, causing the springs to squeal to life.

The new queen-sized bed in the center of the room held the same brown and red covers on it from back in the day.

Mateo placed another one of my duffel bags on my bed and said, "You look like you've never seen this room before."

I found myself sort of staring, looking at everything in the room. I looked back at him and said, "It's just kinda weird, you know? I haven't seen this room in years and when I come back, almost nothing has changed."

Mateo raised his arm, pointing at the bigger bed with his body still facing me and said, "That's new."

I nodded before I looked towards the desk in the corner of the room. The same lamp from my childhood, one with colorful coral reef fish printed on it. "Yeah. But a lot of my old stuff is still here. I mean, it's not exactly the same but it's pretty damn similar."

I pointed to the shelf that lined the side of the window. "Those toys I left here. That's exactly where I forgot them."

"Oh," Mateo said awkwardly. He picked up an old Lego plane I had made as a kid and held it out to me. "You want them back?" he asked.

I couldn't help but laugh. He soon joined and we shared a genuine chuckle. Unfortunately, an awkward silence followed. Thankfully, we both found that funny as well and chucked together again.

"Sorry man," he started, "it's just kind of awkward."

"I know," I agreed.

We both took a moment to appreciate the ice breaker that just happened between us.

11

"Miguel," Mom said from the doorway, scaring the hell outta me.

I did that jump that you do when you get scared and whipped my head around to see my tía and mom standing at the doorway. I put my arm to my chest and began to breathe heavily.

Mateo chuckled in the background and my mom and tía grinned at me.

"Ya me voy, hijo," Mom announced.

My stomach dropped.

"So soon?" I asked.

She gave me a nod. And my tía even looked a little bummed.

We all gathered in the kitchen where my mother and I said our goodbyes and shared a hug. She squeezed me pretty tight, tighter than how I was used to by her, but I didn't mind. I was gonna miss her, too.

Ever since we left this part of Texas and moved into a city, it'd always been me and her—with the exception of close friends and my mom's boyfriends she had over from time to time.

But it'd always sorta been just me and her. With the exception of every other week when I'd have friends over—but that was about it. But even with occasional visits, it'd never not been me and her.

The realization kinda hit me right then and there.

This would be the first time in a really, really, really long time we wouldn't be together. My mom was going to get lonely. I glanced at the familiar strangers I was gonna be staying with. I was gonna get lonely too.

I found myself squeezing her tighter after those thoughts crossed my mind.

After the huge hug, she turned towards her sister and nephew, gave thoughtful goodbyes to them, and I walked with her to her car.

We followed her to the car. After another long hug, and more I love yous, she finally got in the car, looked in the mirror, and looked back at me with a scowl.

"Miguel, I told you not to leave that thing in my car," she barked suddenly.

My face dropped to a frown as the words, "Ohhhh shit," silently left my lips.

Mom hopped out the car and opened the trunk, revealing the dirt bike I had forgotten to unload before we hit the road.

She turned to me and growled, "I have been telling, and telling you, that thing doesn't belong in my car!"

She paused before lecturing me further. She let out a sigh, and her face relaxed. She pulled me in for another hug and whispered, "I

12

don't wanna leave upset with you." She squeezed me with yet another goodbye hug.

"I'm sorry for yelling, hijo," she said after a moment. "I love you, be safe, and behave."

Thankfully, she left with those words and not the ones she'd spoken moments before. After I saw our red SUV disappear in the distance, I turned to face the house. I was also confused that it took her so long to notice that the big blue bike was in there the whole time. I guessed she didn't look in the rear view mirror the whole five and a half hour car ride.

A lot of emotions crossed me. It was nostalgic to be here but also kind of scary. So much had changed. I wasn't the same little kid who was devastated to leave this place. I could hear my mom's car engine and wheels on the path drift more and more away. Once the noise of the car was completely gone, I felt so lonely.

Just until Saturday, I told myself. Next, next Saturday.

CHAPTER 3

After a moment of collecting my thoughts, I took my first step towards the house.

I felt my body tense up just looking at the place where I'd be spending summer break. I'd be outta my comfort zone for a bit. Sure, this place was my childhood—but it's been years. I was not a child anymore. Things weren't gonna be the same. Mom was wrong to bring me here; she believed me and Mateo would be running around the house and fields as we once were. She was wrong.

On my way up the porch stairs something caught my eye. The rows of corn circled the house with the exception of the dirt path leading to and away from us. I focused on that road, watching my mom disappear. Shifting my focus, I could clearly see a spot of corn violently shaking where it stood. I strained my head to look closer, but the movement subsided. I brushed it off as a raccoon looking for trouble. That trouble sure as shit wasn't gonna be me, so I continued my path.

As I walked through the front doors, I was greeted by my tía and cousin. They looked at me, and I could tell that my presence just interrupted a conversation they were having. And I wondered if they were talking about me.

That was when I realized that these guys must also be sharing the same emotions as me. They were as stuck with me for the break as I was with them. Sure, this wasn't exactly the most comforting of thoughts, but it was still a harsh eye opener. I mean, these guys lived here, in an awesome place, in an awesome house. I could be ruining their break, as well.

I felt a sharp stab of guilt impale me. I felt like an asshole for having these thoughts. They didn't ruin my summer break; nobody did. Sure, I hadn't seen them in a while but they were family. Not to mention the amazing childhood they gave me.

I smiled and took a seat on one of the chairs.

"So, Miguel, how have you and your mother been?" my tía asked.

I thought about this question for a bit. There were bad times and good times. But I couldn't help but remember the arguments we had about me staying the week here.

"Uhhh, good," I replied.

My tía raised an eyebrow. "Uh, good?" she repeated mockingly.

I felt my face getting red. And I could even feel my leg tapping the ground. I did that when I got nervous.

"No, I mean, we're good. Nothing bad at all. It's just, we were arguing a lot, prior to coming here. We didn't exactly agree on coming here," I told them. It did take me a second to hear what I was saying. I basically just told them I didn't wanna show up.

"I mean, I wanted my mom to stay here with me," I lied. "I don't like the idea of me being on vacation while she continued to work."

They both looked at each other. Then back at me.

"It also wasn't a—uhhhhh—great surprise that I would be coming here," I stuttered. "My friends and I had made plans that we'd been excited for all semester. Then my mom tells me I'll be staying here, last minute."

Great first impressions, I thought.

"Hey, well, at least you're honest, right?" Mateo said.

Tía gave a sharp glare at Mateo and kicked him.

CHAPTER 4

We talked in the living room for a long time. A couple hours passed by, and I could see that some of the trees turned black as the sun set behind them.

We talked about our lives, and how we lived in a city and how I spent my time. I shared some memories and talked about my friends and old girlfriends and how my mom wouldn't approve of any of them. I told them about my life goals and schools I went to, how I'd dealt with bullying, how my good grades came and went. I told them everything, all about myself and my mom.

And they told me everything—about themselves, about each other, about the farm and their lives. They told me stories about how the horses would escape, about how Mateo learned to ride horses and all the times he got kicked.

It was amazing. We were all laughing and having a good time. My tía brought us drinks and snacks while we talked, and it felt like everything was actually ok.

For the first time since I arrived, I felt relaxed, like maybe I could fall asleep in this house.

"Dude it was so much fun; Trader just wouldn't let her on!" Mateo laughed. "But she just wouldn't stop trying!"

I burst out laughing again, with a bit of chocolate milk spraying outta my mouth.

"Why wouldn't you just stop?! If a horse doesn't want you on its back, it's not gonna let on its back!" I said. "And next time let go of the handle!"

"I don't know what I was doing!" my tía said, pulling her hair out of her face.

She laughed and laughed and showed her age with every giggle. She was still a young woman. "But let's not forget what happened next!" she said.

"Aww no, here it comes," Mateo muttered, rolling his eyes at her.

I looked at her, curious and anxious for the next part of the story.

"I ended up being the only one who can ride that horse," she said proudly. "That animal won't even let Mateo near himself."

"Wait, wait, wait!" I said holding my hands up. "You just skipped to the end."

My tía leaned forward and smugly said, "Well yeah, that's how stories work."

"Well, what happened?" I asked. "How did Trader allow you to ride him?"

"I just wouldn't stop. I wanted to ride him more then he wanted me off. Eventually Trader came to see that he didn't have a say in the matter."

We continued to laugh and chuckle until the light from the sun was completely gone. Several more stories were told. Hours had gone by. And I can admit, I felt pretty stupid for not wanting to come.

My tía had looked out the window, stood up, and told us it was time to call the night.
Then I sorta snapped outta the trance I was in, talking about and in a way embodying my childhood memories that really ran through the day.

I had arrived there on the farm relatively early. Looking back at it, I realized I didn't even check the time, not on my smart phone or my watch.

"Crazy how time flies," Mateo said.

"Yeah, pretty crazy. But it's bedtime. Miguel, the bathroom is the door right next to yours. Do what you gotta do, and then call it quits," my tía said.

Mateo rose from his spot on the sofa and said, "I'll show you where you can put your toothbrush and stuff."

When I got up to follow, Mateo asked me to give him a second and he walked off into the kitchen and left me with my tía.

She turned to me and smiled. "I'm so glad you're here, Miguel."

"Me too," I said. "It's weird being back here. But it feels right, you know?"

"Yeah, I get it. It's been a while since we had our crew back together."

Mateo then entered the sala and gestured me to follow him.

I turned and gave my tía a goodnight hug. She squeezed me tight and whispered, "It's so good to have you back."

After I did my business in the bathroom, I had to fish outta my bag a pair of shorts and a T-shirt, a pair of underwear, and socks.

I was annoyed that I had to go through three bags to get clothes so I ended up throwing my clothes in the closet and its cabinets, putting everything where it belonged.

Another wave of kind memories flew through my body. I remembered digging through this closet looking for clothes to wear on those hot days.

I shut the door and threw myself on the bed.

A nice memory foam bed that I knew for certain wasn't the same spring-powered bed from my childhood.

It's weird how you just know these things. It's weird how memories just linger in the back of your mind and then just pop back up, taking the top spot of images that play in your head.

After I wrapped myself in the soft, thick blanket, and with the rhythmic sound of the cycling fan blowing air on me, I soon fell into a deep, calming sleep.

CHAPTER 5

The morning light impaled the curtains shining on my face. My sleeping body tried to ignore it for as long as possible, but the light inevitably woke me up.

I rose in my bed, sitting up and stretching like crazy.

I stumbled for a bit, doing that 'just woke up' walk that you do when your body is somehow a thousand times heavier in the morning when you wake.

I opened my door and made my way to the bathroom. I enjoyed my morning piss and brushed my teeth. I used some warm water to calm my hair, which looked like a clown's wig.

I walked around the house, and I soon realized that everyone was still asleep. I checked the clock on the microwave. It was 7:50 a.m. exactly.

I felt a sense of awkwardness. I was in a house alone. Sure, it wasn't a stranger's house, but it wasn't my apartment.

With that being said, I stepped out for a while.

On the front patio, I found myself just staring out in the field.

Everything was beautiful. I could even see a couple mountains in the very distance. It all looked like a picture you could see on a computer monitor. Or a painting on a wall.

But something caught my eye.

There was a shift in the corn, and then there was a vibration of corn in the area. It took place within a ten-foot radius...I thought. I wasn't exactly sure. And I wouldn't have seen it if I wasn't paying attention to all the details of the view.

I squinted my eyes, trying to get a look at what could be shifting the corn. Then whatever it was shot to the left at an incredible speed.

Then it stopped, and the wind stopped with it.

I found myself staring at the shifting spot of corn for what felt like an eternity.

Then something slowly began to rise from the cornfields. Something tall and something wrong.

I couldn't move. I couldn't even process what I was looking at. It was a head, but it was hairless and shiny. With no face—in fact, it had no facial features at all. Just a smooth, round oval for a head.

But then it opened its eyes. There were tiny dots of what I assumed were its eyes. They were the reddest red that I'd ever seen. Darker than any crayon, marker, or pencil I'd ever used, but somehow the two spots I was looking at were bright? Not light—somehow, they glowed, enough to glow in the sunlight.

We stared at each other for what seemed like hours. I couldn't stop looking! I couldn't turn away.

Then the front door behind me opened, and the creature instantly sunk back beneath the corn. I saw it take off again in the direction of the sun at an incredible speed that nothing on this Earth could do.

I stood there. Still staring at the spot where it had just been only seconds ago.

What in God's great Earth was that?

I had never seen anything like it. Not from any biology textbooks I'd read, not from any internet video I'd seen.

I felt a hand on my shoulder, and the moment I felt it, I whipped around and screamed.

"Whoa! Whoa! What's wrong, dude!" Mateo asked.

"I don't know," I answered quietly. "There's something out there," I said, pointing towards the spot where I saw the creature.

"Oh yeah. Don't look so spooked, dude, it was our neighbor's dog. He likes to come up here from time to time."

I looked at Mateo. Then I sunk into the rails, exhaling the biggest gust of air I've ever exhaled in my life.

Obviously, it was a dog. What else could it have been? Like, seriously, my morning mind was just playing tricks on me.

"I need some coffee, man, my brain's not fully awake," I said.

"Yeah," he said, "come inside. I'm making some right now."

I followed him inside and into the kitchen, where he poured us both a mug of coffee. He pointed at the fridge and said that if I wanted creamer, it was inside the fridge. I dug it out and unfortunately, it wasn't the hazelnut flavor I was used to at home. It was actually cookie dough. But I didn't mind; it wasn't like they were all that different from each other, anyway. I dumped the sugared liquid into my coffee, took a seat on the kitchen stool, and began to sip the hot liquid.

Mateo joined me, sitting on the La-Z-Boy where I had sat the night before. He turned on the TV and began rummaging through the channels.

While that was happening, I couldn't get that face I saw sticking out of the cornfields outta my head.

It was a smooth, all-black head. Like a balloon, except it was all black and shiny with two glowing red eyes.

But it was a dog. It had to have been a dog; that's what Mateo said it was, and he had to be right, he had to. Nothing else could have explained it.

"I see you guys are up. How'd you sleep, Miguel?" My tía said from behind us.

I was startled and gave a wiggle. "I slept comfortably," I answered.

"That's good," Mateo commented.

"You guys ready for breakfast?" Tía said, walking into the kitchen.

"Sounds good, Mom!"

"Yeah, thanks!"

After a few minutes of silence, Mateo looked at me and asked, "You remember how to ride, right?"

I turned to look at him. "Uhhh—yeah, I think so. It's been a long time since I've done so."

"I could give you a quick lesson if you need to have your memory jogged."

"Yeah, I could use that. That's the plan for today? Horseback riding?"

"Yes and no. We're taking the horses to our neighbors' house."

I grimaced. "Oh yeah? What are they like?" I asked.

Mateo answered, "They're pretty cool. We hang out all the time."

"Mhm."

"They moved here about three and a half years ago," Mateo explained. "Brother and a sister. They're pretty cool, they help me with my chores, and drive me to school."

I smiled at him. And he rolled his eyes at me.

"What's that smile for?" he asked.

"You and this sister a thing?" I teased.

"No, not really. I've known her for a while now, and honestly, I don't think I see her in that way."

I noticed he didn't turn red or even show any type of nervous body language. That meant he was telling the truth.

"She like a sister to you or something?" I asked. "Or does what's-his-face not approve or something?"

"None of that," he stated. "I just don't see her that way. I've got my eyes on this girl in my history class, though."

"Oh yeah?" I said. "Is she hot?"

"Like the sun." Mateo grinned. "What about you? Any special ladies in your life?"

21

I had to stop and think for a moment. There was one girl I knew, Ashly. An attractive black woman in my school, we had a couple classes together freshman and sophomore year, so we became friends. Then good friends, then best friends. I had confessed my feeling towards her this last homecoming.

While she agreed to come with me to the dance, she did reject me. And quite harshly, I might add. She said she didn't see me like that, and was actively pursuing another guy. She, of course, didn't intentionally hurt me. But the friendship didn't last long after that.

I explained to Mateo everything that happened between Ashly and me.

"That sounds about right," he said.

"How do you mean?" I questioned.

"I knew a girl named Amber," he explained. "I thought there was something between us; she informed me that there wasn't. Friendship fell apart soon after that."

"So what's different about this new girl?" I asked.

He took a moment to think before answering. "She seems like she actually gives a shit about me. Like, I'm not the only one doing favors."

"Favors?" I echoed.

"Well, yeah, like, she saves me a seat during lunch. Goes to watch me play, cheers for me. Helps me study."

After a long pause, he said more to himself then to me, "She actually likes me."

"Alright, man, that's deeper than I wanna go," I said sarcastically.

He laughed, a little embarrassed.

A delightful smell of egg and sausage soon filled the room and I damn near floated to the kitchen.

CHAPTER 6

On my way to the beautiful smell of breakfast, a sun ray pierced the window and stabbed me right in the eye. I moved my hand above my face to shield me from the bright sun. Doing so revealed the land outside; the field was as endless as the sky. It made me wonder how the two of them maintained the entire place.

I turned my head away from the window and made eye contact with my tía, she smiled at me before she continued with what she was doing. I thought, I could just ask them. I mean, they were cool about this sort of stuff. They were cool about everything.

"Hey, so how do you guys maintain this place, anyway? I mean, there's a lot of land and there's only two of y'all here. How do y'all do it?"

My tía turned to me, placing a plate full of fluffy scrambled eggs and perfectly cooked and browned bacon in front of me. I was sitting on a bar stool, so I nearly fell off when I realized how great it smelled.

"Well, we really only have to maintain the barn, me and Mateo," she said. "The actual cornfields are managed by workers paid by a company who we sell our goods to."

"This company must really like corn if they willing to do that."

"Yeah, they do so for a majority of the families who live in these areas."

"We?" Mateo said with a full mouth. "Or I maintain the barn, along with our horses?"

My tía shot him a cold stare, and he immediately kept his next comment to himself.

I nearly choked on the eggs I was eating, trying not to laugh.

It was amazing how comfortable I was with these people who I hadn't seen in a while, really amazing.

After breakfast, my tía suggested that Mateo and I take a ride with the horses, an idea I was totally for, and also sort of already had planned. She also told us to be polite with our neighbors, and to have a good time.

I let those old memories of Mateo and I riding the horses sink in. I let the memories run through me like a soft current in a big river.

"So, why'd you get sent here?" Mateo asked as we walked to the barn.

I looked at him, stunned. "Excuse me?"

"Well, I don't know, man, it just kinda seems weird to me, you know? My mom and I haven't heard from you or your mother in years. In a lifetime. Why'd you guys suddenly show up, and why'd your mom make you spend break here with us?"

He looked down at his feet as we walked, almost as if he was ashamed of what he just said. Yet he continued after a short pause.
"Why now?"
I stared at him, because I didn't really know what to say. And to be honest, I wasn't sure how he felt about it. I was sensing that he was somewhat bothered by our actions.
"What do you want me to answer first?" I asked in a soft tone. "If you think we left to spite you, then you're wrong. To be honest, I don't know why we left when we did. And to be honest, I don't know why I'm here now. But I'm glad I am."
"Dude, I'm not mad. I can't speak for my mom, but I'm not mad. But what happened? Why'd y'all leave this place?"
Was my tía upset? I felt a little angry with my mom—she kinda just dumped me here, probably in some kind of attempt to fix a broken relationship.
"Not that my mom's mad or anything. I'm just asking questions, that's all." Mateo choked, trying not to mislead me.
I looked at the path as we walked. It was a stalk that a car had perhaps driven through very often. I looked at the clouds above us, then acknowledged the green around us. And the air was so pure. I knew what Mateo was asking. Why trade this beautiful chunk of earth for a small apartment in a city?
"I can't answer," I said honestly. "We were happy here. We were surrounded by important people, by loving people."
I paused for a moment.
"We simply don't belong here. We simply don't belong to this life." I waved my hands around, gesturing at the farm.
"But you guys could've stayed in touch," Mateo stated.
Even though I stared at the path ahead of us, I felt him looking at me. He waited for a response.
I simply shrugged my shoulders. I didn't know why. I searched my memory and looked for any reason why we didn't stay in touch. But like trying to remember a dream, there were gaps. Gaps in my memories.
I felt his silence.
"I don't know, man. Not to make excuses or anything, but I was too young to really understand. I simply lived here one day, and lived there the next. I vividly remember being sad a few weeks after the move and the culture shock of the move. But after a while, my apartment that I lived in became my home, you know? As I grew older, I began to remember and understand less and less of my years on the farm."
"Yeah, that makes sense." He sighed.

After a few moments of silence, Mateo spoke up again. "Do you think something happened between our moms?"

"I don't know. I'd be lying if I said I'm not thinking it. But you saw how they were. It's not like they were holding grudges towards each other."

"They were happy to see each other. I know what you mean."

Mateo, who was walking slightly ahead of me, came to stop. Seeing him stop, I did the same.

We reached the barn.

CHAPTER 7

Before we entered the barn Mateo turned to me.

"I didn't mean to make things seem awkward between you and me. Nor did I try to call you out or your mom. I was just wondering."

"I know. I've never bothered to think about it, but now that you bring it up, it is an odd situation."

"Would you mind if I asked my mom about it?"

I was surprised that Mateo asked for permission. As if he needed to do so. The situation concerned his mom as much as it did mine. It was just as much his business.

"Dude, you don't need my permission to talk to your mom," I answered. "I'm curious, too."

"I know." He held a hand to the back of his head. "Things are already pretty awkward as-is. Don't get me wrong, it's not like it was when you first got here. It's nice to have you back. I don't wanna make things worse. I probably shouldn't have said anything."

I placed a hand on his shoulder. "It's ok, Mateo. It is a little weird being here. It feels like being with strangers. But yeah, things aren't so weird now. I feel a lot better being here with you guys; we should be able to talk to our moms about it."

Silence followed as our conversation ended. We walked into the barn side by side. The barn was a typical-style barn, the kind of barn you see in movies, with red and brown paint to top it off. It was strange seeing it after so much time. At this point, I was getting used to that feeling.

Mateo reminded and re-taught me how to mount and ride a horse, giving me a few lectures and lessons. Then we let muscle memory do the rest. It was like riding a bicycle; after you learn, you never truly forget. Of course, with a live animal, it's different. Especially one as big and as powerful as a horse.

The horse in particular was a horse by the name of Strawberry Milkshake, named by yours truly. Of course, we just called him Milkshake for short. Mateo and I laughed about the good old days when the topic of this silly name came up, and inevitably it did. We were young, of course, we were young. That was the only other time I'd spent with Mateo.

We had gone out to get ice cream but of course ended up getting milkshakes instead. I got the strawberry milkshake and made the mistake of hanging out with the little horse. The mother horse— whatever her name was, something that I could not remember—

allowed Mateo and me near her young foal, who was soon to be Milkshake. Now, as boys do at young ages, we got into a bit of a rough house, which ended up with me covered in my own strawberry milkshake. Now, being the age that I was at the time I threw a fit, midway through my whining, Milkshake had waddled up to me and in his own way, did me an act of kindness and cleaned me up. He did a terrible job, of course, licking as much of the tasty treat off me as possible. And being the age that we were, we laughed and laughed for the rest of the day. We ended up naming the little foal Strawberry Milkshake. First, we just called him the "milkshake horse," as that was the only way we knew how to identify the horse.

We rode and rode for what seemed to be hours and hours, and yet I was never bored and never felt like I was wasting my time. Riding Milkshake clicked, and I felt like I could do this forever. I felt like I could do this for the rest of my life. I looked towards the star in the sky and let my mind wander in the dream-like state I found myself in. I rode my train of thought through memory lane, picking the best and most relatable stories I could tell Mateo on our ride.

I told him stories of my buddies, stories of my football team, stories of my winning games, stories of my losing games. Mateo shared stories of his own: stories of his girlfriends, and stories of his great escapes from windows of those girlfriends when the crazy father walked in. I found that Mateo seemed to be a bit of ladies' man and a bit of joker.

Of course, I myself wasn't so lucky. I only ever had one girlfriend, a girl by the name of Jenna. The only thing I remembered about her was that she was very good-looking, way out of my league good-looking, but that's the only good thing I remembered out of that relationship. If we weren't making out in the school bathrooms, we were fighting. If we weren't talking, she was off fucking some other guy. At the time, I tried to ignore all of it. But I had to draw the line somewhere. And that's what I did: when she fucked someone on my own bed and in my own home, I damn near grabbed a gun and shot the guy, but he didn't know any more than I did. I broke up with her that night, but I knew she didn't care about any of the yelling I did or the words I said. She just wanted to leave my house and break someone's heart. Of course there was more to the story, so much more that led to the events of her cheating on me. But I didn't find those details important anymore. I just swallowed the pain and moved on.

It took me a while to even consider being attracted to another girl, but in time, I found myself longing for a romantic companion. But I found no luck. I was embarrassed that I couldn't relate to him—that I wasn't a ladies' man like he was. I steered the conversation away from girls and romance, and we began to talk about our versions of the glory days. He spoke of his friends and all the trouble he got into, and I spoke of all the plays I made when I still played football.

After a long yet enjoyable ride, we arrived at the neighbors' house.

CHAPTER 8

The neighbors' house was similar to the house my cousin and tía lived in; almost the same but very different too. On the porch of the house was a set of chairs. After a closer inspection I found that there was a girl on one of those chairs; she sat, leaning back on the chair with her legs on an ottoman reading a book. She looked up at us as we arrived and nodded her head at Mateo, greeting him from a distance.

She had bright blond hair, long curvy limbs, and deep green eyes.

"That's Carly. She's the one I told you about, Lenny's sister." Mateo gestured to her.

I nodded.

I followed Mateo to a hitching stand, and we hitched our horses. We walked up the porch and Mateo introduced me to Carly: "This is my cousin, Miguel." He then turned to me. "And this is Carly."

"Sup," she greeted, nodding her head at me just as she just did with Mateo.

"Hi," I said.

She looked to Mateo. "Lenny's in his room. Go ahead."

She stood up and opened the front door to let me and Mateo in.

On my way in, I thanked her while walking past her.

I took a look around the home, and noticed that they, like my family, had a modern interior, but this home had more of a cabin theme, having polished wood furniture. They even had a collection of deer antlers scattered around the house, and large moose ones too, though not as common as the deer antlers.

I followed Mateo up a set of stairs and into a bedroom. In that bedroom, I found a tall young man who I presumed to be Lenny.

He was tall and husky, with short thick hair that formed into a horn above his forehead. His hair was only a little darker than Carly's hair. Although his physique was manly, you could easily tell how young he was based on his baby face. If Mateo hadn't told me he was about a year and a half older than us, I would've thought he was younger.

He was sitting at a desk using a computer. He appeared to be on some website about the ocean. I saw images of tropical fish and other aquatic life along with some text accompanying it. When he noticed us walking into the room he softly smiled and greeted Mateo with a, "Wassup dude." Before standing and the two exchanged a dap and hug.

Mato turned and gestured towards me. "This is my cousin, Miguel."

I smiled and put my hand up for a wave. Lenny mistook it for a dap as he extended his hand to me. I stared at it awkwardly before understanding what he was offering. I quickly reached out to it, not before he pulled away in his own awkward course correction. This now left my arm out in the open. We awkwardly laughed before preforming the dap and hug properly.

"Sorry about that bro," Lenny apologized.

I shook my head, "No man that's my bad."

All three of us stood in an awkward silence for a moment before Mateo said, "Ok! Moving on!"

Lenny gave a soft chuckle to Mateo before saying to me, "He's told me a lot about you. Welcome back."

"Thanks," I said, "It's great to be back. Although you weren't here last time i was."

"I think they moved in about a year after you guys left." Mateo said. "Not sure exactly when though."

Lenny shrugged his shoulders in agreement.

We talked for maybe thirty minutes, Mateo acting as a middleman, leading the conversations. Eventually, the ice broke, the awkward tension subsided, and soon we were three dudes just chilling and getting along.

Our conversation went from childhood messes we got ourselves into, to girls, and eventually present-day mischiefs.

Which led to Lenny's current conflict.

"So yeah, this dude was trying to sell me weed!" Lenny said, "I told him how I have an off sleep schedule and his response is, 'Hey dude, I have a solution to that!" Lenny paused for comedic timing. Lenny used his best impression of a stoner to say, "Weeeeed, duuuude!'"

"Wait, no way," I started. "This guy tried to sell you weed?"

"Yeah, he totally did!"

"That's crazy, dude, where I come from, nobody ever tried to sell me weed."

Lenny then shifted in his seat. He sat on a large desk chair next to a desk in the corner of his room, while Mateo and I sat on the floor.

Lenny looked up at us. "Have y'all ever been curious?"

Mateo raised an eyebrow. "No manches amigo, you bought some???"

Lenny shook his hands out in front of him. "No way, dude! I'd never buy anything like that. I'm just saying, y'all have never thought of it?"

While I sat there, I did think for a second. Eventually I answered, "No I can't say I have." However, after sitting there for a while and thinking, finally I said, "Well now that I think of it—I am kinda curious now."

"Dude," said Mateo. He looked at me like I just said something stupid. But after a second he turned to Lenny. "You bought some, didn't you?"

Lenny sat up and crossed his arms, "I told you, I'd never ever buy any of that stuff." He paused and with the wheels of his chair, he rolled over to his bed, lifted up the mattress, and pulled out a large bag filled with what looked like chopped up grass. Then he grinned, showing it off to Mateo and me. "But I'm not above stealing it."

CHAPTER 9

After some time, I awoke, a darkness only illuminated by a red lettering in the corner of my vision.

It was an alarm clock. It read 4:57 a.m.

I felt a surge of anger run through my body as I soon realized where I was.

"Hey, hey guys!" I said loudly into the darkness.

I heard movement, sheets being ruffled, and beside me, a body being awoken.

"What's going on?" I heard a deep voice say.

Some more movements took place on the bed and then I heard: "Ah crap, you guys gotta leave."

I had stood up at this point and started kicking the body next to me. "Bro, it's five! Wake your ass up?"

After some time, Mateo rose up, and in what little I could see, I saw he was reading the alarm clock.

"Oh no, dude, it's super late," he said.

"I know, bro, we gotta leave," I said, still in that confusing place sleep leaves you after a sudden wake up.

"Hey, put your shoes on, I'll give y'all a ride home."

"Nah, dude, our horses," I said.

"Oh my god, the horses!" Mateo freaked.

Without missing one more beat of his heart, Mateo rushed outside, and I followed. They were gone. The barn where we had stowed them was empty.

"Oh no, shit!" Mateo yelled. "Where did they go?"

I was cursing under my breath. Out loud I asked, "Would they go home?"

"I don't know? It's been hours? They could be anywhere!"

"Shit dude, what can I do?" Lenny asked. "Let me help you?"

I looked at him and back at Mateo, I waited for someone to have a good idea. I surely didn't have one.

Mateo held his hands on his head. "I'm sure Mom's already looking," he began. "She must've come to get us when we didn't come home when we were supposed to. When she saw the horses weren't in their usual places, she must've gone to go find them."

"You don't think she woulda woke us up to help look?" I asked.

Mateo pointed at the ground. "Well she didn't. Look, come here. There are tire tracks right here." He then looked towards the O'Youngs driveway. "Y'all's parents still outta town?"

"Shouldn't we call her?" I asked. Instinctively, I pulled out my phone and was once again greeted with a black screen.

"Shit." I groaned.

"What?" Mateo asked.

"My phone's dead." I held it up to show him.

Mateo reached into his pocket and pulled out his phone. He stared at it for a moment, I could here him clicking the a button multiple times, perhaps trying to turn it on. Phone in hand, he let his arm drop to his side. "Mine too." He sighed.

Lenny came up to us and offered his cell. "Here, you could use..." He looked down at his devise before he whispered, "What the fuck?"

"What?" Mateo asked.

"Mines dead too." Lenny replied.

My jaw dropped and sarcastically I said, "Seriously? Did none of us charge our phones?"

"No. No. No." Lenny argued, "I did. I took my phone off its charger before I came out here. It was on just a second ago."

I thought back to earlier this morning when my phone, fully charged, didn't turn on. Is this the same thing?

"You're still high." Mateo declared.

Lenny seemed like he wanted to argue but for whatever reason chose not to.

Lenny and Mateo looked back at the tire tracks.

"So are they still out of town?" Mateo repeated.

Lenny nodded but pointed to the tracks. "These aren't knew. They've been there all week, probably from them when they left."

"Ok, so it wasn't their car? Their car ain't even here."

"It was their car, that's what I'm trying to say."

I looked to the driveway—or what I assumed was where they parked their car—and saw it was empty. Next to what I assumed to be Lenny's car was an empty space, with dead grass shaping a large spot on the ground. I looked back to Mateo.

"So what do we do?" I asked, still awaiting instruction.

"Ok. Ok. Ok," Mateo said firmly. "Let's stop wasting time and go find them."

"Where do we go? Where do we look?" I asked.

Mateo looked back at me with his brows furrowed. And in a frustrated and condescending tone, he told me to: "Stop asking me that. I'm figuring it out. Stop just standing there." He then pointed to the spot where we hitched the horses. "The tracks. Do you see them?"

When I looked, I could barely see them. It was dark and what little light that reached us was coming from a house that wasn't surrounded by streetlights.

"Barely. Yeah," I responded.

"We'll just follow the tracks. It's been hours, so they've gone far. If we're lucky, they'd have circled and stayed in the area."

Mateo then looked at Lenny. "Do you think you can drive us?" he asked, pointing to Lenny's small pickup truck.

Lenny, still standing on his porch, jerked his head towards his truck. "Hop in the bed, I'm gonna grab my keys." He turned and rushed into his house.

Mateo and I then made eye contact, and both on cue at the same time, rushed to the bed of Lenny's truck.

After a short time, Lenny came jogging out of his house. He got in the driver's seat and turned on the older vehicle. With a loud rumbling, the truck came to life with a roar, and the headlights flashed on and off a handful of times.

I remembered a conversation we'd had with Lenny about his truck. I recalled him telling me about how every time he turned his truck on, the lights flashed on and off, night or day, for a reason he didn't know. As we began to move, Lenny from the driver's side window stuck his hand out and gave Mateo a flashlight, seemingly to illuminate the trail of tracks where the truck headlights would miss. Mateo started pointing in the direction of the tracks and Lenny followed.

After some time, we began calling the names of the horses to no avail.

I pulled out my phone to check to see if my tía had called me, only to see that the phone was dead. I told this to Mateo, and he pulled out his phone, and saw that he had no messages or calls from his mom.

I raised my eyebrow. "Your mom didn't call you?"

"I guess she didn't," he said, then he just put his phone away in his front left pocket. He looked puzzled but brought himself back to the situation. "Keep calling the horses, I'm going to call my mom later," he instructed.

Only moments later, we found them. It was Lenny who found them. He noticed eyes glowing due to the headlights' glare.

The horses were calm and standing still. Apple, Mateo's horse, allowed Mateo to mount her.

"One down," Lenny said.

34

I looked to Mateo and noticed he was studying the situation.

"We're gonna split up," he said. "You guys stay in the truck and keep following the tracks."

I was confused for a moment. I took the time to notice that the tracks we had been following didn't belong to Mateo's mount.

I turned to Lenny and nodded my head. He returned a nod of his own and we continued our search.

Mateo himself began to search the immediate area. I figured he figured the same thing I did. It was possible that Milkshake was spooked by the truck, where Apple wasn't. Which meant she wasn't far from where we found Apple. However, the tracks still existed and needed to be followed, if that wasn't the case.

It was awkward being stuck with Lenny, a guy I didn't know. There was silence, and every so often, I would shout out for Milkshake. I wished that Mateo was there to act as a middleman. I was sure Lenny felt just as awkward as I did.

I looked at him and decided to take a risk. "You feel as uncomfortable as I do, right?"

He responded, "I do."

A silence filled the air we shared. After a moment I told him, "You know, that does make me feel better."

I looked at him and expected a response. But I saw he had his eyes wider than the sky itself. "What?" I said, trying to see what he did.

"Look! Is that your horse?" he said, pointing at something in the dark and slamming on the brakes at the same time.

I resisted the force of the sudden stop and looked to where he was pointing.

I saw it. I saw what had freaked him so much.

He asked me again: "Is that your horse?"

I didn't answer, I was in pure shock, my jaw was practically dangling near my hips.

Finally, I hopped off the track and approached it. It was Strawberry Milkshake. She was dead. She was in pieces.

CHAPTER 10

I inspected the corpse. It was so mangled and bloody I was surprised we could identify it as Milkshake. But the patterns on her back, the brown spots of fur, were undeniably hers. What few parts of the body that weren't bloody told us this.

I circled her a couple times. The headlights from the truck lit up her poor broken body. As I inspected her, I felt a wave of grief wash over me, water slowly wetting sand on a beach. I recalled early memories of Milkshake when she was small. The first horse I was able to ride when she grew old and big enough. I recalled the fond memories of her training, of her stubborn nature.

My chest felt tight and my legs weak. But I couldn't let grief consume me. Besides, she was just a horse; more would come. None like her would come, but more would come.

I looked at Lenny, who stood close to the carcass. He looked to the ground, studying it. No doubt looking at the hoof prints.

"Dude," he said. "Come look at this." He waved me over to him.

When I stood by his side, I saw what he did. The tracks lead all the way to Milkshake—as if she exploded and collapsed mid-walk. There was no sign of a struggle or fight. The tracks ended where her hooves did.

Lenny was about to speak, but he silenced himself when he heard Mateo riding up.

Mateo took one look at what was left of Milkshake, and he flipped. He immediately turned to Lenny and started cussing him out in español. He dismounted Apple and marched up to Lenny.

He thinks we hit and killed Milkshake, I realized.

"Calm down! I did nothing like that!" Lenny yelled back at Mateo.

"Cabrón! How could you do this?!" Mateo pointed at his horse. "Did you not see her? Are you stupid?"

Lenny tried to defend himself, but Mateo was loud and emotional. I heard both fear and sadness in his voice, obviously due to losing his horse, and the trouble he was inevitably gonna find himself in with his mom.

The argument between the two was getting bad. I had to step in, because at that point, I wouldn't have been surprised if Lenny slapped the holy puto outta Mateo. Mateo was starting to just throw insults all over the place, and based on what I saw on Lenny's face, Lenny was getting sick of it.

"Alright," I said, grabbing Mateo's shirt and yanking him away. "Back it up."

Mateo staggered back. And he instantly directed his emotions towards me once he regained his balance.

But before he said anything, I told him. "You need to calm down!" I pointed at the carcass. "We didn't do this! We found her like this not long before you showed up."

"You mean to tell me she just fucking exploded? Popped like a water balloon?"

"We don't know. We're seeing the same thing you are."

I took a step towards him. "Seriously, look at his truck," I pointed to Lenny's truck. "Not a dent on it. If we had hit a horse half her size, there'd be a dent."

Mateo considered my words for a minute. But he was still pissed. He waved around his body. "So what, a fuckin' tractor ran her over?"

"I don't know, maybe."

Lenny chimed in, "You alright now? Are you done saying all these angry words? Can I finally say what I've been meaning to say?"

Mateo put his hands on his hips and sighed. "What?" Attitude was clear in his voice.

Lenny walked up and stood beside me. "Something killed this horse."

Mateo and I looked at him, both of us wearing confusion on our faces.

"Well, no car hit 'em, or tractor. A car wouldn't do that to her," he circled his hands around Milkshake. "If car was the thing that killed her, it woulda been the force of the impact, whiplash, I think, and a bunch of broken bones."

He stepped closer to Milkshake and after a moment he continued. "No tractor did this, either. If one had run over her, she'd be flat and blood ought to have poured out her like toothpaste."

Lenny looked at Mateo and me with both his eyebrows raised and in a firm voice, he said, "Something tore this poor thing apart."

CHAPTER 11

"How can you tell?" I asked.

"Look at it. The bones are broken, and the skin is ripped," Lenny pointed at the wounds.

Sure enough, everything looked pulled apart.

"How can you be sure?" I asked. "I mean, yeah I see it, but I don't see any claw or bite marks."

Lenny looked back and continued to inspect the carcass. He reached his hands out and almost touched it in an attempt to get a closer look. "I go hunting with my dad a lot. Spent a lot of time in the forest and I've seen quite a lot of dead animals."

"A gun didn't do this." I stated.

"No shit. People aren't the only things hunting animals out there. Ever heard of the ecosystem, genius? Does the food chain ring a bell?"

I immediately felt defensive when he used that condescending tone with me. But the last thing we needed right now was conflict between us. I wanted to say something to defend myself and even insult him back. But even if I was going to do so, I had nothing to say. So I just muttered under my breath, "Dick."

Mateo, with his arms crossed, walked over and repeated my point. "There aren't any claw or bite marks, though. And the only animals that would go out of their way to kill a horse out here would be a pack of wolves. And I'm not an animal genius like you, but I don't think wolves would've left her like this."

"Look, y'all, I know what I'm talking about. I recognize the skin. Something did do this to her. I'm thinking a bear or a pack of coyotes or wolves or something."

Mateo raised his eyebrows and gestured around us. "Out here? There's not even woods close enough? Where would they have come from?"

I took a step back, letting them argue it out. I wasn't confident in my ability to give my opinion. I only knew that a car or tractor couldn't have done this. It just didn't look right.

I listened to them talk it out, trying to solve the mystery of her gruesome death. Personally, I figured that it didn't matter. Milkshake was dead, and we needed to bury her. Regardless of what killed her, we needed to tend to the dead horse in the middle of the cornfields. I knew that the boys were gonna eventually come to the same conclusion I did, and I contemplated telling them this.

Then again, if predators did kill her, or some crazy dude with a crazy tool did it, it was important for them to know. It was important to know what caused her death, because then, we could work on confronting that danger. But whatever could have done this to Milkshake, may very well still be out here.

Right as I turned around to tell the boys what I'd just thought of. I heard a shuffling from within the wall of corn. It was continuing through their talking, and I was the only one who seemed to notice. I did my best to drown out the noise of Mateo and Lenny discussing what animal killed the horse.

And while I wasn't very good at drowning out the noise, to some extent, I was successful. I found myself focusing on the noise and hearing the shuffling in greater detail.

Whatever it was, it was circling us. But when I saw that the exposed path wasn't being crossed, I narrowed it down to whatever it was staying on one side. It was intentionally staying out of sight. It was smart enough to stay within the wall of corn and not show itself.

I also took note that it was walking on two legs. I just barely heard it. I just barely heard one small quiet thump, then another. I could've been wrong, though—I wasn't sure. But there was enough of a pause between the thumps. Unless it was walking on four legs, taking steps in sync.

I turned to the guys. "Listen up."

Mateo was the one who looked at me first, while Lenny was still facing the corpse. So I called him to get his attention as well.

I pointed in the direction of where I heard the shuffling and sure enough, they heard it too. But what made me nervous was that it seemed to be much closer. I didn't even try to focus on it.

"Alright, let's go. We don't know what it is, and we don't have anything to defend ourselves."

Lenny pointed to his truck. "Now hold on. I've got pipe in the back."

"Not good enough. We don't know what it is, let's go!" I was starting to raise my voice in a quiet hushed yell.

They both ignored me, much to my frustration. I was tempted to grab their arms forcefully and talk some harsh sense into them. But the last thing we needed right now was to upset each other. Pathetically, I begged them to leave. "It could've done that to Milkshake! Look at her!"

They both seemed to hear me say that, because they both turned their heads to look at me, then they turned their heads towards the corpse and studied it for a second.

39

Lenny began to make his way towards the truck. Relief filled my body as I followed. I opened the passenger door for Mateo, whom I thought was right behind me, but when I realized he wasn't, I saw that he was still standing where I had last seen him.

"Hey!" I called.

Mateo rolled his eyes and called back, "What?"

I looked to Lenny for help. He was rummaging through some of the junk in the bed of his truck. He seemed to find what he was looking for and hopped out of the bed and started back towards Mateo.

Lenny held what looked like a large pipe. It had a huge bolt at the end and was curved like a crowbar.

They intended to confront it.

At the realization of them confronting the wild animal, I grew impatient and frustrated. I walked up to Lenny, grabbing his arm, and swung him around to face me.

"Listen to me!" I ordered loudly. I pointed to Mateo. "And you listen to me!"

Lenny yanked his arm back and took a few steps back and crossed his arms. Before I could say anything, Lenny spoke up. "Stop being a pussy."

"Or fuck off," Mateo said.

"Fuck you guys! Are y'all stupid?" I yelled out loud, breaking the silence.

The corn, all of a sudden, began to move aggressively, responding to my voice breaking the silence.

All three of us looked towards the noise, and we all flinched in fear.

After a long pause, we heard an earthshaking thump on the opposite side of where we were hearing the movement.

I twisted my body to face in the new direction and I felt my stomach sink.

"The hell!" Lenny yelped. He raised his pipe and took a few steps back. Mateo did the same.

I simply pointed to the truck with the headlights still on.

This time no one argued. We all scrambled towards the truck. My gut told me to get in the truck, but I was compelled to hop in the bed. For some reason, I wanted to see it. I wanted to see what could possibly be running circles around us.

Against my better judgment, I threw myself in the back. Mateo joined me, then Lenny.

It took us a moment to realize that no one actually got in the truck to drive it away. All three of us idiots got in the bed, assuming one of the others was gonna drive.

I felt Lenny roll out of the bed and scramble into the driver's side.

At the same time, me and Mateo were bracing for the quick take off.

Darkness fell on us, surrounding us. The truck headlights died again leaving us at the mercy of whatever was in the void. I felt my eyes grow wide as they searched for anything to cling on to. My stomach twisted and dropped. I would have screamed, but the light returned before I could. Then darkness again, then light, then darkness, then light.

Finally, I heard Lenny scream. I faced Mateo, seeing his eyes grow wide as he spotted something behind me. When darkness surrounded us once more, he screamed. Out of pure instinct, I whipped around to see what it was, what could possibly make these two scream bloody murder—and I wished I had just stayed facing Mateo.

When the lights came back on, it illuminated a large, tall humanoid thing. Everything about it was long: long legs, long arms, a long neck. Hell, its fingers and toes were long. It had smooth, shiny black skin, and the eyes, the eyes were so red, they were almost fuckin' glowing. And it smiled. If it had ears, it would've been smiling from ear to ear in the most literal sense. It almost seemed to stretch in order to be that big of a smile; it was so damn unnatural. It had small sharp teeth, but it was all one row, not individual teeth—like one big tooth that stretched across the mouth. Like a fuckin' child drew the teeth. It looked like this thing had crammed two saw blades into its demonic mouth: one on the upper jaw, one on the bottom jaw.

I tragically took all the details of this damn thing in all at once, even noticing the headlights glinting off the smooth skin.

My head flung forward hitting the roof of the truck as Lenny slammed in reverse.

The pain pulsed through my head for just a moment before adrenaline kicked in.

I composed myself and crouched in the bed to wrap my head around what I just saw. I tried to think of a logical explanation but all I could think to do was grip the rosary that circled my neck.

The little comfort I found in it was enough. Something, anything was more than enough of comfort in the face of this thing.

CHAPTER 12

We all stood in silence. We all stood in the O'Young's living room, no one sitting, no one talking.

The black beady eyes of the multiple mounted heads served as a constant reminder of what we all just witnessed.

After an even longer moment, the sun began to finally show itself.

A moment after that, Lenny spoke. "I'm gonna check on my sister."

Hearing his voice woke me up. I felt my body making sure I was still awake, some part of me hoping to wake up from this nightmare.

"I uhhh, I'm gonna call the police," Mateo said.

When he looked towards me, I simply nodded. "Good idea."

I followed him to the kitchen where he pulled his phone out of his pocket, I asked him to put it on speaker.

Mateo and the operator went back and forth. Mateo explained how there was a tall, crazy man running around the cornfields, killing his horses. I didn't argue, as the operator would've sent men to come arrest us if we explained what we really saw. So tall, crazy man it was.

Eventually Lenny's sister joined us in the living room. Lenny explained that we had seen something in the cornfields, but after I put things together, I learned he did something similar to Mateo: He just told her we had encountered a tall man.

When a sheriff arrived at the house, Lenny and Mateo stepped out to speak to the sheriff. They had asked me to stay in the house and call my tía to come pick us up.

I didn't argue. I didn't feel composed enough to speak to a sheriff right now. I probably would've started crying when he asked me, "What happened?"

So I stayed put and charged my phone. Lenny had also asked his sister to stay in the house. And while she complied, it took some convincing.

After a time, it was just Carly and me in the living room.

We both stood in awkward silence. She, however, didn't seem to notice; she just flopped down on a La-Z-Boy. She flipped the chair and adopted a lazy demeanor.

I had called my tía and, through her obvious frustration, I explained the situation as best I could. I intentionally left out a lot of details, as I intended to let Mateo explain. She'd listen more to her son than nephew.

Carly studied me the whole time. She appeared to be constantly making eye contact. I attempted to ignore her, but she was persistent.

After I was done explaining everything to my tía, and she confirmed she was on her way over to the O'Youngs' house, I hung up and pondered on what the fuck I found myself in. The entire week was probably canceled; when my mom found out about the situation over here, she was sure to show up and take me away.

If I was being honest, I welcomed it. While I had grown fond of this place again, there was some crazy dude running around out there.

I looked out the window and into the sea of corn.

I felt a chill run up my back as the thought of that thing being somewhere in there still crossed my mind.

I turned and studied Mateo and Lenny talking to the sheriff.

He was a tall African-American man. He looked about the same age as my tía. He had a thick, dark, black mustache and had some scruff on the rest of his lower face.

He was also a very well built and strong-looking man, who looked very fed up with the two young boys. As if he could be doing better things.

"Seriously, what's wrong you guys?" Carly asked loudly.

I turned to her, annoyed, and firmly asked her, "What?"

She raised an eyebrow. "What's wrong with you guys? What's got three grown-ass men all freaked out?"

"If you saw some crazy ass dude, naked and big as hell running around out there, at night, in the dark! You wouldn't be freaked out?"

"Well yeah, but y'all are big, too. And my brother's no push over, and neither is Mateo."

She paused and studied me for a few moments. I felt a small hint of insecurity rush through me as she did so.

"You're pretty well-built yourself." She seemed to say this more to herself than to me.

She must've noticed my surprised expression, because she seemed to immediately go back to what she was saying. "The three of you guys could take some junkie," she said.

"You don't know that. What if he knew karate or something? Or had a gun?"

Carly put the chair up and stood, crossing her arms. "Lenny said he was naked, did you not see him?"

43

"No, I did. What I'm saying is, you never know what someone is capable of." I was explaining this while shaking my head. "I mean, we think he killed our horse; he didn't even do that, he fuckin' brutalized it! He fuckin' ripped a grown-ass, big-ass horse apart!"

I caught my fist clenching, and my breathing speeding up. I took a deep breath and calmed myself down. Afterwards, I looked to Carly again and she had wide eyes.

"Lenny didn't tell me a horse was killed," she said and glanced out the windows towards the hitching stick. After a moment, she spoke again in a sad hurt tone. "I've known those horses for a long time."

Dread filled me as well. "Me too," I sighed.

A sort of moment of silence passed. Then Carly turned to me and began again. "Lenny told me he was super deformed. And probably high or drunk out of his mind."

I nodded my head in agreement.

I felt kinda guilty; I felt like I was lying to her. But it also made sense; I saw something that didn't exist. So Lenny, being logical, must've figured that it was some crazy deformation and passed that information to his sister.

I joined Carly in front of the window and studied the scene.

The sheriff looked very annoyed at this point. The expression on his face said it all. His face basically said, "Shut up, you stupid fuckin' kids."

Carly all of a sudden grabbed my shoulders and whipped me around and pulled me close. I almost closed my eyes in anticipation of a kiss. However, the mature part of my brain pulled away. But Carly held me close and tight.

"Hey, whoa, stop!" I cried.

She then let go and flat out said, "Your breath smells like weed."

I choked on my breath and almost shoved her away. In fright, I rushed outside to try and get the boys to back away from the sheriff. If he smelled the weed on them, they'd most definitely be the ones getting arrested as opposed to the crazy, naked, tall dude running around in the cornfields.

That explained the annoyed look on the sheriff; how could I have been so damn stupid? How could they have been so damn stupid to not at least brush their teeth?

But I didn't make it halfway down the porch stairs before the sheriff noticed me and his gaze froze me in my spot.

The sheriff put his hand up to shush the boys' overlapping ramblings.

The boys turned to face me, and embarrassed expressions formed on both their faces.

Really? You assholes are embarrassed on my behalf?

"Come here, son," said the sheriff, waving me towards him.

I wanted to run away but I knew better. I felt like a child who just got caught doing something stupid. It was probably because I *was* a child who was just caught doing something stupid.

I walked awkwardly to the sheriff, stopping at Lenny's side.

The sheriff studied me, looking me up and down. After some time of doing so he finally spoke. "So. What is it?"

"Huh...?" I choked.

"What. Is. It. Boy," he repeated.

I had no answer, and I spoke as if I had no answer. "I...uhhh," I paused and choked on my words even more. "Uhhhhh, I—"

He lifted his hand once more and I immediately silenced myself.

The sheriff pointed to the porch. "You scooted on out here pretty fast. Like you had something to say." He lowered his hand and rested it on his belt. He continued, "So say whatever it is you came out here to say." After he said that, he went silent, waiting for me to answer, never breaking eye contact.

What confidence I had before I met and stood before this man was all gone. Maybe it was his deep voice, maybe it was his killer glare, or even the fact that he was at least six feet five, and super muscular. Whatever it was, I was terrified of him.

I took a second, attempting to collect myself. Only to give a real shitty answer.

"I don't know what to say. I just wanted to see what was happening."

He rolled his eyes. "Bullshit," he said loudly.

"Terry!" a female voice called. "You better not be fucking with my boys!"

We all turned to face the direction of the voice. It was my tía; she arrived on horseback. The horse was clearly the big brute I heard about. The horse itself was bigger than the sheriff.

She came close and positioned the mount close to the sheriff in order to tower over him. But Terry, the sheriff, stood his ground, not seeming intimidated at all.

"Your boys called me. If anything, they're bothering me, Ms. Garza."

My tía, from her mount, eyed Mateo and me. Then she hopped off her mount as if she were skipping a few steps going downstairs.

45

"Porque?" she questioned, walking up to Terry. He towered over her, but she made it very clear how unintimidated she was standing before him.

"Ask your boys," he answered, gesturing towards us, who stood by silently.

She gave the sheriff one last over-the-shoulder glare as she approached us. She then pointed the glare at us, and we all almost stepped back in the gosh damn force of it.

In a super pissed off voice, she growled, "Ok, what the fuck happened?"

CHAPTER 13

We all spoke over each other, mixing and contradicting our lies. Looking back at it, we all should've gotten together and agreed on the same story.

Why not just tell the truth? I squished that thought down as soon as it popped into my head. The truth was, we saw some inhumanly large man out there with glowing red eyes. The truth also was that all three of us smoked weed last night; with that fact, we smelled of weed. No one would believe us. Everyone would think we were just high and hallucinating.

"Ya stop!" My tía barked. She crossed her arms and looked dead at Mateo. "Que paso con mis caballos? Donde están?"

Mateo looked down and a sad expression appeared on his face. "They're gone," he finally answered.

"Where?" my tía pushed.

"They're—" Mateo hesitated, scared to confess to his mom. "They're dead."

I thought of Apple, we never found her dead, but the last time we saw her was with that thing. So she may as well be dead.

Tía got visibly upset at what Mateo said. Her head leaned back, and a long anger-filled sigh left her mouth. "Are you kidding me?" she asked.

"N-no," Mateo answered.

My tía covered her face with both her hands and blurted, "Fuck!" under her breath. "How the hell did this happen?" she questioned.

Mateo flinched but explained to her, "Well, we arrived and hitched them where we always do. Then I introduced Miguel to Lenny and Carly, then we went up to Lenny's room and hung out. A few hours later, Miguel and I were leaving, and they were gone."

"A few hours later, huh?" she echoed. "A few hours? You didn't come home last night! A few hours? Don't you dare lie to me Mateo!"

Mateo stood silently. His mouth opened as if he were ready to argue but he said nothing. The one excuse he had, he couldn't use. But my tía wasn't dumb; she and the sheriff clearly smelled the weed on our breath. Even though I could kinda smell it, because I was searching for the smell, I was aware of it, thanks to Carly. Odds are the boys were, too. If they did, they were playing dumb. If they didn't know they smelled like weed, they were about to find themselves in some deep, deep shit.

"Well?" My tía barked. "Don't just stand there. Say something! Explain yourself!"

Mateo continued to just look at her. He said nothing, only choking on half-baked words, not knowing what to say.

My tía, however, kept stacking the pressure, and dropped the bomb I knew was coming. She uncrossed her arms and placed them on her hips. "Do I have to tell you what happened? Or are you gonna tell me?"

"We fell asleep, Mom! We hung out for a while then we all passed out. We didn't wake up till much later," he blurted.

He was still bouncing around the whole weed thing. I was tempted to just interrupt them and confess the whole weed thing. I mean, they already knew; we were just digging our graves deeper and deeper by lying. Or at least Mateo was. I mean, I knew I might as well confess. I let my feet carry me out here in an attempt to stop us from getting in trouble. And while I didn't have a plan when doing so, I still had to do something—so it might as well be this.

"We got high," I confessed. "We got high on weed and ended up falling asleep. When we woke up, we saw that the horses were gone."

My tía turned her scowl at me, and nodded her head in the way parents do when you're in trouble.

I also felt the gaze of the two boys. Apparently, they didn't put together the fact that we were already caught. Yes, she was pissed cause we caused the death of one of her horses, but that wasn't it. She was mad because we were lying about getting high. We were insanely irresponsible that night.

My tía looked back at her son. "You don't want to tell me the truth? Fine." She turned back to me. "What happened to my horses?"

"Well, we don't know, when we realized they were gone, we went to go find them. We found one. But when we came across Milkshake, she was dead." I paused letting a shiver of ice work its way up my spine. Then I continued. "She was ripped apart. Her bones were snapped, and her skin was torn. We thought it could've been some kind of animal. But then some huge, tall guy showed up out of nowhere. We all freaked out and ran. "

I said all that in one breath. As I was finally taking a deep breath in, my tía questioned me again.

"A tall guy?"

"Yeah, but he didn't look right. He was deformed and clearly crazy."

My tía took a moment and finally said what I was thinking.

"Do you know what I'm gonna say?" she asked.

"Yes, I think so," I answered.

"Then what am I gonna say?"

"You think we were high. I mean, we were, but not so much at this point. You're probably thinking we hallucinated it or something, but we didn't."

"Exactly what I was thinking."

She turned to look at her son and Lenny. "Is what he is saying true?" she said those words, but it sounded more like, "I already knew you idiots were high."

They both nodded their heads, looking quite unhappy with me. But I didn't care. They didn't know it, but I stopped them from digging their graves deeper than they already were.

She looked to the sheriff, who stood behind her quietly. At her gaze he walked up.

"So what do you want to do?" she asked him.

"I want to arrest these boys for smoking an illegal substance," he said firmly, answering her question.

My gut dropped at the thought and realization of actually getting arrested. If my mom wasn't gonna kill me before for smoking weed, she was definitely gonna kill me for getting arrested.

My tía eyed him for a second, then she took a step back and sighed, "Ok."

My knees felt weak and I almost dropped to them when she basically gave him permission to arrest us. But to be fair, we did break the law, and by doing so, resulted in the death and disappearance of her horses.

The sheriff turned to us. But he did nothing. He just stood there, looking conflicted.

What seemed like hours passed as I mentally prepared to be arrested. But eventually the sheriff looked back at my tía, then at us, then at her again.

"I'm not gonna arrest your boys, Sofía," the sheriff finally said.

My tía closed her eyes, showing a visible relief. I, on the other hand, let out a whole sigh of relief.

"No, not your boys. Damn it, not your boys," he said once again. He said it very quietly, almost as if saying it to himself.

"That doesn't mean you're off the hook," he said, immediately going back to his large deep voice. "If I have to come back here for any reason, your asses are going to jail."

He paused again, and for a moment, I felt that he might reconsider his decision and go through with the arrest.

"Let's go see this horse of yours." He sighed.

After another small ass-chewing, we led the sheriff and my tía to where we had found Strawberry Milkshake.

Sure enough, she was still there. Except the smell that was almost minor last time we were here was now horrendous. She was beginning to rot.

"Hoooly fuuck," said the sheriff once he saw the mangled-up carcass.

When my tía saw this, she just stayed silent, no doubt both saddened by the death of her horse and frustrated with the situation.

My tía who was riding the big ol' brute who, I found out after I questioned Mateo, was actually named Brute. Or "The Brute." He told me this with an attitude, no doubt upset with me after I threw him under the bus. Lenny also expressed visible negativity towards me.

But I chose not to be hurt or bothered by this, as I'd be gone soon. And like it had before, years would go by, and I wouldn't have to deal with either of them for a long while.

But my tía had every right to be upset with me. I was just as irresponsible with my mount as Mateo was with his. Lenny, on the other hand, was in deep shit. He was the one who offered, and convinced us to actually try, weed and get high. It was all his fault. And he knew it, but I was the bad guy for telling the truth.

The three of them just stood there, silently. We watched the two go back and forth, mimicking the conversation the three of us had last night.

It was much easier being out there, as opposed to it being dark and nighttime, with the space only being illuminated by the headlights of Lenny's truck. With the daylight, we saw the corpse in much more detail even from where we stood. The sun also probably cooked the flesh, making the smell of decay even worse.

The sheriff and Tía walked up to us and explained the conclusion they came to. They explained that it could've been a bear, or maybe even a pack of stray dogs.

She looked around before landing a glare on Mateo.

"Where's Apple?" She asked.

I hadn't even thought of Apple. I felt horrible knowing that there's a very real possibility that he was killed in the same gruesome way Milkshake was. While I hadn't thought of her since we encountered the tall man, some part of me had hoped she'd made it home. Sadly knowing what my tia just asked, she clearly didn't. Maybe she's still out here somewhere.

After all was said and done, my tia ordered Mateo and me back home. She made us walk back, too, which took us a long ass while. She simply told Lenny to go home.

She followed Mateo and me home on horseback, silence heavy in the air. No one said anything, not until we reached their home.

When we got there, my tía gave us a list of orders. She told us to get some supplies ready as we were gonna retrieve Milkshake, bring her back here, and bury her.

It was all a blur. It all went by so fast. First we dug a grave, then we drove all the way back out there.

We did our best; her body was so broken. It didn't help that she was a big horse. After me and Mateo spend an hour struggling with her, Mateo called Lenny who met us out there. It took all three of us to wrap her up in some sort of cloth—I wasn't sure what it was exactly, maybe some sort of mattress cover—but it didn't matter. It was large enough to cover her whole body.

The hard part was putting her on the flatbed truck. While she was missing parts of her body, she was still heavy. The three of us just couldn't do it.

Despite our efforts for what could've been thirty minutes to an hour, we only managed to get the carcass just a little closer to the truck.

We struggled for so long that Lenny finally made the suggestion to call Mateo's mom and see if there was anything she could offer. Mateo was hesitant at first but ended up calling her and asking for help.

Not long after that, she showed up. Even with the four of us, Little to nothing was accomplished.

This was where I found out something interesting. I saw my tía call Terry, the sheriff. She didn't call 911 and speak to an operator first. No, she called him personally, on what was thought to be his own personal cell phone.

They know each other. On a personal level.

I couldn't help but wonder what their relationship could be. However, it never crossed my mind that it could be a romantic relationship, as the sheriff just didn't seem to appeal to my tía in that way. I could've been wrong, but I doubted it. The fact that I saw him wearing a wedding ring was a good indicator of the lack of romance between them. Perhaps they were friends.

When he arrived, he arrived in civilian clothes, telling me he was off duty for the day.

With his help, we managed to get the horse in the bed. It seemed that he did all the work, since when we all attempted to lift the horse, he was the only one who managed to get it off the ground. He basically dragged the horse in the bed off the truck but at least he got it there.

After all was said and done, he and my tía stepped aside to exchange words.

They were clearly talking about us, Mateo and me, as they kept looking our way and even pointed in our direction.

She was clearly conflicted about me. She was gonna have to call my mom and explain. I contemplated calling her myself and trying to explain. But I wouldn't know what to say.

So like I always did, I did nothing.

Later that day after we had buried StrawberryMilkshake, I collapsed on my bed due to exhaustion. I was certain Mateo must've done the same, as he disappeared into his room as soon as I did, too.

But I was wrong. Mere moments before I fell asleep, Mateo came into my room.

He took a seat on the desk chair.

I sat up straight and waited for him to speak.

"Do you think it's real?" he asked.

I knew what he was talking about. But I almost didn't want to think of it. I turned on the lamp on the nightstand next to my bed.

"I don't know. I mean Lenny said it was some coked-out dude," I answered, "but that's not what I saw."

"Yeah, me neither." Mateo sat silent for a moment. But he eventually continued, "I looked up some crazy, fucked up deformations. Some people can grow up to be wicked tall."

That was all he said for a while. And while I did understand where he was coming from— I mean, I myself have seen videos on the internet showing people growing to freakish lengths—but then what about the skin? The smile? And the eyes?

Perhaps the eyes could be explained as being bloodshot.

Despite trying to rationalize the whole thing, my cousin's voice found its way to my ears.

"Why'd you tell them we got high?" he asked.

I knew he was eventually gonna confront me about it. I was hoping he wouldn't, but knew. However, I looked at him with an eyebrow raised. The question that he had just asked confirmed to me that he, and possibly Lenny, had no clue that our breath stank.

"Our breath," I said firmly. "We smelled like weed, dude."

It was too dark for me to see his facial expression. But the silence told it all.

"And imagine what it all must've looked like to the sheriff and your mom," I continued. "We smelled like weed and all of a sudden, we saw a crazy tall man-monster running around the cornfields. We looked crazy."

His voice poked through my explanation, but I immediately cut him off. I wanted him to hear me.

"On top of that, one of the horses was killed, and who knows what happened to Apple. So, your mom was already pissed. She shows up to your friend's house, pissed off, only to smell weed on us, as if to piss her off more." I paused for just a moment. "Dude, she already knew. Not telling her, keeping it from her—it was only making your mom madder."

Finally, Mateo sighed. "Shit. I never thought to consider how we smelled. I feel like an idiot."

"So, what now?" I asked.

"I don't know," he replied. "My mom's probably gonna call your mom and spill the beans." He shifted in his seat and sighed again. "I'm sorry for being pissy at you all day today."

"It's cool man," I sighed.

Eventually, he left the room, closing my door behind him. Then I heard his bedroom door close. I lay in my bed for some time before eventually turning to my side to sleep. While doing so, I faced the window. I damn near jumped out of my bed when I saw the two glowing red eyes staring back at me.

I wanted to scream but I just sat up and my jaw hung from my face.

My stomach dropped as my brain came to terms with what I was seeing.

It was real. And it was looking at me. It was looking through the glass of the window straight at me.

I knew it was you...

I remembered seeing him earlier that day. Poking his head out of the ocean of corn, watching me, studying me.

I just stood there; I just stared back. It could've been minutes, it could've been hours.

But the thing in the cornfields eventually vanished. It lowered, sinking into the plants.

I sorta wanted to cry. My gut told me to cry. I mean, every single idea of what humanity considers a monster under your bed, boogie man—it turned out it was real. And I had just had a staring contest with it.

I just sat down on my bed for about thirty more minutes just thinking about it.

Despite all my thoughts and my temptation to act. I did nothing. So I closed my eyes and tried to sleep. I failed.

Suddenly my door opened. I was startled but it was Mateo.

"I can't sleep," was all he said to me.

"Me neither," I responded.

I was going to say something about what I had just saw, but he spoke before I did.

"You remember *Resident Evil 5*?" Mateo asked

I was caught off by this random question. "Yeah," I answered. "I remember."

"Let's play it," he suggested.

My first instinct was to decline. Make some excuse as to why I couldn't. But given the fact that I wasn't gonna sleep that night, and had nothing better to do, I decided to join him.

Resident Evil was a video game franchise, specifically a zombie video game franchise. Mateo and I played the fifth installment when it came out many years ago. We played together, shooting zombies and having a good old time.

I'd since come to play the other sequels that would eventually come out, only I played those alone, since we moved when those games came out.

I didn't even know that I missed playing games with Mateo. It wasn't until I sat next to him and played the game that I remembered how awesome a time we'd had.

We still had the memories of the thing in the cornfields in our minds. But it soon faded with a nostalgic video game session.

We laughed over victories, argued over losses, and competed over ammo. As kids, you didn't really think about things like that. You just played. I mean, of course you still argued, laughed, and competed. But it was different. As young adults, you cussed more, said things. It was a different experience; you laughed for different reasons.

I didn't recall how long we played for, but eventually we went to sleep—with no monster in our heads.

CHAPTER 14

In the morning, I considered staying in my bed. I didn't want to confront my tía and the fact that she must've spoken to my mom at some point.

I checked my phone, expecting texts and missed calls from my mom. But I saw nothing. A few notifications from social media, but nothing from my mom.

A rush of relief flew through me. My tía hadn't called my mom yet. Dread soon replaced that relief, as it was only a matter of time before she did.

I took my time waking up and getting ready. I brushed my teeth and took a shower.

I shoved all of last night deep down, refusing to think of it. I told myself it was a dream, a messed-up dream. It had to be. Because things like that didn't exist.

Forcing my thoughts to remain on the current situation, I eventually went back into my room and flopped back onto my bed

I pulled my laptop out of a yet to be opened duffle bag. I turned it on and started surfing the web, landing on Reddit and 4Chan. Perhaps I was looking for answers without knowing it, as I felt myself searching for something, without actually searching for it. Thankfully, after some time passed, I heard a knock on my door.

It creaked open and in stepped Mateo.

"Hey, uhhh," he began, "my mom wants to talk."

I rolled over and sat up on my bed. "Ok," I replied.

I figured that the two of them were already awake and must've heard me waking up. I let Mateo leave my room as I sat there for a few long seconds.

This was it. This was when I dealt with the consequences of my actions. I wondered what she was gonna say to me. I wondered if she was gonna give me any credit at all for telling the truth and spilling the beans.

I didn't want to deal with any of it. I just knew I was gonna get an unfair lecture. I mean, she had to know that Mateo and I weren't to blame. We weren't the ones who stole the weed and offered it to others.

I had to fight tooth and nail to not make some kind of shitty excuse to not go downstairs. I knew I had to eventually, but I just didn't want to deal with it.

I decided to compromise. On my way downstairs, I called out, "Hey, you guys give me a minute I need to use the restroom."

And that's what I did. I went into the bathroom, locked the door, and just stood there.

My thoughts swirled in my head. I allowed the worst-case scenario to run through my brain. I mean, this was the worst-case scenario: I was caught smoking weed. If my mom asked me to do anything in this life, it was to stay away from things like that.

Running out of excuses, I dropped my pants in a pathetic attempt to buy myself more time by reliving myself. Eventually I realized just how stupid I must've looked just standing in my cousin's bathroom holding myself. I suddenly became very aware of how much time had passed with me in this bathroom. I flushed the empty toilet in hopes that if they were suspicious of my prolonged trip to the bathroom, at least they could believe I was actually using it. However as soon as I stepped out of the restroom, I cringed at just how weird and obvious this whole thing was. I now hustled towards my family downstairs in order to avoid overthinking again.

I took a seat on the couch and prepared myself for the lecture. Mateo entered the room and too a seat next to me. My tia sat on the lazy boy across from us.

"Buenos dias," My tía said with a smirk. "You don't look very well."

"Yeah, well, I don't feel very well," I said.

Crossing her legs, she spoke. "You look like you already know what I'm gonna say. You look like you don't want to hear it."

She was right, I didn't want to hear it. I did try and hide it, but I knew better. Moms always know, and she was a mom.

Silence took its time making its way through the room. I did try and find some solace in the idea that I'd be going home soon. It sucked that it was happening like this, but since I've gotten here, I've wanted nothing but to go home.

"Well, I'll be happy to disappoint you. I won't be calling your mother." My tia announced.

I almost let a smile break through onto my face. But I didn't let it. I was more dumbfounded than happy, which helped.

"May I ask why?" Once I heard the words leave my mouth, I felt like the fool I was for saying them.

"Well, if you must know," she began, "I really want this to work." She circled her pointer finger around the room, gesturing towards the three of us.

I didn't understand what she meant by that. So I asked her, "What do you mean?"

"Well," she paused for a second, "I missed you and your mother. Your mom and I have been trying to get us all to reconnect for a long time, we have an incredible bond. And it sucks that we never spend time together."

My heart warmed. My tía's words hit me like bricks, and I felt like a prick for not wanting to be here.

"Now, I understand that things are different, you're not the kid who left us years ago. You're now a young man. But that doesn't mean things can't be like how they used to."

"I miss those days, too," I said.

"Me too," Mateo added.

"I'm not gonna sit here and pretend like you guys didn't do what you guys did. One of my horses is dead, another is missing. But I'm willing to move past it for now." She then looked at me. "Now, Miguel, if you want to go home, that's ok. I can call your mom and ask her to come get you. And I won't tell her what you did, I'll just make something up."

With her question I felt like an asshole. I actually considered the option.

Part of me really wanted to say yes! To go home so I could be in my own bed, with my own stuff, and my own shower.

Was that selfish of me? Was it selfish that I wanted to go home?

I wanted to ponder that for a few moments before I made my decision. It seemed like I already made it, but I wanted to at least give myself time to be absolutely one hundred percent sure. What would happen? Would me agreeing cause a further separation between all of us? We could always try again, right? Maybe they could come over for the holidays. Maybe it would be another thousand years before we see each other again.

My stomach turned at the thought of not seeing them for another long time. I knew then, that wasn't what I wanted.

"Why? I thought you were mad at us?" I asked.

"I am upset with you," She said in her mom voice. She then turned to Mateo. "And I'm upset with you."

Mateo's head dropped and he sighed, "I know."

"As for why," she stated, "I was young once, too. I get that y'all are curious and want to experience things. And that's ok, as long as you're careful. But you boys were not careful. There were consequences for that. And as long as it doesn't become a habit, I'd like to move past it."

Well shit, I already wanted to try some again. The bliss of weed was awfully tempting after you'd already tried it, although the thought of becoming one of those loser potheads was scary. Now, if I could rap or was a good actor, I wouldn't mind. But I had no such talents to speak of, so I'd save becoming a pothead for later.

I was yanked out of my thoughts when Mateo apologized for the entire thing. I soon gave an apology of my own.

"You guys are too old to be apologizing to me like you guys are five-year-old." My tía explained, "You jerks are blaming Lenny, as if he forced the weed down y'all's throats. He offered, you accepted."

I wanted to argue, but she was right. But did Lenny have to offer us weed? I mean, it was still his fault for stealing it and giving it to us.

However, despite my thoughts, I stayed quiet.

My tía stood up, visibly frustrated, and began again. "Boys, I'm not upset that you guys smoked weed. I'm upset that you guys smoked weed, by doing so, neglected the horses, and then lied about it."

She threw her arms up and sighed. Mateo seemed to lean back in his chair, getting comfortable.

Aw, crap, we're gonna be here a while.

"And if it was any other policeman who showed up, you guys would've been arrested. You know why you guys would've been arrested? Because weed isn't legal here."

"How do you know him?" I asked. My mouth spoke without asking my brain for permission.

She jerked her head towards me, wide-eyed. Not from embarrassment or nervousness like I'd hoped, but as a surprise.

"What the hell does that matter?" she asked. She seemed to be waiting for an answer from me. But I had nothing.

"I mean," I started, "lucky us that you did know him, right? Otherwise, we would've been arrested."

"Yup, I just said that."

"I mean, like, he clearly wanted to arrest us. But he didn't."

My tía still glared at me. Waiting for me to say something she didn't already say.

"So I'm just curious. How do you guys know each other?" I asked.

"Miguel," my tía said, "who the hell cares?"

I sat there, stunned for a moment at the sudden raise in her tone.

"I'm short two horses! And you're asking about my relationship with the sheriff?" She paced the room and sighed. "I feel like I'm talking to a wall."

I flinched hearing that from her. My mom often said the same thing when I got a lecture from her. The thing is, when I successfully got her to talk about something else, she often cooled off and let me off the hook. Granted, I wasn't often successful doing this, but it did work sometimes.

"Now, I'm going to ask you if you understand. If you really do understand why I'm upset, you simply say so." She turned to face Mateo. "Tu tambien."

"I understand," Mateo and I answered together.

"Good," my tía replied.

She then sat down and released her frustration in a long deep sigh. "I really want you to stay for the break," my tía said. "But after all that's happened, I'd understand if you want to go."

I immediately got excited, the thought of going home made me so happy.

I was just about ready to make some sorry-ass excuse as to why I wanted to go home. I was thinking something along the lines of being homesick, or forgetting about a project I didn't do, and needed to do at home.

Right as I was about to do so, I looked at my tía. Her face was still stuck in mom-mode. But in her eyes, deep in her eyes I could barely see a glimpse of…sadness? No, was it nervousness?

She genuinely wanted me to stay. She genuinely wanted our family to spend more time around each other.

I looked to Mateo, and he locked his face in "I'm caught" mode.

But when we made eye contact, he relaxed. He then said, "Look, man, you should stay."

Which surprised me. I assumed that Mateo wanted me out of his house as much as I did. "Do you guys want me to stay?"

"Yes," My tía replied. "I miss the way things used to be. I don't want us to drift apart like most families do. Your mother feels the same."

I felt a surge of anger run along my skin. All of a sudden, I was emotional, I was both happy and angry at the idea of it all.

"Why now?" I asked. "After all these years?"

"Because it's still not too late," my tía answered immediately.

"Yeah, mom," Mateo chimed in. "Why now?"

Mateo's sudden words reminded me that he and I were still on the same page of us wanting me out of there. Despite his previous words.

I chose not to be hurt by his words. I'd want him out of my house if he just all of a sudden showed up out of nowhere.

My tía took a seat in the La-Z-Boy to face Mateo and me.

"Well," she began, "for years, your mother and I have been trying to stay more connected. But it's gotten harder and harder. When your mother got the job she's always dreamed of, we both couldn't have been happier for her. She was gonna be a Broadway star!" She paused to find words. "But of course it required her to leave us. Then I finished college and became an accountant. To put it simply, we were just too busy for each other. We talked on occasion, but we were living separate lives." My tía looked up at us. "And you two were growing up, too. You boys needed attention, as well. That took even more time out of our lives."

Mateo and I exchanged glances.

"With my Gaby writing and directing for Broadway, and me with my clients and the farm," my tía paused for a few seconds, "I don't remember when exactly, but we just stopped speaking to each other."

My brain attempted to make sense of this. I was convinced that there had to be more. There had to be more to the story than just "stopped talking to each other."

"And that's it?" I asked. "You guys just stopped talking."

My tía nodded sadly.

"There was nothing?" Mateo asked. "You guys didn't fight or anything?"

My tía looked at him, surprised. "Of course not," she said. "We never argued about anything." She paused for a second then chuckled. "Well, we did compete a little on who had the best kiddo running around."

"I'm sorry," I said, "I don't believe you."

She then turned and looked to me surprised. "Why do you feel that way?"

"How can two people who loved each other so much just stop talking?"

"You guys stopped talking?" she said.

"What?" We asked in sync.

"Yeah," she started. "You boys kept in touch for a while yourselves. But you two stopped talking to each other years before my sister and I."

60

"Tía, I didn't have a phone then," I told her.

She looked up at me surprised. "Yeah, you did, you don't remember?" she asked. "It was an older flip phone, but it worked." She pointed at Mateo. "I know you remember, you still have yours."

I looked over at Mateo and he looked back at me. He didn't say anything, but he nodded. "What? No way."

"No, yeah, I still have it. But I don't remember using it, I mean I'm sure I did, but I don't remember the conversations."

"Well after you stopped talking to Miguel, I stopped paying for it," my tía said.

"I don't remember even having a phone," I announced.

"You were still young," she said. "You two had to come to me and your mother if you ever wanted to use them."

An image flashed in my head, an image of my mom handing me a phone. *Was that it?* I asked myself, *was that the phone?*

"Holy shit," I swore. "I remember."

My tía nodded her head. "We tried to get you two to keep talking when we realized that you guys weren't doing so as much." Said my tía, "But as you guys grew up, you simply became less interested in doing so." She eyeballed Mateo. "Like how you became more interested in that game of yours."

I smiled, I was guilty of that exact same thing. And she was right. I'm sure that as I got older, I become more interested in girls and impressing my friends.

I also realized she was right. My mom was a very busy woman. While yes, she made time for me, she made time for not much else. It was rare when I saw her relax. And when I did see Mom relax, it was her watching her weird sitcom Netflix shows and movies. I didn't remember seeing her on the phone with Tía Sofía. Not till a few weeks ago, when one of them finally reached out, I don't know who, and all of a sudden, my mom was on the phone with her all the time. I was honestly annoyed by it, all that catching up and yapping all the time. But seeing how sad my tía looked while talking about it, it made me realize how happy and excited my mom looked to be talking to her sister.

"To answer your question," Tía said while looking at me, "when your mom reached out to me, we immediately wanted to see each other again. We also wanted you boys to see each other again."

Mateo and I exchanged glances.

On one hand, I missed my home. I missed my mom, and I missed my friends. On the other hand, I could spend some time with my tía and cousin. Two people who, while I may not have known it, I missed deeply.

Memories flashed through my head, memories of my cousin and I fooling around, and my tía and mom taking such good care of us.

So I stayed. I told my tía that I was willing to stay with them for the break. And she looked genuinely happy.

Seeing her happy made me happy.

"Ok," she said. "Well, I'm glad that you've decided to stay."

I nodded.

She stood up and walked over to the kitchen. She poured herself a cup of coffee. "Mateo," she called.

Mateo perked up and called back, "Yeah?"

"Whatever happened to Apple?" she asked entering the room.

Mateo shrugged his shoulders. "I don't know, when we saw the man, we ran. I didn't see where Apple went."

When Mateo mentioned the thing in the cornfields, I felt my stomach twist with fear. I flexed my stomach, forcing the fear out of my body.

"I need you to go look for her," my tía said. "If you can't find her, come back and let me know."

Her tone was a strange mix of both motherly order, and anxious young mother.

Mateo and I exchanged glances. We both were clearly hesitant to back into the cornfields.

"But what about the guy?" Mateo asked.

"Sheriff Terry told me he didn't find anything," my tía replied. "So you should be fine."

Mateo wanted to argue and part of me wanted to argue, too. But when a mom just finished chewing your ass out, you don't say shit.

Mateo and I had a small argument; he had to convince me to go with him. I argued that my tía didn't ask me, she asked him.

"That's the most shitty thing ever, bro!" Mateo yelled.

"Fuck you! I ain't going back out there!" I yelled back.

"Fine," he said. "Let me go ask her and make sure she's just sending me."

He knew very well that I knew that she did in fact mean both of us to go, so to avoid humiliation, I agreed to join him.

"Fine!" I called. "I'll go with you."

"Yeah, that's what I thought!"

We took our time getting ready. Since we didn't get permission to take another horse or use a vehicle, I figured I'd be doing a lot of walking, so I made sure to wear my comfortable boots, and a breathable t-shirt and jeans. I debated on wearing shorts, but the ones I packed weren't very flexible, and restricted a lot of movement.

Mateo's mom was still pretty upset with us. But regardless, she still made us breakfast and sent us on our way.

She really did remind me of my mother. My mom, contrary to what I felt sometimes, had a hard time staying mad at me. When I looked back at my mom, I couldn't help but feel bad for all the crap I put her through.

I then felt worse that it took me pulling some shit with my aunt to see how shitty a son I could be. Why was it that when we're around people who aren't our immediate loved ones, we tend to pay more attention to ourselves? Maybe it's because we're comfortable with them.

Or maybe it's because I know I'll get away with it, I thought.

As Mateo and I reached the edge of the cornfields we paused. We also exchanged glances.

I cursed my tía in my head. Her tone when she ordered Mateo and me to find Apple was so casual, and borderline condescending. She spoke calmly, but also with an attitude of knowing that Mateo and I were listening. She was completely the opposite of my mom, whose tone when ordering me was strict and firm and loud.

Mateo unexpectedly walked forward into the cornfields, which pulled me out of my thoughts.

I hesitated for a few moments.

I grabbed Mateo and pulled him towards me.

"Let's talk to your mom," I said.

"Dude, come on, we have to find this animal."

There was a slight moment of silence between us.

"What if we find a carcass again?" I asked him.

He seemed to listen to that. His eyes grew wide in the slightest way. So I used the events of that night to push him into getting out of going out there.

"What if we run into-" I paused, "-run into that thing out here."

He stayed silent, clearly thinking about it.

"We won't even have a car to drive away if we run into the thing."

He stepped back and I let go of his shoulder.

He released a sigh before simply saying, "Dude."

"What? You're not scared of what is out there?" I said loudly, pointing behind him.

"I am but we don't have a choice!"

"The hell we don't!"

Mateo then put his hand upward and I finished my sentence.

"I asked my mom about the sheriff." Mateo lowered his voice and shrugged his shoulders. "He came out here this morning and he didn't find anything."

Images of that night flashed through my mind. I opened my mouth to argue, but Mateo spoke up first.

"Stop being such a pussy!"

The words cut like knives. And I got defensive immediately. "I'm not a pussy!"

He stepped back and turned walking into the cornfields.

"Well, come on then," he said.

CHAPTER 15

My frustration grew. I was not gonna go back in those damn cornfields.

I almost wanted to beg Mateo to see reason. But my pride wasn't gonna allow it.

"I think I saw it last night," I told him sternly.

He paused in his tracks and looked back at me. His expression wasn't exactly a fearful one, but I definitely got his attention. Realizing that I did catch his attention, I felt a surge of relief flow throw me.

"I looked out the window last night and I'm sure I saw it."

Mateo studied me for a few moments. His attentive expression didn't change.

"Ok," he said. "So?"

I became annoyed that he wasn't budging. He was stubborn. "What do you mean 'so'?" I blurted in frustration.

"It was probably just a dream, dude," Mateo said. "And Mom said that the sheriff didn't find anything."

"No, screw that!" I almost shouted. "I know what I saw, I was awake and I'm not going b—"

Mateo grabbed me by my shoulders and shook me for a half a second. "Seriously!" he shouted. "Calm down."

I got defensive again and pushed him off me. I opened my mouth to speak but before I could, Mateo pointed a finger at me and said loudly, "No! Don't speak!"

Out of instinct, I silenced myself, hating that I did so.

Mateo lowered his arm and sighed. "If you don't want to come with me, that's fine." He raised an eyebrow. "But you're gonna have to be a pussy alone."

I got angry but I had nothing to say.

With that, Mateo turned and walked into the cornfields.

I looked around and called back to him, "We wouldn't even find her here. We lost her way over by your friends' house."

Mateo whipped around and said, "Exactly!" He held both of his fist to his head as they shook in frustration. "We run around here for an hour, then we go back and say we didn't find anything!"

"Now you're being a pussy!" I shouted.

"I'm being smart!"

I exaggerated my jaw dropping and made my eyebrows go as far up as they could. I also raised my arms.

"You dipshit!" I said. "You're scared, too!"

"The hell I am!" he responded.

"I can't believe you called me pussy!" I pointed at his crotch. "You're a pussy! Look! You got a bigger pussy than me!"

"Fuck yourself!"

"Ahhhh, look, you're dripping, your pussy is so big!"

"I ain't got no pussy!"

"BAAAAARRRRRM!"

Mateo and I both jumped and screamed at the same time.

I heard laughing as I tried to look around to see what the hell was going on. My head tracked the laughing down to two people, Carly and Lenny. Anger and embarrassment soon replaced my fear.

"You two fuckers are both scared!" Carly called from the bed of the truck. She began to laugh again.

Lenny, who was in the driver's seat, stopped laughing. His smile lingered, however.

I looked over to see Mateo and he himself was in frustrated shock. When he turned to look at me, and eye contact was made, a sudden grin from his face activated a grin from mine. Then me and Mateo laughed. Not as hard as Carly, but a good chuckle.

Carly hopped off the bed of the truck and Lenny made his way out of the driver's seat.

I took an awful note of Carly. She wore short shorts, and a tank top. I didn't notice before, but now I couldn't help but notice how attractive she was. When she made eye contact with me, I darted my eyes away.

I looked to Lenny, who was still smiling. I was pretty irritated with him, being that it was him who honked the horn, causing Mateo and me to jump and scream.

"Were y'all arguing about which one of y'all wasn't a huge pussy?" Lenny asked.

I didn't say anything. I felt that arguing wasn't a good idea. The fact was that that's exactly what we were arguing about.

"What's going on?" asked Mateo. "Why are y'all here?"

Carly perked up, "We have one of y'all's horses."

The three of us boys looked in her direction.

"You serious?" Mateo asked.

"Yeah, when I woke up I found 'em walking around our property."

"Great," I said. "Let's go get her."

"Let's go," Lenny said, gesturing to his truck.

CHAPTER 16

After the drive, sure enough, we got our horse. Carly filled us in on how she managed to hitch the horse in its usual place.

"How come you didn't just ride her to our house?" I asked her.

"She wouldn't let me or Lenny close. He'd start freaking out whenever I'd try to mount her," she answered.

Mateo and I exchanged a glance. For whatever reason, or at least a reason I didn't understand, the horses only let either Mateo or my tía mount them, unless one of the two was around to assist in someone else mounting them.

Mateo approached the horse and hopped on without any issues.

I glanced at Carly, who looked impressed. A rush of jealousy ran through me.

I shoved those thoughts down, before it began to bother me.

"Ok, let's head back," Mateo ordered.

I nodded.

Lenny offered to drive me back and I accepted. We hopped in the truck with me in the passenger seat. As I was nudging my butt into the seat, a tug on my sleeve stole my attention.

I looked to the right and found Carly. She had a sassy look on her face.

"Yeah?" I asked.

"Scoot over!" she demanded, still carrying that smug look.

I didn't want to scooch all the way next to Lenny; it would've been awkward sitting hip to hip next to someone I didn't know super well. But I wasn't about to pass up an opportunity to sit next to Carly.

"Alright," I answered.

I turned my body to get out of the truck so that she could sit hip to hip with her brother.

To my surprise, she immediately began crawling over me saying, "You're taking too long!"

I felt all kinds of shit as she basically dragged her body over mine. It didn't help that inside the truck was a cramped space.

In my shock of her sitting on my lap for just a second, I managed to squeeze out, "What are you doing?"

When she eventually thumped her butt on the space between me and Lenny, she turned and said, "Taking a seat, duh."

Her smirk never left.

I studied the image of her smirk. Was it either an *"I'm toying with you"* smirk, or a *"Gosh, I'm so much better than this guy"* smirk.

I tried not to think about it. Once again, I shoved that thought out of my mind replacing it with others.

"You know," Lenny began. "What we saw last night,"

I shot him a look. I was stunned. I had for a brief moment forgot about that thing, when I saw how Carly was looking at me. She was looking at me as if I was the one who said something. Except what I said was something completely outlandish.

I corrected my stunned face and replied, "Sure?"

"The sheriff didn't find anything," Lenny said.

I felt kinda angry. More like annoyed.

The fact was, three of us saw it. Yet no one, not even the three of us who saw the thing, wanted to admit what we'd seen.

At least Mateo mentioned that it could've been a person with a huge deformation, and was freakishly tall. But even Mateo gave me the impression that he wanted to ignore it. Just forget that it happened.

"My tía told me," I responded.

Lenny took his eyes off me and put them on the path. Mateo, who was riding his horse, gestured Lenny to follow him.

Lenny did follow him. We matched Mateo's speed, but stayed behind him.

"I don't believe the sheriff," Lenny announced.

I couldn't explain why, but I was so relieved to hear that—to hear someone admit and tell me that we might've still been in danger.

"You don't?" I asked. "Why?"

Lenny kept his eyes on Mateo, but he furrowed his brow so I could tell he was thinking. "I mean," he started, "I believe the sheriff didn't find anything."

He stayed silent for a few moments.

I got the impression he was gonna stay quiet and not say anything, so I vocalized, "Buuuut?"

"But," he said sharply, "I think it's still out there."

I damn near wanted to fist pump the air. Finally, someone said what I wanted to hear. Mateo might've thought that it was still out there, but he wasn't gonna say it. Lenny, for whatever reason, was admitting it. Saying what we're all thinking.

"You guys are crazy," Carly said.

"What?" I asked.

She turned to me. "Oh, I'm sorry, let me repeat myself, louder so you can hear me." She leaned in closer and with a loud tone, she nearly yelled, "You guys are crazy!" She then sat back and crossed her arms. "Hope you heard me that time."

Lenny and I exchanged looks. I leaned back in my seat and sighed.

I couldn't bring myself to argue with her statement. She didn't believe me, and in all honesty, it didn't surprise me.

You heard people sharing stories, beginning and ending them by saying: "And if it didn't happen to me, I wouldn't have believed it." That was never more true than in this situation. Part of me, the logical side of me, was telling me that it was the high off the weed. But it couldn't have been. It was too real. Not to mention all three of us saw the same thing.

I glanced ahead, spotting Mateo riding his horse. He eyeballed the cornfields that surrounded the path we walked.

I looked at Lenny. He completely hid his eyes from the cornfields. At first, I didn't notice it. But then I noticed that he was simply avoiding looking at the cornfields, keeping his eyes either in the interior of his truck or intently studying Mateo. He did anything to avoid looking at the cornfields and risk seeing that thing again.

I then looked at Carly. She had pulled out her phone and scrolled through social media, not a care in the world.

They tried to hide their fear, but I knew. I wondered if they knew how scared I was?.

After some time, we reached Mateo's house. We all hopped out of our rides. Mateo began leading Apple towards the barn where he'd inspect her for any injuries. Perhaps even feed Apple.

Lenny had unexpectedly began speaking to me. "That thing we saw out there," Lenny said. "You think it's real?"

"What?" I asked, looking to him.

"You didn't really respond when I asked you earlier."

I recalled the conversation before Carly put in her two cents.

"I don't recall that you asked me a question," I said.

Lenny's face wrinkled up for a few seconds as he let himself recall the small conversation. "I guess I didn't." He glanced at his sister, ensuring she was distracted by her phone. He then turned back to me. "Do you think what we saw was real?"

My stomach dropped when he asked the question. I almost just answered the question honestly and said yes.

He must've noticed my hesitation. Lenny sighed and leaned on his truck.

"Yes," I said.

He slowly turned his head to me. I felt he already knew how I felt about his question. He knew that I believed what we saw was real.

I crossed my arms and furrowed my brow at him. "Now let me ask you a question," I said. "Us being high on weed that night—you think that had anything to do with our reaction?"

"Wha…?" he asked.

"We were high, right?" I asked.

"Yeah."

"Tell me if you believe it's possible that we didn't see what we saw?"

Lenny looked at me as if I had just shit in my own hands. "Of course, dumbass," he said. "Anything's possible."

I sighed and rolled my eyes at his comment. "I'm just saying. Do you agree that it's very possible we didn't see what we saw?"

Lenny was grinning, but he returned to the seriousness of the conversation after a second. "Yes, it's possible," he answered.

"Then what about Strawberry?" Mateo's voiced chimed in. Hed returned from the barn sooner then I was expecting.

It scared the hell outta me. Thankfully Carly didn't see me jump.

"What?" I asked.

Mateo approached us and crossed his arms. He studied Lenny and me. "If we imagined it," he began, "then what the hell happened to Strawberry?"

Lenny didn't say anything. He simply lowered his head ever so slightly.

"It was a car or something, dude," I told Mateo.

Mateo shook his head, saying, "A car wouldn't rip something limb from limb. Like how Milkshake was ripped limb from limb."

I didn't say anything.

"Let's accept that something is out there. Something scary and dangerous," Mateo said, pointing to the cornfields.

I looked out at the ocean of cornfields following Mateo's finger. Lenny did the same.

The three of us stared into the endless fields. Part of me wondered if the thing was gonna pop his head out like he did in the past.

Screaming from the house behind me proved me wrong.

CHAPTER 17

I darted my head to look behind me to locate the source of the yelling.

Standing right in front of the house was the thing from the cornfields, red glowing eyes and all. The long limbs and shiny black skin almost made me go mad.

The fact that it was once again right in front of me almost blew my mind.

The yelling began again.

It was Carly, she was seeing this thing and like the rest of us, not understanding what she was looking at.

It took me some time to break out of my body, which was frozen in place with fear. I damn near hid behind the truck but the thought of leaving Carly exposed in front of this thing all alone just didn't sit right with me.

She was walking towards Mateo's house when she saw it. It must've just walked right out of the cornfields behind her. And when she turned to look at us, she saw this unholy thing just staring at her.

I looked at Mateo and Lenny, who stood solid in fear. I looked down at the floor and contemplated crawling underneath the truck to safety.

Instead I found my fist balling up and my arm reaching out to Lenny. I grabbed him by his shirt and yanked. He broke from his trance and stared at me.

With my balled-up fist, I pounded on the truck and yelled, "HIT IT!!!"

His eyes snapped to his hands which suddenly held keys. He appeared to contemplate his actions as if he were deciding to fight or flight.

My fist was continuing to pound on the truck. This time instead of me saying to hit it, I yelled, "YOUR SISTER!"

That was all I needed to say. He adapted a determined expression, still with some fear, though. He crawled into the truck and turned it on. The engine roared to life, but the demon wasn't fazed.

I tackled Mateo onto the floor which knocked him out of his fear induced trance. We were on the floor; I looked up at him and saw his facial expression shift from fear, to horrified.

"MOM!" Mateo yelled.

He hopped up from where I tackled him and bolted towards the house. I got up to chase him, but he stopped himself, causing me to crash into him. I was questioning his sudden stop as we tumbled to the ground when Lenny's truck zoomed past us, answering my questions.

I looked up at the monster and truck as they collided.

I didn't know what I was expecting, I really didn't, but seeing that damn monster tumble over as if it were made of feathers gave me goosebumps. The monster rag-dolled down, and its expression was no longer grinning. I saw that it was now making an expression of pain. Its long mouth frowned, and its upper face wrinkled.

I caught a glimpse of Lenny's face. He looked like he was riding a rollercoaster, his eyes were wide, and mouth was screaming.

Carly was no longer screaming; her expression resembled more like someone who couldn't believe what they were seeing. Her jaw was hanging, and her eyebrows were way above her eyes.

I scrambled to my feet and scurried my way to her. I was mostly running for the front door, but she was in the way.

I grabbed her by the arm and yanked her along with me. I damn near slammed into the front door face-first. But I extended my arm and stopped that from happening. Mateo was right behind me; he in fact did slam into the front door shutting it as I opened it. But he quickly corrected himself and punched in the code to unlock the door. He swung open the doors and Carly darted inside. Mateo looked to the truck, and I followed his gaze.

Lenny was in his truck just staring at the monster. His eyes were so wide I damn near expected his eyeballs to roll out of his head.

But he wasn't doing anything. He just stared. The monster began to get up. Its expression was irritated.

I couldn't blame Lenny for getting stuck in fear. It was incredible to see this thing. It wasn't supposed to exist, so to see this thing, here, existing, it was hard to take your eyes off it. It was hard to wrap your brain around what we were seeing.

Mateo and I stood on the front porch. Lenny's truck was maybe a few feet away from where we stood and a couple inches from the small gate that surrounded the porch. Part of me assumed Lenny hit the house.

Then the monster stood up and towered over the truck, as well as the house. At least from my perspective, I believed I was wrong about how tall I thought it was.

The monster, in rage, made a banshee scream and brought its fist down on the hood of the truck, leaving a dent. A very large dent.

The loud pounding seemed to smack Lenny out of his fear, and he put the truck in reverse and backed up.

The monster stood tall and just stared at the truck reversing, gritting its teeth.

Lenny did the same, his eyes still wide with fear. Even with the new and huge dent on the hood, the truck went flying towards the monster.

The monster was slow to react. Lenny's truck once again hit it, and the monster fell easily to the ground. The monster released a howl of pain as Lenny's truck began to bounce over it as he ran it over.

Some confidence arose in me as I saw the monster fall over and rag doll for the second time. But that confidence quickly subsided as the monster adjusted his long limbs under the truck and with Lenny still in it, sent it flying.

The truck went air born, it flew at least nine feet into the sky!

My stomach twisted with the fear of Lenny getting hurt. As the truck smashed to the ground, the monster gave it no time to breathe.

The monster hopped onto the truck and began pounding its fist on it.

The truck had landed upside down. It was shaking with the force of the thing hitting it over and over again.

I damn near shit myself when I caught a glimpse of the monster grinning wickedly as it beat the living shit out of the truck.

"What do we do???" Mateo asked in a loud desperate tone.

I whipped around and looked at the front door. I instinctively wanted to run inside the house and hide somewhere in it. I began to turn towards the door, ready to run into the house.

But Mateo's mom, my tía, ran out of the house and got in my way.

I saw the moment her eyes landed on the monster. Her expression went from, "What the fuck is happening out here," to "What the fuck is that thing?"

I debated running past her into the house but she immediately whipped out a shotgun that I didn't see she had concealed.

She raised it towards the monster and fired.

With a bang, my ears rang, and with a bang, the monster's head whipped suddenly to the left.

I didn't realize I had fallen down, instinctively ducking at the sight of a gun. I rolled around to see the monster had grabbed its head where it had been shot. It began to scream in pain again.

I didn't realize I was covering my ears. I also didn't realize that Mateo was calling out to me.

He had pulled me up to my feet and through my ringing ears, I heard him say, "Let's get Lenny!"

He didn't drag me with him as he has done in the past as when we were kids. He expected me to follow him. But I wanted to run into the house.

I couldn't talk myself into it, I couldn't convince myself to abandon Lenny. I really needed to help Lenny. I was surprised that I cared enough to go help him.

Would he come help me?

I shoved that thought away. And I shoved my feet below me. And ran behind Mateo.

It took me a second to realize that as we were running towards the truck, towards Lenny, that we were also running towards the tall, thin monster that was howling in pain.

CHAPTER 18

Another bang from my tía's shotgun hit the monster in the shoulder, which had whipped it around. The monster moved his hands from the spot where he was hit in the head to the spot he was hit in the shoulder. Another banshee-like scream roared from its mouth.

Mateo and I ran around to the driver's side to Lenny.

"MATEO NO!" My tía's voice ripped through the cries of the monster. When she had seen me and her son near this thing.

"RUN!" she called.

I wanted to listen to her and run in the opposite direction. But I couldn't leave Lenny. I thought of the night we met, how we smoked weed and shared many laughs. How was that enough? How could a couple decent memories I have with someone keep me from abandoning them?

Lenny and I were still strangers. More or less.

He was Mateo's friend not mine, he was a good guy and all but why should I care? I don't know why, but I couldn't let him die.

The monster continued to squeeze his wound on his shoulder, gritting his teeth.

My tía was calling out, but I couldn't hear what she was saying. I did, however, hear the bang of the shotgun and the monster's head fling back. He once again moved his arms from his shoulder to his face and began to scream in pain.

"LENNY!!!" Mateo called. Mateo fumbled around the truck door and when he found the door handle, he began to yank and tug on it.

The door wasn't budging. The truck door was smashed closed.

Mateo, however, didn't notice that was why the truck door wasn't opening. He was calling to Lenny, shouting for him to unlock the door.

Neither of us could see his condition, as the windows were cracked. We could only see his figure. I began checking the other doors to see whether or not they would open, but none of them would.

Another shot from my tía's shotgun rang in my head.

I ran back to Mateo as he was still struggling to open the door. I grew frustrated, from the shotgun bangs and the monster screaming from pain. The loud noises were irritating me both from physical pain and not being able to think clearly.

That frustration encouraged me to run and kick the driver's side cracked window. The glass shattered much more easily than I had thought it would have. My foot went right through the glass and landed next to Lenny.

I immediately yanked my foot away. And Mateo shoved his upper body into the truck. After a couple seconds, he began to drag Lenny out.

I scrambled to help Mateo, and the two of us got Lenny out of the truck.

Mateo held Lenny's upper half, and I held his legs. We ran as fast as two people carrying a man could run. I felt my grip on Lenny's legs slipping as we skipped steps above the stairs. But I held tight enough to get through the front door.

Once through the front door. My tía unleashed another four rounds into the monster.

More screaming came from the monster. I ran to the window to see what it looked like.

I saw it was holding its face again, which told me my tía was a good shot, as it seemed she'd hit the head, when she wanted and hit the body when she wanted.

"FUCK!!!" My tía shouted.

I turned my head to look at her and saw that she was reloading. She appeared to be shoving shells into the weapon.

Terrified, I looked at the monster and saw that it was still wailing in pain.

My childlike instincts told me that it was gonna be safe inside the house. With those instincts, I grabbed my tía and pulled her into the house. The speed and sudden weight shift caused the two of us to fall, thankfully inside the house. Before I could think to do anything else, I kicked the front door. I slammed the door shut. Seconds later, my tía locked it.

The reassuring click of the lock made me relax for the first time since this thing showed up.

My tía ran from the front door to a window located next to it. I followed her and looked out the window.

The monster was no longer holding his head. The thing from the cornfields now held a confused expression. His face darted from left to right. It moved its eyes around itself.

"It's looking for us," I said thinking aloud.

Someway, somehow, it didn't see us run into the house.

It looked around for a few more seconds, then slowly walked into the cornfields.

"H-how could it not know where we are?" I asked, thinking out loud.

"What?" a voiced asked from behind me.

"It lost us?" I stuttered. "It's-it's gone."

Mateo stood up from where Lenny laid on the floor. I believed he was treating him for a wound I wasn't aware of yet.

He walked to me, then past me to the window.

"It's gone?" he asked.

CHAPTER 19

Lenny woke up some time later. The sun hadn't gone down yet, but it was getting there.

When Lenny woke up, we saw that his head wasn't physically injured, at least no bumps or open wounds we could see. He had a bit of a headache, but Carly concluded that he had no concussion. Of course, Carly wasn't a doctor, so for all she knew her brother was dead with his eyes open.

Regardless, he looked fine to me.

His arm, however, was dislocated.

"That's fuckin' nasty," Carly expressed.

And she was right; the arm dangled unnaturally, and it made me wanna puke.

"Ummm," I started to say, "does anyone know how to relocate an arm?"

I looked at Carly and she shook her head. I looked at Lenny and he did the same.

Mateo raised his hand as if in school. "Let me try," he said.

"You know how to relocate an arm?" I asked.

"I mean, in school I've seen trainers do it," Mateo explained.

"What?" Carly chimed in. "Our school wouldn't allow that."

"I don't know if it's allowed or not, but I saw them do it once," Mateo answered.

Among our chatter, Lenny made it clear that he was in pain, groaning and whenever someone got a little too close to his arm, he'd yell, "FUCK OFF."

"Man, y'all, fuck!" Lenny yelled. "No one is touching me!"

Lenny was still on the ground where Mateo and I had left him. Every other movement he'd make would result in his noodle arm moving, which in turn, resulted in pain.

"Can someone take me to a fuckin' doctor?" Lenny asked loudly.

"If we leave you like this, your arm could get more damaged," Carly tried to explain.

But Lenny was stubborn and didn't wanna hear it.

I kinda just stood there and studied the noodle arm. It was weird to look at but I couldn't take my eyes off it. It didn't help that he was wearing a shirt with short-short sleeves.

Part of me wasn't even staring at it to see if I could find a solution. Part of me was just looking at it in awe.

Mateo grabbed my arm and pulled me aside. We stepped from the living room to the dining room. The others were still in sight. But with Lenny groaning in pain, he sucked up all the attention. We were also still in earshot but if we kept our voices down, we'd be relatively in our own space.

Mateo looked at me with a serious stare. My stomach dropped when I felt he was gonna talk about the thing in the cornfields.

"Have you ever relocated a shoulder before?" Mateo asked.

"No," I answered, relieved.

"Ok," Mateo said. "Just hold him down."

"What?" I asked. "No way."

"Dude, you gotta."

"The hell I do."

Mateo waved his hands towards Carly. "You heard what Carly said. We can't just let him sit there."

"Do you even know how to reset a shoulder?" I asked. "Like, for sure know?"

"Yes!" he shouted. "I've seen so many people do it!"

"But that doesn't mean you've ever done it!"

"I can do it, Miguel!"

His force and tone didn't sit right with me. So in response, I stepped aside, revealing a path directly towards Lenny who was still on the floor, loudly moaning in pain.

"Ok," I said. "Then be my guest." I waved my hand toward Lenny.

Mateo nervously studied Lenny. He looked at Lenny, then at me, then back at Lenny. After a few moments of silence, he began forward.

I stayed where I was. I could make out some words, but most were lost due to the distance. Finally, I noticed the conversation became a loud argument. Regardless of the raised tone they all now had, I still couldn't one hundred percent make out the words.

Finally, I heard, "AW HELL NO!" from Lenny.

I watched, doing nothing, as Lenny kicked and screamed as Mateo began the struggle with Lenny's arm.

Eventually, I heard Mateo call out to his mom, who showed up and after a second of lecturing and arguing, she joined Mateo.

She shoved him out of the way and ordered loudly, "HOLD HIM DOWN."

The pair still struggled to aid the large young adult.

Lenny was only a little taller than me and Mateo. If I were six-foot, then Lenny was six-foot-one. His body was also a little bit huskier.

Regardless of how much bigger Lenny was compared to Mateo—enough to be noticed while looking at us if we stood side by side—but it was clearly enough to give two grown adults a hard time, not to mention giving two grown adults a hard time with only one arm, and also in pain caused by a dislocated shoulder.

My tía was now the one who was gonna relocate the shoulder. And Mateo held Lenny down. Lenny was bigger than Mateo, but with Mateo using his full weight with one hand on his chest, the other hand on his good arm, and Mateo's knee was on Lenny's stomach, he kept him still.

You should help them.

I began to talk myself out of that thought. There was no way I was gonna go help Mateo and my tía. I wasn't about to go watch someone shove a body part back into place. I also wasn't gonna risk getting hurt, especially not if medical professionals were much more qualified to do what they were trying to do.

After a while of Lenny screaming profanity at my tía and cousin, he soon began to sort of beg them not to do anything.

"Please don't!" he begged. "Wait, wait!"

You should go help them.

I once again began to push away that thought. I wouldn't know what I was doing; I'd probably end up hurting him.

"Guys, please just wait!" Lenny pleaded.

"Stop!" I called. I immediately hated myself for saying what I just said.

I didn't know why, but I couldn't bear to hear Lenny's agony. He was in pain. And we weren't helping. They were not helping.

Everyone turned their heads to look at me. They all relaxed, including Mateo, who got off Lenny.

"Please just take me to a doctor." Lenny begged.

His voice filled the now-silent room.

I walked up to the group of people. I looked at Mateo, ready to say something. But nothing came out of my mouth. I did the same to my tía. I was about to speak to her, but nothing came out.

It was because I didn't wanna say anything to them. I wanted to talk to Lenny.

I kneeled down and waited for Lenny's eyes to meet mine.

"Hey," I said. "We need to relocate your arm."

Lenny threw his head back and closed his eyes in frustration, saying, "Noooo!"

"Hey, come on," I said. "We can't leave it like this."

I looked to Carly, and she nodded.

"Fuck you man!" Lenny said. "Don't touch me!"

He scooted his body away from me.

"Damn it, Lenny."

"Nooo!"

"Let us help you!"

I looked at my tía, who was studying Lenny's arm. She had a look of confidence on her face that Mateo didn't.

"My tía actually knows how to relocate your arm," I said looking at Lenny, then I shifted my attention to my tía. "Right?" I asked.

"Yeah," she said, nodding.

"Look, dude, let us do this," I asked.

Lenny didn't swear or even say anything. He just shook his head *no*.

I was getting frustrated. I didn't wanna be in this house, this place, any more. I wanted out. And because of Lenny, we couldn't leave.

"Either you get up, sit on that chair, and let us do this," I said gesturing at a chair in the dining room, "or we're gonna do it here."

Lenny didn't say anything. He looked at me and the chair. He began the process of shaking his head, but before he could, I grabbed his good shoulder and squeezed, saying, "Make the smart decision."

Lenny scrunched up his face, as if he were a ten-year-old who had lost an argument. "Fuck," he said quietly.

He began to stand. We helped him and escorted him to the dining room.

Carly rushed ahead of us and pulled out a chair and met us halfway. Lenny sat down and adopted a determined look. Mateo gave him his arm and Lenny took it.

I was about to step back and let my tía do whatever she had to, but she called me to assist her.

"Can you hold him from behind?" she asked.

"Umm, how?" I asked, nervously.

She pointed to his back. "Keep him as straight as possible," she said. "It's gonna hurt, he's gonna flinch and resist."

I positioned myself behind Lenny, and sort of hugged him from behind.

The tension in the room was so heavy, you could damn near taste it.

Lenny began breathing heavily. Mateo positioned himself in the front, holding Lenny's good arm. Mateo also raised his knee and placed his leg on Lenny's. The two of us made a makeshift restraining vest, and my tía crouched down and studied Lenny's noodle arm.

She then placed her arms and hands around Lenny's dislocated shoulder, and I felt Lenny tighten up.

"Don't," Lenny began. "Don't tell me when, ok?"

My tía looked up and met Lenny's eyes.

"Ok," she said. Then in a swift powerful motion, she shoved that arm right back into place.

Lenny's whole body shook and flexed in pain. He let out a loud yelp of pain.

Mateo and I continued to hold him, not realizing that my tía had already relocated the shoulder.

"Get off him!" My tía ordered.

And we did. I backed up into the hallway wall and almost knocked down a hanging painting. I watched as Lenny held his arm, moaning and groaning in pain.

What the fuck am I doing here?

I was watching my cousin's best friend in pain. My cousin's best friends' car was also crashed like a tin can less than a few yards away from the house I was currently in. Crushed by some kind of monster.

I looked around the house I was in. It no longer felt like my childhood home. It no longer held some kinda nostalgic grip on me. This place used to mean so much to me only a couple nights ago. It was where many of my childhood memories took place.

Now, it was merely a wall between me and whatever the hell that thing was outside.

I glanced out a window and saw pieces of Lenny's truck, a headlight and some sort of pipe.

Not a very strong wall.

If that thing could do that to a car, the walls of a house gave little protection for me.

A loud, hard knock at the front door made us all jump with fear. We all yelped.

It was Carly who was closest to the door. She leaned to her left to glance out the window. She released a sigh of relief and turned to us.

"It's the sheriff," she said with her thumb pointing behind her, "from the other day."

My tía walked past us and swung the door open.

"You mind explaining that?!" asked the sheriff, pointing to the mangled-up car.

For the first time in my life, my tía had nothing to say. What could she tell him? My tía just stood there, looking at the sheriff, then the car.

"Come inside," she finally said.

The sheriff stepped inside, and my tía closed the door behind him. He looked puzzled, noticing the fear in the room and on our faces.

"The hell happened to him?" he asked, pointing to Lenny.

"His shoulder," I answered, but it sounded more like a question. Like I was suggesting it.

"What happened?" he demanded, staring daggers at me.

That's what I got for being dumb enough to answer him.

"He was in the car," I said, "he was in the car when..." I trailed off.

"When that fuckin' happened?" he shouted at me, pointing at the truck. "What the hell happened?"

"Uhhhh…" was the only noise I was able to make.

"Uhhhhhhhh," the sheriff repeated, mocking me.

"Hey!" My tía chimed in.

"No, no, no, no, nooo." The sheriff said, "Someone better start talking!"

"We were attacked!" Mateo called.

"Attacked?" the sheriff asked.

"Man, I don't know," Mateo said. "I don't know what to tell you."

The sheriff walked to a window and stared at the mangled-up truck. "Sofía," said the sheriff turning to my tía, "What the hell happened. Now I'm getting real tired of asking that question."

My tía just stood there for a minute. She didn't say anything for a while. "Lenny over there," she said pointing to Lenny. "His arm was dislocated. I put it back in place."

"You what?" he asked, looking frustrated.

"Hey, I've relocated yours a few times!" she snapped back.

At this being said, Carly's surprised look made its way to me, and we ended up exchanging confused and surprised glances at the news of Sofía, my tía, apparently relocating the sheriff's arm.

I was also a bit hit with a wave of emotions with sharing that glance with Carly. I looked at Mateo and Lenny. They were both in her eyesight, and she chose to share that glance with me.

I decided to let go of those thoughts of Carly and focus on what was happening now.

"I don't care!" the sheriff said. "You're not trained to do it right. You could've made it worse. For all we know, you did."

"I didn't, Terry," my tía told him firmly.

Terry raised an eyebrow and crossed his arms.

The frustration visible on his face made my stomach turn.

"Alright girl," he said. "Fine." He uncrossed his arms and placed one on the belt and the other fell to his side. The sheriff calmed his eyes and looked at my tía. "You best tell me why the hell that truck looks like..." he paused and looked at the truck outside. "Shit, like that."

My tía looked like she wanted to answer, but she refused to speak.

I looked around the room. Carly just looked at the floor. Lenny, while his face held a pained expression, looked conflicted. Mateo simply stared daggers at Terry, the sheriff.

"You hear me?" Terry asked.

"Yeah," she answered.

"Then please answer me," he demanded.

My tía shrugged her shoulders and smirked. "Alien," she stated.

The sheriff just looked at her for a minute.

"Wow," Carly blurted out. "Is that what they sounded like?"

Carly pointed at us boys trying to pick up our jaws off the floor.

The sheriff let out a small genuine chuckle at Carly's comment. He then turned back to my tía and repeated what she had just said. "Aliens?"

"No, not aliens, an alien," My tía said, nodding.

"It's true!" Mateo exclaimed.

"No, it's not!" Terry snapped back.

"Ok, well, maybe not an alien," Carly explained. "But definitely something."

I debated chiming in. But I had nothing to add, so I stayed quiet.

Terry laughed sarcastically. "So a little gray spaceman swooped down here with his flying saucer spaceship and decided to beam up a few cows, is that it?"

"You sound super old," Carly whispered loudly.

"And you all sound crazy."

I sighed and rolled my eyes, which got the sheriffs attention.

"You got something to say?" he asked me.

I looked at him and decided to at least appear as less intimidated as possible. I crossed my arms and straightened my posture.

"I don't know what to tell you," I sighed. "I don't know what it is out there."

Terry didn't say anything. But the amused look on his face told me he wasn't buying it.

"It wasn't an alien in a flying saucer," I explained. "It was like a person, it's humanoid, I mean. But it's unnatural, it doesn't make sense, and I don't know how to explain it."

I unintentionally uncrossed my arms and began to move my hands in sync with my words. "It's big and tall, and surprisingly strong?" I explained.

"What do you mean by that, son?" Terry asked.

"I mean," I tried, "it doesn't look strong. In fact, it's real skinny. Yeah, it's tall as hell, but it's really skinny."

I let fear into my voice, and realized I was close to shaking. Just describing the monster, picturing it in my head, freaked me out— but I didn't stop talking.

"It's strong enough to do that to Lenny's truck." I pointed at the truck outside. "It's the same thing we saw the other night. Exact same thing."

Terry didn't say anything. Instead, he opened the front door and walked outside.

For a moment I thought he was leaving, like he'd heard enough of all this nonsense. But my eyes followed him to the truck. He turned toward the house and motioned for us to come to him.

My tía was the first to walk out the front doors to join him. Then Mateo. I didn't wanna seem like a pussy in front of Carly, so shortly after Mateo hesitated to walk outside, I did the same.

But I turned to Carly, who was about to follow me out the front door, too.

"You should stay with your brother," I suggested.

Her eyes met mine and she just nodded.

Still trying not to look like a wimp, especially knowing her eyes were on me, I marched out the front door, although I sped-walked to meet the others at the truck less than halfway.

My tía was explaining the whole thing to the sheriff.

"After he hit it," she explained, "it threw the truck off like it was a plastic toy. Then it jumped on the car and began to just smash."

"And that Lenny kid was in the truck when all this happened?" Terry asked.

My tía nodded.

The sheriff paced the area where Lenny hit the monster, and I assumed he took note of the obvious disturbed grass and dirt.

He then looked at my tía and asked, "I also saw some shells on the porch. I take it you shot at the thing?"

My tía nodded. The sheriff sighed and took a few steps back.

"You all do understand what you're telling me, right?" he asked.

None of us said anything. We did. We were all very aware of what we were saying.

"What are you gonna do?" Mateo asked.

"Shit, I don't know," he replied. "Let me go ask my partner, Robocop."

"Come on, Terry," my tía voiced. "We honestly don't know what to say. Because we don't know what the hell happened."

Terry seemed to soften up at my tía's tone.

"There's nothing I can do for y'all," he said. "The most I can do is report a car crash."

My tía clenched her fist and raised them to her face, saying, "Please! Will you at least look around?"

Terry sighed, "Don't you think I've looked around enough?"

"Terry, please!" My tia begged. I've never heard her voice sound so desperate before.

Terry shook his head but agreed. "If y'all are so scared, then you should get off the property. Head to town, get a hotel and call their parents," he suggested.

He walked over to his cop car and spoke to someone over the radio. Perhaps calling for assistance.

My tía turned to Mateo and me and ordered us to pack for a night or two and insist Carly and Lenny come with us.

Mateo and I ran to the house and met up with the two siblings. Carly and Lenny were talking about the thing in the cornfields, trying to figure out what it could be.

"Hey," I began, "my tía wants to head to town for a night or two."

"And sleep in a car?" Carly asked.

"No, we'd get a hotel somewhere," I explained, "and you guys should come with us."

Lenny and Carly hesitated for a moment before eventually agreeing. They weren't gonna stay surrounded by cornfields where the thing could pop out of at any time.

"But we should stop by our place and grab some clothes," Carly commented.

"No, fuck that," Lenny told her. "I don't mind wearing the same clothes for a night or two. We'll just tough it out."

Carly looked like she wanted to argue but decided not to. I understood her completely. But the faster we got out of here, the better.

"You know what, yeah," Mateo agreed. "Let's get the fuck out of here."

Mateo ran into the dining room and fished out a set of keys that were in a bowl on a counter.

The sudden urgency to leave the place became overwhelming and the fear that twisted up in my stomach and spine at the thought of sticking around this place only encouraged us to move faster out the front door.

Lenny was still in pain, but he was moving. Carly kept an eye on him but she herself was in a rush. We all scampered down the porch steps and ran into my tía.

"We're not packing," Mateo said to his mom while handing her the keys.

She didn't argue. She turned and gave one last look at the sheriff. Then we all rushed to the soccer mom car in the driveway and got in and drove away.

CHAPTER 20

The drive was quiet for the most part. But Carly being Carly decided to be funny and ask a question.

"So, what's up with you and the sheriff?" she teased.

I grinned. I had the question in my head, as well. We all did.

Carly and I sat in the middle seats. Mateo sat in the passenger seat. And Lenny was in the very back. I saw my tía's eyes through the rearview mirror use the mirror to glare at Carly.

"That's the question you have to ask?" My tía said ferociously.

Mateo turned his head at his mom, looking horrified. "What are you so defensive about?"

My tía turned her head to Mateo but said nothing. Silence filled the car again, with the exception of the humming AC.

"Sooooo?" Carly pushed.

"¡Callarse la boca!" My tía shouted.

Carly turned to me and asked, "What did she say?"

"She told you to shut up," I answered.

"Mom," Mateo called, "what's up with you and Terry?"

I'd never seen my tía look scared. Fear was an emotion we all felt. But I'd never seen my tía scared; she never was scared. But today, with all that happened, she looked horrified. She also looked desperate while begging the sheriff to look around the property. The expressions didn't suit her. They didn't belong on a person like my tía.

I'd seen my tía break a door open when Mateo was locked in a room with a rattlesnake.

The memory came flooding back. Mateo and I were playing hide and seek one day. And Mateo locked himself in my mom's bedroom at the time. Unbeknownst to him, a large rattlesnake somehow made its way into the house and into my mom's bedroom. When Mateo saw the snake, he jumped on the bed and screamed for his mother.

When his mom eventually got to the door and saw it was locked, she asked loudly, "What's going on?!"

"SNAKE!!!!!" was all Mateo screamed.

That was enough for my tía. She struggled with the locked door for a few minutes. She got frustrated and stressed at her child's situation. At some point, she walked away from the door and opened a closet that was located down the hall. She fished out a machete and walked back to the bedroom door.

I remembered thinking she was gonna start chopping down the door. Instead. with her hand that didn't hold the machete, she gripped the round door handle and in a swift motion, she ripped the door open. By doing so, she completely destroyed the locking mechanism and even destroyed a hinge.

I didn't see what happened after she entered the room. But I knew what happened regardless.

She chopped up the snake and saved her crying, scared son.

Even then she didn't wear a scared look on her face. But she sure as shit had one now. She even looked like she was blushing a little.

"No way, Mom, what the hell?!" Mateo exclaimed.

"Watch it!" she ordered, pointing a finger at him.

"Well?" Mateo asked.

My tía sighed. She looked like a child who was caught doing something she wasn't supposed to be doing.

"Terry and I are friends. We're long friends, since middle school," my tía explained. "That's it. We've just known each other for a long time."

"Friends? Really?" Mateo asked. "Is that why you're blushing?"

My tía didn't say anything. She just kept her eyes on the road.

"Mom?" Mateo pushed. "Are you guys fucking?"

"Hey!" my tía snapped. "I'm not your friend, you don't talk to me like that!"

Mateo flinched. "Sorry." Mateo adjusted himself and took a couple deep breaths. "Are you guys a thing?" Mateo asked his mom.

"We're," my tía paused, "something."

"What? You're *something?*"

"We're not together, together."

"Mom, you're not making sense."

"Mateo, yo no sabe."

I felt a hand on my thigh, and I damn near had to punch myself in the balls to keep my body from getting excited. It was Carly's hand; she was trying to get my attention.

"W-what?" I asked.

"What did she just say?" Carly asked me, not even recognizing what her action of placing her hand on my thigh that close to my area was doing to me.

"She's saying she doesn't know what she and Terry are, ok!" I told her, sternly grabbing her hand and getting it off me.

"You assholes enjoying the show?" Mateo asked loudly, looking at the three of us in the back.

Lenny and Carly both answered at the same time. With Lenny saying no, and Carly saying yes. I decided not to say anything.

"Calm down!" my tía called to Mateo. She shifted in her seat. "To tell you the truth," my tía said, "I like him. And he likes me."

"And you both know you like each other?" Mateo asked.

My tía didn't say anything. She just nodded.

After that, the car went silent. And it stayed silent for the rest of the ride.

Eventually we got to a hotel. And I was secretly grateful. I was expecting us to arrive at some cheap motel, but we ended up somewhere better. We all stepped out and entered the hotel.

I felt very odd not having to unload any luggage. But I was mostly grateful to be surrounded by roads and a few other buildings, instead of being surrounded by cornfields.

We all walked into the hotel and my tía got us rooms: a two bed and a pullout for my tía, my cousin, and me, and a two bedroom for the siblings.

The two rooms were right across from each other in the hallway, and they were located on the sixth floor. The hotel was generic, nothing super fancy. But it also wasn't a shit hole at all. Just a regular hotel.

The pullout couch wasn't too bad. Not as comfortable as my own mattress, of course, but from what I was expecting, I was delightfully comfortable.

The sun was setting around the time we arrived at the hotel. By the time we got to our rooms, it was dark.

Laying on my bed, I pulled out my phone and called my mom.

"Bueno?" she answered.

"Hey Mom," I said.

"Hey, mijo. Sofía told me what happened. Are you ok?"

"She did?" I asked, surprised.

"She did," she said. "You're ok, right?"

"Yeah, I'm ok, Mom."

The tone and concern in her voice, the voice of my mom who loved me so much and took such good care of me, made me feel safe.

"How is Mateo?" she asked.

"He's ok," I replied. "Scared, you know."

"Si."

There was a pause in the conversation.

"I'll be there in a few days, ok," she said in a motherly tone. "Take you back home."

"Ok," I said, almost choking up.

I didn't even know that I was crying softly. I missed my mom so much. I felt like a child. She must've heard me crying over the phone.

I wanted to hug her and be away from this shitty nightmare. I wanted my mom to protect me. Like she always protected me when I was young and scared.

"Are you sure you're ok?" my mom asked.

"I'm ok, Mom," I answered. "I just wanna go home."

"Yo se. Ya voy."

"Gracias, madre."

I felt small. I felt helpless. But that was ok. My mom made me feel like I was safe and ok. Hearing her voice made me homesick. The mattress I laid on, comparing it to my own, made me homesick.

"Thank you, Mom," I whispered softly.

"Of course," she replied. "I'll see you soon. I miss you and I can't wait to see you."

"Yo también."

I didn't hang up. I didn't want to. And my mom knew this, so she didn't hang up either.

The sudden urge to pee is what finally got me to hang up the phone with a final goodbye and 'I love you.'

I walked to the restroom located right next to the pullout couch and closed the door behind me.

I relieved myself and washed my hands. When I eventually looked in the mirror and saw what a mess I was, I almost laughed. I was an ugly crier. I may as well have been wearing mascara. You could see the remnants of the waterfall my eyes just produced on my face. Not to mention the color of my eyes, all red and swollen and shit.

"Fuuuck," I chuckled to myself.

I washed my face and walked out of the bathroom.

Mateo and his mom were kinda just in the room on their phones. They were clearly avoiding each other. One did wanna talk about the elephant in the room and the other didn't.

I decided that I wanted some time to myself. And I also decided it was best that they talk it out.

"Sorry y'all had to see that shit show," I said pointing to the pullout bed where the shit show just happened. "Imma take a walk." I pointed to the door. "I'll be back."

My tía didn't say anything, she just nodded her head. Mateo smiled and waved me goodbye.

"It's none of my business," I said, "But you guys should talk it out. I'll be a while so y'all should take this opportunity and talk it out."

I didn't wait for a reply, I just grabbed my phone charger sitting on my mattress and walked out the room. I memorized the room number and started to the elevator.

I figured I'd visit the pool. I caught a glimpse of it earlier while checking into the hotel. I'd figured a swim ought to do me some good.

CHAPTER 21

On my ride in the elevator down to the first floor, I simply couldn't get the anxiety out of my head. I couldn't get the urge to run out of the hotel and run in the direction of my home to just get away from all this. Every time I looked out a window, every time I gazed into the distance, I'm afraid that I'll see the red eyed monster. The elevator offered a surprising amount of comfort and relief. No windows and no distance, just cold metal walls. With every ding that sounded when it passed a floor, I felt a surge of anxiety. The opening of the doors when I reached the bottom floor would mean exposure and vulnerability to the red eyed monster again. The thought of sprinting home somehow made sense to me.

But I couldn't. I mean, sure I could, I had the ability to do so. But I decided I'd rather just wait for my mom to show up and come get me. It was the only realistic thing to do.

The thought of my mom made my head heavy again. I never wanted to see my mom more than right then. I wanted her to show up in her small red Ford Fusion. I wanted her to take me away from all of this, all the awkwardness from my family, the not being around my own friends, the not being in my own room, on my own bed, and away from whatever the fuck was out there.

I just wanted everything to go back to normal. I wanted to get away from all the awful things that had happened.

A ding from the elevator snapped me out of my thoughts. The ding from the elevator also informed me that I was holding my breath, letting all the frustration swirl around in my head.

I awkwardly shifted through a young family trying to enter the elevator as I tried to exit. We exchanged the usual, "Excuse me," and "Have a good night." When the elevator closed behind me, I began my walk to the pool.

I passed the main entrance lobby, which held the usual waiting couches and potted plants. The check-in desk was empty, making the place feel bigger than what it actually was.

I eventually reached the pool entrance and swung the doors open. To my delight, the entire pool was empty, and it was a decently well-sized pool, too. So if at any point I was interrupted and joined, I'd probably be ok just sticking to just one side of the pool.

I fished my phone out of my pocket and checked the time. Odds were no one was gonna show up, either. It was past ten, so it wasn't very likely for anyone to want to go swimming at this hour.

I began to unload my pockets on one of those picnic tables that are always surrounding public pools. I took a seat on one of the chairs circling the table. I began to unlace my shoes. Of course flip flops would've been ideal for pools. I cursed the fact that I was wearing socks and would inevitably have to either shove my wet feet into my only pair of shoes or walk barefoot back to the hotel room.

At the realization of this, it finally hit me that I didn't have any swim shorts or clothing in general. My options were to swim wearing my jeans or to not wear my jeans and show everyone who might be looking or checking out the pool what kinda boxers I was wearing.

I sighed. I decided that it's better to leave all my clothes off and simply wait till I was fully dry to put everything back on. I began the process of doing so when I caught a glimpse of someone.

It was a girl.

Suddenly insecure, I shoved my shirt back on my body. I stared at the girl, wondering how I'd missed her.

It was Carly.

With the realization that it was Carly, yet another surge of insecurity pulsed through my body. To my relief, I saw that she wasn't even paying attention to me.

She was laying down on one of those sun tanning chairs. Her eyes were closed, and a pair of white wires ran from her ears to a metal box on her belly.

She was listening to music.

I wondered how'd I missed her, she had headphones on, so she wasn't making any noise. Her eyes were closed so she was probably sleeping. She was out of sight because the chair she was laying on wasn't in its usual place. I concluded that she had moved the chair to the edge of the pool, allowing her to put her feet in the water.

Welp. Time to go.

I wasn't about to swim around in my red boxers and possibly wake her up to see me like that. I also didn't wanna just sit around in an empty room and not do anything. I gathered my things and began to put my shoes on.

"Heyyy!" Carly called.

Her loud voice echoed through the big room, causing me to jump.

I again cursed myself for not bailing sooner and letting myself get caught. "Uhhhh, hi," I called back.

She sat up. "Going for a swim?" she asked.

"Nah, I'm gonna head on back." I replied.

She shook her head and lay back down.

I shoved my feet back into my shoes and didn't bother to tie them up.

I began speedwalking to the exit when Carly called back out, "Hey, wait!"

I gritted my teeth at my constant failure to remove myself from this situation. "Yeah?" I called, turning to her.

She was sitting back up.

"I'm a bit embarrassed to ask but—" she continued to speak but with the echoing and the water, I was having a hard time hearing her.

"What?" I asked loudly, putting my hand to my ear.

She repeated herself, but once again it got lost in the echoes and water.

"I can't hear you," I called to her.

At this point, I was more annoyed by the back and forth then I was nervous of being in a room alone with Carly. It didn't help she was a fast talker.

She eventually rolled her eyes and waved me over to her.

I almost just continued on my path out of the room. I wanted to avoid an awkward moment that would surely come from me, talking to a pretty girl. However, by doing so, I'd be entering a hotel room with my cousin and Tía having an equally awkward conversation. At least it would be awkward for me to be there.

So with that in mind, I chose to see what Carly wanted to say. I walked along the edge of the pool to where Carly sat. When I reached her, she took her feet out of the water and turned to face me.

She looked like she was about to say something, but she retreated. An awkward silence filled the air.

"I'm sorry," she finally blurted out.

It caught me off guard to hear her apologize for no reason.

"You're sorry?" I asked. "For what?"

"Don't hate me!" she ordered. "Promise you won't be mad!"

"Whoa, whoa," I voiced, "what the hell did you do?"

Given her sincere tone, I was thinking she had done something bad.

"Can you just promise?" she begged. "Please?"

I side-eyed her accusingly. "Okayyy," I said. "What did you do?"

"I didn't do anything," she explained, "I just—" She paused for a second, and broke eye contact and pointed her head to the pool.

"I forgot your name," she sighed.

Part of me was hurt. Yeah, it sucked that this girl I was developing a crush on didn't remember my name. But I was mostly relieved it was nothing totally serious.

"What, that's it?" I asked.

She looked embarrassed. And refused to look at me.

That was weird. Earlier she showed completely different character traits. She seemed loud and jumpy, all energetic. It seemed like she always had a smart-ass comment to make.

But now she appeared totally different. And just for forgetting my name? We'd met like a day ago. On top of that, we'd only really talked a couple times.

"There's no way you're bothered that much," I said.

"What?" she asked.

"We met recently," I began, "you probably only heard my name once, when we met."

"Well still," she sighed, "it's kinda not cool of me."

"I think you're making a big deal out of something that's not a big deal."

I took some time to really think about it. It didn't add up. Something else was bothering her. She clearly had more to say. Maybe more to apologize for.

"Something else is bothering you," I stated.

She didn't say anything. Instead, she just turned the rest of her body to the pool and placed her feet back into the pool and sighed.

"I'm sorry for being an asshole," she said firmly. "Earlier I was talking shit to you and the other boys for being scared."

A long pause flowed through the air. The thoughts and images of that thing in the cornfields flashed through both our heads.

I didn't say anything. I didn't even know what to say. It's not like she'd done anything wrong. Her apologies were sincere, but they didn't matter.

"I didn't know." she whispered.

When she said that, I understood. I looked around and with my foot, I reached out and dragged a chair near me. When it reached the back of my leg I took a seat.

The three of us, Mateo, Lenny and I were decently big guys. We were still clearly kids in high school, but we were tall and in shape. Carly seeing all of us as scared as we were, we must've looked pathetic, like three pitbulls scared of a poodle. The three of us together could possibly take down a freakishly tall and skinny person as we described.

She must've thought so little of the three of us. Yet when she encountered what we did, she must've felt like an asshole. She basically

96

realized she was making fun of and talking shit to three guys who were in genuine danger.

"It's ok." I finally said.

She didn't say anything. She just continued to stare at the water.

I understood her. Not too many hours ago, she had come face to face with something completely unnatural, something inhuman. Her mind was probably racing, trying to make sense of what happened. To put words to something that didn't exist, something that didn't belong.

I wanted to say something, something that would comfort her. But what could I say when I myself was horrified and my own stomach twisted when I thought of it.

"I'm scared too." I muttered. The words just left my mouth. For some reason, I felt like that was the right thing to say.

Carly looked at me. "What do you think it is?" she asked.

"Fuck if I know," I replied in a matter-of-fact tone.

Carly grinned, finding humor in my response. "Yeah, that was a dumb thing to ask," she said. "Who the fuck knows what that thing is."

Carly's face scrunched as if she were thinking of something. "Your aunt said it was an alien. What do you think?"

"Me?" I said, "I don't know."

She continued to look at me as if waiting for another response.

"A demon?" I guessed.

"Maybe some lab experiment gone wrong?!" she cried sarcastically.

I chuckled. It was nice to see her hyper and loud tone return.

What she did next surprised me. She got up from her seat and sat directly by the pool with her knees now in. She looked at me and patted the edge next to her, inviting me to sit next to her.
My teenage boy hormones spiked. Thankfully, I hid it pretty well.

Eagerly I shoved my jeans as far up my legs as they would go, and took my shoes off. I joined her sitting on the edge of the pool and putting my feet in the water.

"So, why'd you come down here?" she asked.

"Mateo and his mom needed some privacy," I answered.

"Oh yeah," she said. "What do you think of all that?"

"Of my tía and the sheriff?"

Carly nodded.

"It's weird," I said honestly. "Mateo and I don't have dads. Neither do our moms or their moms."

"Seriously?" Carly's jaw was hanging open, her eyes wide.

I nodded.

"So you don't have a dad, either?" she asked, then flinched and said, "Oh my shit, I'm sorry, that was not ok to ask!"

"Hey, whoa, it's cool," I said. "No, I don't have a dad."

Despite my reassurance she still held an embarrassed expression. "Sorry," she mouthed softly.

"It's really ok," I emphasized. When she relaxed, I continued, "But it is weird. Mateo probably thinks his mom is trying to get him a new daddy."

"Yeah," Carly agreed.

"So," I said, "why'd you come visit the pool?"

She shrugged. "I wanted to think," she explained. "About what happened today, you know?" She paused. "Plus Lenny's a loud snorer."

I laughed. "Speaking of Lenny," I said, "How's he doing?"

"He's ok," she answered. "His arm is sore and it hurts, but he's feeling better."

"That's good." I commented.

"Yeah, your auntie is something else." she said in awe.

"I know."

She excitedly moved her arm, mimicking the way my tía relocated Lenny's army. "Like for real!" she blurted. "She just shoved that thing right into place."

"Yup. I was there." I leaned back on my hands. "She's always been like that," I explained. "It's easy to forget how much of a badass she can be. Especially considering how sweet and kind she is."

She nodded. She swished her feet in the water. "I really am sorry," she said apologetically. "I feel awful."

"I know, it's ok," I said. "I would not have believed it, either." Without thinking I placed my hand on her thigh. "Stop feeling so bad."

When I felt her leg tense, I immediately snapped my hand away and awkwardly tried to play it off.

I was just about to get up and leave. I felt my face get red, and my body sink. I couldn't understand why I thought it was a good idea to put my hand on her thigh. But it was time to retreat.

Then I caught her smile. And once again, for some reason, I couldn't explain, I made a decision without thinking.

I decided to stay.

I recalled my past experiences with other girls. I was a good-looking guy, so I did get a fair share of attention. However, I never made a move myself. I always let the girls come to me and either say yes or no when they inevitably asked me out. It was the only way I was comfortable with. Just letting the girls come to me.

Yet with Carly, all of a sudden, I made a move on her. It was instinct, it just happened. And I was ok with it because she was ok with it.

"So why'd you come to the pool?" she asked, "Were you gonna go for a swim?"

"I was at first," I answered, "but I don't think so any more."

"Why not?" she asked, raising an eyebrow.

"I don't have any clothes." I grabbed my shirt and jeans. "This is all I have to wear."

"Oh yeah, none of us packed," she said, nodding.

A couple seconds passed and neither of us said anything. Suddenly, she stood up and used me to get up. She grabbed my shoulder and propped herself up.

"I'm pretty sure there's a laundry room somewhere here." She grunted as she stood up.

"Is there?" I asked.

She stood on one foot and shook her feet, shooting water everywhere. "Yeah, most hotels do," she answered. "Wait here!"

Before I got a chance to question her, she walked out of the room. About a minute later, the doors swung open as she returned.

"They do!" she called.

"They do?" I repeated.

"I just asked the front desk!" she replied. "Had to ring the bell a few times, but there's definitely a laundry room somewhere.

To my shock, as she was walking towards me, she began to unbutton her shorts.

When she fully unbuttoned and unzipped her shorts, she slid them down her legs.

I froze. I didn't say anything or do anything.

She eventually got to where I was still sitting.

"Come on!" she ordered.

I looked up and saw her taking off her shirt. But then she stopped suddenly and brought the shirt back down to show her face but held it there so she was still showing her stomach.

Our eyes met. I recognized that I didn't look away. I thought back to other times when I'd been caught looking at girls. Normally, I shot my eyes away as fast as possible.

But I didn't this time, for some reason I didn't know.

"Before I continue doing what I'm doing," Carly said, "do you have a girlfriend?"

The question caused an entire tsunami of feelings to rush through my head.

"Nope." I said as fast as possible. I almost blurted it out.

"Great." she said, then continued to take off her shirt.

She stood in front of me only wearing underwear and a bra. Her body was amazing. Just as beautiful as her face, if you could even compare the beauty of the two.

The best part was her expression. She was smiling. And she was turning red, red as a tomato. Her expression told me she was nervous. Combine that with the question she just asked me, and I came to the conclusion she liked me.

My jaw must've been on the floor because she giggled at my face.

She then walked to my right side. Held her arms out and fell back into the pool resembling a trust fall, her smirk never leaving her face.

Well, I was no fool.

In a rush of confidence, I stood from where I sat and ripped off my clothes as fast as possible, leaving only my boxers on. I hurled my body into the pool as fast as I could. I damn near had a heart attack when the pool was deeper than I had predicted.

I emerged and held myself above the surface. I completely forgot to feel insecure about my body and just let myself have a good time with Carly. We splashed around, throwing and swinging foam pool noodles at one another.

At first it was awkward, and I was only humoring Carly's childish, playful nature. Despite this, I eventually grew to let myself be childish, too.

An hour must've passed because I felt my body grow sore and tired.

When Carly swung a pool noodle at me, I caught it and yanked it out of her hand. Continuing to try and act cool, once I got it out of her hand, I tossed the pool noodle away.

I raised my pool noodle in an exaggerated manner. I raised it past my head using both my arms. Carly, not being an idiot, splashed water on my now exposed face. Water got in my eyes, nose, and mouth as I was inhaling. I let out a small yelp before I began to cough my way down to the floor of the pool.

I eventually recovered enough to swim back up and when I broke the surface of the pool, I only heard the delightful noise of Carly's giggle.

I rotated my body to face her.

She sat at the stairs that led into the pool. She held her belly with one hand and her mouth with the other, chuckling.

I squeezed my nose and cleared my throat as I made my way to share the stairs with her.

"Laugh it up," I coughed.

"I'm sorry!" she laughed.

I crawled and sat next to her. "Yeah," I said. "Laugh. It. Up."

"I'm sorry." She chuckled as placing her hand on me. "Oh my god, are you ok?"

"No," I choked out, still clearing my throat.

All of a sudden, her grin was replaced by embarrassment and shock. "Holy shit!" she yelped. "Holy shit! Holy shit! Holy shit!"

"Whoa, what?!" I yelled.

She shook her head and faced me. "I'm so sorry!"

"For what??" I asked.

"Dude, what's your name???" she finally asked.

CHAPTER 22

I made sure to evade my eyes away from Carly as I followed behind her while we walked up the steps.

I couldn't get over how attractive she was. She could've been a model.

We walked in silence towards a shelf that held towels. I made sure to memorize every detail of her before she wrapped her towel around herself. Regardless of her covering her body, I was still entranced by her amazing face and beautiful smile.

"Come on," she said, "I know where the laundry room is."

I nodded.

We walked back to where we were sitting and collected our things. Carly, never failing to find a way to be attractive, struggled to keep her towel on and carry all her stuff.

"You need help?" I offered.

"No, I got it." she replied.

We walked out of the huge indoor pool. I held the door open for her and before I shut it behind us, I took one last glance at the pool and thanked it for giving me this awesome bunch of moments.

Carly and I walked the hallways of the ground floor of the hotel until we finally found the laundry room. It was exactly like a laundromat setting in other establishments, only smaller and no arcade machines anywhere. Just a small room, with washing and drying machines covering the walls. A small bench in the middle of the room called to me as my sore body ached.

Still in our towels, we bunched up our clothes and threw them in the washer.

"I'll be right back," she said. "Can you watch our stuff?"

"Sure," I replied.

She disappeared and in a couple minutes returned.

To my shock yet again, I noticed she tossed her bra and panties in with our other clothes. My teenage boy hormones went crazy, but I managed to hide them by sitting on the bench. After I gained some control of myself, a battle I fought all throughout my time with her, I told her to wait and watch our stuff as I did the same.

When I returned, she explained that she didn't have any change to run and start the washer and dryer.

I was carrying my cell phone in my hand, removed from my jeans to avoid being washed. I took off the case and out clinked a multitude of change. I got on my hands and knees and searched the floor. I somehow managed to pull together five dollars' worth of quarters.

"How the hell is your phone not broken?" Carly asked.

"No idea," I answered. "I'm just glad it's not."

Some time passed as we waited for our clothes to wash and dry.

"Miguel!" Carly kept saying. "Miguel, Miguel! I'll remember this time."

"You sure?" I asked sarcastically.

"You dick! Yes, I'll remember! You know why?"

"Why?"

"Because this is probably the first time you told me your name." She crossed her arms and smirked, in a sort of *gotcha* way.

"Not true," I said, "I told you my name when I introduced myself."

She frowned, "Doesn't count, I wasn't paying attention."

We laughed and talked for what seemed like hours. Only stopping to transfer our clothes from the washer to the dryer.

Another ding sound interrupted our conversation about my name. We reached into the dryer and pulled out our warm clothes. They stunk of chlorine, it was to be expected given we had no detergent. But it was still better then nothing. Our clothes themselves weren't even dirty or wet, we'd removed them before entering the pool, tossing our underwear in a cycle with clothes that didn't need to be washed causing them to stink of chlorine was turning out to be kind of dumb. Still, I wasn't gonna admit defeat if she wasn't.

I put my boxers on with my towel still covering me. After that, I put everything back on, appreciating the warmth that came with clothes fresh out the dryer.

Carly, understandably, used the restroom to get dressed.

We made our way back to the rooms. Carly and I surprisingly spoke very little, only holding a small conversation on how names are hard and easy to forget.

When we got to our floor, we stopped in between our rooms.

"I'll be sure to remember your name," Carly said. "*Miguel.*"

"I appreciate it," I said.

I dreaded the fact that this amazing time with her was coming to an end. But I also couldn't think of a way I could drag it out.

"Ummm," she said nervously. "Can I have your number?"

"Of course," I said, grinning.

She blushed, failing to hide her smile. I took her phone and punched in my number.

"When my parents show up," she began, "and your mom. We should stay in touch."

"I'd like that," I said softly.

A voice in the back of my head kept nagging me. And with each step she took to get to her room, the voice got louder and louder.

"H-hold up," I called.

"Yeah?" she answered.

I couldn't find any other way to phrase what I wanted to ask—so I just went ahead and asked it.

"Why did you ask me if I had a girlfriend?" I asked sheepishly.

She raised an eyebrow and smirked. "Why do you think?" she asked sarcastically.

I couldn't respond after she said that. I wished she had simply said what I wanted her to say, because we all knew it could mean something other than what I wanted it to mean.

She continued to look at me with that look on her face.

"I don't want to interrupt anything that isn't there." I explained. "I don't want to think one thing, and something else is actually the case, you know?"

"Miguel, I just asked for your number," she said. "Put two and two together."

"But—" I began to say before she cut me off.

"Miguel," She said addressing me by name for the first time, "we're friends."

The words cut me like a hot knife through butter. I tried not to let my face drop and show visible emotion.

"Ok great," I said. "See? Now I know."

She smiled. Then walked into her hotel room and closed the door behind her.

I did the same.

The silence in the pitch black room told me that my tía and cousin were sleeping. I'd hoped that whatever issues arose due to the recent events had been solved.

I crawled into my bed and instinctively plugged in my phone to its charger.

When I did so the phone lit up to reveal that it was now charging. When it did so, I got a text. It was from a number I didn't recognize.

The text read: "I'd like to be more than friends."

For the first time since I'd been there, I didn't fall asleep thinking about some monster running around in the cornfields, I didn't think about how awkward things were between me and my family. I didn't think about how much trouble I was in.

When I fell asleep, I only thought of Carly. It led to a peaceful rest.

The following morning brought every issue the previous night had washed away back.

Mateo and his mom didn't speak of Terry. They acted somewhat normal. Of course they had that awkwardness looming over them, but it appeared they had worked things out the night before.

While the morning consisted of Mateo and my tía getting ready, taking showers and brushing teeth with whatever the hotel provided, I was slow to get up. I wasn't sure what time I had returned to my room, but I did know I only got about three hours of sleep max. At least that's how I felt.

It wasn't until the door opened and I heard the familiar voices of Lenny and Carly that I forced my eyes open and the first thing my brain registered was the three teenagers teasing me for drooling in my sleep.

"Let me be." I groaned.

"This is borderline a wet dream." Lenny giggled.

I dragged my body to sit up.

"Morning sunshine." Carly chimed. Carly, for whatever reason, despite probably going to bed the same time I did, showed no signs of being tired.

I had nothing to say. Without saying anything, I simply got up and walked over to the bathroom. At some point in the night, I must've taken off my shirt as I found myself putting it back on.

"Is anyone in the restroom?" I asked in a deep tired voice.

"No." answered Mateo.

"I can hand you your pillow and give y'all some privacy if you'd like?" Lenny said.

"What?" asked Mateo.

"You know," said Lenny, "because he clearly makes out with it."

Mateo didn't say anything, and neither did Carly. We all just looked at him.

"Because he drooled all over it." Lenny tried to explain.

I just turned and walked into the bathroom. I struggled to lock the bathroom door, as was typical with hotel rooms; they always seem to be broken. Without even thinking, almost instinctively, I began to shower. I turned the heat to the maximum hotness and flopped my naked body in.

While showering I almost fell asleep. The warmth of the hot water apparently did the exact opposite of waking me up. Considering I was swimming around in a pool and only washed my clothes, I figured I may as well as actually shower. The shampoo and conditioner was, of course, provided in the smallest bottle the hotel could possibly get away with.

I washed myself as well as one can without a shower scrubber. When I was satisfied with how clean I got myself, I stepped out of the shower and searched for a toothbrush.

Through my heavy eyes and muffled ears, an hour earlier I had heard that there were toothbrushes and toothpaste somewhere in here.

I opened every single container that could be found in a hotel bathroom until I found a cheap pack of toothbrushes. I fished one out and brushed my teeth with, once again, the smallest tube of toothpaste these monsters could get away with.

After I was done, I dried myself and forced on my clothes, dragging them upon moist skin. The most horrible way to put on clothes.

I finally exited the bathroom to find everyone except my tía watching tv. They were arguing over what channel to watch.

It mostly consisted of Mateo and Carly, with Carly wanting to put on some kids cartoon channel, and Mateo wanting to watch some movie he had seen while on the guide.

I just dropped my body back onto the mattress pulled from the sofa. I grabbed my phone and replied to notifications sent from my mom.

"I'm leaving today, see you later tonight," she sent with a smiley face.

My heart once again felt small and childlike. I yearned for the safety my mom would bring. She'd take me away from all of this.

With that thought, I glanced at Carly, who continued to argue with my cousin.

I wanted my mom to come and take me away from all of the scary shit that had happened. But I didn't think I wanted her to take me away from Carly. Or even the others. Despite my efforts, I had grown attached to them.

But I was more attached to my home and the safety it provided.

Even though the shower woke me up a little, sleep was still a dominant force in my body. I let it take me, drowning out the voices and sounds of the others in the room.

I wasn't sure how much time passed, but eventually I was woken up by Lenny.

"Miguel," Lenny called, "we're leaving."

I peeled my eyes open and saw everyone was exiting the room. "Where?" was all I managed to groan out.

"Breakfast," Lenny answered.

I stood up and joined my companions. Still fighting sleep, I heard very little of whatever they were talking about. The trip to the breakfast area also seemed to flash by.

The only thing I really noticed was how Carly, despite going to sleep at the same time as me, was wide awake. She was loud and cruel with her jokes, and buzzing around the group like a bee searching for a flower. An audible crowd of people buzzing with talk and noise consumed the air.

"Over here." Mateo said.

We all lined up, following him and weaving through a maze of hungry people probably enjoying their summer vacation. When we reached the destination, our table, I took immediate note that Terry was sitting with my tía.

Terry was once again dressed in civilian clothes. I took note of how much less intimidating he was outside of his uniform. He looked a lot more human. Normal.

We all sat around the round table, with Mateo landing next to his mom, Lenny next to Mateo, Carly next to Lenny, me next to Carly, and sure enough, me next to Terry.

"Good God, son," a rough, deep voice said to me. "You look like shit."

"I feel like shit," I answered.

Surprised expressions coming from the other teens made me realize who I just said that to. But I was way too tired to be scared and intimidated by the sheriff. So I leaned back in my seat, turned my head to make eye contact with the sheriff and said, "Good morning, by the way."

To my surprise, Terry nodded and smiled replying, "Morning." Terry turned to the others and said, "Can someone please get this kid some coffee?"

Not a second passed before Carly stood up and disappeared into the crowd of people.

"You don't have to," I called to her. But she turned to face me with a smile and waved her hand.

"Are any of y'all gonna grab something to eat?" Terry asked the others.

His tone was strange, he still had a terrifying deep rough voice. But he wasn't using it to terrify us. He was being nice. It felt like a parent trying to talk to you after they just whooped the shit outta you.

When nobody moved, apparently preferring to stare at the sheriff like he was a difficult math equation, my tía cleared her throat.

"Boys," she said getting our attention. "Go get something to eat."

She glanced at me. "Can y'all bring something for Miguel, too." She ordered.

"No," I said, "I can get my own stuff."

My tía looked at me, concerned.

Did I really look that bad?

"Really," I said, "I'm ok. Just tired."

My tía gave me a reassuring smile and nod.

I stood up and walked around the area. The whole place gave me flashbacks to the school cafeteria back in my hometown.

I once again had a hard time staying awake and hence staying focused on what I was doing. I grabbed a paper plate from one spot in the big room, and collected my food from other places. I grabbed waffles, scrambled eggs, and of course, bacon. The anticipation of eating this food woke me up a lot. Not to mention my hands warming, a result of the foods' heat seeping through the paper plate.

I didn't know if I was hungry. But this food looked delicious. I had a struggle within myself, trying to keep me from eating the food off the plate where I stood.

I began to rush to the table where my companions sat. Lenny had already returned; he was already eating. It was at this point that I noticed that my tía and the sheriff had empty plates sitting in front of them, with the exception of crumbs.

On my way, I felt a hand grab my arm.

I felt annoyed and anger. Someone was keeping me from my breakfast.

"Miguel," Carly said.

"Huh?" I said. "Oh hey."

She held up a small foam cup with a dark liquid in it with steam escaping into the air. "Do you like cream?" she asked. "Or are you more of a dark black coffee person?"

"Oh," I voiced, "lots of cream."

She nodded and turned away. Guilt compelled me to grab her arm the way she took hold of mine.

"Wait," I began, "I can make my own, it's ok."

"No, it's ok," Carly said. "I got it." She gestured towards the table. "Go sit down," she said—but it sounded more like she was begging me.

I noticed she herself didn't have a plate of her own.

I glanced at the table where the others sat and saw there wasn't one there for her. No one had gotten one for her.

"What do you want?" I asked. I held my plate up to her. "There's sausages if you don't want bacon," I explained, "and there's sunny side up eggs if you don't want scrambled."

She didn't say anything. She simply beamed happily at me, which filled my heart with joy.

I had wanted to talk and spend more time with her after she had texted me what she did last night. However, with Lenny around I couldn't find any courage to do so. Not wanting an awkward silence to fill our air. I spoke up.

"Pancakes if you don't want waffles," I said nervously and flustered.

She continued to smile at me. Even if it wasn't the case, I decided to accept the smile as her giving me affection.

"The variety ends there," I once again said awkwardly.

She chuckled. A noise that now meant something more than it did in the past. She looked down at my plate and studied it for a moment. "The same as you," she requested, "with sausages instead of bacon."

"Ok," I confirmed.

"I'll finish making your coffee and get my own. Thank you."

She turned and disappeared into the sea of people.

I quickly collected a second plate and filled it with Carly's requested food. I made my way to our table. I placed my plate in front of me and slid Carly's plate in front of her. Carly in turn slid my coffee to me.

With all that out of the way, ignoring the talk of the others surrounding the table, I snatched a plastic fork from the center of the table, almost knocking over the lazy susan that held them. I immediately began to shove the cheap hotel food into my mouth. I took breaks from shoving my mouth with food to occasionally sip my hot sweet coffee.

My eyes were still heavy. But I felt better and more energized.

"Eat up, it's on me," Terry said.

Without thinking, along with a mouth full of soft waffles, I asked, "Why are you so nice all of a sudden?"

Terry raised an eyebrow. "It must have something to do with you boys not breaking the law," he explained bluntly.

Not wanting to open my mouth and risk losing the food within it, I nodded my head and shrugged my shoulders. Agreeing with him.

"Mateo," Terry called turning to him, "I was just telling your mom what I found."

Anger filled my body. An hour couldn't go by without someone wanting to talk about the monster in the cornfields.

My monstrous appetite crumbled a bit. Enough for me to eat like a normal person, but not enough for me to stop. I rolled my eyes as my stomach twisted and turned with fear.

Mateo just looked at the sheriff. I had no doubt that Mateo had a lot on his mind concerning his thoughts on the sheriff.

"Ok," Mateo replied.

"Have you seen this thing before?" Terry asked.

I was surprised—had Mateo encountered this thing before? Prior to me and Lenny.

"What are you talking about?" Mateo asked.

"Have you seen it before?" Terry repeated.

"No, I haven't," Mateo answered, shaking his head.

"Your mom told me about nightmares you had when you were a kid," Terry said.

"Nightmares?" Mateo asked. Suddenly his eyes went wide with realization. He spoke again, mainly to himself and only managing to say, "Night—?"

His last word came out in a small whisper. If I wasn't paying attention, I probably wouldn't have heard him.

"You've dreamed about…" Carly paused for a second, trying to put a name on the thing in the cornfields, "about it before?"

"Seriously?" Lenny accused.

Mateo just stared at his plate. He looked to be searching for a specific memory.

"When you were young, your mom told me about you. Said you were having bad dreams," Terry explained.

Mateo didn't say anything. He continued to search his mind when suddenly his eyes went big again. His jaw dropped just a little. "I remember," he said.

Terry leaned in and rested his crossed arms on the table. He looked like he was interrogating someone. In his line of work, I was sure he had before.

"Tell me about that dream, son," Terry ordered.

"S-someone used to come to my window every night," Mateo said. "This thing I dreamed about, it would look through the window and look for me." Mateo hunched in his seat, disturbed at the memory. "It made me think of…" Mateo paused. "I-I felt like a baby bird in an egg. The egg was chipped, had an opening, and something would look inside the egg to see what I looked like."

Terry let the words Mateo just said sink in for us all. "Go on," Terry said.

"It…" Mateo paused again. He didn't continue his sentence. He closed his eyes, collecting himself, but with a still puny tone he said, "It had red eyes."

CHAPTER 23

"You've seen it before?" I shouted.

Mateo didn't answer me. He continued to stare at his plate of food. "Mom," Mateo said. "What do you remember?"

My tía shifted in her seat, adjusting herself. She exchanged a look with Terry, which told me they had been talking about Mateo.

"Well," my tía said, "I didn't think anything of it."

"What do you mean?" Mateo asked.

"Kids have nightmares," My tía explained. "When your tía and cousin lived with us, it wasn't uncommon for one of you two to enter your mom's room upset and scared."

At the mention of my mom and me, I leaned in close.

"Maybe a month after they moved away," my tía explained, "you started having this nightmare. You described a man with red eyes coming and looking through your window at you every night. I didn't think much of it. I assumed it was because you were missing **tu tía y primo.**"

Carly turned to me. Before she asked, I translated, "Cousin and aunt."

"It went on for weeks," my tía said. "Eventually you stopped."

"That's it?" I asked.

My tía shot a look at me for my question. "Yes. That's it," my tía said, glaring at me.

"I'm sorry," I choked. "It just went away?"

"Evidently not," Terry said.

"Wait, we don't even know if it's connected," I said.

"Is it the same thing?" Lenny asked, leaning forward.

"I don't know," Mateo answered honestly.

I had my own questions. I wanted to ask Mateo and his mom if they ever saw anything anywhere else other than the bedroom. Did my tía ever go and investigate outside after Mateo described a man watching him sleep through his window?

I wanted to ask, but my arms were being controlled by some other force that wasn't my mind. Every time I swallowed a mouthful of breakfast, I'd just shove more in my mouth.

"Years ago, your mother told me about this dream of yours," Terry began to say. "Like Sofía, at the time, I thought nothing of it. But now it seems a lot more relevant." He pointed at Mateo and then pointed at my tía. "You two gave similar descriptions of whom ever is out there at two different points in time."

"And?" Carly asked.

Terry turned to face the girl who was giving him sass. "And?" Terry repeated.

"And did you see it?" Carly asked.

"Yeah, while you were out there looking for it," Lenny chimed in.

Terry leaned back in his seat and crossed his arms. "No," Terry answered. "But let me tell you all. I know a crime scene when I see it. I've seen hundreds. Where you guys tell me Lenny over here hit it with his truck, I found some kicked up dirt. Looks like someone was hit and slid across the floor. And going from the tire tracks of the truck, it…" Terry paused. "Well, they vanish."

"What do you mean?" Lenny asked.

"I inspected what was left of your truck, son," Terry explained. "I especially took note of the crater it seemed to make on the ground. With the pushed-up dirt around it, and the top of your truck being caved in, well, call me crazy, but from what it looks like, it looks like it dropped and landed where it lay now."

"Mom and Dad are gonna kill you," Carly teased Lenny.

Lenny's face dropped. "What am I gonna tell them?"

Mateo shrugged his shoulders. Everyone else stayed quiet.

"Ok, so what are you saying?" I asked Terry. "Do you believe us?"

Terry shifted in his seat, adjusting himself. "Think about what you guys are telling me," Terry said. "It's unbelievable."

"But you just said—" I paused. He never really said he believed us.

"You saw the evidence that there was a struggle of some kind," Carly continued my sentence.

Terry nodded, looking from me to Carly.

"Do you believe us?" my tía asked.

My tía's tone sounded desperate and shy. It was a tone I almost never heard from her.

I didn't know why, but it frustrated me. Made me feel awful.

"Why does it matter if Terry believes us?" I asked in a frustrated tone.

Everyone turned their eyes to look at me, making me want to hide and shove the words I said back into my mouth.

"I'm just saying," I began, "what happens next?"

I got weird looks from around the table. They didn't know what I was talking about.

"I mean," I said, "Do we all just go home? With that thing out there?" I gestured at the sheriff. "No offense, but it doesn't matter if you believe us. That thing is still out there. It's probably still lingering around our homes."

Everyone around the table adopted the same type of look on their faces. They all knew that what I was saying was true. Yes, we weren't in there at the houses now, but were we just gonna avoid Magnolia Falls forever? Based off their defeated expressions, they had not given thought to it.

"The problem is still there," I continued. "If you believe us, what can you do to solve the problem?"

"Ok, we get it," Mateo said sternly.

"He can get the rest of the policemen," Carly explained. "You can go get him! Kill him!"
Carly stood from her seat excited by her words. "When Sofía here shot it with her gun, it hurt it, remember!?" Carly yelled.

Lenny seemed to pay attention to Carly's words more intensely than the rest of us. It must've been because at the time my tía shot at the monster, he was unconscious. It was most likely the first time Lenny was learning of this.

No one responded to Carly. So Carly faced my tía and the sheriff and asked, "Right?"

Neither of them answered.

"That's what I'm saying," I answered her finally. "What would you do?"

"Personally," Terry said, "I'd find and kill it. But realistically, that seems impossible. Sofía shot it with her shotgun. Not just that, but with fuckin' slug rounds."

I wasn't super educated on guns and bullets and how they worked. But I knew that slug rounds were a serious thing.

"If what you guys are saying is correct, and that thing survived multiple slug rounds, then consider the truck, whatever it is, it is strong."

I'd considered this myself. It survived my tía's shotgun. It crushed and threw a large truck like a soda can. Killing it wasn't even an option. How could we?

"Hypothetically speaking," Terry continued, "we don't want other forces getting involved. Your lives will never be the same."

"What do you mean?" Carly asked.

"With this discovery," Terry answered, "you and your homes will become a biohazard."

That's a thought I hadn't considered. How would people react to this thing? How would they react to us?

"So," Lenny said, "we're really not gonna do anything about it?"

Terry looked sad for us. He was basically telling us we were in a lose-lose situation. They'd go back to their homes with that thing hiding just behind their crops, or see how human race will react, see what the human race will do to them.

"I don't know," Terry said.

"Seriously?" Lenny exclaimed. "That's all you got?"

In my experience with Lenny, he didn't get loud very often, with the exception of the events of the past couple of days. That would get anyone to get loud.

From what I understood about Lenny, he was probably more or less on the quieter side. Unlike his sister, the complete opposite.

I felt so bad for them. Their homes were taken from them by some force we didn't understand. How frustrating and scary it must be to be them. I looked at my aunt and cousin. I felt pity for them too.

And yet here I was, about to be taken away from all of this. My life would probably go back to normal, or as normal as it could be, after all that's happened. But still, I was going to a home that didn't have what they had.

"You guys, I don't know what to tell you," Terry said. "I'm not even sure you guys are telling me the truth."

"Fucking seriously?" my tía said. "I've never lied to you in the past. But I'm lying now?"

"Think about what you're telling me!" Terry said coldly. "What do you expect me to make of it?"

"I expect you to trust me."

"Yeah? You think I don't?"

"I don't."

Terry and my tía were both sitting up, glaring at each other. Since I couldn't see my own reaction, I turned to see the others' reaction to this clash of the titans. But to my despair, Mateo, Lenny, and Carly just looked sad. Not scared, sad. No doubt because they'd lost their homes.

"I believe you," Terry said.

"I don't believe you!" my tía said, sticking her finger at him.

"I believe the sincerity of your voice," Terry said calmly, but with emotion. "I believe the fear in your kiddos' eyes, in your eyes. But I can't believe what you guys are telling me."

He relaxed his shoulders, inciting my tía to do the same.

My tía sighed and calmly whispered, "Ok."

My tía turned to look at us. Her motherly instincts broke through her tough skin; the raw concern was obvious.

It cut me like a hot knife through butter. All a parent wants is to keep her children safe. My Tía Sofía never had an issue doing that before. Nothing ever got between her and her child. I had no doubt she also felt a sense of protection for the O'Youngs, loving them because Mateo loved them.

"So what happens now?" I asked. Repeating the same question again.

"We'll have to figure something out," Terry answered. "First priority is keeping you guys safe."

My tía glanced at the sheriff after he said that. I could tell a lot from that small glance. I somehow understood that they cared deeply for each other. But they'd never act on it. Partly because of Mateo.

He clearly cared for her and cared about what she cared about. He wanted her to be ok. I also knew that she cared for him. Men didn't exactly hang around our family for one reason or another. My mom and tía didn't have a dad themselves; they didn't know what it meant to put trust in a man who wasn't their kid. It must've been hard for my tía, to care about someone and not know how to act on it or not want to act on it.

Sofía would not want to push a father figure on Mateo. Especially after all these years. I believed Terry felt the same.

I studied his hands. He had no ring on his fingers. No wife, and I assume no girlfriend. Which meant he probably didn't have kids of his own.

Through the conversation between those around my table, I couldn't help but think what if. What if Terry and my tía became a couple years ago? Would things be different? I thought about how having a father figure of some kind in the family, how it would've changed the family dynamic, if at all. What dynamic? I hadn't spent time with my cousin and Tía in years.

I decided to put these thoughts away for now. I attempted to tune in to what the table was discussing now. To my horror and discomfort, the young ones were going back and forward on what the monster could possibly be.

"Alien?" Mateo suggested. "It does kinda look like the grays, right?"

"No," Carly responded. "Government experiment gone wrong."

They were apparently pitching ideas to Lenny, who shook his head no with every suggestion. Lenny was thinking the same thing I was. He didn't care what it was.

I decided to push away my fears for a moment to think for myself what it could be.

The first thing that came to mind was a ghost. When I was a kid, I had a huge fear of ghosts. My little kid brain chalked everything scary up to being a ghost. I blamed the film, *Ghostbusters*, and their goofy, oddly shaped ghost for this.

Of course, when I got older, I stopped believing in anything supernatural. That didn't mean that my mind still didn't go there from time to time.

"It could just be a regular guy," I said, and their heads turned to face me with confused looks. Understanding what I said sounded like I continued to say, "What if something happened to him? What if he's just some inbred deformed guy?"

"The eyes point to something else being the case," Lenny said.

"What?" I asked.

"No matter what happens to the human body," he explained, "bioluminescence doesn't happen to us."

Never hearing that word before, I asked, "Bio what?"

"We don't glow," he answered, rolling his eyes. "There's only a select few species on the planet that can naturally glow. Mainly aquatic animals. Humans and other mammals simply don't glow."

"Ok?"

"Look, you're implying that something happened to some guy or something right?" I nodded and Lenny continued, "It might be the case, but his eyes are red, right? Not red like popped a blood vessel red, but glowing red."

"Ok, so what are you implying?" I asked.

"Personally, I don't think it matters what it is. Even if knowing what it is would make us feel better," he explained. "But if I had to answer the question we're all asking, then I believe it's something supernatural."

"Like a ghost?" I asked as if I were a child.

"I don't know," he answered. "Glowing red eyes is a monster trope we all know and recognize. So to put it simply, it's just a monster. Nothing more, nothing less."

Lenny wasn't talking to me at this point. He was talking to himself. He was speaking his mind. "It can be anything," Lenny continued. "Literally everything's a possibility. The glowing red eyes, in my opinion, point in the supernatural direction."

Lenny said the same thing he said before. Just used different words. This said a lot about where his mind was concerning thoughts on our monster.

Going off Terry's expression, he pitied us. After a moment of silence, he said, "You guys really saw something."

"The evidence is all there, too," Sofía said.

Terry nodded and said, "I'm gonna assume whatever is out there has been there for a while. At least since his nightmares." Mateo and Terry exchanged looks. "I'm gonna grab some friends of mine," Terry said. "We're gonna investigate the cornfields."

"And when you find it?" Sofía asked.

"I'll cross that bridge when we get there.," Terry answered. "I need to see this thing for myself."

After some time, we all tried to steer the conversation in a direction of some sort of normality. We failed hilariously. I got desperate and tried to talk about diarrhea. This led to a conversation that spawned a couple chuckles and not much else.

We eventually finished up our food, throwing away what was on our plate due to our appetites being a thing of the past. We eventually made our way back up to our rooms.

It was at this point where I realized I was feeling much better. My eyes, while still heavy, stayed open with much less effort. My body felt less fatigue. I was still tired and suffering from not sleeping a full night's sleep, but it felt a lot more manageable. It was worth it. Spending a large majority of the night with Carly was totally worth losing a few hours.

I glanced up at her and felt a stab of hurt and jealousy when she was speaking to Mateo. We were inside a moving elevator, a cramped elevator, so they were close to each other. I envisioned myself stepping between them and stealing the attention away from Mateo. But it was just a thought.

Carly said some things last night. I realized I should trust her and let things play out comfortably for her. Exposing myself as a jealous person wouldn't help my case.

Lenny shoved into me by accident. A result of the elevator being so crowded with Terry now joining us. I knew Terry was a big guy. Since I first met Terry, it was obvious he was a huge dude, easily over six foot three. But being this close to him in the elevator really showed me just how big and tall he was.

A ding from the elevator allowed us all to scatter into our hallway with relief.

We entered our rooms. Lenny and Carly disappeared into their own room, leaving me with the sheriff, my cousin, and my tía.

"Describe it to me?" Terry asked.

My tía didn't expect this question; she wasn't sure what he was referring to at first. This confusion on her part led her to ask, "What?"

"Our monster," Terry clarified. "Tell me what it looks like."

"Didn't I tell you already?" Sofía asked.

"Tell me again," Terry demanded sternly. Terry took a seat on one of those cushioned chairs that's always in a hotel room. On his way down, he let out a grunt.

My tía walked around the bed and took a seat in front of him. The conversation, to my amazement, sounded like two professional talkers.

"It's tall."

"How tall?"

"Over eight feet tall."

"And?"

"It's skinny."

"Skinny?"

"It looks malnourished."

"Ok. The face?"

My tía took a second to think about her answer. "It's bald, has smooth shiny skin, and it doesn't have a nose or lips."

"It doesn't have a mouth?"

"No, it has a mouth, just not lips."

This time Terry took some time to think about what he wanted to ask. "Tell me about the eyes."

"They're glowing red."

"I got that part. Tell me what else."

"That's it, the eyes glow the color red. And they glow bright."

A silence once again broke the flow of their conversation. Terry was clearly picturing the thing in his head. "It was naked? It wasn't wearing anything?"

"Yeah, yeah, it was naked. But it didn't have any genitalia."

"It didn't?"

"No."

Yet again, a silence filled the air between them. Mateo and I gave each other wide-eyed looks.

"Its skin was black," my tía finally said.

"He was Black?" Terry asked, confused. He perhaps thought my tía was talking about a skin tone typically seen in our society.

"I mean," my tía said. She looked around the room and her eyes landed on a trash can with a black plastic trash bag. "That black," she said, pointing at the trash can.

Terry stood up and gave a goodbye to us all. The goodbye he gave us all was a strange reminder of the fact that he was human. Then he left the room.

"That's it?" I asked.

"Yup," my tía answered.

"What's he gonna do?"

"What he said he would do."

With nothing to do or say, I decided to sleep. While I was feeling better, I still felt like ass. Without waiting for the others, I stood from my seat and headed up to my room. I guess all that could be done has now been done, at least from my end.

I yanked out the bed from the couch and immediately threw myself on it.

My eyes didn't wait for the rest of my body. They shut as soon as my head hit the pillow. Not long after that, I lost all consciousness.

Hours later, I awoke. Regardless of my sleep, I still felt like shit. My eye lids opened, dragging themselves across the surface of my eyeballs. My body felt heavy and lazy.

I never thought I'd think such a thing. But I somewhat regretted spending the night with Carly. This thought was immediately withdrawn after images of that night flashed through my head. It still sucked though.

But I didn't want to throw my sleep schedule off, so I forced myself to sit up and stay awake.

I was surprised to see that the room was empty. Mateo and my Tía Sofía were not here with me. I wondered for a moment where they could be. But before I could wonder for too long, I noticed the chair that Terry was sitting on earlier wasn't where I last saw it. In fact, it was missing entirely.

I instinctively scanned the room, looking for the chair. When I eventually turned my head to the left of my bed I found the chair, and someone sitting on it.

My mom had finally come.

"Hi-" she began.

Before she could finish her greeting, I shot off my bed and threw my hands around her.

My mom stood from where she sat and did the same.

My eyes began to water up. I was so happy to see her and so relieved she was here now. I was so overcome with emotion I was on the verge of crying.

My mom's embrace made me feel safe and comfortable for the first time since I left home. I felt like a child, crawling into my mom's bed after a nightmare. For the longest time, we just stood there, hugging.

I eventually backed off my mother and when the back of my legs hit the edge of my bed I sat. My mother did the same. I didn't know what to say. Neither did my mom.

"It's so good to see you," I finally whispered.

"I missed you, too," my mom replied.

"Umm," I hesitated, "how was the drive?"

"*How was the drive?* How are you??" my mom shouted.

"What?" was all I managed get out.

"Baby, you've been through a lot," my mom explained. "Are you ok?"

I sat and stared at her for a second. I thought of lying and telling her I was ok. But I never got away with lying to her before, so I told her the truth. "No."

My mom smiled reassuringly. The concern she felt for me was obvious. "It's ok," she said. "Tell me what happened."

I almost went on and on about the thing in the cornfields and how it terrorized us. But I remembered my tía must've told my mom something completely different than the truth.

"What did Sofía tell you?" I asked.

My mom leaned back in her chair, the gears in her head turning. From my question, she put two and two together. She then told me, "Your Tía told me someone broke into the house. Now tell me what really happened."

I felt guilty, throwing my tía under the bus. But my mom was gonna find out eventually. She wasn't stupid. It was hard putting everything into words, but I still tried.

I tried to sound as serious as I could, but what came out of my mouth sounded as stupid as you'd expect. I said, "We were attacked by a monster."

"A monster?" my mom asked. "What kind of monster?"

"I don't know," I said honestly. "I wish I knew how to explain it."

"Try your best," my mom sighed.

"One night, Mateo and I were spending time with Lenny, a friend of his."

"Mhmm."

"We ended up staying late and losing track of time. We went outside to go home, and the horses were gone. We found Milkshake, but she was destroyed."

My mom simply raised an eyebrow and I knew that I needed to elaborate.

"Milkshake was dead," I explained. "And it was bad. She was in pieces and twisted all over the place. She was killed."

My mom's face was scrunched up. She was confused, but she was listening.

"We found the monster that killed her. It's big, dark as a shadow and strong with red eyes." I used my hands to visualize my words. "It chased us. Then it showed up again. Lenny hit it with his car and the monster crushed the car like it was nothing."

My mom's face showed disbelief, which encouraged me to shut up. I felt stupid trying to explain this to her. For some reason, I assumed she was gonna believe me.

"Then what?" she asked.

"Then we all ran. Ended up here," I answered.

"And your tía knows?"

"About the monster? Yes."

My mom still looked concerned about me, but it was clear she was frustrated with my story. She didn't believe me.

Desperate for her understanding I nearly yelled, "But there's a lot more details. I probably said all that too fast!"

She didn't say anything, just nodded. She stood up from her chair and took a seat next to me on the bed.

"Stop, Miguel," she said. "Just stop."

"I'm telling the truth!" I barked.

"Watch it," my mom said coldly.

I relaxed and apologized. "I'm sorry, but—"

"No buts!" my mom ordered, cutting me off. "Miguel. Tell the truth."

"I am," I said, my voice cracking.

"Do you think I'm stupid?" my mom accused.

"Noooo!" I begged. "Mom please!"

My mom held her hand up, which led me to instinctively silence myself.

Well, this was awful. All I wanted was to see my mom again. I wanted her to tell me everything was ok, comfort me. She was supposed to take all of this away. Make everything go back to normal.

Instead, she was giving me those eyes, the eyes where she thought I was lying or keeping the truth from her.

But what did I expect? Did I really believe she would believe me? I didn't know what I thought. I thought she would instantly take care of me. No matter what. Instead, she was questioning my fear and stress.

"Whatever!" I said loudly. "Never mind!" I waved my hands in the air with tears sneaking up on my eyes. "I lied!" I lied. "We were robbed at night!"

"Bullshit," my mom commented.

"Well, what do you want?" I lashed out at her. "You want me to make up another story?"

"Hey!" My mom yelled. "Don't talk to me like that! I'm not one of your friends."

"I know," I said defiantly. "You never fail to remind me."

My mom stood up, and in a cold yet stern voice, she said, "If I have to tell you again to watch your tone, you'll be sorry."

Her threat finally got me to calm down. I slumped on the chair with my mom sitting on the bed, flipping where we originally sat.

"I didn't drive all the way here, put everything I was doing on hold, just to be lied to," my mom said.

Really? I thought. *You're upset for you? What about your clearly fucked up kid?* Regardless of my thoughts I didn't say anything.

"Miguel, I know it's been awkward," she said. "But the fact that you couldn't spend a couple days with them before all this happened is ridiculous. I was so worried! I rushed all the way down here I thought something bad had happened."

Her last sentence quite literally made me laugh. I couldn't explain it, maybe I thought it was ironic. I laughed like I laughed when I was with friends of my own age. Even my mom glaring at me because of my laughter couldn't get me to stop.

"No way!" I finally said through gritted teeth and a smile.

"What?" she asked, confused and offended at my words.

"I can't believe I thought you'd believe me?" I explained through tears. "I mean I'm pretty much telling you that my family and new friends were attacked by some slender man monster. And I told you with such confidence." I paused in my rant only to take a breath. "I mean, I laid it all out for you just like that! Gosh, how stupid and ignorant of me! How could I have expected anything else to happen?!"

"Miguel," my mom said softly. "What's wrong with you?"

"What's wrong with me?" I repeated. "Mom, I encountered a literal nightmare. And regardless of what you think, that's what happened. And instead of my mom, who I wanted to see so badly after all the shit that's happened to me, comforting me and at least humoring me! She gets upset the first chance she gets!"

My mom just sat there, stunned. She was both angry at my outburst and disrespect towards her and concerned at what the hell had gotten into me.

I waved my hands downwards at her, brushing it off. "Can you please just take me home?" I asked defeated. "Seriously, that's all I want."

Mom just continued to stare at me. She didn't say anything.

"Oh, what, you think I'm crazy?" I said. "Is it because it's obvious I'm telling the truth? Because I clearly believe what I'm saying, but what I'm saying is nonsense, so I must be crazy, right?"

My mom just continued to stare at me, in shock of my words and actions.

Seeing her face finally brought me back down to Earth. I realized I was just yelling at my mom. My mom who did everything for me. Guilt and sorrow consumed me.

"I'm sorry, Mom," I apologized.

Regardless of my apology, I was still frustrated, and angry. I was done wasting my time trying to get my mom to believe me. And I was done wasting her time with me.

"Where's everybody?" I asked.

"They went out to get some food," she answered.

"Already?" I asked looking at the clock. To my surprise, it was already late afternoon. I must've slept for a long time. "Now what?" I asked.

"That's it?" she scoffed.

"Uhhhhhh, yeah. That's it."

My mom's face scrunched up and she yelled, "No, that's not it!"

I threw my hands up and let them drop and slap my sides and sighed, "I don't know what else to tell you, Mom. I honestly don't have anything else to say."

"Why can't you just tell me the truth?" she pleaded.

"Because I can't come up with a lie right now, Mom," I said honestly. "I just can't think of something you'd believe. I don't even think you'd believe anything I have to say anyway."

I got up and threw myself on the bed my mom currently sat on. I pulled out my phone and started scrolling through social media.

"I'm so sorry, Mom. I know this sucks."

The words left my mouth, and I was being genuine. But I was also frustrated, and I made no attempt to hide it.

It wasn't all bad; my mom was finally here. I was finally gonna go home and all this bullshit would become some bad fucked-up memory.

I wasn't sure how much time passed. Maybe about thirty minutes. The others finally showed up to the hotel, and all piled in the room.

Lenny and Carly only dropped off some of the food they had brought before retreating to their room. However, only a couple minutes passed before they once again joined us.

It was the best thing ever. I was in a room with people who would believe the story I told them. It was an odd comfort, but a welcome one. Maybe it was because we all shared the same traumatic experience that made me feel less alone. Or maybe it was simply being around other people my own age.

My comfort was immediately ripped from me when my mom, without missing a second, jumped on my tía.

"What the fuck happened?" my mom asked.

My tía closed her eyes. She was caught in her lie. "What did he say?" she gestured to me.

"All kinds of bullshit!" my mom said. "I'm now asking the one other adult around to tell me the truth."

"I told her about the monster," I chimed in. "I told her everything."

My tía nodded reassuringly. "Welp," my tía declared. "A wickedly deformed man attacked us. We don't know what it is, so we've been calling it a monster."

"No!" My mom called, "No, no, no, noooo! Tell me the truth."

"Hermana," my tía said calmly, "we are."

I could tell my mom was ready to argue some more. So I stood up and made my way to my mom.

I put my hand on her shoulder and turned her around to face me. Once she faced me, I put my other hand on her shoulder to grab her tightly.

"Enough, Mom," I said. "You hear what you want to hear."

My mom surprisingly took the hint. She sighed and looked down. I didn't wait for her to say anything or do anything. I let go of her shoulders and walked over to the food.

I was wildly delighted to see they had gotten McDonald's. My delight only increased when Carly passed me a ten-piece chicken nugget with sweet and sour sauce.

I looked around and saw only my tía and mom were not eating. So I wasted no time and consumed my meal.

A loud awkwardness filled the air. We all ate with the lingering fact that my mom was in the room and her thoughts on the rest of us were less than great.

"Are you guys fucking with me?" my mom asked.

At the same time, we all answered, *no*. Carly chuckled at the unified answer.

"I mean seriously, Tía, read the room," Mateo said.

"Don't be a jerk, Mateo," said Mateo's mom.

Some moments went by. We ate our fast-food dinner while watching TV.

"Welp," I said, "I'mma head out."

"Where?" my mom asked.

"I'm just going to hang out at the pool," I answered.

Before my mom could give me approval, I turned and left. I made my way as fast as I can to the pool. I didn't want my mom to stop me. The frustration and anger had really gotten to me. It was stupid. I was angry for a stupid avoidable reason. I should've just gone along with my tía's lie. Although it would've been nice to be clued in on what she said. Not my fault we couldn't get our stories straight.

But for some reason, I'd really wanted my mom to believe and understand me. I wanted her to know what happened to me. I wanted her to feel bad for me, I wanted her to coddle me and comfort me.

I got none of that. All I got was my mother thinking I was full of shit. The worse part was, it wasn't like she was being unreasonable. I'd just told her that monsters exist, like actual monsters from fairy tales.

I flung the pool doors open and flopped down on a sun chair. I laid there for a bit,
before letting my thoughts go round and round in my head just getting worse. I sighed and pulled out my phone and scrolled through social media. I saw a post from friends, having a way better summer break then I was. I saw a post from my friend, Peter Castilanos. He was at a water park. Having a great time with our other friends. I remembered us planning that trip to that exact water park.

That was before my mom told me I was gonna spend the summer with my cousin and tía.

"Fuck you," I whispered to my phone.

I hated that my friends were having a normal vacation. Doing what people should be doing while on summer break. I should've never come, I should've fought harder to not come.

It's all my mom's fault.

"Wipe that shit off your face!" a voice called.

I turned to face where the voice was coming from.

It was Lenny, Carly, and Mateo. They had followed me.

"I said," Mateo began, "wipe that shitty look off your face, please."

"What look?" I asked.

"That one," Carly said putting her finger an inch away from my face. "You look like you wanna do something stupid."

"Like I wanna do something stupid?" I repeated. "I've already done something stupid."

"Yeah, you didn't finish your food," Lenny chimed.

I rolled my eyes.

Mateo studied the pool area. Like yesterday, the pool was empty.

"We should jump in?" Mateo suggested.

"Yeah, no way," Carly said. "I don't have a bathing suit."

I shot her a look. And she very briefly smirked and winked at me.

"We can just run to the store real quick," Lenny offered, "I saw a Walmart on our way, its like a minute drive from here... probably."

"Oh yeah?" Mateo said. "Have you forgotten you no longer have a car?"

Lenny slapped his cheeks with both his hands and dropped his jaw, then in a sarcastic tone he cried, "My what is whaaaaat???"

"Lenny's car wasn't the only car in existence," Carly laughed.

"Yeah, I'm sure your mom would be cool with letting you drive her car over to the Walmart," Lenny explained.

Mateo thought about it for a moment. Then he said, "I guess I could ask her."

"Great," Carly voiced. "Let's go."

After some light begging from Mateo to his mom and a couple side eyes from me to my mom, we were allowed to go to Walmart, with the promise we'd be back at a decent time.

"Make sure you bring your phones." Sofia ordered. More to her son than anyone else.

I felt around in my pocket and pulled mine out, the battery was almost dead.

When my mom spotted me holding my phone she repeated Sofias order to me. Maybe it was the fact that my phone would've been all but useless by the time I left this room, or maybe I wanted to somehow get back at her for hurting me. But instead of listening to her I walked over to the nightstand where someone's charger, maybe mine, laid, and plugged it in.

I avoided her gaze and exited the room before her eyes burned a hole through my head.

"You sure you can drive?" I asked.

"Duh," Mateo shot back,

"I've literally never seen you drive before," Carly chimed in.

Mateo turned to face us all as we walked behind him and called, "Shut uuuup." He eyed Lenny for a moment. Then said, "Unless you want Lenny to drive. And we all know how his vehicle ended up."

"Fair enough," Lenny sighed.

We piled into the car like clowns. Not two minutes later, we arrived at Walmart. We wandered around the supermarket until we landed on what we were looking for. Brightly colored swim gear hung from racks that surrounded us. I personally couldn't find anything I liked, so I ended up going with something cheap.

"Yo Miguel!" Carly called. "You wanna see me in this?" she asked with a flirtatious smile.

What she held was basically red string,

"Uhhhhhh—" was all I managed to get out, before she chuckled and tossed it over her shoulder and into the sea of racks.

"Whatcha gonna get?" she asked, as she walked to me.

"Just these," I said. "Nothing fancy."

Carly took them from my hands and while she studied my trunks, she said, "I think I'm gonna get a one-piece. Something cheap, too."

Not really knowing what to say I just nodded in agreement. Carly shoved the trunks back into my arms and crossed hers.

"What?" I asked.

"What's with you being all awkward all of a sudden?" she asked.

"I don't know," I shrugged. "What will your brother think?"

"I talked to him already," Carly said. "And he's not from a bad '80s movie."

"Really? What did he say?" I asked.

"He knew," Carly answered. "He said he'd caught me stealing glances."

"You were?"

She smiled flirtatiously again and nodded her head excitedly.

I smiled at her. Then I looked back to the shorts I was gonna get. I'd noticed a rack filled with men's swim shorts, with a label that read $4.99. I fumbled with the shorts in my hands and found the label. The price read $6.99. I flung the shorts in my hand back where I found them and made my way to the cheaper shorts.

"Hellooo?" Carly's voice called.

I didn't hear her at first. Not until she yanked at my shirt. And repeated, "Helloooooooo!"

"What?" I asked.

"Where are you?" she asked.

"In a Walmart?"

"No, I mean where are you?"

I raised my shoulders and arms saying, "I don't get it?"

Carly whipped her arms towards me, raising her eyebrows. "You've clearly got something on your mind," she said. "Spit it out!"

"What are you talking about?" I asked, backing away from her. She took a step closer to me, closing the distance I had just made.

"Well, I'm over here tryna flirt with you," Carly explained. "And all I'm getting is one-word replies?"

Her words of admitting that she's flirting with me filled my stomach with butterflies.

"Can you at least flirt back?" she demanded.

I thought about it for a bit. Based on Carly's face, she did not like that at all. Maybe it was the confused expression I had.

"You've got a nice smile," I tried.

She rolled her eyes.

"Sorry, I'm not very good with flirting," I apologized. "All I can think about is that creature that attacked us."

"Well," she began, "can you at least not ignore me?"

"I'm not ignoring you," I said firmly.

"It feels like it."

"Look, I'm just distracted. Right now feels like the quietest it's been in a while."

She looked at me thoughtfully before saying, "I know what you mean. It's hard to think of anything else."

We continued walking for a moment before she stopped me again. "Can you at least keep an open ear, so I don't feel like I'm talking to a wall."

"Yeah," I replied.

"See? Like that!" she said, pointing a finger at my face. "I feel like I'm barely talking to anyone right now!"

I pushed her finger away from my face before saying, "You do enough talking for the both of us, don't you think?"

I hadn't realized what I said could be hurtful until I saw the look on her face. She looked pissed and hurt.

"Screw you!" she said loudly pointing another finger at me. "I—"

She stopped mid-sentence, as if she didn't know what to say. She opened and closed her mouth a couple more times trying to find words. But I guess nothing came to mind. Maybe now that I'd said something, she was more aware of her excessive speaking.

"Look, I'm sorry," I said. "That wasn't a cool thing for me to say."

I got nervous with the words I was about to say. I almost stopped myself, but decided to say what I was gonna say. "I think you're beautiful. I find all that you say and do cute."

She blushed, which made me feel better. But she also held on to her angry look.

"I honestly don't know what to say. I'm sorry." I sighed.

She thankfully took pity on me. "It's ok," she said. "It's just, one night we're flirting getting all chummy and the next day, nothing?"

It was odd how open she was about the situation. But it was also comforting. It told me she liked me.

"I'm sorry, I didn't mean to seem like there's suddenly nothing happening. Like I said, I have a lot on my mind right now." I waved my hands around, gesturing at everything. "Being here right now, in a Walmart. I feel like I'm pretending, like I'm acting. I'm actively trying not to freak out as if there is nothing going on? As if what we all just went through doesn't change everything? Now I know that that thing exists."

Carly looked at me and softened her expression. She reached for my arm and wrapped herself around it. She quietly whispered, "I'm sorry."

Feeling her wrapped around my arm and pressing herself against me made me feel strange. It felt like being somewhere I hadn't been in a while. Like being back at an old house. I was strangely aware of her body, her warmth, I could feel her muscles, small and soft yet undeniably filled with strength.

"And—" I began before stopping myself. "Sorry, there's more."

She tilted her head, "Like what?" she asked. "Other than the obvious, I guess."

"I guess it's my mom," I said.

130

Carly raised an eyebrow.

"I guess we had an argument," I explained.

"You guess?" she asked.

I hesitated, not knowing how to explain. "I was expecting a different outcome," I explained. "When she finally showed up." I looked down at the floor in disappointment and said, "I wanted her to comfort me. She argued with me instead."

Carly looked at me with sad eyes.

Saying what I said out loud must've seemed pathetic. I was embarrassed to say it.

"I'm sorry," Carly finally said, putting a hand on me.

Her comfort was appreciated. But I still felt pathetic for expressing my feelings.

"I want my parents, too." Carly sighed.

I looked at her, surprised.

"Seriously," she said, noticing my disbelief. "For whatever reason, as unreasonable as it sounds, I feel like everything will be ok when I finally see my parents."

"Like they'll fix everything," I said.

Carly nodded, then looked at me empathetically and said, "It's comforting knowing you feel this way, too."

"Me too," I said, not realizing how ridiculous my words sounded. "I mean," I stuttered, "it's comforting for me, too."

Carly beamed at me delightfully.

We regrouped with Mateo and Lenny. They had picked out items similar to mine. Cheap items. Lenny kindly offered to pay for all our stuff, and after some arguing I and Mateo gave in. I thanked Lenny. I made sure to tell him that I would pay him back. I took out my wallet and offered some cash. Lenny waved both his hands at the sight of my cash.

"Seriously buddy," Lenny said, "don't worry about it."

As we walked back to the car, Mateo quietly told me that Lenny did this kind of stuff all the time. "He'll never let you pay him back." Mateo explained.

"Why?" I asked.

"That's just how he is I guess," he answered.

I thought about that for a moment. Where I was from, unless it was a date of some kind, you paid for yourself. It wasn't just money. If you had a problem and needed someone's help, you owed them.

I thought back to my best friend, Josh. A couple months ago, I had asked him for a ride to an auto repair shop. I was picking up my mom's car. As my friend, he, of course, agreed. However, he made it clear I'd be paying for gas. And I officially owed him a favor.

Stuff like that was normal at my home. It wasn't even considered rude; that was just how people were.

That wasn't the case here. When the horses went missing that night, Lenny immediately offered to help us look. I didn't realize till then he had yet to ask for anything in return. I recalled he'd offered to drive us back to my tía's house.

Now he'd bought me a pair of trunks. They were cheap, sure, but still.

As we drove back to the hotel, we passed a frozen yogurt store. Carly begged Mateo, who was driving, to stop so that we could all get some. He agreed, and then Mateo offered to pay for us all.

An argument formed between Mateo and Carly. Carly argued that since it was her idea, she should be the one to pay. Mateo argued that since he got the most expensive cup, he should pay.

Carly won the argument and paid for us all. The only thing that came close to her asking for something in return was her demanding a taste of everyone's cup.

It was strange but I decided to appreciate it, rather than try and understand it.

"You guys are all nice here," I stated.

"Fuck you," Lenny sarcastically replied.

I exaggerated my surprised expression, saying, "I take it back."

"How are people nice here?" Carly asked.

"I don't know." I said. "You guys are."

"We don't make up the whole of the city," Carly said in her smart-ass tone.

"I know," I said. "I guess things are just different where I come from."

Nobody said anything. Perhaps they understood what I meant.

We eventually pulled up to the hotel. I was in a rush to get to the pool but before I could open the door, Carly thanked us all.

"For what?" Mateo asked.

"Hanging out like we just were. Like we are. It helps with everything I've been through."

My gut sank. This whole time, I'd only been concerned with how I was feeling about this demon in our yard. I wasn't so stupid to completely disregard the fact that other people were going through the same thing I was. I knew that the others were as scared as I was. But I put no more thought into it. That was pretty selfish of me.

As we all hopped out of the car, Lenny's phone went off.

"It's Mom!" Lenny cried to Carly, waving a hand at her to come to him. "Hello?!" Lenny answered the phone.

Mateo and I watched them have a conversation, only hearing one side of it.

"W-what?" Lenny said nervously.

Silence followed that heart-pounding word. What could possibly cause a stoic-ish person like Lenny to sound like that?

"N-nooo!" he cried into the phone.

"What!" Carly called. "What's wrong!"

"I told you guys!" Lenny shouted. "No, we're not home!"

CHAPTER 24

"Hey!" Mateo called. "What's going on?"

"Hold on!" Lenny answered. "I don't know." Lenny put a hand up to shush Mateo. "Mom! We're not home. I texted you!" Lenny said loudly. Lenny darted his head towards his sister and glared at her. "You didn't tell them!?" he shouted.

"I did!" she replied, frustrated.

"Fuuuuuuuuck!" was all Lenny managed to make out.

Carly grabbed her head and began to cry out, "Oh my god! Oh my god!"

"Call your mom!" I ordered Mateo.

Mateo took out his phone and called his mom.

"I DONT HAVE MY FUCKIN' TRUCK!!!" Lenny yelled, stomping the ground in frustration.

"Hey, he's calling his mom!" I said. "Calm down!"

I felt stupid for saying those words. I told a guy whose parents could be terrorized by a literal demon to calm down.

The look Lenny gave me was both understandable and terrifying. He looked at me like he was ready to not only destroy me but hide the evidence.

"Panicking isn't gonna help," I said nervously. Then I looked at Mateo and noticed he looked visibly disturbed. "She didn't pick up?" I asked.

Mateo shook his head, with his phone still to his ear.

Minutes went by as Lenny was begging his parents to exit their home. He was growing more and more frustrated as he was dodging questions like, where was he, and what happened to his truck.

I felt so bad for the siblings.

His parents were more upset at the missing car and were attempting to lecture Lenny on it. I could tell they were getting mad at Lenny's refusal to listen to them.

"We're not going home," Lenny begged. "Please, Mom, just listen to me and come to the hotel."

I felt all kinds of useless.

Mateo was attempting to get a hold of his mom. Meanwhile, Carly and Lenny were dealing with their parents possibly being in danger. I pathetically just stood there not knowing what to do. What could I do?

"Let's just go!" Mateo said coldly.

I took a step towards the hotel, thinking he meant to just go get his mom.

"W-where?" Carly asked.

I turned to explain but I saw Mateo was climbing into the car.

"Let's go get your parents!" Mateo answered.

"What?!?" I asked loudly.

"No!" Lenny shouted. "They just need to listen, and they'll come to us."

"They're not listening though, are they?" Mateo shot back.

The driver's door was still open.

"No!" I said. "No way, we're not going back!" I pointed my hands at Lenny. "Just let him talk to his parents!"

To my surprise, Mateo listened; he paused as he was about to turn on the car.

"Let me!" Carly growled, yanking the phone away from Lenny. She put the phone to her ear, slapping her brother's hands away. "Dad! I need you to get Mom and come to the hotel we sent you!"

Silence followed as we listened.

"Just do it!"

More silence.

"Please!"

More silence.

"There's a murderer or something!"

Silence.

"WE'RE NOT COMING HOME!"

Carly's sudden scream shook me up.

"I'm sorry for yelling, but there's someone killing horses and trying to break into the houses! That's why we left!"

Silence.

"Yes, I'm serious!"

Mateo's phone buzzed. It was his mom calling him back.

"Mom?! Hey, listen." Mateo's voice trailed off as he walked off to explain everything in silence.

"Please don't get mad! We'll explain everything once you get here."

Silence once again followed Carly's words. She put her hand to her mouth and closed her eyes.

My stomach dropped.

"Please..." Carly's voice was barely louder then a whisper. "Guys please..."

Carly began to cry as she continued to beg for her parents to come to them.

"They're not responding anymore!" she sobbed, looking at Lenny.

Lenny snatched the phone away from his sister and put it to his ear, calling for his parents.

"What happened?" he asked Carly.

"I don't know," Carly said through tears. "They just stopped talking it went silent!"

Carly began to breathe heavily. Lenny was pacing. There was absolutely nothing I could do.

I recalled how my phone just stopped working whenever the creature was nearby. Nothing but pure dread filled the air like a fog as we all came to that realization.

"It's ok," I tried. "Terry is there."

My attempt at reassurance fell on deaf ears.

Finally, my mom and Mateo's mom burst through the door.

"What happened?" Sofía asked.

"Ask them," Mateo answered, pointing to the stressed-out pair of siblings.

"What happened?" my mom asked, pulling me aside.

"Their parents went back to the ranch," I said.

"So?" my mom asked.

"So?" I repeated. "So that's bad!"

"Why?"

"Haven't you been listening?!" I shouted shoving myself away from her. "Haven't you even thought about the fact that everyone here is saying the same thing!"

My mom's hand was around my arm. Even though I was much bigger than her, her mom-strength was still very much a factor.

"Holy shit, son," my mom said. "How many times do I have to tell you to stop talking to me like that."

"I'm sorry." I said. "But come on, you have to admit it."

My mom rubbed her forehead. "Don't you hear what you're telling me!" she growled. "Don't you know what you're saying?"

She was right.

I was pretty much talking nonsense. No matter who else backed up my story, we were pretty much telling her the sky wasn't blue.

"Ok fine," I sighed. "But her parents are in danger."

"It's ok," my mom said. "The police are already there."

Even if that were true, Terry and whoever else was there wasn't a lot of comfort. If that thing could crush a truck the way it did, and take a bullet the way it did, it didn't matter.

I turned away from my mom, not knowing what to say to her anymore. That's when I saw all of them getting into my tía's van.

"Hey, whoa," I voiced.

"Come on, let's go!" Mateo said.

I instinctively took a step forward when my mom grabbed my arm.

"Hold on," my mom said.

She walked past me and spoke to my tía. My tía nodded and turned to her son. Some words were exchanged between them; I didn't hear what they were saying. But eventually Mateo's face scrunched and he said, "No way!"

"I'm not asking," my tía said.

"Mom, there's no way," Mateo said. "Please don't make me!"

She's gonna make him go back to the house.

"I'm making you," was all she said.

"No!" Mateo yelled. "No, no, no!"

"Mateo!"

"No, Mom, I'm not gon—"

"This is not a negotiation! This is not a conversation! This is a direct order that you will follow."

"No, I won't!" Mateo shouted. "They're my friends!"

Mateo's loud tone towards his mother caused a surge of awkwardness. We all stared at his mother, waiting for a response, a response appropriate to someone's son yelling at them.

"As your mother," Sofía whispered, "I can't let that happen."

"Mom, I can't abandon my friends," Mateo looked at Lenny and Carly. "I won't."

Mateo took a couple steps back and flung his arms open, saying, "Even if you make me stay, I'm just gonna find a way back to Magnolia Falls!"

Sofía stared at her son empathetically. I was surprised to realize that Mateo was actually getting to her. And it almost got to me too. The sudden guilt I felt for assuming he was arguing against going back to Magnolia Falls, as if he wanted the same thing I did, made me pathetic.

"What kind of mother would I be if I let you come?" she asked.

Mateo shook his head, "I gotta be honest, I don't care about that. I wouldn't be able to live with myself if I didn't go. What kind of person would I be if I didn't go?"

"And do what?" my tía questioned. "What are you gonna do other than just go?! Than just be there!"

Mateo choked on his words; some sounds came out of his mouth but nothing more than that.

"You're staying. Listen to your tía." Sofía ordered gesturing to my mom. She then turned to her sister, "Don't let him try anything." She then walked past Mateo, who just stood there.

Mateo didn't have a good enough argument to go. Even if he did get to his mom a bit. But she was right. Mateo would only be going just to go. What would he do? It wasn't like Mateo had any special talents that would be essential to simply going to pick up the O'Youngs' parents. If something were to happen, Mateo would be an unnecessary casualty.

Sofía, my tía, was simply protecting her son from that very real possibility.

But then why take Lenny and Carly?

"Why take them, then?" I asked, pointing to the worried siblings.

My tía glanced at them. "You guys are staying, too," she stated.

"Like hell!" Lenny shouted.

My tía was about to argue, saying, "I'm not as—" she paused, being cut off by Lenny as she was climbing into the car.

"No!" Lenny shouted. "If you think I'm not gonna personally see to my parents' safety," Lenny sarcastically chuckled, "you're crazy."

Lenny and Carly shoved themselves into the car before she could argue.

"This is not happening," Sofía stated.

"You're gonna waste time trying to drag us out of this car. Time that should be used getting to our house."

My tía eyeballed them for a couple seconds: first Lenny who sat in the front, then Carly, who was in the back.

Then my tía cursed under her breath as she slammed the car door.

"Fuck this," Mateo growled. Then he ripped the back door open and jumped in.

Some shouting followed. I didn't hear all of it, but after some begging from the O'Youngs to just go, they went.

My mom and I just stood there. Alone.

CHAPTER 25

In silence, my mom and I made our way to the room. When we walked, the absence of our companions was obvious and heavy. That was topped off with the awkwardness that followed an argument between a mother and son.

"Grab your things," Mom ordered.

Her words were so sudden and stern that all I managed to respond with was, "Huh?"

She turned to me and sighed with her eyes closed, visibly stressed. "We're leaving," she said. "Collect your shit."

A bunch of emotions filled my head. On one hand, I was finally going home. The thing I'd wanted since I'd arrived, even before I encountered the thing in the cornfields.

On the other hand, I didn't get to say goodbye to any of my friends and family, which bothered me.

I looked around and noticed all I really had to pack was my phone and charger. They sat on a nightstand next to the bed. Instinctively I checked to see how much power the phone had been charged up to, and I was delighted to see it was fully charged. I grabbed it, rolled it up, and shoved it in my pocket. Then I stood there awkwardly. Waiting.

"You ready to go?" Mom asked.

"Yeah," I whispered.

"Let's go."

We turned and were about to walk out when I asked, "Do you believe me now?"

I asked this without really thinking about it. But it was in my head, and I wanted to know more than anything.

"Excuse me?" Mom asked.

I took a moment to collect my thoughts. She understandably didn't believe what I had tried to tell her. Who would? If someone told me that a literal monster was terrorizing them, I wouldn't believe them, either. However, after my mom saw how everyone reacted or was acting about everything, she was bound to believe us now, right?

"Do you believe me now?" I repeated. "After seeing how everyone is acting about the whole thing?"

My mom didn't answer.

"Do you still think we're lying?" I pushed.

"I don't know?" my mom finally answered.

Her answer filled me with hope. It wasn't a no and that was more than enough.

"I believe you guys saw something," Mom explained. "I believe you guys got scared, and you guys are scared. But I don't believe you guys saw the Slenderman."

I chuckled at my mom's mention of the Creepypasta.

Slenderman used to scare me. But part of me knew that it wasn't real. It couldn't have been real.

If Slenderman was real, he was on our land.

"Mom," I began. "We saw something, something we can't explain or even really describe. Maybe it was a man. A really fucked-up man."

"Watch your language," Mom ordered.

"Sorry," I apologized. I sat at the edge of the bed closest to the window. "What do you think it is we're so scared of?" I asked.

My mom looked annoyed at my insistence on having this conversation. She hovered around the door and jangled her car keys often. Regardless, she humored me.

"What do you mean by that, son?" she asked, sitting down on the other bed.

I sighed and shifted where I sat. "You know we're all very scared," I explained. "You don't believe what we're scared of, but you know that something must've scared us, right?"

My mom didn't say anything, she simply studied me.

"You just told me that you know we're scared, you know that something scared us. You know this enough that you haven't questioned why all my stuff that I brought here isn't with me." I stood up and counted my fingers. "My clothes, shoes, and toothbrush are not here. The two bags of luggage I brought with me are still at their house. There's no way you didn't notice that. You're way too smart. So you've already figured out that we must've left the house in a rush, right?"

My mom didn't say anything.

"Right?" I repeated.

My mom gave me a glare at my tone, but answered, "Right."

"Soooooooo," I pushed, "what do you think scared us? Since what we're telling you isn't true."

My mom thought for a second before answering, "I think, like you said, some crazy man."

My mom's answer was genuine and sincere. I wasn't sure why it was so important for me to get an answer from her. But I guess I wanted her to admit that she at least believed me partly. She at least believed that something scary, like a scary man, scared me so much.

However, even with her answer, I wasn't satisfied. But I took what I could get.

"Terry can handle it," my mom said.

No he can't, was all I thought.

Mom stood up and headed to the door. I followed with nothing more to say. We walked what seemed to be a mile from the door to the elevator.

My mom was finally taking me home. She was finally gonna take me away from all of this. And hopefully, I could put this all in the back of my head. I could go back home and see all my friends and enjoy a real summer break. I no longer had to be somewhere I didn't want to be.

I looked at my mom and noticed something. She looked sad, with a hint of anger and also, defeat.

"What's wrong?" I asked instinctively.

"Hmm?" she looked at me, perhaps not hearing me.

"Is something wrong?" I repeated.

"Why do you ask?" she questioned.

"Because it's obvious something is bothering you."

"I'm just tired. It was a long drive here and now I've gotta drive back home. I'm not super excited to do so, you know?"

I couldn't help but feel like she was lying. I mean, I was sure it must have sucked that she did just drive a long way and now had to drive some more. But things like that didn't bother my mom. Not really.

"I can drive the first half," I offered. "Give you some time to rest."

"No way," Mom laughed sarcastically. "You're not driving."

"Whaaat? Why not?"

"Because you're a terrible driver, that's why."

"You taught me how to drive!" I teased, pointing both hands at her.

"And I'll regret it forever," Mom shot back.

I rolled my eyes. Even with our light exchange I still felt that something was bothering my mom.

I let her check out at the front desk, then I asked her again, "What's bothering you? I know that all this isn't super great mood-inducing, but there's something else. What is it?"

As we walked to the car, weaving through a parking lot, she seemed reluctant to answer me, shaking her head and answering with, "Nothing, I'm fine."

As we got into the car, I continued to push her. "Mom, please," I begged.

She sighed and leaned back into her seat.

"Did your tía explain everything to you?" she asked.

"Explain what?" I questioned.

"I thought she told me she told you about why we haven't seen our family in so long."

"Oh yeah, she did."

"Well, I thought this would be it. I thought this would be the great Band-Aid, the one to fix everything and bring us all back together."

"I don't understand," I said. "We did all come back together. Didn't we?"

Mom looked at me thoughtfully before saying, "Well yes. But not really."

I looked at her questioningly.

"I know you didn't want to come here. I know that you wanted to spend summer with your friends back home. I get that, but I believe that it's important for you to also be with your family. When your tía and I reconnected, it was like no time had passed; it was wonderful to have my sister and best friend back. Oh, and I remember how close you and Mateo used to be. Inseparable. Sofía and I had wanted you and Mateo to hopefully rekindle that. I wanted you to have your best friend back."

With the words best friend, I thought of Peter, whom I considered to be my best friend as we did nearly everything together, spent most of high school together.

"Mom, I'm not a kid anymore." I said coldly. "I don't need my best friend back; he's back at home. Peter."

Mom sighed. "That's not what I mean. I know that you and Mateo aren't kids anymore and I'm also very aware of the fact that you two have lives with different people in them."

"Then what did you mean?" I asked.

"I mean..." my mom paused for a moment. "We don't have a lot of family. I pray that will one day change for you when you get older. But as of now and since you've been born, we've had almost no one. You've had no one, no one except for me. No father, no siblings, just your mom. But what family we did have was beautiful. What we did have was special. I'll never stop regretting that I let it get away. When I got it back, even though it was just over the phone, I was so happy. And I want you to have that, I want you to have your family."

Silence filled the air. My mom continued.

"Your tía was so excited to see you again, she missed you so much. And I missed Mateo. I couldn't wait for all of us to be back home together again, even if just for a little while. I couldn't wait for him to come spend time with us at our home. Sofía and I were so happy to get our family back. But then our worst fears had come true; too much time had passed. You and Mateo were different and were strangers to each other. Sofía told me about the awkwardness between you two. It was heartbreaking." Mom frowned, she looked as though the separation between me and Mateo hurt her physically, "Then Sofía began to tell me about how you two were starting to get along, started acting like cousins again. Oh, we were so happy. She told me how Mateo took you to see his friends, how you guys rode horses together, and played video games together. We knew you two weren't kids; we were not expecting you guys to play together like kids. We hoped you guys would spend time together like young adults and you guys did."

My mom's words felt heavy in my body. I'd never considered any of what she was saying. She was right; my mom and her sister and my cousin were all I really had to call family. My mom and her sister had missed being a family and wanted us to be a family again.

"Then I get a call from Sofía," Mom blurted suddenly, "telling me to get you. And all that I get as an explanation was some monster attacked. Then Sofía starts telling me that some crazy drugged-out dude was running around the cornfields." Mom sighed and leaned forward to turn the car on.

The car sprang to life, lighting up the dashboard and stereo.

"We tried to get our family back," Mom explained, "we failed. Now who knows what will happen from here."

"What could happen?" I asked.

"How do we come back from this?" she said. "We can't just continue doing our little thing."

"This isn't as huge a setback as you think, Mom," I explained. "Hopefully if everything works out, we can try again."

"After this?!" Mom cried. "After some guy terrorizes the house? After some monster attacked you all? After all the lies? We can try again, sure, but this ruined everything." Mom sighed in defeat. "After years, we finally start to come back together, and this happens!"

It seemed my mom said that more to herself than to me. Regardless, I still understood where she was coming from.

It was like graduating, walking the stage to get your diploma. Then you fall, trip on your own gown. Sure, you can get back up and continue walking and receive your diploma with a handshake. But you still fell. Fell in front of everyone and possibly a camera. The moment has been tainted forever.

"I'm sorry," I told my mom. "This sucks."

"Yeah," was all she said in response.

We sat there for a while. Not saying anything.

Images of Mateo and Tía flashed through my head as I thought about my time spent there. Images of Lenny and Carly soon joined them. I thought of the good times we did have there, even if they were short-lived. I thought of the video games Mateo and I played and the weed Lenny shared. I thought of Carly, a girl I really liked. A girl who liked me. I thought of the time we spent together in the pool. I thought of how kind Lenny was to help Mateo and me find our horses. How Lenny bought me a new pair of swim shorts and asked for nothing in return.

Mom put the car in reverse and began to back out of her parking spot. My gut sank. I came to the realization that it would be a long time before I saw any of them again.

My gut sank even more when a new thought popped into my head. It would be a long time *if* I ever got to see them again.

What if they encountered the monster? The fucking bulletproof monster that crushed Lenny's car like it was nothing?

It sucked. But at least I was finally going home. I was no longer in danger and would soon be miles and miles away from that thing.

Even though my tía didn't kill it with a shotgun, she still hurt it. Terry and his friends definitely had weapons to fight it off. They'd be fine. Besides, what could I do other than add to the number of people Terry and his buddies had to protect? I had to trust that God would keep them all safe. I had to thank God that He was pulling me out of danger.

Then, thinking of God, I thought of the Bible. I didn't read it much, in fact, I recall reading through it only once. Maybe that's why I only remember one verse, that verse being John 15:13.

"Fuck," I said out loud.

"Excuse me!" my mom shouted.

"Sorry!" I tried, but it was too late.

Dozens of slaps began to hit my body, as my mom lectured through gritted teeth, "Stop having such a vulgar mouth!"

After she stopped, I had to speak fast. "Mom, we can't leave."

"What?" she asked, still mad with me.

"I can't leave!" I cried.

My mom stopped the car with a screech and turned to me with a finger pointed. "No!' she growled. "I'm not having this conversation. We're going home."

I didn't really know what to say. I knew for a fact that I wasn't gonna convince my mom. I still had to try.

"The entire time I've wanted to go home, even when I was having a good time. But now that I'm actually going home, I feel so sour and rotten inside. I feel like I just gave everyone the finger!"

"What's wrong with you!?" Mom shouted.

"You weren't there!" I said as I opened the door and stepped out. "You could never understand what I just let happen!"

I shut the door behind me and prayed for what I was riding on. My dirt bike was still where I left it.

It was a new habit I had just gotten into a few months before summer. It was sort of a trend at school. All my friends got one, so I did as well.

My friends and I would drive to rural parts of our city and ride our bikes until either someone crashed, and the party was over, or until we had somehow had enough. Normally, it was the latter.

The dirt bike I had ended up with was a 2021 Suzuki. I had been the one to end a party one day and had to take the bike to a shop for repairs. When I got it back for maybe a week, my mom begged me to get it out of the car and my lazy ass never did.

Boy, was I happy to be a disobedient little shit.

I got it out of the car, ignoring my mom's protest.

She had enough. She grabbed my hands and whipped me around to face her. "If you think I'm gonna let you just go ride off, I have failed you as a mother," she told me angrily.

"I don't think you're gonna just let me," I said. "But I also can't let you stop me."

My words fell on deaf ears as she continued to speak, "If you want to go back, we can go back, but you're getting in the car."

"You're not going anywhere with me!" I said loudly and flinched at my mom's inevitable slap.

But nothing came.

When I opened my eyes, I saw her jaw was hanging.

"What," she said, although it sounded like a "How dare you."

"Mom," I began, taking my hands away from hers, "there is something in the cornfields, I don't know what it is, but it poses a threat to my family and my friends. I'm not going home until I know they're safe."

"Stop!" Mom barked. "Stop! Just stop! You are not going back. And if you do it is with me."

"But you see, Mom," I said sarcastically. "I'm not gonna put my mom in a situation where she's in danger."

"Likewise!" she called. "If you truly believe that they're in danger, I am going, too."

"NO, YOU ARE NOT!" I shouted at her.

This time she did slap me. But I shrugged it off.

"Mom," I said softly, "Please just go back to the hotel."

Mom didn't say anything.

"I should've gone with them," I said, "I'M going with them. I'M going to make sure everything is ok. Then it will be ok. Then we can go home." I shrugged, "Look, I'm going to go whether you say so or not. So, this argument is pointless."

"I'll meet you there, then," she said and began to make her way to the driver's side door.

"You are going to the hotel," I ordered.

My mom scoffed. "Now who the hell are you to tell me what to do?"

"I'm turning eighteen this spring!" I called. "If you don't go to the hotel and wait there for me and all of us to come back, you will never hear from me again."

My mom's expression went from anger to fear and hurt.

"What?" she whispered. "What are you saying?"

"I was already planning on moving out on the day of my birthday," I lied. "If you don't do this for me, then I'll make sure I never see you again."

The look on my mom's face broke my heart. But I had no choice other than to use her love against her. I justified it by promising to apologize later. But as of now, I had to ensure she would stay safe. I was sure she'd see though my harsh lie eventually, she always did. But I'd hoped my words, and threat would be hurtful enough to buy me some time. So, I couldn't give her time to figure me out.

"Stay at the hotel," I demanded. "Agree."

She said nothing, only looked at me with sad eyes.

"Say yes," I demanded again.

After a moment, I heard her quietly whisper, "Ok."

With that, I hopped on the bike and sped off.

The look on my mother's face, the sound of her voice. It was a lot, and I was lucky it was dark. If she saw my face, she may have called my bullshit.

At a red light on the way, I took out my phone and texted my mom.

"You track me through my phone. I can track you too. If I see you anywhere other than the hotel, I'm gone."

I hoped that that was enough. On my way and in my head, I began to go over the apology I had to give her. I also had to explain myself to my tía and cousin as my mom no doubt would contact them.

But at least for now she'd be at the hotel.

I, on the other hand, was going back to my old childhood home. And unlike the first time I'd returned, I'd ensure that nothing would keep me away.

The gravity of the choice I made to return didn't hit me the whole ride back. It didn't even hit me when the headlight on my bike showed nothing but a dirt path and the towering corn that surrounded it. It hit me when it was already too late to turn back. It hit me when I slowly approached the old metal overhead sign welcoming me back to Magnolia Falls.

CHAPTER 26

I ran up to the door and almost busted my face bouncing off of it. It was locked, which was a good thing. It told me that people were inside.

Unless, of course, my tía locked it behind us as we left.

The door swung open, and a huge arm shot out and gripped my shoulder with an unimaginable force. I was whipped inside before I could even comprehend what just happened.

I stumbled as I entered the house. I was about to fall on my ass when a couple bodies caught me. I looked at who it was and was filled with joy as I realized I was surrounded by my friends and cousin.

"Guys!" I exclaimed.

A flurry of hostile shushing was shot at me.

"W-what?" I stuttered.

Mateo gave me another hard, "SHHHHHHHH!!!!"

I finally got the hint and shut up. However, I made sure to hold my questioning look. But nobody said anything. Everyone just darted their heads around the room.

I realized that they were all looking at the windows. Mainly the ones in the living and dining room.

My stomach dropped with fear as I came to understand what was happening. I was outside with it. I should've known that it was a possibility I'd encounter the thing on my way to the house.

"Holy crap," I whispered.

My tía had just entered the room, coming from the kitchen, hissing, "What the hell was that?!?"

"Lookie over here," a deep voice called.

I didn't recognize the voice. I turned my head in the direction where it came from to see a bigger man. An older man. I knew he was on the older side as he had white thinning hair, and a thick white mustache stretching along the top of his wide lips. He was a bigger guy, but not overly fat. He resembled an NFL lineman.

"What the fuck!!!" my tía called. "Why the fuck are you here?!?"

I whipped my head around to see my tía, who looked pissed.

"I came to help you guys!" I replied.

"Help!?" my tía began. "Help with what???"

I opened my mouth, but nothing came out. I figured telling her that I came to help with saving the O'Youngs' parents didn't sound right.

My tía, noticing my silence, didn't say anything. She just held her head and gritted her teeth.

"You dumb fuckin' kid," said a voice. A voice I recognized as belonging to Terry, the sheriff.

Looks from those who were my age didn't help with the humiliation I was feeling. They all looked at me with frustration, confusion, and discomfort.

Then again, I didn't expect much else. I was aware that chances were I'd be putting myself in unnecessary danger. I wouldn't change a thing, though. They were in danger, and I didn't just go home.

"What's happening?" I asked. "Where's your parents?"

At this point Lenny and Mateo had stood up. They had broken my fall when I was yanked in the house.

Lenny looked down at me and answered, "They're back at my place." He paused for a moment. "With Carly."

Hearing those words, I scanned the room.

I counted my tía, Mateo, Lenny, and Terry. Along with three new people. The first one was the person who I assumed yanked me into the house; the NFL lineman-looking guy. There was also a younger-looking guy, and a middle-aged looking dude.

The younger guy had longer hair. Long for a cop. He was white as snow, with freckles, and red hair. He was tall and thin, but he did have some muscle.

The middle-aged dude was perhaps about Terry's height and age. However, he had an average build. He was also white, but not as white as the younger guy. He had dark brown hair.

Despite noticing these new people, what took center stage in my head was the absence of Carly.

"Did y'all get separated?" I asked.

Mateo nodded.

"How?" I asked, standing up.

"We arrived at their house and tried to get them to come with us," Mateo explained. "But they argued. Eventually we got them to come with us, but we couldn't all fit in my mom's car." Mateo looked at Lenny apologetically before continuing to explain. "Lenny's mom just had hip surgery. We couldn't exactly pile up in the car without somehow hurting her or risking hurting her."

"We decided to make a trip back here," Lenny chimed in. "We figured it was worth a try flipping over the truck and seeing if we could get it to start and work."

"You're kidding," I said. "Your truck is fucked up."

I stood up and walked towards the window. I cupped my eyes and spotted the truck and sure enough, it was fucked up.

I was gonna continue to trash their terrible idea when I noticed something.

The truck was fucked up, there was no question about that. However, the wheels, and engine seemed more or less intact. Even so, the top of truck was completely caved in. Should someone manage to drive it, they'd have the hardest time.

It couldn't be Lenny. He was far too big to fit in there.

"How would y'all flip it over?" I asked.

"The horses," Mateo answered.

"They're still there? They're ok?"

"We'd have to check." Mateo shrugged.

I stood and paced the room we were in. "So then what? How'd y'all end up in here?" I asked.

"Red Eyes popped up. We all ran in here," Mateo explained. And that was enough.

Terry eventually approached me. "You dumb fucking kid," he said.

When my friends said that kinda thing to me, it was really no big deal. But when a six-foot-three ripped sheriff said it, the way he said it, I damn near shat myself.

Not wanting to discuss my dumb kid-ness, I asked, "Those your friends?"

He smirked at me. He knew exactly what I was doing by asking him that. He knew that I was changing the subject.

"That's Greg," he said, pointing to the old man. He moved his finger to the redhead, "That's Phill." Finally, his finger landed on the middle-aged fellow. "And that's Simon."

"From the force?" I asked.

"Yeah," Terry answered. Terry sighed and pinched the top of his nose with his other hand on his hip. "Why are you here?" Terry asked before eyeballing me.

"Well," I began, "I simply couldn't stop thinking about it. The guilt was killing me."

"Guilt?" Terry repeated. "Seriously? You have absolutely no obligation to anyone here. No obligation to put yourself in harm."

I damn near scoffed at him. I would've if he wasn't glaring at me. I knew that Terry constantly went out of his way for Sofía. He felt some obligation towards her and her son. But instead of telling him that and risk pissing off this brute, there was something else on my mind I felt was worth risking.

"Did you see it?" I asked.

Terry raised an eyebrow. "What?"

"The monster," I explained. "Did you see the monster?"

Terry's face relaxed. He still held his glare on me, but something clearly changed in his face. "I did," he finally said.

Not having anything to say to that, I stayed silent.

"Sorry you went through that. Sorry I didn't believe you," Terry eventually said.

Once again, I had nothing to say. I just nodded in acknowledgment. A hand gripped my shoulder and whipped me around. I now faced my tía.

"Donde esta tu madre?" she asked angrily.

"She's at the hotel," I answered. "Don't worry."

"Why aren't you at the hotel?" she asked.

People kept asking me that and I still couldn't put together a good answer.

"I should've come with you guys," was all I was able to say.

"No!" my tía shouted. "You should've stayed at the hotel! You should be safe!"

"I don't mean to make you angry," I said, backing up from my tía. "But I couldn't stop thinking about how I should've just come with you guys to help."

My tía shook her head. "You shouldn't be here!"

"Well, I am! I'm here." I argued.

"NO!" She shouted. "NONE OF YOU SHOULD BE HERE!!!" She waved at Mateo, Lenny, and I.

She was gonna keep arguing with me, telling me the same thing everyone else was, and I was sick of hearing it.

"Why aren't there helicopters circling us?!?!" I shouted to everyone, turning all their heads. "How has this thing not been kidnapped by the FBI and taken to Area 51?! Has no one called anyone yet?!?!"

Many voices answered at the same time. They all said more or less the same thing: *Nothing that would allow us to make any kind of communication worked, and no one's coming because no one believes us.* It also didn't help that technically police were already here.

I ended up asking why they hadn't lied yet. Lied to get other people to show up.

This time only Terry answered me. "We would if we could," he said.

"Why can't you," I asked.

"Check your bars, kid," he answered.

My stomach dropped as I ripped my phone out of my jeans. Sure enough, my phone was now useless. I only saw a black screen staring back at me as if it was dead. Despite being fully charged when I left the hotel.

"But you just said you talked to them," I said. "How'd you do that?"

"I don't know," Terry said honestly. "All of a sudden, none of us had shit to work with."

"Like literally every horror movie ever," Phill chimed in.

"No kidding," I sighed.

"So now we're just sitting here," Lenny said. "Waiting for a miracle."

I wanted to make the joke that I was the miracle that they'd been waiting for. But considering the seriousness of the situation, I wisely chose not to.

"Are we just gonna wait here?" I asked.

"Yes," Greg answered.

"No," Terry answered.

They both looked at each other with a clear ancient resentment.

"You wanna die!" Greg called. "Then die! Don't bring other people into it!"

Greg's voice was very scratchy, most likely from smoking for a ton of years.

"We can't just sit here and wait to die!" Terry groaned. "And don't fucking talk to me like that."

Greg said nothing. He merely continued to stare at Terry.

Terry turned to face my tía. "You got them dragon breath rounds?"

CHAPTER 27

"I told you, Terry," my tía said, "bullets didn't do much."

"No," Terry said grabbing his belt. "But they did something. I'm willing to bet them rounds from hell ought to do a lot more."

Sofía considered his words for a moment. After some time, she shook her head. "I prefer the slug rounds," Sofía stated.

"You tried those already," Terry said. "We're trying something else now."

My tía thought for a moment, then nodded. She turned and exited the living room disappearing into her bedroom.

Greg scoffed and stepped in her way. "This isn't happening!" he said loudly.

Terry opened his mouth to speak, calling Greg's name before Greg cut him off.

"No!" he said. "Our best bet is to wait for backup."

"We're not even sure they're coming, Greg," Terry argued.

The old man paused at Terry's words before responding. "They're coming. We told them enough; even if they don't believe us, they're bound to send someone to investigate the call."

"And you feel like waiting?" Terry pushed.

"Look, we should only act unless we need to," Greg argued.

"Yeah, let's do that," Terry growled, "Let's wait till after something happens to do anything. Let's wait till someone gets hurt before we make a move." Terry shrugged sarcastically.

My tía placed her hand on Greg's shoulder, giving him an empathic look. Greg's body language clearly went from tense to calm.

Sofía followed her shoulder touch with a soft, "Hey." My tía then used her arm on his shoulder to shove him aside. As big as Greg was, he flew aside with a pitiful ease. "Stop being a bitch." Sofía said sternly.

Greg's eyes were wide. He was both humiliated and pissed. He also was smart. He didn't retaliate in any way.

Then as casual as ever. She turned and walked back into her room as if she forgotten something.

"Greg," Terry called.

Greg turned his head to face Terry.

"Get over here," ordered Terry.

Greg reluctantly approached Terry, who signaled the other police officers to him.

"Long story short, we're gonna light the fucker up," Terry said firmly.

"What if that doesn't work?" Greg questioned.

Terry clearly heard Greg but didn't give him a response. I figured it was both from annoyance and not having a good answer.

Terry took a breath then said, "That thing flinches, it feels pain. So we're gonna give it a whole lot of it."

"Oh, shut up," Greg complained. "Talking like you're some kind of action hero."

Greg crossed his arms and sighed, "Does no one know what's happening? We are looking at some kind of demon. A demon who can somehow block us from calling for help." Greg rushed over to the windows and pointed at the truck, still looking at Terry and the others. "And it did that to a truck."

The other two officers looked nervous at his words.

"Enough," Terry ordered.

Greg rolled his eyes. "We don't even know what that is, everything ever known to mankind is out the fucking window!" Greg's voice cracked as he said this, however, he didn't seem to mind. "It could be fucking anything! Literally nothing's off the table."

"Dude," Phill said, "shut up! Let's see what he has to say."

Greg looked at Phill with wild eyes.

Seeing Greg this way felt pretty odd. It didn't help that he was a pretty ugly guy. Seeing this old man act like a child didn't make me feel better about cops being here.

"I want to get out of here," Phill explained. "Sooner than later. Terry will help make that happen." Phill approached Greg and grabbed his shoulder and lead him back to the other officers. "Don't you see, man," said Phill, "we're trying to run away."

Phil's words apparently helped Greg, because Greg didn't say anything after that.

Terry went on to explain what the plan was. They were all gonna make a break for the barn, get the horses and whatever else they needed in order to get them to flip the truck. Then, after the truck was flipped, we'd hope that it would start, the kids would get in and get out. The sheriff, my tia, and the others would then ride to the O'Youngs' house, hope the car they arrived here with still worked, and drive away.

If the monster showed up, they'd simply shoot it and hope it was enough to scare it off.

It was a simple plan. Of course, it had a few holes in it, like if it were even possible the horses could flip the truck over. Then there was the possibility the truck wouldn't start or even be drivable.

It sucked, that this was the best we could do. I decided to take these odds regardless. The sooner we got outta there, the better. I was already starting to regret showing up back here.

"I don't understand," I said.

Mateo was keeping an eye out for his mom, so he didn't hear me. Lenny did and responded to me genuinely confused, "It's pretty self-explanatory Miguel."

"No, I mean I get the plan and all, but shouldn't there be like a million cars here? What happened to the car y'all showed up in?"

"What do yah think?" Lenny said, "it smashed them to hell."

"All of them?"

"All of them."

"How could that happen? How'd did y'all end up separated?"

"When we arrived at my house we were all prepared to leave. The sherif was already there and had gotten my folks to agree to leaving. We had practically met them on the way out." Lenny paused as if disturbed by the memories he's recalling. "It just appeared out of nowhere, walked out of the cornfields as if it fucking owned the place. The creature then began to rip and tear every single car apart."

"Whoa..."

"Yeah, we hid in the house for a while. Some of us decided to make the trip here and do what we are currently doing."

"And what are you doing here?" I asked. "Why didn't you stay with your family?"

"I can't help them by staying there." Lenny said.

His words summed up the reason why I myself came back. And given that all goes to plan, I'd be leaving pretty soon not having done a damn thing.

"You guys made the trip back here on foot?" I asked.

Lenny didn't say anything, he just nodded.

I wasn't so stupid to ask why no one has tried to simply make a run for it. I'd prefer my chances in a moving vehicle then on foot. And since we're taking a chance on Lenny's truck, we're most likely taking a chance on another car back at Lenny's home.

Footsteps echoed through the room as my tía appeared, holding a shotgun. Sofía and Terry exchanged a look, then a nod.

It wasn't the same gun she used in her first encounter with the Red Eyes. Even though it looked well maintained and polished, it was still very visibly older. The wood stocking and pump were so aged and worn.

"Sticking to the original plan," Terry explained to her. "If it shows up, we shoot. Simple."

"Simple," Sofía agreed.

Terry walked up to my Tía Sofía and held his hand out. He wanted the gun she held. Sofía raised an eyebrow and brought it closer to her chest. Terry backed off.

When he did, Sofía turned to Mateo, Lenny, and me.

"You boys stay here," Sofía ordered. "Once the truck's flipped, you boys hop in and get the fuck out, understand?"

None of us answered.

"UNDERSTAND?" she said louder.

We all nodded hurriedly, with Mateo giving his mom the classic, "Yes, ma'am!"

"Ok," Terry said. "Let's go get the horse."

"Hold on! Hold on, hold on!" called Lenny.

The adults turned their heads to face him. Lenny was clearly taken aback by the sudden attention.

"I mean—" he tried. "You—" Lenny took a deep breath, slowly in and out. "This is stupid!" he finally exclaimed.

The adults still didn't say anything.

"The plan y'all have is stupid," Lenny said. "This isn't going to go well at all. When it shows up, you can't depend on just shooting it. Even with those fancy bullets."

"Lenny, we don't have much of a choice," Terry said sympathetically. "If someone was gonna show up for help, they would've been here hours ago."

"Fine, we get that," Mateo chimed in. "But is this really the best we can do?"

"We have to get out of this place," Sofía answered. "We should take the opportunities we have to escape."

Mateo and Lenny stayed quiet. They looked pretty defeated.

Personally, I was fine with staying put. I was perfectly fine letting the badasses do what they need to do. And as much as the plan relied on hopes and prayers, it's not bad.

Before I knew it, the adults marched out of the house. The door closed behind them and with the slam, Mateo and Lenny rushed up stairs. I followed quickly, not wanting to be alone.

We piled against a big window that showed the whole scene. From the window upstairs, we could see the truck, the barn in the distance, and the adults tactically moving towards the barn.

The sun was down so it was dark, but the scene outside was illuminated by a small streetlight and the lights on in the house.

As they passed the truck, they took a moment to study it. Perhaps looking for any reason why the truck wouldn't start. They pushed on, all of them constantly turning their heads, looking for a pair of glowing eyes.

I'd say they made it halfway to the barn when Mateo spoke.

"I have an idea," he said.

Lenny and I both responded to him with, "What?"

"They can only see what the light allows," he explained. "If the monster is out there, they won't know it until it's already on them."

"Ok, so what's your idea?" Lenny asked.

"We have a flare gun," Mateo explained. "We could shoot a shell on each of their sides, left and right. Light up more of the area."

"I think you're just itching to do something, buddy," I said.

Mateo looked at me. "Aren't you?" he asked.

I thought about his words for a second. I did want to help. But not more than I wanted to stay safe. "We'd just be putting ourselves in danger," I said. "A flare gun isn't a Glock or a shotgun."

"No, but it's something!" Mateo argued.

"It's a stupid idea!" I shot back. "If we shot a flare into the cornfields, we'd just start a fire."

"That's not a terrible idea," Lenny said. "Burning it."

"Or we might just flush it out in the open where it could get them!" I argued.

The boys actually thought about it. Then Mateo finally sighed in defeat, saying, "There's gotta be something we can do to help."

"There is," I said. "Stay safe and out of their way."

"We could just shoot it towards the sky," Lenny said. "I agree with Miguel, we'd start a fire which would only put everyone in more danger." Lenny pointed a finger upward. "But if we shoot it up, we could light up the whole area."

"Wouldn't the shell rocket too far in the sky to actually shine light down to us?" I asked.

Lenny looked at Mateo for an answer. Mateo nodded his head.

We all redirected our attention back to the window. The adults made it to the barn. We knew this because the barn light was on.

"Talk about drawing attention to yourself," Lenny said.

He was right. If that thing was out there, it definitely could see the barn lights on.

"How long do you think it will take to get the horses to flip the truck?" I asked Mateo.

Mateo thought about it for a moment before answering, "It's going to take a while. They're going to have to find a way to keep one half of the truck still while the other free to move in order to keep the horses from just dragging the truck."

Lenny suddenly gasped! He shot his hands out to grab and touch Mateo and I. "I see it!" he said.

"What?" I stuttered.

"I fucking see it!"

At his words, I turned my head to see the monster had appeared. Sure enough, it was investigating the lights in the barn. It just walked upright, towering over the corn. It swung its long arms as it stomped towards the barn.

Mateo didn't wait for anyone to speak. He rushed past me and Lenny, almost knocking me over. Lenny let out small grunts of pain due to his arm as he hurried behind Mateo. My stomach dropped as I found myself behind Lenny.

Once I got downstairs, I heard a smash. Mateo disappeared into his mom's room. He emerged from the bedroom holding something with both hands.

It didn't take me long to put two and two together. He was holding a gun of some kind. It was a pistol, possibly the flare gun.

We all rushed outside, nobody saying a word. The three of us stepped outside into an eerie silence. We all just stood there. None of us said a word. It was awfully quiet, as if we'd just stepped onto the moon.

I decided to be a smart ass by saying, "That flare gun better be—"

BOOM!!!

A loud bang tore through the night sky. A bright flash of light accompanied the noise. Then the banshee cry returned! It sank my stomach all the way to my balls.

I might've collapsed on the floor with fear when the other two boys ran towards the barn.

"No," I whispered pathetically as I gave chase.

BOOM!!! BOOM!!! BOOM!!!

The loud bangs were followed by more of the banshee screams! Flashes came from the direction of the barn.

"Holy crap," Lenny said. "They're shooting at it."

We bolted in the direction of the barn. If the other two boys were scared, they didn't show it. It embarrassed me how scared I felt. But I decided to keep quiet and hold it to myself as much as possible.

When we came in view of the barn, I immediately came to a stop.

There it was. In all its skinny, tall, horrible glory.

The creature was gritting its teeth. It held an expression as if it were in pain.

BOOM!!!!

A bright light ripped through the darkness, almost blinding me.

It was as if the sun personally came to say hi to us. The light struck the creature dead in the chest, exploding on impact. The monster was flung back and howled in pain some more.

Seeing the creature hurt boosted my confidence immensely. I caught up to the other boys, who continued to run towards it.

Mateo himself raised his pistol and fired. A beam of red light whipped through the air and hit the monster on the shoulder.

It did nothing. It bounced off and died on the ground.

The beast, however, noticed it and turned its head towards us.

I became increasingly horrified as a smile appeared on its face.

My fear once again dissipated when yet another sun blast blasted the thing in the face, which officially threw it on its ass.

"WOOHOO!!!" I cheered as I raced to the barn.

Before I could finish celebrating, the thing was on us. It had a handful of corn crops in its hand. It flung the crops towards the barn, presumably at Sofía. The sheer force and strength of the throw shook the entire barn.

It screeched at the barn before looking at us.

Mateo shot another flare at the thing which did nothing; it bounced off its face.

It reached out and grabbed Mateo. It lifted him up with an unfathomable amount of ease. Lenny screamed a word that I didn't register, something about the monster.

I damn near shit myself as the monster opened its mouth, perhaps to shove Mateo into it.

"NOOO!" I cried as I threw a rock at it. Thank goodness I'd tripped on it, because there was nothing else around me that I could've thrown.

Unfortunately, it did nothing but temporarily take its attention off of Mateo. It eyed me for just a moment before tossing Mateo into the air as if tossing a crumpled-up paper. He landed with a gut-wrenching crunch.

But before I could react, the monster wrapped its fingers around me and threw me in the direction of the barn.

We were quite some distance from the barn so the thing threw me with such force that I glided right through big barn doors. If I screamed, I didn't hear it; the wind tore through my ears so I couldn't hear anything but a loud, violent whistling.

I hit the ground well past the barn doors. I rolled past many wood structures before I crashed into something. I hit the thing hard enough that it knocked all my air out.

The adrenaline didn't help; it allowed me to stand up instead of staying on the ground, but I still couldn't breathe.

My legs wobbled, but before I could fall, I leaned against a wood pole and gripped my gut. I gasped for air but was denied. My body began to seize and shake violently as I struggled for air. Finally, I pushed out a breath and breathed in a large gasp of air.

As I recovered my breath, heavily breathing in and out, I realized that my vision had somehow disappeared. Thankfully I knew it was temporary blindness because my sight was slowly returning to me.

I began to sob, the pain and loss of breath had finally caught up to me. I had to set aside my pain though; I had to make sure Lenny and Mateo were ok. I tried to run but my legs failed me. I fell on the ground and groaned in pain. My back felt like it was one giant bruise. It hurt to breathe and walk, the muscles on my back stretched with a pain that stopped me in my tracks. I stood up and grabbed a hammer and stumbled out of the barn.

My logic was all gone. I was gonna try and hit that thing with a hammer when bullets didn't do a thing. Before I could exit the barn, arms wrapped around me and gave me a painful squeeze, my back bursting with pain.

It was my tía. She was in the barn with me. I somehow hadn't noticed her. She laid me down gently, not saying anything. She then turned and bolted outside the barn, carrying something that I concluded to be her shotgun.

I stood and chased her. She ran ahead of me, getting to the monster faster than I could. I noticed that Terry and the other officers had already beaten us there. They each held pistols that popped with fire.

I noticed the red-headed one: he fired at the monster only a couple times before the monster faced him. I somehow knew he was gonna die. Maybe it was the way the monster eyed him, maybe it was the way time itself seemed to slow, or maybe it was that Phill screamed as the monster balled up its fist and brought it down on the man.

He was squished flat like a pancake, with blood exploding from where he once stood. He popped like a fucking water balloon, his arms poking out of the now-paste that Phill was.

Blood pooled from the monster's fist as it lifted it from Phil.

I had just seen someone die! I'd just seen someone killed! This wasn't some old man or woman, surrounded by loved ones as they slowly and peacefully pass away.

This man was flattened! He died in fear!

Part of me hoped that he died instantly. If he'd even felt an ounce of pain from that death, he'd perhaps suffered a pain more severe than anyone had ever suffered before.

The monster turned its attention at my tía. It reached out an arm to grab her.

Sofía acted fast though. She leaped back, cocked the gun, and fired at the giant hand.

The monster's arm jerked back. It gritted its teeth and extended its other arm towards Sofía.

Sofía wasn't as fast this time.

She leaped out of the way, avoiding her upper body being crushed by the monster, but her legs were still gripped. She fell back, dropping the shotgun as the creature lifted her up by the legs. She hung upside down, struggling against the monster.

Meanwhile everyone else who had a firearm continued to shoot at the thing. They were clearly hitting it, because points of the creature's skin would suddenly vibrate with force.

They were doing absolutely nothing to the creature.

Sofía had gotten out a combat knife and began to stab and shank the fingers that gripped her. They blade didn't pierce the monster's skin, they simply bounced off.

I found myself running towards the shotgun that was laying on the ground. When I reached it, I picked it up. I was surprised by the weight of it. Weapons seemed lighter in movies.

I looked up at my tía and my jaw dropped.

The monster raised Sofía, with the intention of smashing her on the ground.

Without thinking, I fired the weapon, but instead of releasing a blast of fire, a click was the only thing that came from it. I panicked and hurriedly pulled back the pump and fired.

The entire area lit up with a yellow light. A stream of dragon breath shot out of the barrel, hitting the monster in the face.

By the time I had done so the monster had already begun to swing Sofía down towards the ground. She hit the Earth with a breathtaking thump. She moaned in pain after hitting the ground.

Whatever I'd done was enough. After a second, Sofía gathered herself up and continued to stab at the monster and struggle.

I breathed a sigh of relief but didn't take too long doing so, as she was still in the clutches of the monster.

I pumped the shotgun and fired again! This time I hit the thing square in the chest.

The thing recoiled! It released my tía and gripped its chest with both its hands. It screamed in pain as it looked at me.

It suddenly leaped forward and slapped me with its ginormous right hand. I went flying to the left. I landed and slid across the ground.

Someone was in my path and I knocked them over as I passed under their feet. It could've been anyone. I took a moment to recover and stand.

"Ahhh shit," was all I managed to say.

When I stood, I was immediately lifted off the ground by the thing. It didn't give me a chance to process what was happening.

I was suddenly dropped from the air, and I hit the ground, landing on my back. A burst of pain exploded in my body. I saw the red eyes whip away from me and look at my tía.

She had shot the beast with the dragon's breath; it's why it let go of me midair.

I managed to stand again and stumble away. Something suddenly prevented my left foot from moving forward. It had caused me to fall forward right on my face. The way I fell and landed bent and arched my back leading to another wave of pain.

I realized that it was Mateo, the thing I had tripped on. I only recognized him because of his red sweater.

He was facedown and not moving. Noticing this, I become horrified of what could be wrong with my cousin.

"Oh God!" I choked. "Oh God, Mateo!" I scrambled to my knees and turned him to face me. "WAKE UP!" I shouted.

His eyes shot open!

I didn't know what I was expecting. I don't know what I would have done if he was hurt, but I was so happy to see him awake.

He looked at me for a second and then turned his head around to look at where all the noise was coming from, where he could see the officers and his mom surrounding the creature and unloading all the ammunition they could on it.

"Whoa!" he yelped. He struggled to his feet, and I did the same.

The monster began to reach out towards Simon, who wasn't paying attention. Simon had taken his attention off the monster to reload his pistol. By the time he was done, the monster had already formed a fist around him.

The creature lifted him off the ground and brought him close to its face.

Simon, thinking quickly, wiggled his arm out of the monster's grip and pointed his weapon directly at the monster's left eye. He fired multiple times, but on his first shot he hit the monster's eye, causing it to scream in pain.

This wasn't a good thing for Simon, because unlike me and Sofía, the monster didn't let go.

Instead, the monster furiously screamed in pain and anger. It squeezed Simon and his scream was suddenly cut off by a loud pop.

Simon didn't explode with blood like Phill; instead, blood began to pour from between the monster's fingers.

My stomach sank with dread. I'd just watched another man die.

The thing in the cornfields grinded his fingers, sloshing around Simon, causing him to fall from the monster's hand in pieces. First his legs, then his right arm, and then the rest of his torso.

Vomit emerged from my stomach and sprayed from my mouth. I tasted this morning's breakfast along with the McDonald's I'd had earlier.

"Lenny?!?" Mateo asked loudly.

I looked at him. I couldn't find my voice, so all I did was look in the direction where I'd last seen him.

He wasn't there.

Horrified, I scanned the area looking for at least a body. I sighed with relief when I found him. He had a pistol in his right hand, but he wasn't shooting. It took me a moment to notice that his gun was empty due to its shape.

When Mateo spotted him, he immediately bolted in his direction.

I wasn't as brave. I just stood there. I prayed that the beast didn't see me and decide to come for me again.

The monster's head whipped to the side as another blast of dragon's breath hit it. It looked directly at Sofía. The monster's eye suddenly twitched with pain when Terry shot it in the eye.

Terry clearly took note of how Simon had seemed to hurt it before he died. The monster then looked at Terry, growling and clearly pissed.

A thought came to me as I saw this whole thing unfold.

The monster would rush towards Terry and Greg, then would get hit by Sofía. It would then rush towards her.

From watching this cycle, I came to the realization that the monster could only focus on one thing at a time. Not only that but it was very distractible. Its attention went from Terry and Greg to Sofía.

With this knowledge, I rushed towards Mateo and Lenny. I went the long way. I circled around the entire area, opting to stay as far away from the monster as I could.

About halfway to their position I called out, "GUYS!!!"

Only Mateo and Lenny moved their heads at me. Terry and Greg focused on the monster, their pistols still popping.

Lenny and Mateo just looked at me. I couldn't find the words to explain what I had just discovered.

"Look!" was all I managed to say while pointing a finger at the creature.

They looked but only saw the monster. They didn't see the pattern.

"Yeah, we see it, genius!" Mateo yelled.

I tripped on my own feet, but I was close to them. I crawled the rest of the way and shoved my body in front of them, I faced them forcing their attention on me and pointed at the monster.

"It can't stay focused!" I said loudly. "Loooook!"

This time, the boys looked and saw what I saw. They saw the monster's attention go from Terry to Sofía.

Even though I tried to explain it, the constant popping of gunfire, the dragon's breath, and the monster's banshee scream kept them from hearing me.

A strong pride filled my body. I had found a weakness! A flaw! There was something we could use against the monster.

"We need to distract it!" I yelled, my words finally cutting through all the noise. "Take its attention off of us!"

Lenny's eyes lit up as he spotted something behind me. Mateo's eyes followed Lenny's gaze, and his jaw suddenly dropped.

In fear, I turned around, only to see the monster approaching us.

It marched towards us gritting it's teeth. It began to extend its arm towards us. But with another wave of gunfire, instead of going for us, the monster went for Terry and Greg, who fired their weapons at the beast. The gunshots got faster and more desperate and aggressive as the creature's hand closed in on them.

The two men were going for the monster's face, trying to hit its eyes. But the monster used its other hand to shield its face from gunfire.

Why wasn't Sofía shooting?? Did she run out of ammo???

I looked past the monster, taking a few steps away.

Sofía was reloading. She looked from us to her gun with a scared expression. She desperately shoved shells in her shotgun but gave up halfway, not reloading it to its max capacity. She pointed the gun at the beast and fired.

The monster jerked forward as the dragon's breath hit it in its ass.

Terry and Greg dashed out of its way. Greg tripped and fell and crawled as fast as he could away from the monster. Terry rushed towards us. He grabbed me first, then used the rest of his huge right arm to also scoop up Lenny. In the blink of an eye, he holstered his pistol and grabbed Mateo by his hoodie. In only four steps, he was able to get a good distance away from the conflict.

"Bomb!" Lenny shouted as Terry threw us on the ground.

Terry turned and drew his weapon. "We don't have any!" he responded.

Terry ran back to the monster as fast as he could. Meanwhile, Sofía held the beast off. The dragon's breath was very effective. With every shot the beast would recoil greatly.

Sofía shot the thing in the head causing it to whip back. Unfortunately, that was the last of her rounds.

The monster recovered and continued its march towards Sofía. Instead of trying to reload, Sofía brilliantly turned and ran in the opposite direction. She disappeared into the cornfields.

"WAIT!!!" I called to Terry.

He kept running, ignoring my calls. He did look back ever so slightly, so he was at least listening.

I wasn't able to put together a good enough sentence to explain my findings so all I called was, "DISTRACTION!!!"

If he heard me, he didn't show it. Quite frankly it didn't matter. One word wasn't enough.

"What can we do to take its attention?" I asked, sitting up to face Mateo and Lenny.

They looked at me, dumbfounded.

"What?" Mateo asked.

"Didn't you see??" I groaned. "Its attention span is horrible!!!"

Mateo and Lenny just looked at me as if I were speaking some foreign language. Regardless of their looks, they both stood and helped me up.

"What are you saying?" Mateo asked.

"Didn't you see all of what just happened?" I asked. "It went from Sofía to Terry to Sofía to Terry! It can't multitask; it gets easily distracted! It was like monkey in the middle!" I explained. "Just think about it."

"I get it," Lenny confirmed.

"We need to take its attention off of us!"

"How?" Mateo asked.

"I'M ASKING YOU!!!" I shouted, pointing at them.

Mateo raised his eyebrows and shoulders.

"The flares?" Lenny suggested. "The flares!"

"We tried that!" Mateo replied.

"How about noise?" I suggested. "We can set something loud off?"

"I have a loud Bluetooth speaker!" Mateo said.

"Go get it!" I ordered.

I was sure that Mateo's speaker was at the house somewhere.

Looking at where the flashes and echoes of gunfire were in the cornfields, I could see as the flashes of gunfire occasionally lit up the creature, which towered over the cornfields. I could tell that it was only a matter of time before the creature killed Terry and Sofia.

So, I couldn't wait for Mateo to go to his house and come back. I had to at least try to get its attention somehow, if just for a couple seconds.

Before Mateo turned to run to his house, I grabbed his shoulder. "Do you have flares?" I asked.

He raised the small orange pistol.

"No, separate from this!" I pushed the gun away. "Something that'll last longer?"

"There might be some in the chest," Mateo said pointing to the barn. "On the second floor in the left corner."

I nodded. And with that, Mateo ran towards his house.

I pumped my legs as much as my bruised body would allow. I entered the barn and for the first time I noticed the horses. They were freaking out, grunting and snorting.

"I know it's scary," I said, comforting them.

I was expecting to see a staircase of some kind, but I ended up with a ladder that led to the second floor. I climbed the ladder. Every time I raised my shoulder above my head, a burst of pain would flow along my back. Not to mention how bad it hurt just pulling myself up.

When I finally reached the top, I saw nothing. No flares, or even any boxes or tools of any kind.

"Shit!" I cursed.

I rushed around the top floor, looking for any sign of flares. But I found nothing. I did find a large hunting rifle. But no bullets.

166

Even if I had found ammunition, my aim was not good enough to hit the thing's eye.

I rushed to the window in the barn located on the front. It gave a clear view of the field. I had to step over a couple metal boxes that blocked my path to the window. Once I reached it, I undid the latch and pushed open the doors.

I saw nothing, however, not the beast or gunfire.

My stomach dropped as a thought crossed my mind. What if it got them? What if they were dead? I had no words to describe that kind of fear.

Suddenly, the red eyes flashed about four feet above the corn. Then they vanished, one before another.

This happened a couple more times. I came to see what was happening.

It was searching for them. They had somehow managed to hide from the creature. Either they knew that shooting it would only draw its attention to them, or they ran out of ammunition and simply hid.

But this was all a theory. For all I knew, it had already destroyed Terry and Sofía and hadn't gotten to me yet. I couldn't help but feel that it was looking for them and they were hiding. Otherwise, it would be coming for me.

I turned to continue my search for flares and ending up tripping on a metal box. I noticed a pile of large boxes stacked in a sort of pyramid. An old-aged blanket covered them. I figured it was a decent place to hide should it come to that. Given that my plan was to draw the monster away from Sofía and Terry, I was most likely going to end up hiding.

The noise made me flinch. I believed if I made too much noise, I'd draw the creature to me. Small cylinder objects rolled across the floor, some softly bouncing off my body.

They were bullets. I wasn't knowledgeable on firearms. But they looked like they could fit in the rifle.

Holy shit, I thought, *I'm about to shoot this thing.*

I was able to handle the shotgun. I could handle this.

I scooped up a handful of the bullets off the floor and shoved them in my right pocket. I filled my hand once more and made my way to the rifle, which lay on a desk. I picked it up, surprised by the weight. I inspected the gun. I grabbed the handle and pulled it back. A loud click came of it.

I fumbled with my fingers and eventually carefully inserted the bullet into the hunting rifle. I pushed the handle back towards the gun. And it clicked again.

The gun was loaded.

"Ok," I said out loud. "Now I need a clip thing." I didn't think it would be wise to have to put a bullet in every time I fired it.

I scanned the desk where I found the gun and got lucky. To the right-hand corner lay a clip. I picked it up and began to load bullets into it. Thankfully, I'd played enough video games that I had a decent idea of what I was doing. Once the clip was full, I felt around the rifle. I felt the clip, and figured where it was supposed to go.

The gun was now ready.

I made my way back to the window. I looked down the sights and hoped that video games would serve me right.

I mimicked how the gun looked on games. I placed the iron sight on the creature, which was more visible being closer to the light.

My plan was simple. Draw it to me, and away from Sofía and Terry.

I took a breath, coming to terms with the fact that I could be bringing the thing right to me.

I pulled the trigger with a loud BANG. The gun jerked.

I wasn't sure if I had hit it or not, either way red eyes now faced me. They glared at me, with both hate and curiosity.

"Ooowaaahh!" I screamed as the creature began to march to me. "I did not think this through!" I said to myself.

I rushed to hide in the boxes and blanket. I became more rushed and scared as I heard the Earth shake with that monster's footsteps. I yanked the blanket around my body, and a huge puff of dust formed a cloud around my surroundings.

I rolled to the wall next to the pyramid and made sure that every part of my body was covered. Thankfully, the blanket appeared to belong to a king-sized mattress. The dust burned my eyes and scratched my throat.

"*Where...?*" a voice said, "*I saw you in here. Where...?*"

The voice had multiple tones, one loud and one quiet. It scratched the air with its sound. As loud as it was, it was also somehow transparent, like it was whispering.

I couldn't believe it! I couldn't believe that this thing could talk! Not only that, but it was talking to me!

My first instinct was to scream! Scream and lose myself into insanity! It was appropriate to lose my mind! It was natural! But I couldn't afford to go crazy. Doing so would certainly mean my death, and I wasn't ready to die yet.

I bit my tongue. The pain distracted me; with every breath I took, I bit harder.

"Tell me!" the thing demanded, *"Tell me where you are!"*

I began to hold my breath. I wasn't risking making any noise at all. I tried to focus on biting my tongue, along with clenching my fist.

I couldn't see the creature as I faced the wall. But I could feel what it was doing. I heard it crawling around the bottom floor of the barn.

The horses were going crazy. They were snorting in fear and adrenaline. Part of me hoped that the thing would focus its attention on the animals. Their pens were rattling as the horses jumped around and kicked.

The monster's thumps told me that it was crawling towards the pens. It must've stopped and studied the animals because it went quiet, no longer thumping around, bumping into tools and wood pillars.

I found myself relaxing. I felt the pressure I was putting on my hands and tongue slowly going away.

If the thing was focused on the horse, I could possibly make a run for it. The horses could keep its attention if I was silent enough. The poor horses were still going crazy. And the monster wasn't making any noise.

In a moment of courage, I shifted in the sheets, with the intention of peeking out. But with the soft sound of cloth ruffling, I froze. My fear of being caught took hold of my body.

I heard hardwood snap! I heard a horse snort and screech. Then I began to hear ripping and tearing.

It was fucking demolishing a horse again.

The noise the poor animal could vocalize came to an abrupt halt. But the tearing went on. I could hear the flesh being smashed, and the bones being cracked.

We were now down to four horses.

I mustered up all the courage I could, I forced myself to unclench my fist. I felt the blood fill my hand back up as I did so. I gently shifted the blanket slowly across my face, and it dragged along my forehead, then my nose, then it gently fell off my chin. Even though my face was uncovered, I couldn't see anything. My eyes were still closed, and my breath was still being held.

Cursing myself, because I didn't think I could cover myself back up, I forced open my eyes.

Sure enough, it was there. Thankfully not looking directly at me.

I saw its elbows poking through my line of sight. It was on its hands and knees, with its chest close to the floor, causing its arms to poke through where the second floor began.

I scanned the rest of the floor and saw two possible exits.

The barn's two large front doors had a window above them, where I had shot the monster. The left wall and right wall each held a window of its own. I couldn't risk the front window because dropping from there would expose me to the monster. Dropping from the left window wasn't an option either, as it was closed with a potentially loud latch.

The right one, however, was definitely the way to go. It was already slightly open, and dropping from that window would put a wall between me and the monster. From what I saw, it wasn't a big drop from the window to the ground.

That didn't mean it couldn't break my legs or ankle in a stroke of bad luck.

"WHERE!!??" the creature called. It's voice sent shivers down my spine.

It was still looking for me. It knew I was in here.

When it finally began to raise its head to my level, I decided to just roll the fuckin' dice.

I jumped up as fast as I could, pointed the barrel of my rifle at the monster's face, as soon as our eyes met I pulled the trigger. I didn't stick around to see if I landed any critical hit on it.

I bolted as fast as I could to the window! Thankfully the adrenaline hid the pain I would've felt due to my back and let me run.

When I reached the window, I used my hand to vault through it, with my other hand holding the rifle as tight as I could.

The adrenaline was a lifesaver for the mad dash. But it couldn't help with the landing. Because of the way I flung myself out the window I ended up kicking both my feet in front of me. Gravity showed no mercy as it pulled me down to the floor in such surprising speed. I landed right on my ass, sending a blunt wave of pain through my body. My tail bone felt like it had shattered. Unfortunately, there was no amount of adrenaline that could help me with losing my breath. Not like it was helping much anymore.

I barely had time to get to my feet when the wall of the barn exploded, unleashing the monster on me. Pieces of the barn smacked me in all parts of my body as the creature let out a spine-chilling roar.

I rolled to my left as the monster swung its clenched fist down on me. The ground shook with the thump that came from the impact. If I had been a second late, I would have surely been killed.

I sprung up to my feet and ran as fast as I could to the cornfields! I figured the crops could offer me some sanctuary like it did with Terry and Sofía.

A horse had somehow made its way in my path. Two thoughts crossed my mind when I saw the horse. The first one consisted of me cursing the animal, as I would surely find myself bumping into the animal, bouncing off it, slowing down my escape.

The second thought simply had me acting fast! Using my bruised ass and legs, I leaped as far and as high as I could. Unfortunately, the horse had no saddle on it, which would make the task of mounting it harder. The horse was huge, and was running away from the barn wall, meaning it faced my left. I kicked out my right leg, which thankfully went over the horses back. The rest was easy after that.

I used my free hand to grab its mane and pull the rest of me on the horse. I didn't bother to try and steer it. I just let him run as fast as he could.

It took me a few seconds, but I eventually recognized the horse I was on. His name was Grundy. I had no idea what breed he was, but thankfully he was all white with brown spots, so I could see him in the dark.

Grundy was as panicked as I was. I could feel his heartbeat damn near bursting through his body. He ran wildly, taking no care that I was on him. But I held on tight; I was not about to lose my only chance of escape.

Grundy sprinted towards the cornfields but at the last second, he turned at its border. His sudden turn almost threw me off. I yanked myself back on him before I slipped off.

While I was struggling on Grundy, I got a glimpse of the monster. My stomach dropped as I saw the uncanny sight of the thing full-on sprinting in my direction. It was pumping its legs and arms, the way they flew around caused my stomach to turn. It didn't look right, this oddly shaped thing running.

"Just get me outta here!" I said to Grundy.

The horse didn't argue. He continued to run. For whatever reason, he didn't want to enter the cornfields. I felt like I could possibly lose the monster in the fields, but that wasn't part of the plan.

Grundy began running towards the house, which was awfully convenient for me. I turned my head towards the beast and to my absolute delight and relief, Grundy was outrunning it. There was noticeable distance between us. However, that didn't mean the creature couldn't catch up.

Once Grundy and I reached the front yard of the house, I took control of Grundy. I got him to slow down, to his resistance.

I scanned the area for Mateo. He wasn't out yet; he was still inside the house looking for the speaker. If he was outside, I would've seen him.

The door swung open and out came Mateo calling, "I got it!"

"Give!" was all I could respond with. Grundy was still trotting so Mateo had to toss it to me. Thankfully, he got it to me the first try.

"Red Eyes is right behind me!" I called. "Hide!"

Lenny popped out from behind Mateo and tossed me a trash bag filled with hard cylinders. Catching it caused me to drop the rifle but I didn't care. I figured if the thing was gonna run past me, I should at least leave the boys something.

Holding the bag and feeling around it, I assumed they were flares. This would only help my plan. If I could get the thing to focus on something far away enough for us to flip the car, we might just make it out alive.

A wave or sadness and grief washed over me as I recalled Terry's friends. It wasn't fair. I survived this creature by dumb luck.

I couldn't let my mind wander. Not even for those poor souls. I had to save who was still here.

I kicked Grundy to go faster and sure enough, the creature was chasing. Thankfully, I wasted little time with Mateo and Lenny. I still had its attention, it wasn't gonna go for the others. I was gonna have to ride past it in order to comfortably get it as far away from the rest as I could.

Shockingly it dived for me! But thankfully, Grundy was fast, and in a moment Grundy jolted out of the way. To my horror, we rode past the two bodies. I tried not to look but the sight held my gaze like a magnet.

Focus, I told myself.

I pulled out my phone and turned on the speaker. Juggling the bag, the speaker and Grundy, I failed to realize that my phone refused to turn on. To my horror, it was dead. I cursed myself for forgetting phones didnt work with this thing around.

"Fuck." I cursed.

I found myself riding past the barn. I was on the right, the side with no giant hole in it. That's when it hit me. I wasn't gonna be able to lead this thing away the way I wanted to. I couldn't get a Bluetooth connection, and without a saddle or some way to keep the speaker on Grundy. I was just gonna have to drop the speaker off somewhere and hope it would keep the monster's attention.

"Plan B." I said.

I reached into the bag of flares with the hope that this would be enough. As I did so I felt my hand push something on the speaker. As luck would have it, music burst from the speaker filling the night sky.

I turned my head to see if the beast was behind me. When I saw it once more pumping its arms and legs to me, I was both relieved that it stayed on me and didn't go for the others and horrified that it was gaining on me.

"Fuck it!" I said. I really had no choice but to keep going. I prayed that my plan to get its attention away would still work. We rode into the cornfields, and a couple crops smacked me.

THUMP THUMP THUMP.

It was getting close; I could hear its heavy footsteps when I couldn't before.

It was dark, so I had to feel around the speaker looking for the volume control. When I felt the same knob I felt earlier, I turned it. The speaker cycled through channels splitting and cutting through multiple songs. I felt around some more and felt another bigger nozzle. I turned this one and the music got louder.

THUMP THUMP THUMP!

It was getting closer; the footsteps were louder and closer.

Thankfully Mateo was right: the speaker was loud, really loud. I felt it vibrating in sync with the words and music of the song. I could hear the sound pounding in the inside of my ear. It blocked out the creature's footsteps, which put me at ease.

There was no promise that a loud song would be able to match the attention getter of a dragon's blast to the face, but it was worth a try. Hopefully it would be enough for it to stop chasing me.

The thought of the thing catching up to me and doing God knows what when it got me was almost enough to get me to drop the speaker and bolt. Doing so would only park the thing some little distance away from the barn. I had to get this thing as far as possible.

The speaker took up my whole arm just carrying it. With my other arm, I juggled the contents of the plastic bag. Using my mouth, I fished out a couple flares. If only I knew how to light one up. I figured instructions had to be in the flare somewhere, right?

It was dark as hell, so unfortunately, I had to struggle to use what little light the moon offered to illuminate the small metal cylinders. Thankfully, a small bold lettering on the side of the cylinder simply instructed me to pull off the cap and use it to ignite the flare. I did so and a bright green light damn near blinded me. It did for a moment before my vision returned to me.

When it did, I just continued to ride. I had to gain a significant amount of distance before I could comfortably drop the speaker and flare. Then hopefully it would stay away for a while.

The music and flare became more and more annoying. It was getting hard to stay focused. At some point, the flare started to die out. When it did, I popped another one. With this, I decided that it was enough.

I dropped the speaker. In a normal situation I would've hated hearing it hit the ground so hard. The speaker was clearly expensive. However, dropping it was like removing a splinter. I felt free and unburdened, like a bird flying for the first time.

But I couldn't bolt away yet. I got Grundy to slow down, just a little bit, to his dismay.

I popped all the flares in the bag. I tried to juggle all of them at first, after a few burns I just let them fall. As soon as I got the last one, there were maybe five or six, I kicked Grundy with a "GRAHH!!!"

He didn't argue, running fast as if he hadn't been running this whole time and was out of breath. I was sure we were running back in the direction of the house and barn. But I didn't want to risk bumbling into the monster, so I forced Grundy to sort of wide turn our way over. Instead of going in a straight-line back home, we made our way back in a "C" shape.

I could still hear the music loud and clear. And when I looked back, I could see the flares illuminating their light. I prayed that it was enough to save the others.

I felt awful and sick, thinking about Phil and Simon. I felt both sadness and disgust, sadness from their unfair deaths, and disgust from their horrific deaths.

Eventually I got clear of the cornfields. I had ended up at the barn with a clear view of the broken open wall. I scanned the area for the monster and my companions. I searched for anything.

Silence was all I found. There were some crickets going off somewhere but not much else. I didn't wanna call out for anyone. I didn't want to draw any attention to me.

Grundy passed around the barn, I kept an eye out for the monster, looking for any sign of him. Thankfully, every corner I turned was met with emptiness.

After I circled the barn, I decided to make my way to the house. When I turned, I saw three figures standing out in the open.

It was Sofía, Terry, and Greg. They were alive. I rushed to them, not being able to hide the big grin on my face.

When I reached them, Sofía let out a huge sigh of relief, bending down, laying her elbows on her thighs, and saying out loud, "You're ok."

I simply said the same thing.

"The music?" Terry voiced. "Was that you?"

I nodded.

Terry gave me a thoughtful look and said, "Fucking brilliant."

I looked to see Greg, who was looking all over the place, presumably for the monster. I felt my eyes and stomach tingle with the thought of Terry's friends.

"Simon and Phil," I choked. "I'm sorry."

Terry visibly looked pained, clenching his eyes closed for a moment. Seeing his pain just made mine worse. But I couldn't cry. For some reason, I didn't let myself cry.

Terry didn't respond to my condolences, he grunted and turned to Sofía. "Let's go," he said.

"Get the fuck off the horse!" Greg said suddenly.

He marched towards me and before I could react, he grabbed me by the leg and shirt and ripped me off Grundy. I hit the ground hard which knocked my air out for what was probably the thousandth time that night.

But as soon as I hit the ground so did Greg. Sofía had knocked his ass down.

Terry came from behind her, jumped on Greg, growling, "The fuck is wrong with you!"

"I'm fucking leaving!" Greg snapped back. He tried to throw Terry off of him but failed.

Terry then raised his giant right arm and fist and struck Greg square in the nose. Greg instantly stopped struggling. He wasn't out cold, just dazed.

"Don't be a pussy!" Terry said through clenched teeth. "You can go when we're done."

I could tell Terry used a lot of his pent-up grief in his actions. I stood and made my way to Sofía, who looked just as pissed with the old man. Terry stood and walked to Sofía. He gestured her to get on the horse and she did so.

"You don't even know how to ride one, dipshit," Terry said.

Terry then helped Greg up but brought him close. "You can leave when we flip the truck," Terry scoffed. "Pussy."

"TO HELL WITH YOU!!!" Greg shouted, "IF YOU GUYS WANT TO STAY AND GET KILLED BY SOME MOVIE MONSTER, THEN DO IT!!!" His tone softened but was still loud for my liking. "But I'm taking off!"

That was when a thought occurred to me that hadn't in the past. "What about their cars?" I asked. "You and my tía got here separately, right? Where's your car?"

Terry took his attention off of Greg and looked at me. "Red Eyes must've gotten it," he answered.

"Must've," I echoed. "You don't know?"

"When we arrived, we parked the car in front of Sofía's house. We investigated the area for a while, then it was suddenly gone."

"What?" I asked.

"I don't know," Terry sighed. "It was like one second it was there. The next it wasn't."

"How far away were you guys from the vehicle?"

"Not far, within eyesight."

"You guys didn't hear it?"

"We heard nothing."

"So what? It can just make things disappear?"

"It didn't just vanish if that's what you're thinking." Terry explained. He dropped his harsh tone towards Greg a little bit while talking to me. "It was dragged a yard or two then possibly launched somewhere into the fields."

Terry didn't say anything more to my to comment. So not only was this thing somehow blocking communication, but it could talk, and make things vanish.

It probably wasn't likely, but then again, what is? We don't know the rules anymore.

Terry looked at Greg. "You lay another hand on anyone, and I'll kill ya," he said.

Greg said nothing. Which said a lot.

Terry was clearly capable of fucking him up. And Greg knew this, he didn't dare say shit to him. Terry was clearly in charge. Not to mention the wrath he'd surely suffer from Sofía.

I myself had so much anger towards this man. He fucking threw me off the horse after I just saved his ass. I thought about taking a cheap shot at his jaw. I knew that Terry and Sofía would back me up. The priority, however, was getting everyone the hell out of here. If that was even possible.

176

This creature was somehow capable of insane things. For all we knew, it could do so much more.

We all began making our way back to the barn. I explained to all of them what I discovered. I told them about the creature's short attention span.

"That's why the music was so effective," Sofía pointed out. "Smart."

We could still hear the music, booming loud rock music.

Inside the barn we found the mangled-up horse, along with three spooked but safe and sound horses.

Sofía silently mourned her horse. She took a moment, looking at it. That was all, though, she immediately saddled up the other four with my help. She and I instructed Terry how to mount and ride.

"He'll mostly be following me," she explained. "So don't worry."

Terry and Sofía denied Greg a ride.

"You'll walk," Terry said.

Greg didn't argue. He just glared at the two.

On our way back to the house, I decided to make clear what was on my mind. "What do y'all think this is?" I asked, not to anyone specifically.

Terry and Sofía both turned their heads at me. Greg just kept his head straight. Greg walked alongside Terry at the far left of the line we made, with Sofía on the right of Terry and me at the far right.

"Well?" I pushed. "We can talk about it."

"I don't know," Sofía replied. "Things like this aren't supposed to exist, so technically it could be anything."

"What do you mean?" I asked.

Sofía thought about her words for a bit before responding to me. "For all we know, it's a person. Could be a witch, or some government experiment gone wrong. It could also be a demon, like an actual demon from the Bible, bending reality."

"You think it could be any of those?" I asked.

Sofía shrugged her shoulders. "That's the thing, kiddo, I don't know. Maybe it's all a trick, maybe we were drugged by some crazy scientist and were just seeing things. Hell, it could be a prank, a very elaborate prank." Sofía sounded frustrated with the thought of the possibilities she was up against. She was right, this creature could be anything.

"So, what do you believe it is?" I asked.

"You asked me that already," Sofía answered.

"No, I mean, of all the things it could be, what do you feel is most likely?"

"Same as you, kiddo."

"A demon?"

Sofía nodded her head.

"Really?" Terry asked suddenly. "You think it's a demon?"

Sofía turned her head towards Terry. She didn't say anything, she just nodded her head again. Terry accepted her answer with, "Hmph."

"You got another idea?" I asked Terry.

"No," Terry said. "I'm just starting to think God is real."

Terry didn't believe in God like my family sort of did. At least he didn't use to; the creature was beginning to change that. But this creature could easily be proof that God wasn't real. Why would God allow such a thing to come into existence? I thought demons were less physical and more like spirits.

"But," I began, "couldn't this thing easily not be a demon? And aren't there rules to demons? I thought they were more like ghosts."

"Demons could be a lot of things," Sofía answered. "You're right, it may not be a demon, it could be anything, could be an alien. Like I said, we don't know what it is, other than it defies everything we've ever deemed to be normal." Sofía looked at me thoughtfully. "Just take your pick, Miguel."

I wanted to talk about it more. But at this point we were already closing in on the house. I could still hear the music playing all the way where I left it. I was shocked at how effective the music was. I had thought that the most it was gonna do was take its attention off of us just for a moment. But it's already been a few moments.

The image of the creature just staring at the speaker formed in my head. If only we could be so lucky to have the monster suddenly become a statue itself. I knew the loud music wouldn't last long. We were already lucky enough that it had been lasting as long as it had. The fact that my idea worked at all was a blessing I wasn't gonna take for granted.

A blessing.

The word bounced in around in my head. A blessing? In these times?

We stopped at the flipped truck. I hopped off Grundy and handed him to Sofía who was already off her horse.

Lenny and Mateo came running out of the house. The two of them approached me and Lenny said, "It's so fucking good to see you, bro!"

"It worked! Your idea worked!!!" Mateo called.

I didn't know how to respond to this praise. It was nicer and definitely tickled the balls of my ego. But I was just glad to know that they were safe.

"Come on!" I said, deflecting their attention. "Let's get this done."

I turned to the truck to see what I could do to help. I met the gaze of two disapproving adults.

"The plan is now back to normal," Sofía said. "Get in the house and wait."

CHAPTER 28

Mateo and Lenny argued. They wanted to help. Me, on the other hand? I was so ready to go back into the safety of the house. I was not gonna argue—and I made that very clear.

"I am not arguing. I'll be ready if you need help," I announced as I turned my back on them and proudly marched my way up the stairs and into the house.

Mateo and Lenny followed me soon after.

I wasted no time. I found a La-Z-Boy and sat down. My body was covered in bruises and scratches, not to mention possibly a few broken bones. Most likely nothing was broken, but if a doctor told me something was broken here, there, and right there, I wouldn't have been surprised.

As I sat down, I let out a huge audible sigh. I let my muscles relax and let everything untense.

Mateo and Lenny stood at the front windows. They studied the adults out there doing their thing. I was still in danger, sure, but for some reason I wasn't panicked or freaked out. I was just glad to not be in so much immediate danger or being chased. I guessed after I'd gotten so close to death, being a little further away put me at ease. Or maybe with the sudden calm I found myself in, I was just feeling tired.

"What if it doesn't work?" I heard Lenny ask.

"What?" Mateo replied.

"What if my truck doesn't turn on?" Lenny repeated.

Mateo looked offended. "I think it's a bit too late for second thoughts."

"I'm just saying," Lenny said defensively. "This whole plan is riding on a miracle."

"We've had plans that rode on miracles," Mateo shot back.

I was jealous hearing those words. Mateo and Lenny had history; they were close friends. And hearing that made me feel left out.

"Like what?" I asked.

I faced away from them. But their sudden silence told me they heard.

"A year ago, we had bet on Chowder. Like in a race," Mateo said stepping to me.

"Chowder? Really?" I asked.

Chowder wasn't a very fast horse. She was always a bit slower and weaker compared to the others. She was a good girl, though.

"And?" I asked.

"And a miracle happened," Mateo said.

"She won??"

Mateo nodded while grinning.

"What did you win?" I asked.

"Money," Lenny said. "What do you think?"

"How much money?"

"Well, a good chunk of the school pitched in. We won around five grand."

"Fuck!" I gasped. "Wait, what do you mean 'around'?"

"Like five thousand dollars and some change," Lenny answered.

My jaw dropped.

"Too bad we spent it all," Mateo said.

"On what?" I asked, shocked.

"Trying to impress girls." Mateo laughed. Then he thought for a bit before saying, "Turns out, money really is everything they look for in guys. Suddenly every girl in school wanted to date me."

"Must be nice," I said sarcastically.

After hearing what the boys had to say I wanted to ask how they got Chowder to win a race? Was there some awesome training montage? Did they cheat? And what school is involved with some horse race event?

Lenny turned and looked outside.

Silence fell on us after my last comment. Reality set in again. The severity of the situation came back to us.

I stood from the La-Z-Boy and walked over to them. The adults had straps to the horses and were in the process of trying to flip it. Surprised to see it was actually working, I found myself smiling. Genuine joy came from the thought of being able to leave this nightmare.

There was a problem, however. I saw that the horses were able to move the car, but not in the way it was intended. The vehicle was being dragged. Mateo's concerns came true.

"We should go help them," I said, surprised by my words.

Without even questioning me, the two boys moved right out the door. I followed, disappointed at the lack of an argument. But they did need help.

Terry was a big guy. And he was able to move the truck upwards ever so slightly. He was positioned at the opposite side of the horses. The three of us walked out and were immediately confronted by my tía.

"Go inside," was all she said.

"Mom please!" Mateo argued. "We'll help push!"

"You have been arguing with everything I've been saying," she barked. "I'm sick of it! Go inside now or I'll drag you all inside."

Well, I was sold. I wasn't gonna let myself be dragged inside a house. It wasn't like she had to convince me to not put myself in danger.

"If we help you guys, we can leave sooner!" Mateo argued. "Come on, we're so close."

Sofía thought about her son's words. She eventually caved and gestured towards the truck. Without missing a beat, the three of us rushed to join Terry and Greg.

"Thank you, guys," Terry whispered.

I made sure to stay on the opposite side of Greg. Lenny took his place right next to Greg. Lenny was taller than him, not by a lot, but enough. Enough so that I didn't worry about Lenny.

I held the truck, ready to shove, at the bed. Being this close really did show how intact the vehicle was. Excitement was crawling all over me seeing this. We were actually going home.

But the music kept my expectations low. It echoed through the black sky. At any point, the music could stop, I knew the flares already had. For all I knew, the creature had already lost interest and was coming for us.

"Ready!?" Sofía called.

"Ready?" Terry asked us.

We all nodded.

"Ready!!!" Terry called back.

The truck began moving so I used all the strength I could to push the truck upward. With all of us, the truck moved in the correct direction. But it began to drag again. We heaved out, and the truck fell.

Mateo said through heavy breaths, "We have to keep the bottom still. That way it won't hit a point we can't go past."

"How?" Terry asked. "It's not like we can hold it from the bottom."

Mateo walked over to the bed and pointed at an opening to the bottom. "All we have to do is bring one of the horses around this way and hook the line from down there." Mateo waved his arms around the truck. "So we'll have one moving this side, and the others moving that side."

What he said made sense. Sofía and Terry had a face of understanding and recognition. With that, Sofía brought a horse to our end, opposite the others.

Mateo crawled under the bed. Shuffling and movement came from underneath. When he emerged, he said, "Got it."

While this was happening, I kept an ear out for the music. I had a gut feeling that when the music stopped, we were in trouble. To my relief, the rock music still played.

Terry walked up to me and asked, "Something wrong?"

I gave him a look that would make anyone feel stupid. Even a badass super cop like Terry. "There's no way you just asked me that." I laughed.

"Fair enough," he said. "What's on your mind?"

I thought for a moment before answering. "I don't know how long the speaker is gonna hold it. Or if it even is holding it anymore."

Terry nodded. Terry approached Sofía and they talked out of my earshot. I saw her nod at some point then disappear into her house.

"Alright!" Terry called, clapping his hands together. "Let's do this!"

Everything was set. We had one horse hooked on one side, with **four** hooked on the other. We all got in position. And with Mateo guiding the horses, we began to push.

With a dozen good shoves, we managed to get it further then we did last time. We were all grunting and groaning.

A loud creaking noise emerged from the scene, and after a few more inches—we did it! Gravity and the strength of the horses soon took over. The truck was on its side. From there, all it took was a few more shoves. The truck crashed on the floor. It sounded bad, but it was on its wheels again. The sound it made, however, was loud and echoed through the night.

We all thought the same thing. We exchanged looks of horror and fear.

"Fuck!" Greg cried. "Keys! Gimme the keys!"

Lenny gave him a pathetic look, walking to the driver's side door. "Back the fuck off my truck." Lenny said sternly. Lenny proceeded to walk past Greg, giving him no attention.

Greg was about to say or do something before he caught Terry's gaze. Terry gave him a look that said, *Back off or else.* And sure enough, Greg backed off.

Lenny went for the door. It clicked open, but the dents it had on it caused a loud and painful squeal as Lenny opened it.

The noise was making me anxious. I was so scared that the monster would hear us and come for us.

When the door was opened, Lenny crawled in and took a seat. He inserted his keys into the keyhole and turned. The truck's engine made a whole lot of noise. Struggling for only a couple moments before turning on.

"Hhhhholy shit!" Lenny cheered.

A loud burst of laughter and cheers soon followed from Terry and Mateo. While I didn't cheer myself, I was just as happy and relieved. I felt my face stretch as a huge smile formed.

"YYYYYEEEAH!!!" Sofía cheered.

Her sudden appearance shocked me. When I saw it was her, though, I felt a whole lot safer.

"Come on!" Lenny said while hopping out of the vehicle. "Let's get the roof off."

Mateo, without missing a beat, bolted into the shed near the house. He later came running out leading a wire.

Sofía approached one of the horses, dropping a duffel bag on the floor. It must've been what she disappeared for but its contents were unknown to me.

Sofía shuffled in the sack on Grundy. She pulled out a large saw. We were now gonna begin the process of cutting the roof of the truck off.

I hated that we had to make more noise and take more time doing this. But none of us were gonna be able to drive the truck unless we made at least some room. Even Sofía, who was shorter than all of us, wouldn't be able to pilot the vehicle.

Not wasting any time, Sofía made her way to the driver's side door. Mateo met her there shortly after and plugged in the tool. Terry took the tool and began cutting. Sparks exploded from where he was cutting. Sofía took many fast steps back avoiding the sparks.

She spotted me and walked to me. "Hey," she began, "help me with this."

She grabbed my arm and pulled me towards Grundy. We stopped at the duffel bag she had dropped on the ground.

She squatted down and unzipped it, revealing a large speaker. It looked heavy-duty, as if its purpose was to be mounted on large pulls to play music and audio in sports stadiums.

"Why do you have this???" I asked, genuinely surprised. "What would you need this for?"

"We had a theater experience here about a year ago," she explained.

"Really?" I asked.

"Mhmm," she said while pulling the thing out of the bag. She handed it to me and told me to join her on Grundy.

"Isn't it weird how convenient this is to our current predicament?" I asked.

Sofia chucked. "Yeah, I guess now it is."

"Now?" I echoed, struggling to join her on Grundy.

"Not an hour ago, having some leftover dragon's breath from years ago seemed convenient. If I had known that this would've been more useful than I would've brought this out sooner."

Her words resonated with me deeply.

We went immediately left from the house, opposite of the O'Youngs' house. Grundy ran fast, taking us far into the land. We went far enough into the land that I could ever so slightly hear the music played by the speaker.

I was shocked to see just how far we had traveled. It was incredible how fast Grundy was.

"If you want to play something, we might be too far," I said nervously.

"This thing is loud," Sofía explained. "It's more than enough."

She hopped off Grundy and I did the same. She snatched the speaker from me, turned her back, and planted it right in front of us. She stood and faced me.

She cleared her throat before saying, "I can set the speaker up. You're gonna set up fireworks."

I didn't argue or say anything at all. I immediately understood what was needed from me.

I turned to Grundy and searched his saddle for fireworks. I had to rush to his other side and search that sack. Sure enough, I found everything I needed.

There was a huge shell, and a huge tube. Much bigger than any I'd ever seen. This thing was big and bad. I wanted to ask about the context of this firework, but I didn't. I placed the tube on the floor and inserted the shell in it.

I made a trip back to Grundy and grabbed a large roll of fuse. I fished in the tube for the shells fuse and when I pulled it out, I twisted them together.

"Where's the fuse go?" I asked.

"Bring it to me."

I rolled the fuse all the way to Sofía, who was focused on what she was doing. When she spotted me hovering over her, she said, patting next to her, "Just leave it here."

I placed it next to her. Still watching her, I made my way back to the tube. I inspected my work and felt like everything was good.

"How will you light it remotely?" I asked.

"The light bulb on the speaker gets pretty hot. It lights up when it plays audio. I don't know if it'll be hot enough to light a fuse, but I think it's worth a try."

"How hot does it get?" I asked. It had to be hot enough for her to put her trust in it.

"Fucking hot," she answered.

"Convenient," I joked.

She stood and rushed me on Grundy. She hopped on first before helping me on. She was wasting no time at all.

"I hooked it on a timer so hopefully the creature will be drawn here!" Sofía shouted over her shoulder.

I didn't answer. Sofía knew what she was doing. I trusted her plan would work. It wasn't a Hail Mary like mine was.

After a couple minutes, we were back in sight of the house and the little project everyone was working on. As we pulled up to everyone, the roof of the truck was already detached. The boys had grabbed one end and were already in the process of sliding it off the truck. When it hit the ground, everyone took a second to appreciate their work.

"Alright," Sofía said, "get going guys."

I hopped off Grundy and joined Mateo and Lenny.

"Please just go. We're right behind you," Sofía said to Mateo.

When I looked at him, I could tell he was ready to argue. "Dude," I said while grabbing his shoulder, "we need to leave. There's nothing else we can do to help."

He took his eyes off his mother and placed them on me. He looked concerned and emotional.

Lenny stepped up to Mateo and said, "Dude, I know you wanna help. I want to help my family, too, but I think it's in our best interest to keep to the plan."

The word "plan" was starting to sound annoying. Regardless, Lenny was right. I admired Lenny, being able to make the most logical decision, and not jumping to help his family.

"This isn't up for discussion!" Terry shouted.

I jumped at his words. Mateo and Lenny also recoiled.

Terry marched up to the three of us. "Two men! Two very good men are dead! If you think for a second you're gonna waste it, I'll pound in your faces, break your legs, and throw you assholes on that damn truck.

The memory of Phil and Simon popped in my head. I barely had a chance to know them. But they were here, put their life on the line for these two families.

186

The images of their deaths shook my body. I was so close to experiencing a similar death, it chased me closely and almost caught me. I could still feel it's grip around my body. So many emotions swirled around me as I thought of Simon and Phil. I could only imagine how Terry felt.

Terry didn't say anything. He just stared at Mateo. Waiting for some kind of response from him. Mateo wisely agreed to just leave.

I, on the other hand, was already getting in the fucking truck. No one had to convince me. I came here to help, and I did just that. I saved everyone, which was more than enough, I was the last person who needed to stay.

Mateo hopped in the bed. He was joined by Greg.

I spotted the dashboard, which had every single light on. It was a miracle that this thing was on at all. It would be a miracle if the thing could drive us out of here.

Lenny took his spot on the driver's side. Not before saying, "Bring them back," to Terry, who nodded.

We began to move. I felt like we were peeling off a bandage. I was so relieved.

Terry and my tía were right behind us. All they had to do was make it back to the O'Youngs, try and save whatever vehicle their hopes were riding on there, and drive away.

Lenny circled Terry and Sofía, who stood in front of the house. Sofía waved at her son. Terry was already eyeballing the path leading to the O'Young's house. Once Lenny cleared the front of the house, he drove onto the red gravel driveway leading away from Magnolia Falls.

"Come on kid, hit the gas!" Greg called from the back.

Lenny went to look in the rearview mirror, but then saw that there was no longer one.

I almost smiled at the thought of actually leaving this place. This place once brought me so much joy. It made up the majority of my childhood's memories. Now this place housed a creature beyond imagination. This place would now represent nothing but nightmares to me.

I almost smiled at the irony of it all.

CHAPTER 29

The truck's engine made all kinds of noises. You could actually hear the gears turning, the belt squeaking, and the bolts rattling. The ride was also bumpy, a side effect of the trucks newly messed up body.

We were maybe seven minutes from exiting Magnoila Falls. It was going to be the longest seven minutes of my life. It didn't help that only one headlight was working. Our path was lit up, but very little. Other than the light that the truck provided, we were surrounded by darkness.

"Can't this thing go any faster?" Greg called.

"What do you think?" Mateo laughed. "We'll be lucky to make it all the way out of here."

Greg snorted.

"I'm going twenty," Lenny said turning his head towards Greg. "Believe me when I say I'm flooring it. This is as fast as we're going."

Greg didn't say anything.

Unlike Terry, Greg was not growing on me. I wondered why Terry asked him to come at all; it wasn't like Greg showed any signs of being reliable and trustworthy. Perhaps being in this situation changed how he normally acted and behaved.

"Aye, Miguel," Lenny called, "look in the glove box for me, maybe I got a flashlight in there."

I did what he asked and thankfully pulled out a large heavy flashlight. "Alright nice," I said.

I felt around the metal cylinder, looking for a button. My pointer finger dragged across a rubber button. I pushed down on it and the other half of our path lit up.

It wasn't a very powerful light; it lit up only a small perimeter of what the left headlight was lighting up. It was also a different color.

"Better than nothing," Lenny sighed. "God!" Lenny shouted before slamming on the brakes and putting the truck in reverse.

My head flung forward! I threw my arms on the dashboard, smacking it to catch myself. When I bounced back and got my composure, I saw what had freaked Lenny out so much.

It was the fireworks; they had gone off. It was huge and bright, and it lit up the whole sky.

Not long after that, slow jazz began to echo through the cornfields.

"It went off!" I screamed.

"What?" Mateo asked loudly.

"Your mom set this up as a distraction!" I explained, more yelling than not.

"Does that mean they are encountering it?" Mateo asked.

I didn't know, it was possible. But it may also be possible that my own makeshift distraction stopped working so they activated this new one.

"I don't know," I answered honestly.

The jazz was insanely loud. It helped a lot that we weren't in very populated area.

"We're pretty close to it," Lenny said.

"What?" Greg chimed.

"We're close to the speaker and fireworks," he repeated.

When I looked in the direction of the fireworks, I saw that he was right. The fireworks were almost directly above us. We all must have came to the same conclusion because no one questioned or argued with Lenny's claim.

"Let's keep going!" I called over all the commotion. "We don't wanna be here when that thing shows up."

Lenny, after putting his truck back in drive, pushed the gas and moved us forward.

Dread was all I felt as we pushed on. We'd have to hope and pray, that if the creature showed up while we were in the area, it wouldn't notice us. I continued to scan our surroundings. My mind was starting to play tricks on me. Crops were being shaped into looking like the creature.

The fireworks died out, leaving only the music. A saxophone was playing a solo. Then it was soon replaced by drums and soft vocals. As calm as the music itself was, its volume damn near made it hellish. And it only got louder as we got closer.

"You can't drive around it???" Greg asked from behind.

Lenny shook his head.

"Why?!" Greg pushed.

"Because there's no path," Mateo explained. "Driving over all those crops would only damage our already screwed-up truck."

Greg visibly got more anxious and frustrated. "Shit at least floor it, kid!" he growled to Lenny.

Lenny turned his head to face Greg. "SIT THE FUCK DOWN AND SHUT UP!" Lenny barked.

Greg hesitated before moving his head closer to Lenny's. Greg's eyes grew large and wild. "Move the fuckin' car!" Greg whispered aggressively.

Mateo grabbed Greg by the shirt and pulled him back. "Can you fucking hear?!" Mateo asked. "The truck can't go faster!"

"Bullshit!" Greg cried before shoving Mateo aside and crawling for Lenny's seat.

Lenny flung his fist back, but Greg evaded the blow. Greg grabbed Lenny by his left arm, which was holding the wheel, and pulled. The truck jerked to the right as Lenny's grip failed. Greg demonstrated a surprising strength by yanking Lenny right out of the driver's seat. Lenny was soon face-to-face with Greg, and Lenny took the opportunity presented. Lenny head butted Greg right in the mouth. Greg's head whipped back but not much else. Greg used the momentum to pull Lenny the rest of the way out of the driver's seat.

I finally decided to do something, I stood up on my seat. Greg saw me; he held Lenny with one hand, with the other he shoved his hand in my face and pushed me back. I landed on the shattered windshield. It shredded my back like cheese.

I cried in pain. I used my elbows to lift myself off of the windshield, cutting myself on my way up as well.

I'd never thrown a punch that knocked someone out before, I knew throwing a haymaker in an attempt to knock out Greg would most likely fail. It was dark, I'd most definitely miss any swings I swung at his head. Going for his body was my best bet to land any sort of blow. I kicked off my seat and shoved Greg. But he stood his ground. I was only able to push him back into the bed of the truck. He corrected himself immediately. Thanks to Gregs iron grip, he dragged Lenny with him.

Thankfully, Lenny was able to break free of Greg's grasp. Mateo got to his feet and the three of us braced for a fight. Even though Greg was a bigger guy, and had years of experience as a cop, he was older, we could take him. The three of us were all pretty able, and Greg knew this. So he did the smartest thing he could've.

He pulled his gun.

CHAPTER 30

"Cheater!" Mateo shouted.

I immediately felt weak in the knees. I felt powerless and so much fear.

Lenny tensed up, taking a step back. The truck was still moving, and it was a matter of time before it rolled into the cornfields.

"Get the fuck out of my way," Greg ordered.

We all did so. We cleared a path for him to get to the driver's seat.

Greg instantly knew he was in control of the situation. His giant grin said as much. He moved past us, still holding the gun. He was smart, he pointed it right at Mateo's head to keep me and Lenny from trying anything as he faced away from us. He hopped in the driver's seat and corrected the truck, which was a few seconds from entering the cornfields. The sudden jerk of the car made the three of us in the back stumble and fall. My back and my body were beginning to feel all that it has been put through. Even breathing became uncomfortable.

Pushing away the pain, I scrambled to my feet as fast as I could. I couldn't see the gun, which made me all kinds of nervous. The other two boys did the same.

When the altercation occurred, Lenny took his foot off the gas, which slowed down our vehicle. Greg hit the gas which made us all fall again. Unfortunately for Greg, he didn't get what he wanted. The truck couldn't go faster than twenty miles per hour.

Greg screamed in frustration. At that point, we were closer to the speaker than before, so he screamed loud enough for us to hear him. Greg's grip on the steering wheel tightened, as if trying to will the injured truck to go faster.

The slow jazz continued to get louder and louder and louder.

Then we saw it. The creature.

We saw it for sure; it was the red eyes.

Greg stopped the truck. He had no choice; we couldn't risk getting closer.

I didn't understand why the fireworks and radio weren't working. My tía and I definitely placed them a good distance away from both the house and the road. At least we thought we had. Evidently, we were mistaken.

It was possible that it heard the altercation we'd just had in the truck. But the speaker had to be loud enough to cover up the noise we made.

I gritted my teeth, the realization of our mistake hit me like a train. The speaker and fireworks worked exactly the way we wanted them too, It drew the monster to it. Sadly, it was drawn towards our way out.

Greg put the truck in reverse, and we started to move backwards.

My gut dropped as the realization of ending up back to square one became the only thing I could think of. All I had done, all the work we had done, was for nothing.

Greg moved the truck slowly though. With that thing near, Greg was playing it safe.

The three of us huddled down in the bed of the truck.

"How is it here?" Mateo whispered.

I didn't answer, I just gave him an "I have no clue" face. I scooted back and huddled at the door. I felt a warm goo slide down my sides. It was blood, from being shoved on the broken windshield.

Maybe it smells blood, I thought.

It was possible. Technically anything was possible. Apparently, it could speak, which was something I hadn't considered at all. It was the only real explanation as to why it was closer to us than it was to the speaker. Maybe my scent caught its attention, took its focus off the distraction.

With this thought I looked up and studied the creature. It towered over the corn scanning its surroundings. It didnt see us, not even with Lenny's single headlight.

This didn't explain why Simon and Phil's bodies, which reeked, didn't take its attention off us. Maybe because it didnt have to look for them?

I decided to stop trying to understand the nature of this thing. It would only prove a pointless endeavor. Of course, smelling me was only a theory. It could be anything.

I had to come up with a way to get it off us.

I slapped at my pockets and felt nothing. I searched my head for anything I could do to make some kind of distraction. My mind came up with almost nothing.

Searching for a solution, I recalled all the events of the past couple days. Weed came to my mind, the night where everything began. I recalled the night where the three of us smoked weed, and Lenny used a BIC lighter to smoke. I'd hoped that I could start some kind of fire.

I scooted back to Lenny, who held his arm, the bad one. It was the arm Greg had grabbed him with, no doubt hurting him.

"Lenny," I said. "Do you have a lighter on you?"

Lenny's eyes lit up; he was instantly on the same page I was on. Lenny crawled to the two front seats and opened the glove box, and after some ruffling, he retrieved a lighter. Mateo was studying us. After a second, he came to the same conclusion.

"Tell me we have some fireworks on us somewhere?" Mateo asked.

Lenny shook his head. But he didn't look distraught. Lenny shoved his hand in one of his many cargo pants pockets and pulled out a handful of bills. My heart broke, knowing that he was about to light up money. But better the money than us.

Lenny sparked up the lighter and released a small flame that quickly died. Standing on the bed of the truck, we knew immediately how to fix that problem. We huddled around each other and Lenny gave the lighter a few more flicks.

A small flame appeared. Lenny began to bring the money close to the flame. The light of the flames showed the money Lenny held to be a couple of twenty-dollar bills.

"Wait!" Mateo whispered. He used his hand to lower Lenny's. Mateo proceeded to take off his flannel; he wore only a deep blue t-shirt underneath. "Just burn this," Mateo said, lifting up his flannel in a ball.

"Will y'all quiet the fuck down back there," Greg hissed.

I was beginning to feel a hatred towards that fucking coward.

We huddled around the lighter and in time, Mateo's shirt was set ablaze. Lenny wasted no time chucking the shirt away. With a whoosh, the fireball landed somewhere behind the wall of corn. Lenny grunted in pain as the heat burned his hand; thankfully the burn was mild and left no wound.

We moved away from the fire painfully slow. If the fire were to catch and it were to get the creature's attention, we'd take its attention soon after. Thankfully we cleared the fire, if you could even call it that. The jazz music continued to play. The songs became more and more distant.

A pair of red eyes continued to flash, tearing through the darkness.

Mateo approached Greg, and Greg pointed his gun at him.

I froze in fear. The possibility of Mateo getting shot ripped my guts apart. I couldn't bear the pain it would bring. Not just to me but to his mother.

"Hey whoa," Mateo stuttered. "Turn the headlights off."

Greg kept his weapon on Mateo but did what he said. Greg fumbled with the controls before he found the headlights and shut them off. In a second, we were swallowed by darkness. Even with the headlights illumination being significantly reduced, it was pure luck the creature didnt spot us.

My eyes went wide as they searched for any glimpse of light. The thought of finding light here, in the middle of these damn cornfields, seemed pointless. But it wasn't; somewhere in the distance, my instinctive action of searching for light found what it was looking for.

In the distant horizon, a warm, dim light was visible. The sun was rising, blanketing the endless Earth. Daytime was approaching, and it would bring an end to this infinite darkness-filled night.

It looked heavenly and beautiful. The night sky went from pitch black to a deep, dark, blue.

"Get down!" Mateo whispered loudly.

I instinctively threw myself to the floor. The truck suddenly stopped, then began to move forward. We were back on track to leaving.

"We good?" Mateo asked Greg.

"I think so." Greg answered. "I think it wandered off."

We were moving at twenty miles per hour again. We approached a close distance to the speaker again but cleared it just as soon as we arrived.

We were so close to making it out. I could barely hear the sound of cars driving along a highway.

Out of nowhere, I found myself bouncing off the front seats as the truck came to a sudden stop.

"NO ONE LEEEAVES!!!!" said a loud horrible voice.

The monster had found us! It stood behind us with its big hand wrapped around the bed of the truck. Its red eyes glowed all over us.

Before anyone could react in any way, the creature whipped the truck so that we were facing in the direction of the house. I barely had time to recover my composure when the creature began to drag the whole truck.

Greg pulled his gun in the direction of the monster.

The creature stood tall and breathed heavily. Its chest rising and falling. Every step it took covered a huge distance.

Six loud bangs rang in the air! Greg shot at the creature. With each shot, different points on the creature's body would shake insignificantly. There was nothing a 9mm could do against this thing.

The creature began to slowly walk the truck back to where we came. One large step after another.

Greg wasted no time putting the car in reverse and trying to speed us away.

The creature never loosened its grip, if anything it got tighter.

Lenny thought fast, he pulled the cash from his pocket and lit it on fire. He for sure burned his hand as he pressed his palm against the creature fingers where it held the car.

Unfortunately, it did nothing. Lenny eventually whipped his hand away in pain, grunting and hissing loudly.

There was nothing we could do.

I crawled to jump out of the car and make a mad dash! But Mateo grabbed my shoulder, stopping me.

"Let it!" He whispered loudly. "It hasn't killed us yet!"

His words gave me an idea. "Go back to the house!" I called to Greg. He looked at me like I was insane. "We need to give it what it wants!" I yelled.

Greg hesitated before he put the car in drive and ran the engine. The sudden jerk caused by the sudden movement of the truck gave the creature a slight tug. It caused Red Eyes to study us for a moment before letting us go.

CHAPTER 31

By the time we made it back to the house, the sun had turned the sky a beautiful orange and blue. Unfortunately, I wasn't able to appreciate it. My mind was on the creature.

"So it speaks now?" Mateo laughed sarcastically.

"Who cares that it speaks!" I said harshly. "We're right back where we started!" I jumped out of the truck and started to pace the area. "I don't get it!" I exclaimed. "I don't get it! What does it want? Why didn't it just kill us?" I could feel tears building behind my eyes. The regret of returning to this place never felt so strong.

They all gave me weird looks as they individually hopped out of the truck.

"The noise, the light," I began, "They worked perfectly. Why didnt it work this time? What led it to us? What needs to change?"

I was facing my companions, but I was clearly talking to myself. Thankfully, I was listening.

"Change!" I cried loudly. "It doesn't like change!"

"The hell do you mean?" Lenny asked, holding his arm.

I pointed at Mateo. "You said you'd seen it, right? When you were young?"

Mateo nodded, saying, "Maybe, yeah."

"Sofia explained that that didn't start happening until after my mom and I left. Maybe it was here the whole time and whenever something changed, it would investigate."

They all adopted thoughtful expressions.

"Then for years nothing happens, right?" I began again. "Then I showed up, causing that thing to investigate again. Or it wanted to see who the new guy was, which was why I saw it the first day I was here. Then the horses go running in the cornfields, probably something that doesn't happen often."

"Dude, summarize, please!" Mateo demanded.

"Just think about it," I said. "Every time, maybe with exceptions, there's a significant change of some kind in this place, that thing pops up. Change causes it to react."

"That's why it didn't want us to leave," Lenny said. "Maybe it got used to us being here or something."

"That doesn't explain why it didn't stop us from leaving the first time," Mateo argued. "I can see where you're coming from, but it doesn't make that much sense."

"No, I think he's on to something," Lenny said. "Maybe it didn't stop us because it was hurt. I did hit it with my truck, and your mom did shoot at it."

"It clearly wasn't hurt," Mateo argued.

"It screamed like it was," I countered.

Mateo thought about our words for a second before explaining, "If this is the case, why let me leave for school every other day? Why not pop up during any of the holiday breaks?"

He had a point. I didnt have a good answer for him.

"And," he continued, "why not show up whenever Lenny moved in? Doesn't that count as a huge change?"

I had to think about his words. It was very possible I was wrong about everything.

"I guess it got used to the routine?" I tried.

The answer I gave must've been satisfactory for him because Mateo thought for a second before he eventually just asked, "Ok, so now what? We're back here. No offense Miguel but how is this helping?"

"We just need to cause a distraction," I said.

"We tried that," Lenny sighed, "It didnt work."

"No, we need something big enough to get it away from us. Preferably not in the direction of our exit," I explained. "It has to be something big and crazy! More then just a loud noise!"

"I know!" Mateo said. "Every other car we have was destroyed, all except for two. We just park one far out somewhere, blast the radio, and rig it to explode."

"How do we rig a car to explode, dude?" I asked. "This ain't *Mission Impossible*."

"We just pour gasoline all over it and light it on fire," Mateo explained matter of factly.

It could work on paper. But that didn't mean the actual car would explode or cause a significant enough boom to harm Red Eyes.

"It works on grand theft auto," Lenny chimed in.

My jaw genuinely dropped at his words. "No, yeah, let's take a video game's advice on how to blow up cars," I said sarcastically. "You guys don't understand. We need to do something crazy. Something that would cause some sort of change to the status quo."

Mateo scoffed, "Red Eyes himself isn't enough?"

"No." I said. "We need to rattle the bored."

Before I could continue my explanation a movement in the distance caught my eye. I almost panicked in fear of it being the monster but was quickly put at ease when I realized it was someone I recognized. It was Grundy, and with him a few other caballos roaming around the now destroyed barn.

Unfortunately, I wasn't able to point them out to the others. The next thing I knew, my eyes were instinctively closed in pain. It was dirt, dirt was thrown into my eyes. I dropped to the ground and ferociously began to rub. I heard a loud noise, like something being dragged across the dirt. I also heard an engine rumbling, along with Lenny and Mateo coughing.

"That asshole!" Mateo shouted.

"MY TRUCK!!!" Lenny called.

I put together that Greg took the truck and took off. But where would he go? It wasn't like he could outrun the demon. I felt a large hand grab my armpit, helping me to my feet. I blinked away the pain and my vision slowly returned to me.

"Let's go!" Lenny said.

"Where?" I asked, still partially blind.

"He's going to my house!" Lenny answered in a rage-filled tone.

As we made chase for the stolen truck, I began to wonder why would Greg go to the O'Youngs house? It made more sense to me that he'd just try and make another run for it.

"We can't catch up!" I coughed.

"Yeah," Mateo said sprinting alongside us. "But we can't just stand here and do nothing!"

"The horses!" I called.

My words caused Mateo to stop running, and I took the opportunity to join him.

"I saw a couple horses," I said pointing in their direction. "There."

Grundy and the other horse were sort of running around in circles. But they were there. Mateo, without missing a beat, ran down the two mounts. It took him a few minutes, but he managed to get a handle on both, something I doubt I could've done.

Mateo rushed towards me and Lenny who stayed where we stopped. Mateo didn't even say anything, he let go of one, and jumped on the other.

I made my way to Grundy and mounted up. It was a completely different feeling now riding with a saddle. I felt more secure and in control, like a perfect piece of a puzzle. Unfortunately, Lenny was out a horse.

"Welp!" Mateo began holding his hand out to Lenny. "Looks like you're riding bitch!"

Lenny pulled his hand away from Mateo's. "What? I don't want to ride bitch!"

"Come ooon!" Mateo teased.

"No way!" Lenny argued. "Don't call it that!"

"Lenny, shut up!" I spat. "You're riding bitch and you're gonna like it!"

Lenny looked like he was ready to argue with me now. But I turned to chase Greg before I could hear it. I'd hoped that Lenny seeing me ride away would get him to man up and just hop on with Mateo. I looked back and was pleased to see that I was right.

Greg disappeared into the cornfields, but before I knew it, I could hear the engine of Lenny's truck. The horses were easily gonna catch up to the truck, especially one that could only go up to twenty miles an hour. Before I knew it, I could see the truck with Greg in it. And before I knew it, Mateo had caught up.

"What's the plan?" he called to me.

Why the hell would he ask me that? I had no plan. All I knew was that I was chasing Greg. So, I just pointed at him.

"He's going for my dad's car!" Lenny called from behind Mateo. "It's in better condition than mine!"

Mateo nodded and continued riding. We picked up the pace and were making pretty good distance. It was an amazing idea; horses could easily run faster than 20 miles. We'd be on him in no time.

I took the right side of the truck and Mateo took the left. Mateo and Lenny came face-to-face with Greg, and to get his attention, he kicked at the door. Greg looked horrified at the two boys, probably expecting the beast.

"What the hell are you doing?!" Mateo shouted.

"Piss off! You stupid kids!" Greg responded.

"Stop!" Lenny barked.

"I'm getting out of this place!" Greg screamed before slightly jerking the truck towards the boys.

Mateo jolted away, looking quite pissed. What could I do? There was nothing I could do to stop the truck. And Greg punched first, so we were now in a fight.

I was thinking about using one of the extra hooks in Grundy's sack to maybe throw at Greg, but too much could go wrong. And it wasn't like a panic snap could do much. I had no other useful tools to stop the truck.

"Dude!" Mateo called to Greg.

"Back the fuck off!" Greg yelled, pulling out his gun.

Mateo and I instinctively slowed our rides to escape the gun.

Greg fired off a warning shot, causing us all to duck our heads. We had no choice but to follow him. If we came any closer, we'd be shot. Mateo, however, didn't come to the same conclusion; he rode on ahead catching up to Greg.

"He's gonna die!" I said out loud to myself.

"Just stop!" Mateo shouted.

If Greg heard Mateo, he didn't care. Greg just fired another warning shot dangerously close to Mateo, close enough that he may have just missed an actual shot.

How much ammo did this guy have??? I was sure he emptied a bunch of clips into the beast earlier and even before that.

Mateo backed off, and joined me some yards behind the truck. He still rode some feet ahead of me so i was able to see Lenny lift up his right arm while using his left to push Mateo out of his line of sight. I heard a loud pop and a flare shot from Lenny's arm and fly directly towards the truck.

The glowing green flare struck Greg in the back of the head with a satisfying thud.

Greg took the arm not holding the pistol off the wheel and held his head where he had been struck. With his hands still off the wheel he turned his torso to face us and fired a few more rounds.

I yanked myself closer to Grundy trying to make myself as small of a target as possible. Bullets whistled by missing me possibly by inches. I jerked Grundy side to side hoping not to put him in the direction of the incoming fire.

Thankfully it appeared to only have been two shots fired. I shoved away the urge to stay down and matched Mateos speed.

"You g-good?" I asked shakily.

The two boys, wide eyed, nodded, visibly freaked out.

"We need to reach the others!" I said to Mateo. "Terry will deal with him, we can't!"

Mateo reluctantly agreed and we just kept our distance behind the truck. We had to be a couple minutes away from Lenny's house now.

I looked up to see Greg was no longer facing us. I could see he still held the pistol at the ready. Thankfully he made no further attempts to shoot at us.

The sun was starting to take primary hold of the sky. It made it easier to watch Greg closely. It also meant we could spot the creature without having to depend on its glowing eyes. With that thought, I scanned around. When I looked behind me, I saw nothing but a huge black hand.

200

I screamed and kicked Grundy to speed up. Mateo and Lenny heard my scream and looked at me to see what I was freaked out about. When they saw who was chasing the chasers, they too picked up the pace, with fear plastered all over their faces.

Thankfully, the horses were fast and immediately passed the truck, leaving Greg to be the first to be caught. I gritted my teeth and braced, sure that Greg was about to open fire. I hoped that the creature would reach him before he did. A small part of me dreaded the idea of losing another vehicle.

Before I could even start thinking about how we'd have to cram all of us in one car with Lenny's mom's surgery problems, I heard a loud bang. I hoped Greg was shooting at the creature, but seeing the ground coming to me all too fast brought me to another conclusion.

I hit the ground hard and so did Grundy. I knew I couldn't let myself get pinned under a large horse, so I took my feet out of the saddle. It didn't help much, I only managed to kick my left leg out, which was the side we were gonna land on. I smacked the ground way too hard for what was probably the hundredth time.

The two of us tumbled and rolled bouncing off the ground. I slid under Grundy as he himself slid across the ground. My body stopped him from moving. The whole left side of me was basically pinched. My skin was painfully squeezed under Grundy. The horse on top of me wept in pain, he attempted to stand relieving a lot of pressure off my body. However, his wounds must've been too great because he collapsed on me again shooting another more intense pain through my body.

I saw Red Eyes making its way towards me. I didn't have time to react or do anything at all. Red Eyes was gonna get me, and it was gonna kill me.

I saw a white and brown horse dart past me, with two screaming boys on it. The creature took its eyes off me and put them on Mateo and Lenny, who were trying to save me. Dread filled my soul as the creature tried to snatch at them, missing by inches.

I tried to push Grundy off me and failed.

That's when Greg and the truck whooshed passed me blowing dirt in my eyes. It must've startled Grundy too as he ever so slightly jerked away. It was enough for me to free my pinned arm and grab a corn stock.

I pulled with everything I had making absolutely no progress.

Looking at Grundy, I saw he had a hole in him. It was gushing what looked to be liters of blood.

I didn't know what to do, I held the dying animal struggling with my own injuries.

I reached down and put pressure on the hole, trying to stop the bleeding. Blood started to cover my hands, creating a thick layer over them.

Grundy was weeping in pain, and I could only stare at him. Grundy struggled less and less, as his movements slowed and so did his breathing.

Inevitably, Grundy passed.

I was sad to see him go; I'd grown fond of him. His death however did bring me some comfort. At the very least, I wouldn't be dying alone.

The monsters aggressive screech pulled my eyes off of Grundy. I spotted Mateo and Lenny heading for me. Lenny was leaning down the side of the horse and held out his hand.

They were approaching fast; I had little time to react. I sprung out my arm and Lenny grabbed and squeezed.

Screaming in pain I was violently pulled from beneath Grundy. I was hurt, but I was free!

However, I soon found myself rolling along the ground again. Lenny must've lost his grip, and unfortunately, I hadn't been able to grab onto him when he grabbed me.

"HEYYY!" I coughed as the boys whooshed passed me.

Mateo didn't need any more than my pathetic call for him to turn and scoop me up.

I still laid on the ground, and I could see the creature stomping its way to me. I was relieved to see its attention still on the boys.

They simply turned around and passed me along with the creature, leading it away from me. Mateo leaped through the corn on one side of the creature, then jumped on out in the open on the other side.

The creature turned its head to face us once again before marching towards us.

Mateo and Lenny stopped at me and dragged me onto their ride. I laid on the horse's ass, making no effort to sit upwards.

"He's on! Go!" Lenny demanded.

Mateo took off.

I kept my eyes on the creature, and it kept its eyes on us as it moved into the cornfields like it was sinking in water.

I didn't bother to think why this creature didn't chase us. I had to stop trying to understand it. At this point, who cared? It wasn't worth the headache.

My body was throbbing in pain, my ass hurt, my ribs, my back, my arms everything. Even my head hurt from all the motion I was involved in. Surprisingly, nothing hurt as bad as my feelings. Watching Grundy die was horrible; it twisted up my guts and my mind. I had gotten attached to him, he saved me, and we saved the others together.

I thought of Phil and Simon and how unfair their deaths were. They maybe had families, who'd they'd never see again, all because of this nightmare, all for a couple of little shitheads. All because Terry asked them to. They were probably damn loyal friends. Friends now lost.

CHAPTER 32

We rode behind Greg, not passing him, knowing he was more than ready to kill our horse to save himself. So we just kept a good distance away from him.

Soon we approached the O'Youngs' home. We cleared all the corn and Mateo circled the house, keeping distance away from Greg.

I managed to pull myself up, my body aching, to see our surroundings. I saw Terry, Sofía, and Carly, along with two other adults who I presumed to be the parents of Lenny and Carly. They were all talking in a circle; they seemed to be arguing about something.

They all turned to see Greg pull in half a truck. Greg already had his weapon drawn and pointing at the biggest threat to him, Terry. Terry was forced to be still and so were the rest. Unfortunately, they were caught off-guard. I knew immediately what had happened to catch them off-guard. It was us, our little scuffles we had with Red Eyes and Greg.

"Hang on!" Mateo called, speeding up his horse.

I didn't need any more than that, I was ready to get my hands on Greg, screw everything else. Greg quickly noticed us approaching fast, and he pointed his gun off the others and at us—something I assumed Mateo to have wanted to happen.

Terry took the opportunity and lunged at Greg, who unfortunately jumped out of the way, but by this time, we were inches away from him. Greg was now the one who was caught off guard. With every last ounce of strength I had left, I hurled myself off of Mateo's ride and collided with Greg. I was a heavy guy, so I immediately took Greg's **skinny** ass down.

I made sure to grab whatever I could on my way down to hopefully keep him down. We rolled and the ground hit every bruise and wound that had formed on my body. I had almost no time to recover before Greg threw me off him.

I found him standing over me, staring down the barrel of his gun. I was shocked to see how ready I was to die. There was something comforting about not having to deal with this nightmare anymore.

Terry's large, hulking body smashed into Greg's, who went airborne. Terry, at the same time, managed to take the gun from his hands.

"I told you what would hap—" Terry's words were cut off as he was grabbed from his leg and thrown one hundred feet into the air.

My jaw dropped when I saw his body get smaller and smaller in the air.

The creature was back. It WAS chasing us.

I didn't care to see where everyone else was, I got onto my feet and ran towards the house. I pathetically thought the house would save me from this creature. On my way to the house, I saw everyone else rushing through the doors.

I jumped, skipping all the stairs, and flying through the two front doors. My body hurt but not enough to keep me down. Mateo and Lenny caught me as I came through the doors. They were eventually slammed shut and to my pleasure, with Greg on the other side. He wasn't in here with us.

The O'Youngs' parents were both going off, saying things like, "What was that thing!" "Oh my god!" "What's happening!"

But all I could think of was Terry. He was thrown into the air like a fuckin' toy!

Finally, I broke, I began to cry at the hopelessness of everything. Tears streamed down my face like a slow, calm river.

Terry defended me like I was his son. He put his trust in all of us without any hesitation. How many people were going to die before the rest of us did? No one here had to die, no one here deserved any of this. I felt my brain instinctively try and rationalize everything that's been happening again, but I caught myself this time.

The only thing that made sense now, was that nothing made sense. Yes, I should've died instead of Terry. And yes, I should've stayed away from this place. Unfortunately, nothing that should be happening was happening. So I needed to move on.

I couldn't feel my legs. Mateo and Lenny were basically carrying me. Not wanting to be a burden to anyone, I forced what little strength I had left into my legs and stood. I felt like I was on clouds.

"W-where's Terry?" I heard a feminine voice ask.

Sofía was studying the room, eyeballing everyone. She was searching for Terry.

Please. Not me.

I started to pray that someone else saw what happened. I didn't want it to be me. I didn't want to be the one who told Sofía that Terry, someone extraordinarily important to her, was just killed.

My eyes darted around the room, searching for someone who was gonna speak up. Mateo began to do the same, waiting for someone to answer. Then Lenny, then everyone. They all just looked around, both looking for Terry and someone to answer Sofía's question.

At first, I cursed them all for their cowardness. Then I realized that when the creature emerged from the cornfields, everyone must've seen it and ran. Everyone except me and Terry.

"Where'd he go?" Sofía asked more aggressively. "Terry?"

I began to beg the universe to make anything else happen than what I knew was about to happen. "He—" I choked, nearly crying.

Everyone looked at me and it suddenly became harder than it already was.

"Whoa," Lenny's dad said.

"Oh my god," said another voice.

All their faces scrunched as if they were looking at something awful. I wasn't that ugly, was I?

"Oh my god," a familiar voice said. "Are you ok?"

It was Carly. She emerged from behind her parents. She wore black leggings now instead of her short shorts, along with a bright green hoodie and athletic shoes. She was still very beautiful, and I became shy and nervous in her presence.

A pause followed those words. "That was a dumb question, you're not ok."

"What's wrong?" I asked. Could she see in my face that I had witnessed something horrible? Was I in shock? Maybe they could see that I was in shock?

"What's wrong?" Carly repeated. "What do you mean what's wrong! You need a hospital!"

At her words I flung my hands around my body, feeling for any open wound. Maybe my legs were broken? I looked down and saw nothing wrong. I felt around both my legs and felt nothing. I flexed my muscles to see if pain would help guide me to whatever was wrong with me. Of course everything hurt, but nothing was out of the ordinary. I looked up at the others and they all held the same expression towards me they did before.

"What?" I challenged, getting frustrated.

Mateo took some steps towards me reaching a hand out for my shoulder and asked someone to bring a chair. Lenny brought one and Mateo made me sit down.

Mateo looked me up and down and said, "Miguel, you look horrible."

Lenny's father grabbed a mirror that was hung up on a wall and faced it to me.

I understood what they meant now. I was fucked up. I had a black eye, bruised all over and bleeding from my back. "Fuck..." I whispered.

Carly walked up to me and placed her hand on my thigh. "What happened?" she asked.

What the hell didn't happen? My mind flashed through everything I went through the past couple hours where something hurt. Needless to say, it was a lot. Mainly my back.

"A lot," I eventually answered.

I overheard the O'Youngs' parents talking.

"Where's the first aid kit?" the Mrs. asked.

"Upstairs," said the Mr. "In the guest bathroom."

She rushed upstairs, leaving Mr. O'Young to introduce himself to me. "Hey kiddo," he said. "You're going to be ok. I'll patch you up the best I can, alright?"

I nodded.

"This is Miguel," Carly said, removing her hand from my leg. She turned to me and gestured at her dad. "This is my dad, Adam."

"It's a pleasure," he said, shaking my hand. My hands were tiny in his. I can see where Lenny got his huge husky form from.

"What happened to you?" Adam asked, studying me. He looked genuinely concerned.

"Ummm…" I began. "You got all day?"

Adam smirked at my little joke. "You're pretty beat up, don't like how swollen the left half of your face is, but it doesn't look like there's any permanent damage. What I'm concerned about is your back."

Adam spun his finger in the air, gesturing me to turn around in my seat and show him my back. I did so obediently. I felt his hands feel around my back and slightly putting pressure on the more swollen parts. I winced and hissed in pain. I was embarrassed to have done so, especially so pathetically in front of Carly.

"Would you mind lifting your shirt?" he asked me.

My first instinct was to say no and come up with some BS as to why I couldn't. I realized this guy could help, however; at least he made it seem like he could.

"Are you a doctor?" I asked.

"Pediatrician," he answered softly.

I found myself pulling up my shirt to just expose my back. I felt both dry and wet blood as my shirt peeled off my skin. I heard Adam gasp quietly and judging by Carly's face, it was bad news.

Holding it, I could now tell the back of my shirt was soaked in blood.

"What the hell happened to you?" Adam asked. "No jokes."

I thought for a moment. "I hit the ground quite a bit, landing on my back, I mean. And I was thrown into broken glass."

I heard Adam thinking out loud at my words, humming.

"Ok," he said. "You have glass shards in your back along with some loose skin. I can pick out some of the bigger pieces and try to bandage you up, but you need a hospital."

A hospital sounded nice. At the very least, a mental asylum. The thought of having drugs pumped into my body to take all the pain away was a very welcome thought.

A small woman shuffled into the dining room, joining us. It was Carly's mom, Mrs. O'Young. When her eyes eventually landed on me and my wounds, her eyes went wide and she choked on her words, saying, "Oh my god."

"Is it that bad?" I asked.

"It looks bad," Adam said. "But from what I can see it's just one giant flesh wound. Or multiple flesh wounds in one place."

"Ok but is it bad? Should I be worried?" I asked nervously.

"While there appears to be no permanent damage, that doesn't mean you're ok. So, to answer your question, you'll be ok, but are not ok right now."

This guy answered my questions in long sentences. I appreciated it, but I'd appreciate it more if he got to the point faster.

I looked at Carly, who looked at me sympathetically. Now I knew where she got her constant talking from. She spotted my eyes on her, but I didn't look away. She knew I liked her, so it was pointless to try and hide the fact I was checking her out. Besides, I was already caught.

She smiled and introduced her mom. "This is my mom, Daisy."

I smiled at Daisy and said, "Hi Daisy, I'm Miguel."

"Oh, you're calling us by our first names?" she said sarcastically. I stuttered out an apology before she said, "I'm kidding, don't worry."

The more I interacted with these people, the more I traced the traits from parents to child. It was comforting to see a healthy family. Sure, it made me feel like shit for not having a dad, made me a bit jealous. But it was nice to be in a warm and loving environment for a change.

I felt Adam place a hand on my shoulder. He handed me some pills and ordered Carly to bring a glass of water.

"I'm gonna get started," Adam said. "I won't bullshit you, son, it will hurt. But I don't want you to get an infection."

I cursed in my head. Unfortunately, Carly showed back up with some water, so I had to act tough now. I accepted the water she handed me and downed the pills.

"Those will help," Adam said. Then he began.

CHAPTER 33

I found myself lying belly-down on a couch. If I wasn't done before, I was done now.

Despite my back holding most of the pain I felt, Adam took the liberty to treat every other wound on me. Thankfully the throbbing stopped. So I just laid there, half-asleep.

Everyone in the house was in the living room with me. I guess no one wanted to be alone. We were back at square one. Stuck in a house, hiding. Everyone tried and failed to make a plan. No one wanted to go outside; some even avoiding looking out the windows. Yet no one closed the blinds or shut the curtains.

I only got bits and pieces of what everyone was saying. Even though I was in pain, I was managing to drift in and out of sleep. This went on and on for a while, but I eventually did fall asleep.

The first thing I remembered was shaking. Someone was waking me up. I sat up and faced who was waking me up. It was Sofía.

In a groggy voice, I asked, "What's going on?"

She checked me up and down, studying my wounds. "Are you ok?" she asked.

"No," I answered honestly.

She frowned and looked like she was gonna say something, when the sound of breaking glass erupted from another room.

My tía stood, immediately ready for action.

The master bedroom door suddenly flung open and in burst fucking Greg. He must've jumped through a window, escaping the monster.

Why did it take so long for this fool to show up? I thought he was dead. Part of me even hoped for it, hoped Red Eyes had gotten to him.

"Holy shit!" Sofía cried. She barely had a chance to form some kind of reaction before Greg pulled his gun.

The others rushed into the room, responding to the loud noises but at the sight of the gun, we all froze.

"Now, now," Greg said. "Everyone calm the hell down."

"Don't make it too easy for us, dickhead!" Mateo yelled.

"Oh, piss off!" Greg screamed. "I want what we all want! I want out of here away from that!" Greg pointed a finger at the broken window behind him. Greg breathed heavily. He'd been running. "Whose car is that?" he asked.

Everyone stayed quiet.

Greg began to twitch and shake. This fucking guy was genuinely slipping. "WHO!!!" he yelled, slipping his finger on the trigger.

"Mine," Adam said, stepping up.

Greg held his hand out with the other hand holding the gun. "Keys," he demanded.

Adam felt around his pants and sighed. "They're not on me."

Greg's eyes went wide, and he raised his eyebrows. "Then go get them," Greg said through his teeth.

"We can do this without that gun," Carly said.

Greg turned his attention on her, which quickly drew all the color from her face.

"Please just don't point that at us," she stuttered.

Greg gritted his teeth. "You fuckers are making this so much harder than it should be. I should've been gone yesterday!"

"We all want to get the hell out of here!" Sofía said sternly.

"You could've fooled me."

"Please just put it down."

"NO!"

Greg was squeezing his pistol so hard it was shaking in his hand. "I should've never come here!" Greg said.

"You weren't even invited!" Sofía shot back.

Greg, hearing her words, looked pissed. He did not like what she just said.

"But your nosy ass couldn't stay away!" She continued.

I loved my tía, but she was basically asking to get shot. I'd seen movies where the hero would get in the villain's head by insulting them, which somehow lead to the hero gaining some sort of advantage over the situation. But there was no advantage to be had here.

"Alright, everyone, calm the hell down," Adam said. "I'll get you the keys, just don't shoot any one, mmkay?"

Greg darted his eyes around till he spotted Adam. When he finally did, he answered, "Hurry."

With that, Adam took some steps back into the hall and stepped away. Adam totally took his time with getting the keys, because we were at the mercy of Greg for way too long. When he finally showed up, Adam approached Greg confidently and handed his keys over as if it were no big deal.

Even Greg picked up on this. Greg looked confused as he took the keys out of Adam's hands. Greg had a huge problem with not being in control of his situation. He hated that Adam wasn't scared of him.

When his hands were empty, Adam said, "Now please put the gun down."

Greg hesitated, thinking about it for a couple moments, but he was determined. "Everyone get the hell out of my way," Greg said. When no one moved, Greg got angry again and screamed, "MOVE!"

Everyone suddenly scurried out of the way to the front doors. Sofía and Mateo were, however, the last to move. Standing their ground.

Greg marched his way to the door, keeping his gun on the group of us. He turned and opened the door, then slammed it, screaming, "FUUCK!!!"

"What?!" Carly asked shaking..

"It's fucking out there," Greg shouted.

With his words, the window closest to the front door burst open, throwing shards of glass everywhere. And just like that, he was back inside the house.

Coming from the window he had just jumped through, followed a black arm. It reached around to grab Greg, but he ducked and rolled out of the way. Everyone, even me, scattered out of the way. And we watched in a mix of horror and shock as this thing felt around the entrance hallway.

Seconds later, the window to the left of the front door shattered open as well. The creature's right arm was then slowly reaching in, feeling around.

Furniture crumbled and slid around the floor. Its large hand slid across the couch I had just been laying on. As if it knew what it was holding, it crushed it as if disappointed that it was empty.

A loud bang rang through my head as Sofía began to unload into the arms, using her shotgun. Greg followed suit; he raised his pistol and began shooting the arms. The creature's arms flinched and soon retreated away.

We heard a banshee-like scream, which sent shivers down my spine. Everything this creature did reminded me of how unnatural it was.

My ears rung from the gunfire, my hands covered them instinctively.

After the monster's cries faded out, we all braced for its return. Fortunately nothing came.

"Red Eyes doesn't quit," Carly said, breaking the tension.

I couldn't help but smile at her comment. I appreciated her crusade to make people laugh, wherever they were. I looked around the room to see how terrified Adam and Daisy were. They held each other tightly.

Sadly, I noticed that everyone else in the room looked a little less terrified. Mateo, Lenny, and Carly both looked more alert than anything. Sofía just looked determined. Seeing their calmer than expected reactions made me feel insecure. They were a lot tougher than me. I was still scared shitless.

I looked at the windows, the glass dripped down like water drops. My gaze drifted towards the now destroyed living room. Through all the destruction a wheelchair stood out to me, even though it was bent out of shape from the attack. The house was no longer a safe place.

"Ok," Daisy said. "We just cram ourselves into the car outside."

"But your hip!" Adam tried.

"Screw my hip! We need to leave." She motioned forward, but Adam held his wife tightly.

"It's still out there, honey, we can't," he said.

I got pissed at her words. I couldn't believe that now she was ready to share a seat. Now we were gonna do what she should've done a fucking day ago! Three people were dead because of her! Not to mention how close we all were to fucking dying.

Her words were soon met with protest from her family. All of them kept saying there was some way they could figure it out. I felt rage towards all the O'Youngs now. They couldn't just be smart and listen to her.

Lenny's voice cut through all of theirs. "Mom, we can't. Even if we're careful, yo—" Lenny was cut off.

Daisy reached out and grabbed the shoulders of her son. Lenny winced with pain. "It's better to be alive, and safe," she paused for a second. "Then to be here."

More protest erupted from the family. I hadn't realized just how bad her condition was. Bad enough that her family didn't want to do the smart thing and just cram ourselves into the car. I peeked outside. There I saw the car. It was a four-door vehicle. Even though it was pretty smashed up, it looked to be in much better condition than the truck. The windows were all shattered, and the roof caved in a bit, but it looked like it could still hold us. There was me, Mateo, Lenny, Carly, Sofía, and Mr. and Mrs. O'Young.

Looking through the other window, Red Eyes stuck his hand in, I spotted Lennys truck once again upside down. Red Eyes probably flipped it over during the scuffle outside earlier.

"Guys! Guys! Guys!" Daisy said, shaking her fist in the air. "We'll make it work! Sit on laps! Throw someone into the trunk! We can't stay here anymore!"

I could hear the fear in her voice. She was genuinely scared and wanted out of this place. We all did. But she was scared enough to set aside her physical pain.

"Fine, then we'll make trips!" Carly suggested.

"No, we're not leaving anyone here!" Daisy said. Even in her fear, she wasn't willing to abandon anyone.

I glanced at Greg and felt even more disgusted and angry towards him. He was more than willing to sacrifice others to save himself. With my glance, I became stiff and alert.

Greg had his gun raised at Sofía, Sofía had hers raised at Greg.

No one had even noticed this standoff happening. The argument between the family was absorbing the whole of everyone's attention.

Sofía must've been waiting for an opportunity to point her gun at him. Red Eyes sticking his arms in the house was a perfect one. To my surprise, Sofía lowered her weapon, unprovoked. She stared at him calmly and with assertiveness.

"There's nothing you could do," Sofía said. "That thing is out there. So let's just calm down."

"Fuck you!" Greg said.

"No, just stop! You know I'm right," Sofía said.

"Yeah, dude, listen to her," I said.

Greg pointed the gun at me, which led to me clenching my ass like I never had before.

"Hey, hey, hey, heeyyy!" Sofía called. "You don't have to threaten or kill anyone. We all want the same thing."

To my shock, Greg lowered his gun. He brought it to his head and inspected it. "I'm out of bullets anyway," he mumbled.

"Took you long enough," I said.

Greg shot a look at me. My little comment pissed him off. I didn't care, he was empty. The three of us just stood there in an awkward silence. It was broken by Mateo entering the room.

"It's gone!" he exclaimed. However, it sounded more like a question.

"It vanished?" Sofía asked.

Mateo nodded saying, "It went back into the cornfields."

"Let's go!" Greg called as he began to march towards the front door.

"Wait," Sofía began.

"Aww, no!" Greg shouted. "Stop stopping!"

"Just think about it! It could be hiding, waiting for someone to go out there," Sofía explained. Her words got through to Greg. He paused and looked behind his shoulder at Sofía. "I know you don't want to! But we have to figure something out. Before we can make a run for it."

Greg sighed and took his hand off the door handle. I couldn't believe he was so ok with standing so close to the door after what just happened.

"Fine," Greg huffed.

Mateo and I stood with Sofía. The only noise was from the arguing O'Youngs. I decided not to hear whatever they were saying. I needed to keep my eyes on Greg. Even if he was out of ammo, he was still dangerous. He was willing to attack others to ensure his safety. I couldn't take my eyes off him. Sure, we had Sofía there, but we didn't have Terry. We might've outnumbered him, and he was out of ammo, but I just couldn't take my eyes off him.

Sofía placed a hand on my shoulder. "Do me a favor," she asked. "Go get something to eat," she ordered me. She looked at her son. "You go break up that argument," she said, nodding at the O'Youngs.

I was a little hurt to see that she sent to me to simply grab something to eat, and Mateo to intervene in an argument.

"I'm ok," I said.

"Please," she said, "just go. You're gonna need your strength."

I didn't know what to say to that. Everyone needed strength. So I decided to find something to bring to everyone.

I wandered around the house until I found the kitchen. Then I wandered around the kitchen until I found the pantry. When I opened it, I searched for anything that could be distributed amongst the others. I found cereal, chips, and a couple of granola bars. I was gonna just go with that when I spotted peanut butter. After some searching I found a jar of jelly. Then bread.

Perfect, I thought.

I once again wandered around the kitchen, looking for spreading knives.

I suddenly jumped when I heard a voice talking to me.

"W-what??" I stuttered.

"Whoa, it's just me," Carly reassured me.

I sighed in relief, saying, "Oh hey."

Carly studied the counter that held the jars and bread. "Whatcha doing?" she asked.

It was already weird, making food in someone else's kitchen. Now I had to explain myself making sandwiches. I felt like I had been caught.

"I uhhhh…" I began. "I was gonna make everyone sandwiches."

"Oh," she said.

Why was I embarrassed? It wasn't like I was doing anything wrong or suspicious. Maybe her presence just caught me off-guard.

"We all ate already," she explained.

"You did?" I asked.

"Yeah. You were asleep."

Apparently, I took a longer nap then I thought. "Oh," I said.

"Don't worry, I saved you some," she said reaching into the fridge.

Funny enough, it was a peanut butter and jelly sandwich. I guess someone else, and I had the same idea.

She slid the plate over to me and poured me a glass of Kool-Aid. I thanked her but took my time eating. I was insecure about eating in front of her. What if she thought I was a nasty eater or something? But after the first bite I couldn't help but chow down the rest in a hurry. I then inhaled the Kool-Aid.

Apparently, I was much hungrier than I thought.

"Thank you," I said.

She smiled at me before taking a seat next to me. "I know people keep asking you but are you ok?" she asked.

"I'm ok," I answered.

She didn't look convinced, but she didn't press the matter any further. I felt pretty sweet knowing she cared so much.

She looked bothered, like she wanted to say something but didn't know how.

"Are YOU ok?" I asked. She gave me a puzzled look. "Looks like you got something on your mind."

She looked down at her hands and leaned on the counter. "I feel like I owe you an apology," she said.

"Why?"

"Because things are awkward between my family right now."

Was she really about to apologize for her family arguing?

"There's no way you're gonna apologize for that," I said. "You're just looking out for your mom."

I felt a little guilty saying that just after I had the thoughts I just had about their whole family. I sort of hated them for not just cramming themselves into their car, which they arrived in, and leave.

They should've never given Red Eyes the chance to destroy their vehicle, 'cause now we're down to one.

Despite my thoughts, what I said was sincere and the truth. If it were my mom, I probably would've wanted her to ride as safely in a car as possible.

"Seriously. You guys are just looking out for each other. Never apologize for that," I said.

She smiled and giggled a bit. "Yeah, that's not what I meant," she explained. "I'm sorry for the awkwardness between you and my family."

"Why me?" I asked surprised.

"Well, because you hurt me," she explained.

"What???"

"Just hear me out before you jump to conclusions!" she said, waving her hands at me. "When we all decided to come back to get my parents, I was a little disappointed that you didn't come. You didn't even fight with your mom to come, you just took a couple steps back." She paused and looked thoughtful for a moment. "I thought we were friends, and I thought you cared. Cared enough to come help us. I mean, I know that we shouldn't be putting anyone in harm's way, but Mateo came."

I felt like an ass, being called out on my cowardness. "Well," I began, "I've only known you guys for a couple days."

I immediately wanted to take back my words. Not because they weren't true, but because the excuse I gave was a piss-poor one.

"I know," she said softly. "I don't know why I was asking so much of you." She got red and held her forehead. "We had a good time the other night and I thought it was enough."

"It was!" I exclaimed. "I know I've only known you for a couple days but that was more than enough time!"

She held her hand up and shook her head, "You don't have to explain, I get it. In all seriousness, I shouldn't've gotten so butt-hurt about it. It's just," she hesitated, "I like you. At first, I just thought you were cute and nothing special. But I'd be so full of crap if I said I didn't fall head over heels for you."

My heart skipped a beat. I damn near grinned at her words.

"I told my parents about you," Carly admitted. "Told them that you were a coward, and scaredy pants."

Now I was the one who was disappointed, and butt-hurt. The only thing I could say to her was, "Wow."

"I know! I know! It was fucked up of me to expect so much of you. Then talk shit about you to my parents! Then suddenly, you show up and all my parents know of you was all the bullshit I told them!"

I didn't really have much to say. Actually, I thought it was kind of funny. Everything she must've said, and then I come in riding bitch times two and fling myself at Greg.

After a long silence she sighed and said, "I'm just, I'm so sorry."

Part of me was actually upset. She went on and talked about me in negative ways to her family. But another part of me understood: after she showed me her body, and was so intimate with me that night, she got the impression that she could trust me, that we were becoming something more than what we were. She wasn't wrong; I cared deeply about her, I'd never crushed on a girl so hard.

That made what I did so much worse, even though I felt so strongly for her, and not just her but for her brother, who at this point I'd like to think was becoming a good friend of mine. And yet I still bitched out.

"It's ok," I said. "I can't believe I ditched a girl so beautiful and worth every second of my time. I will never forgive myself for that. Not to mention ditching some of my only family, and new friends."

She had the slightest smile. She placed her hand on mine and leaned in close.

"I'm really, really, glad you're here." She whispered.

Genuinely perplexed at her words, I asked, "Why?"

She locked eyes with me and squeezed my hand a little tighter.

"After everything," She explained, "Everything that happened. All you've been though, you chose to come back. And now that you're back, I know now I'm much safer."

CHAPTER 34

"What's next?" Carly asked.

Sofía answered by pointing through the window at the last car.

"All we can do is make a break for the car," Mateo said.

"What?" I said. "There's no way that's all we've got?"

Sofía answered, "We've exhausted every idea and resource we had. This is our only real play, our last chance."

"So that's it?" Lenny asked. "We're just gonna make a run for it?"

"Yes," Greg answered. "And if no one is in the car by the time I turn it on—"

Sofía cut him off, turning to him. "No one will be left behind."

Greg glared at her. But before he could say anything, I spoke up. "We need to at least find some way to draw Red Eyes away," I said.

"Your auntie already spoke to us about that," Adam explained. "Unfortunately, we don't have the same gear as you guys. We only have hunting supplies."

I turned to face Lenny. "You have speakers for your computer, right? Let's set it up at the back door and then we could make a break for the car."

"That would be a good idea," Lenny started, "but those speakers aren't louder than a car engine."

"We gotta do something!" I cried. "Making a break for the car, trying to cram us all in, is suicide!"

"Hijo," Sofía said, "there's nothing more we can do."

"No! Don't you dare give up! You gotta think of something! We have to think of something!"

"This is it! This is the plan! This is our best shot!"

I stared at her for a moment before saying, "Fuck that! We won't make it."

Sofía rolled her eyes. She held her head with one hand and another on her hip.

"There's nothing else we can do." She said again.

"Yes there is!" I begged. "We just need to do something much more drastic, noise isn't enough. Like our plan before!"

"Clearly that plan fell apart," she argued, "hence why you're still here."

"I'm with the kid," Adam spoke up. "A Hail Mary isn't a good play."

"It's the only one we have." Sofía argued. "You told me yourself, you have nothing that could draw that thing away from us."

"What about the guns!" I explained desperately. "Remember earlier, its attention broke every time someone shot it. Someone could shoot it from afar and lead it away."

"We don't wanna risk someone getting hurt, Miguel," Sofía said.

I thought hard, trying to come up with some kind of plan.

"I know nobody likes it," Sofía announced to us all. "But we have no choice."

"Mom," Mateo said, "what about the TVs?"

Sofía looked at her son, confused, "What about them?"

Mateo turned to Adam. "How many TVs are in this house?"

Adam took a second before answering. "Living room, upstairs living room, guest room, and Carly's room, and master bedroom."

"So, five?"

Adam nodded.

"Ok, we turn each one on and turn their volume up full blast. It'll be loud enough."

"Yeah, loud enough to bring that thing in here," Sofía argued. "The houses are not safe places anymore. That thing just reached in here, and eventually it will stop being stopped by this!" She held up her weapon.

"Mom, all we need is enough to get that thing in here and not out there. We can at least put some distance between us and Red Eyes."

"We can light this place ablaze while we're at it," Lenny chimed in.

We all looked at Sofía for approval. She looked like she wanted to argue but she ended up softly nodding.

"We have gasoline in the shack outside," Carly said. "It's safe, only a couple steps away."

"Someone should still go with you," I said.

"We will," Mr. and Mrs. O'Young said at the same time.

Sofía shook her head and threw her hands up. "No. No way!" she said. "We're not doing this."

We all stood silent, looking at her.

"We're not poking the bear again," she said. "Miguel and I were safe when we set up the distraction. And even then, Red Eyes could've popped out at us at any point."

"Mom," Mateo said, stepping up, "we don't have a choice."

"We do," she said. "We wait it out. Eventually someone will come looking for us."

"And what if that person is my mom?" I asked, challenging her. "I have no doubt that eventually my mom will call the police and send them here, along with bringing herself here."

Sofía looked conflicted. "But at least she won't come alone, she'll be showing up with multiple police officers."

"So did Terry," Mateo said. "And it's not like he brought a bunch of knuckleheads, he brought very capable men. And we're down to one."

"And say a whole lot of police men show up. It will be some time before they do. We may not make it that far. And I won't risk my mom, knowing she'll be searching for us alongside them."

"Guys, I get it," Sofía said. "But we can't risk anyone else getting hurt or killed. I guarantee someone will get hurt or killed if we do this, if not all of us."

"We cannot just sit here either," I said. "Think about it! If we cram us all in a car, we could all be killed if the creature catches up to us."

"It's a lose-lose," Carly said. "But the odds would be more in our favor."

I caught myself checking her out as she spoke, using the fact that she was talking as an excuse for looking in her direction. I looked away and nodded my head.

"You guys should listen to her," Greg said.

"There's no way you guys think it's a good idea to bring that thing in here."

We all turned towards Greg.

"Let's just wait for Red Eyes to disappear, then make a B-line for the car," he said.

"Even if Red Eyes is out of sight, he's never far," I said.

"Yeah," Mateo agreed, "in fact, it seems like he's always just out of eyesight."

Greg threw his hands in the air and argued, "Well does it fucking matter?! We ain't gonna kill it."

His words shook me. Even though it sucked, he was right. We simply didn't have the means to kill this creature. We didn't even know if it could die at all. But it did have one weakness, and that's what we were riding on.

"Well, no shit," I said. "We're not trying to kill it. We're trying to distract it. It almost worked before."

Greg rolled his eyes, condensing, "No, no, no, no, you guys aren't paying attention. The thing was barely able to catch up to the horses, the car can go way faster than the horse. We'll be ok."

"I don't think so," Lenny said. "The first night we encountered Red Eyes, it kept up with my truck."

"THEN WE FUCKING GO FASTER!!!!" Greg yelled.

His yell made us all jump. It actually irritated me. This fucking man-child was throwing a tantrum 'cause he's not getting his way. I let the anger I felt cool off by staying silent and taking deep breaths.

"Dude, calm down!" Mateo barked. "We're telling you it's not a good idea, we're trying to figure out a good idea."

"Fuck you!" Greg shouted. "No idea is a good idea."

"Stop," Sofía said firmly. She turned to Greg. "They're right. There's no better option. And if there is, we can't think of it."

Greg visibly grinded his teeth. "You guys want to risk your lives? Fine! Do it!" Greg spat. "I'm out of here."

He turned to walk out the door.

Sofía lunged forward and grabbed his arm saying, "No!"

Greg whipped his arm away and with the other, he struck Sofía in the jaw. Her head violently flung back, and she fell. Before she hit the ground Mateo, Lenny, and I were rushing him. I knew he was gonna go for his gun so I focused on his right arm, where he holstered his pistol. My stomach dropped as I saw his hand wrapping around his pistol, but I was able to shove my hands on his before he unholstered it. He did say it was empty earlier, but I wasn't going to risk it.

At the same time, Lenny kicked Greg in the gut while Mateo attempted to break his mom's fall. Lenny's kick sent Greg stumbling back. I almost lost my grip when he did so, but I held on tight. I managed to wiggle his arms away from his firearm. I gripped his wrist and twisted to the floor in an attempt to throw him to the ground. He corrected himself and used his momentum I provided to whip me around and throw me on the ground.

Before he did, I was able to grab the pistol on his belt and bring him down with me. When I landed, I landed on my back and it hurt like hell. The pain caused me to delay my recovery, and Greg was able to crawl on top of me.

He pulled back his fist and brought it down right on my nose. The force of the strike caused my head to bounce off the floor. I used my arms to shield my face in anticipation of more punches. But thankfully Lenny and Mateo yanked him off me.

I ignored the daze and ringing in my head, along with the throbbing pain coming from my nose. I got up as fast as I could; I was pissed off now. I saw Mateo and Lenny holding him down as they beat him with their free fist. Seeing Greg getting beaten was satisfying, but it didn't last long. He managed to wrestle Lenny off him, but it left an opening. A big opening; I would've smiled if I wasn't scrunching my face in pain.

I jumped forward and stomped on his chest, a great deal of pride swelled in me as I stomped out his breath. I could see it in his eyes. I prepared to stomp again but he kicked at my legs, causing me to fall. His kicks didn't hurt, it was more of him tripping me.

When I got to my feet, I saw that so did Greg. He tossed Lenny away. But by the time he did, Mateo kicked the back of his knees and Greg buckled to the floor.

Greg scrambled his hands around his pistol but he felt nothing. I had taken it while he was on top of me. The look on his face was priceless when he realized it wasn't there. I gripped it tight.

Mateo backed away from Greg but kept his arms up and ready, and was pulling back for a punch. But before he could, Sofía stepped in, and kneed Greg in the jaw as he was trying to get up. He fumbled to the floor again. He was about to get up, but Sofía cocked her shotgun. The sound stopped Greg. He once again felt for his firearm, but nothing came of it.

I held it up and shook it. The rattling of the gun rang through the air. I saw out of the corner of my eye, Carly grinning.

"Out of ammo huh?" I taunted.

"Mata a este cabrón!" Mateo called.

With his words, my stomach dropped. Was I about to see another bloody death? The anger and rage I felt were immediately washed away from me as the thought crossed my mind.

I looked at Sofía for a reaction. She was baring her teeth and her eyes looked wild. I got scared but calmed when I saw her face relax.

She turned to her son while keeping her barrel on Greg and said, "What did you just say?"

Mateo's face turned guilty and he didn't answer. They stared at each other for a while, bringing an awkward silence to the room.

"Alright," Carly said, "moving on!"

"What do we do with him?" I asked.

Sofía took her eyes off of Mateo and ordered me to find zip ties. She spotted the gun in my hand and held out hers, and said, "Give me that."

I did as she asked and walked into the kitchen, where I hoped to find something to restrain Greg. I started opening drawers and cabinets, only finding utensils, silverware, and cups of various kinds.

I could hear my tía ordering Greg, "Stand up! Turn around!"

I jumped when Carly popped out of nowhere.

"Hey," she said. "Are you ok?"

"Zip ties?" I answered sick of being asked that question.

"Uhhhh, we don't have any," she said. "None that would hold him."

"Tape?" I asked.

She nodded nervously. She turned and walked away and I followed her. She led me into their laundry room and opened a toolbox she pulled out of a cabinet. She pulled out a large roll of bright yellow duct tape. I reached for it, and she pulled it away. I looked at her and she looked concerned. Before I could say anything, she spoke.

"Are you ok?" she asked.

"Yeah," I said, nodding.

"Seriously," she said, "are you ok?"

"Yes!" I answered, much more firmly.

She recoiled at my answer and smiled smugly. "No, the fuck you are not!" she said. "Now calm down, let the adrenaline go away."

She leaned forward and wrapped her arms around me.

I didn't know what her logic was. Her hugging me wasn't something that would calm me down. It, in fact, actually made my heart beat faster. But I wasn't about to tell her to back off. I did pull away after a second.

"We shouldn't leave them waiting," I said. She nodded and we walked back to the living room.

I wasn't feeling any sort of adrenaline; I was just pissed and in pain. Maybe I was acting weird because of that.

When Greg spotted me, duct tape in hand, he said, "Fuck!"

"Shut the hell up!" Sofía growled.

"Ruuuun! We need to RUUUUUN!" Greg shouted.

"Shut. Up," she said.

Greg didn't understand why we couldn't just drive away. He didn't understand that Red Eyes would reach the car before we did. It wasn't even about that at first. It was about getting everyone out safely. He just wanted to run.

"Hands," I ordered as I walked up to him.

He hesitated, but one look from Sofía and he complied. I layered his hands together until a thick ring of adhesive and cloth circled his hands. I stepped back and looked at Sofía.

"On the ground," she said.

Greg looked like he was about to argue but once again, one look from Sofía and he was on the floor. It took me a second, but I eventually understood. I taped his legs together, rendering him immobile. I damn near smiled to see him lying on the floor hogtied. It was where he belonged.

"You two," Sofía barked at Lenny and Mateo. "Get him outta here."

"Where?" Mateo asked.

"Bathroom," she answered.

The two boys dragged Greg away. Sofía flopped down on the sofa behind her and let out a huge sigh. I did the same.

When I spotted Mr. and Mrs. O'Young, I felt a small rage for Lenny's father. Why the hell didn't he jump in and help? He just let a couple of kids fight a grown-ass man.

He saw me and must've read my mind because his face adopted something as if he was both sorry and mad. But not at me. He looked mad at himself. My first thought at seeing his face was, *You should be sorry*. He stepped away and tended to his wife, who was freaking out a bit.

When Mateo and Lenny showed back up, they also took their seats on the sofa.

A moment of silence passed before Carly said, "What now?"

CHAPTER 35

The plan was to be continued as intended. We set the house to blare loud noise and pray that it was enough.

There was one problem, though. And no one was willing to say anything about it. It was what to do about Greg.

It was clear that some of us wanted to save him. And some of us wanted to leave him here. What was weird about this particular issue was both options were justifiable. Or at least the idea of leaving him tied up in the bathroom was justifiable. In truth, doing so was still considered killing him. Even though his actions led to us almost being killed, was it our place to kill a man? We all sorta just dodged the topic all together.

Until, of course, Carly had to say something about it.

"So we gonna talk about the elephant locked in the bathroom?" she blurted.

We all were regrouping in the living room, collecting ourselves when she said what she said. When no one answered her, she followed up with a big fat, "Hellooooooooo!" Her mother looked at her with a disappointed expression. To which Carly responded, "What? We gotta do something about him."

"For now, we do nothing, ok?" Lenny said.

"We're just about ready," I said. "We decide what to do now, or never."

Mateo looked at his mom. He knew better than to put his own two cents into this conversation after what he just said. In his defense, it was the heat of the moment.

Adam and Daisy looked at their daughter with a mix of emotions. What parent wants to hear their child talk about this sorta thing? Eventually, Adam spoke up.

"We shouldn't kill this man," he said.

His choice didn't surprise me. He was a doctor, after all. His wife, on the other hand, clearly had her thoughts and opinions based on the look on her face when Adam gave his answer. But she kept quiet. It was clear that despite their different opinions on what to do about Greg, she trusted her husband.

"Well," Daisy said, "that's our vote. What's y'alls?" She looked around the room and stopped at her kids. She was waiting for an answer from them.

They looked confused and nervous. It wasn't something that suited either of them.

"Before you guys answer," Adam said, "you guys should tell us if you even want to answer."

"Your dad's right," Sofía said. "But you guys are a part of this just as much as any of us here. If you want to say something, speak up."

"He tried to kill us." Lenny said, gesturing to himself and me and Mateo. "Not to mention all the times he almost got us all killed." Lenny took some time after speaking before saying, "He's dangerous, we shouldn't bring him with us."

His dad nodded in understanding.

"We can't," Carly said. "He's a piece of shit, but we can't just leave him to die."

Lenny looked at her and his face clearly said he wanted to disagree with her.

"This whole thing is a nightmare," she said. "All of this. I won't wish this nightmare upon anyone."

Her reasons were solid. And I was surprised she would feel the way she did. I thought she'd damn him without a second thought.

"So that's three votes for taking him, and one vote for not," Sofía announced. She turned to her son, who visibly turned red. She sent him a reassuring smile and nod.

"Like Lenny said," Mateo began, "he's dangerous. He almost got us killed too many times. I say we leave him."

It was now three votes to take him, and two votes to not.

Sofía looked at me.

I wish I could say I had a long discussion in my head about what to do and what was morally right. But I knew deep down what I felt was the right thing to do. Unfortunately, I was more interested in keeping everyone safe.

When Sofía's eyes landed on me, I felt my stomach drop. I took a deep breath before speaking. "Greg's been nothing but trouble. We're already in enough trouble with what's waiting for us outside. I can't think of a logical reason to take him with us. But I don't believe we should leave him to die." I paused for a second before saying, "We're not the monsters here."

If my words meant anything, it wasn't much. Yes, we were having a discussion about it, but we all knew what was gonna happen. At least I could say, I spoke up about what I thought was right.

Sofía cleared her throat before giving her vote. "That fucker tried to kill my kids," Sofía stated firmly. "I'm not going to help him." Sofía scanned the room, waiting for an argument in response for her words. When she heard nothing, she spoke again, "We're leaving him."

I tried to take comfort in the thought that I'd voted against leaving a man to die. I told myself the decision wasn't mine to control, but maybe it was. I told myself maybe I could sneak a kitchen knife into the bathroom, slipping it under the door.

I knew better, though. I knew that if I were to do something like that, I'd probably end up getting all of us killed.

I regained my focus on the moment when everyone suddenly scrambled. Lenny and Carly made their way around the house, disappearing into rooms and exiting when noise was emitted.

Sofía approached me and held my shoulders. She scanned me but I shook her off and said, "I'm ok."

Sofía nodded and turned to Daisy, who was leaning on Adam for support. But before she could approach Daisy with the concerns of her disability, Daisy answered, "You're a mother, too, don't question the sacrifice I'd make for my children."

Sofía didn't even respond, she just pointed them to the front door and said, "Get ready."

Here we go.

"Matches?" I asked Adam.

"There's a lighter in the laundry room," he answered.

I almost didn't hear him; the noise coming from all the TVs and radios in the house were starting to pile up.

I rushed to the laundry room, thankfully it was somewhere I knew I could find. When I reached the laundry room, I tore the place apart. I looked in every cabinet, drawer, and compartment I could find. Eventually I found a lighter but not until after dumping everything out everywhere and searching the pile I made.

The lighter was clearly older and on its last legs. My stomach dropped at the thought of it not being able to produce a flame. When I flicked the lighter, a big bright flame shut me the fuck up. I couldn't contain my smile at the relief I felt.

"What about the lighter we used for the weed? What about the one Lenny had earlier?" I asked myself out loud. Before I answered, *Who cares*, in my head.

I made my way back to the living room to see everyone huddled at the front door, ready to run. Even though it was a Hail Mary, if it worked, we could all get out of there alive. All of us but Greg. Some guilt flowed through me for a second, but it was crushed by the images of his violence and cowardness to us.

I couldn't hear anything at this point; the media playing from everything in the house made that impossible. But I didn't need to hear anything. I just needed to see from where I was going to the door then to the car.

I looked for anything that would catch fire, and my attention landed on dark blue curtains hugging the window in the living room. I scrunched over them and peered out the window. The window faced the front of the house. I had a clear view of the car and no sign of Red Eyes.

I grabbed a handful of curtains and flicked the lighter on. The big, beautiful flame drew close to the blue cloth. I looked at the O'Youngs, and they all watched me with what seemed to be every emotion ever on their faces.

I was about to burn down their house. I was also about to save their lives.

I winced at the sudden heat my right hand felt. I took a step back and watched a fire slowly grow, then it quickly grew to engulf almost the whole window.

I wasn't sure what happened next. Two senses that I relied on the most were partly impaired. I couldn't hear a thing, and the bright flames made it hard to see. I just found myself on my back, wondering how I got there.

My answer came in the form of a huge black hand slamming down on my body. Not hard, but firm. It wasn't trying to kill me; it was trying to grab me. I felt its fingers slither their way under me and wrap around me.

I struggled as best I could, but my strength simply could not match Red Eyes. I thought I'd find myself being pulled through the flames to meet this creature, but the opposite happened. Instead, Red Eyes began to slowly crawl into the house, ducking through the window, which was now bright with yellow flames.

The fire was spreading to the roof, and the grip of Red Eyes was beginning to become painful. A strange calm washed over me as Red Eyes brought me closer to his face. Something about knowing I was about to die was a strangely comforting thought. It was all about to be over, it was all gonna end soon. All the madness, all the physical pain, all the horror was over.

Red Eyes' head jerked violently to the left as my tía shot him point blank in the face. I was dropped and I rolled to the right towards my people. But before I could stand, I was swatted at by a large shiny black arm.

I managed to shove my feet below me and launch myself away, evading its attacks. Lenny grabbed my arms and pulled me away. When I was clear, my tía unloaded shot after shot after shot on the creature. I was shocked that I could hear the gunshots, each one louder than the next.

The creature flinched, howling in pain. It wasn't enough; the creature was becoming numb to the gunfire because he extended his arm at my tía and gritted his teeth when she fired at him instead of pulling away.

Mateo rushed to his mom and shoved her away before the creature could grab her. They both tumbled on the ground for a bit before standing.

No one had to say anything, we all shoved our way through the front doors. But we didn't make it halfway to the car before Red Eyes popped out of the house and began stomping towards us.

"SCATTER!!!" I shouted, and thankfully, everyone did so.

We all scrambled away.

I stopped myself when I saw that Red Eyes was going for Sofía. She had shot at him last, and it didn't forget.

So I had to make it forget somehow.

Our plan had failed; the loud house and flames did nothing to take Red Eyes' attention.

"Stop shooting!" I called at Sofía. Either she heard me or was out of ammo, 'cause she turned and bolted, grabbing her son and going for the car. I thought she was gonna leave us for a moment when she was making her way to the car with her son. But they both took cover behind it.

Once the creature caught up, it just stood there, hatefully watching them. It began to walk towards the two when it turned its head at me. My stomach dropped when it smiled at me. I didn't even do anything to get its attention, I guess it just had a grudge.

It turned to me and started in my direction. I was unbelievably screwed; I couldn't take shelter in the house or go for the car. I also didn't like my chances going for the cornfields.

I decided to turn and run and hope I got lucky somehow.

Thankfully, that's exactly what happened. As I ran to the house, I saw Lenny waving me over. He was sticking halfway out of the ground. It took me a second to see that he was in the doorway of the house's basement. It was the classic two-door entrance.

The creature gave chase and I could hear the Earth shaking with every footstep it took towards me.

I was smart enough not to look back. When I got to the door, Lenny grabbed my arm and yanked me in. We both went tumbling downstairs, falling over each other. Thankfully the fucking concrete floor broke our fall.

I had no time to feel any pain or relief as I felt a force grab my leg as I was being dragged back up the stairs. I looked up to see Red Eyes had reached his arm down through the doors and grab my left leg.

Lenny jumped on me and began pulling against Red Eyes. If he made a difference, it wasn't much 'cause he found himself also being pulled away. Adam and Daisy gave their son a huge bear hug and started fighting against the monster's pull.

To my surprise, it actually did something. I felt Red Eyes' grip loosen and my ascent slowed. When Carly joined in saving me, there was an even bigger resistance. I felt hope that I could be saved. I began to struggle as best I could; maybe I could wiggle my way out of his grip.

I used my free arm to pound at Red Eyes' fist. It did absolutely nothing. So I opted to use my arm and burrow it under its fingers. I thought if I could shiv my arm down there and wobble it, I could potentially loosen its grip.

I managed to get my forearm about halfway in when I saw that I was already exiting the basement doors. I screamed in fear.

"DONT LET GO OF HIM!!!" Carly cried, as I was pulled fully outside. When I was pulled out of the basement, the monster was no longer limited by a small hallway. It quickly shook off Lenny and his mother. Adam and Carly still held onto me tightly. The creature picked the three of us up and held us out.

I forced myself to scream, "Let go! Run!"

Adam dropped to the ground first, leaving his daughter up there with me. Part of me knew that he didn't let go of me, he just lost his grip. I repeated myself; I couldn't bear to let Carly die for me.

"LET ME GO!" I yelled.

Carly didn't say anything, her struggle to hold onto me continued. Red Eyes grabbed her with his other hand and ripped her off me.

It held both of us in the air. It smiled and kicked at the others below us, sending them flying. It opened its mouth wide and brought me close. Suddenly the sound of an engine came roaring to us.

The beast toppled over as it had once before.

I was released and hit the ground hard. I crawled over to where Carly had been dropped and picked her up back on her feet. She grunted in pain but hurried to her family.

The creature was on the ground once more, but before it could crush the car, the car backed off of it. The creature stood up and jumped for the car, but it drove out of the way.

This was it, this was our last chance, and we blew it. Now our only hope was to hide, wait, and hope that people would come looking for us.

"Why did I come back?" I asked myself aloud.

Thoughts of driving home with my mom filled my head. Then thoughts of touring around while I was on my dirt bike took over.

What the hell was I doing here? Why didn't I just send an anonymous call to the police, say some shit like there was a drug lord on the property or some human trafficker? I'd seen streamers, cops storm a guys' house live on camera. Why didn't I just do that? Why was I back here fighting for my fucking life?

I remembered Terry's response to that suggestion. It was still better than sending myself and having all of us here face this thing.

I stood up and began to make my way for the basement door. I felt a soft heat on the right side of my body. It was the house; the flames were spreading, and the house was beginning to be more fire than house, I wondered if the heat would actually burn the creature if it was in the house while it was on fire. I didn't think it would.

I got to the basement and practically threw myself down the stairs. Thankfully, all of the O'Youngs were in there too. They'd all made it in here.

"The house is gonna fall on us," I said.

"It won't," Adam said without looking at me. He was tending to his daughter. She was in pain, holding her chest. Unfortunately, his words didn't convince me. He sounded more hopeful and in denial than anything else. Carly squeezed her father's arms as they tended to wounds. Her fall must've hurt her.

Yet again, another rogue thought came flooding into my head. *That's why I'm here.*

I was here because I cared about these people. I had to find some way to help. That was why I came back, after all.

I peeked out of the doors leading out of the basement. I saw no monster. That didn't mean he wasn't out there. I could hear the engine of the car driving around and the thrashing of a giant.

I made my way up the stairs. I didn't have a plan; I'd have to let one come to me in pieces.

When I popped out the doors, my eyes instinctively landed on Red Eyes who was doing his best to catch Sofía, who was practically doing doughnuts around the creature. I wasn't sure where Mateo was. I hoped he was safe. But boy, was I glad Sofía was behind the wheel.

My eyes spotted the shed hiding behind the house and before I could talk myself back into the basement, I pushed my bruised body towards it. Maybe there was something in there that could help. I hoped that there was at least something that could throw off the creature, if just for a moment.

When I reached the shed, I let out a loud "FUCK," when the shed doors remained shut with a jiggle. It was locked.

I backed up and apologized to my shoulder. I glanced back at the chaos behind me and thankfully saw that crazy game of chase was still tied.

I flung my body into the shed doors, forcing myself to not flinch as to not dampen my blow. I was suddenly falling forward, with dust flying into my eyes with a sting. I blinked the sting away and stood. I was sorta satisfied with the results. There was an assortment of tools and chains. Up until I thought, *the fuck am I gonna do with that?* A dragon's breath round didn't do shit. Even when shot in the face.

I then recalled a couple seconds ago, when I'd gotten dust in my eyes. I looked around and to my delight and pride, I found a bucket of paint. When I picked it up, I found it to be a full gallon of dark brown paint. Unfortunately, it was sealed shut. I looked around the shed, looking for something that could be used to open the paint can. I scrambled on the counter filled with tools and tried to jam a flathead screwdriver into the can as I tried to pop it open, but it didn't work. I once again scrambled around the shed, looking for anything. I even abandoned my bucket of paint, trying to find something to use.

I eventually found an axe lying against the wall. I picked it up and was filled with dread when I found how heavy the thing was. Not at all like the movies.

"Shit," I muttered dropping the axe.

When I picked it up again, a small hatchet was revealed to be hiding behind it. It fell and clanked on the floor. I picked it up and went for the paint can. When I had my fingers firmly wrapped around the handle, it immediately fell out of my fingers, and I fell over, with the shed coming apart around me.

When I collected myself, I put together that the car crashed into the shed. I got a glance of the back left wheel before the engine revved and it sped off. Whatever was left of the standing shed fell on me as the car tore away from it.

The sudden brightness of the daylight caught me off-guard. And my body felt like hell while being covered in tools and half a shed.

For a moment, I believed that a lot of time passed. It was the ground shaking with each stomp Red Eyes took and the tires dragging on dirt that told me otherwise.

I flung as much of the debris from my body as I could. I stood and faced the battle between a giant and a fuckin' Honda Civic.

Red Eyes was getting impatient. It was practically throwing itself towards the car, and the vehicle managed to ram into Red Eyes, buckling his knees from behind. It fell hard, but as hard as it had fallen, it always scrambled back to its feet.

Sofía was getting ready to ram it again, but the creature was ready this time. As my tía sped towards the creature, the creature dove head-first towards it.

My tía was about to die. I wasn't gonna watch that happen. I turned my head away before I could see the collision.

My eyes landed on the paint bucket; it was underneath what was left of the shed roof but still visible. I winced at the noise of broken glass and crushed steel.

Don't think about it! I told myself.

I reached out and wrapped my fingers around the handle of the bucket. It remained stuck after my rage and frustration-filled attempts of yanking it towards me. I used my free hand to lift the roof when I saw I was still gripping the hatchet, my knuckles white as snow.

I dropped it and lifted the surprisingly light roof and wiggled the rest of the bucket to me. I scooped up the hatchet, grabbing the blade before the handle. But I didn't care, I just had to do something, anything.

I began sprinting towards the cloud of dust and dirt. To my relief, I could hear the car racing around.

It didn't take me long to see Red Eyes. He was far more aggressive, pouncing on all fours, desperate to obliterate his pray.

Sofía wasn't even able to attack anymore, she was only able to dodge Red Eyes. He was closing the distance each time he pounced for the car.

I wasn't gonna make it to them on time before he eventually caught them. But to my surprise, Sofía whipped the car, using the ass of the car to crash into the monster's left leg, tripping it to the ground. But it caught itself and pushed its body off the ground.

Thankfully Sofía managed to put the car in reverse and just sped off in one direction. I was relieved until the car smacked into the house, which was almost entirely engulfed with fire.

The creature wasted no time and bolted towards his prey. My cries and screams did nothing to pull him away from my family.

I was at this point using the small axe to open the can. The blade bounced off the metal with each attempt.

As I closed the distance to the creature, who was now looming over the car, I thought the worst. I believed they were about to die. Thankfully, my tía proved me wrong. She hit the gas and drove into the creature's legs, flipping him forward and smashing him into the house.

The car zoomed past me, and I made brief eye contact with my tía and spotted my cousin. They were both in there. Why Mateo was in the passenger seat, I didn't know; it seemed he was in there to die. But I knew deep down, I'd never let my mother die alone, either.

I fixed my attention back on Red Eyes, who had finally spotted me. Panic didn't set in until I realized the can still wasn't open. Without thinking of the consequences, I dropped the can on the floor and along with the thump it made, I swung down the hatchet as hard as I could. The can top half finally split open.

I would've smiled, but the creature had already made its attack on me. All I saw was the large black hand quickly moving on me; I had little time to react and dove out of the way while managing to grab the bucket and take it with me.

When I landed, a great deal of paint poured out of the can. I was so focused on that that I didn't notice the creature reach out and grab my left leg.

My face slammed against the ground, and I was dragged into the air, coming face to face with Red Eyes. He snarled at me, a mixture of rage and amusement emitting from his person.

All I could think to do was swing my hatchet around hopelessly. It brought me close to its face once again. I swung my hatchet. When it made contact with its face, the axe bounced off pathetically. But I swung still, I refused to die without fighting.

The battle cry of an engine pulled our eyes away from each other, and to the Honda speeding towards us.

All I could do was reach out as the monster stomped on the car, stopping it instantly. When it lifted its foot off the flattened hood, it merely kicked the car away like a small tin can.

I screamed in horror! The pain of seeing my cousin and aunt die destroyed me. Tears poured out of my eyes like a hose.

"NOOOOOO!!!" I cried, thrashing around.

The monster shook me and brought my eyes to his. The faintest sign of pupils locking with mine.

Only rage escaped my mouth. "FUCK YOU MOTHERFUCKER!!!"

A long, wicked smile formed along his face. It disturbed me when I saw that it never finished forming, it continued across his face as his mouth opened.

It was my turn to die.

CHAPTER 36

I could only scream and cry as he slowly brought me closer to his large mouth.

My only hope was to somehow complete the plan, get the paint in his eyes. As fast as I could, I tried to position my arm to somehow throw the paint in his eyes' direction. But it was useless, I knew it was useless. But I still attempted to jerk the bucket enough to shoot out a stream of paint.

Gravity forced it down before it could get anywhere near his eyes.

I felt his grip around my leg loosen ever so slightly and panic set in at the thought of entering this thing's mouth.

In a last moment of desperation, I threw the empty paint can down in the monster's open jaws. The can dropped past the teeth, past the tongue, and right into the center of the throat, where it suddenly came to a stop.

The monster's grip on my leg tightened, so tight I mentally prepared for my leg to break off, but as sudden as the grip tightened, I was released.

Time stopped as I unwillingly made my way towards the monster. All I could think to do to defend myself was to spring my arm, holding the axe out, at the monster. I expected to bounce off his face, but I didn't; my arm was somehow stuck on something.

I had no time to wonder how my hatchet could possibly pierce the skin of this thing when all else failed. I kicked out, getting away from the giant jaws. But holding onto the hatchet, I found myself quickly swinging right back towards its mouth. I once again kicked out my legs, positioning myself away from its lips.

I gathered as much strength in my legs as I could. I only had so much time to launch myself away. I twisted my upper body around to gauge just how hard of a fall I'd be taking. I was half-expecting to see two large black hands speeding towards me. To my surprise, I saw nothing but the fields.

I looked down to see Red Eyes had his hands around his neck.

That's when I noticed a bunch of abnormal sounding coughs and wheezes. My eyes and jaw both opened wide enough to rival the monsters. He was choking on the can.

I was so wrapped up in all the crazy shit happening, I barely noticed the body I was dangling from vibrate violently with every noise the thing made.

Speaking of dangling, I looked up to see the hatchet, expecting it to somehow be piercing the skin but to my shock, the blade had slid right between the eye and its socket.

"Holy shit…" I scoffed.

I pulled myself up and with all the power I could muster, I shoved my whole arm as far into the blood red eye as I could, screaming, "DIEEEE!!!"

The huge eye closed, sealing my arm in him. I knew what was coming next, so I positioned my feet and placed my knees as close to my chest as my body would allow. With one final burst of strength, I shot myself away and to my surprise, my arm slid out of its eye.

I collided with a couple giant fingers, dribbling through its hands, which thankfully somewhat broke my fall. I landed on my feet but still collapsed to the ground.

I bear-crawled away from that creature as fast as I possibly could before my legs assumed their rightful place and carried me away. I barely ran a couple feet before I fell to the ground.

The brief moment of stillness calmed me down enough to stand and turn to face my foe.

Red Eyes was practically digging into his eye socket where I left my ax. Before I knew it, a small stream of blood began to pour out of its eye.

I would've smiled at the fact that I managed to hurt the monster, no matter how small and insignificant the damage I caused may have been, but the smoking, smashed car where my family was wouldn't allow it.

I sprinted to them, but Red Eyes stumbled in my way, stopping me in my tracks. I had no way of fighting the creature; my only weapon was lodged deep in its face.

I looked up to the monster and to my shock, he was no longer rubbing his eye, he went back to holding his throat. I guessed my small attack was just that: small.

The monster still coughed and wheezed, failing at each attempt to suck in air. I found myself staring in awe as the creature began to look more and more panicked. It grew weak in the knees. It almost crushed me with its body as it fell to its knees, still trying to suck in breath with inhuman sounds. I flinched away, still in awe at its sudden weakness.

It began to roll around on the ground, its blood-red eyes somehow even more red. Tears began to swell in its eyes, blood seeping out of the heavily damaged one.

The creature, spotting me, flung a hand out to me, but I was ripped away by strong arms. It was Lenny. We both fell to the ground but soon enough resumed our stare when Red Eyes didn't make any further attempts on our lives. I guess choking left no attention to spare.

Lenny and I just sat there, looking at the creature thrash around and struggle, the sounds it made becoming less and less frequent.

"Holy shit," a voice said. "Is it... dying?"

I turned my head to see Carly equally as shocked as Lenny and I. Her parents formed in my peripheral vision, surely as shocked as me.

I turned back to the creature, which now lay on its back, gasping for air. If its skin wasn't shiny black, it would have looked blue. Its movements were now slow, only a loud silence emitted from it.

It must've been hours we sat there. I didn't think anyone noticed when it finally stopped moving and nothing more came from the creature.

My frozen body only broke free when I heard crying. I sprang to my feet and willed them to carry me to my cousin and tia.

Next to the vehicle sat Mateo. Tears were pouring out of his eyes, and he made the most horrid sound, crying.

In his lap was my tía's limp body. He held her tight, crying, "NO, NO, NO, PLEASE!!!"

I collapsed to Mateo's side and joined his cries. I held him and my tía, and pleaded with every fiber of my being for it not to be true.

Adam approached us with Carly and Lenny in his shadow. He knelt down and began to inspect my tía. He tried to move our arms, but we wouldn't budge. We held her tight and in our hysterical state, we could barely comprehend his presence and willingness to help.

Once again, it felt like hours went on. Through the sound of my cries, something broke through. A sound ever so faint softly brushed through my emotions. The familiarity of the sound allowed me to gain enough of myself to open my eyes. Through my tears, I could see my mom on her knees, her hands on her face. Soon, her quiet sobs were the only thing I could hear.

I released my tía and lunged for my mom. I wrapped my arms around her and held her tight. In that moment, I knew that only one thing mattered. And there was only one action I could take. I had to be strong for my mother. I buried my cries and emotions deep down within me.

I held my cries through choppy breaths, and whispered, "It's gonna be ok. Everything's gonna be ok."

I knew my words were little comfort, if any at all. All I could do was echo the words long told to me. Every time I needed my mother, she used those words, and it never failed to be true.

The dread and emptiness I felt at the thought of Sofía being gone made me question my words. But I had to stick to them. I needed my mother to know that she wasn't alone. Her only sister may have been gone. But she wasn't alone.

I repeated my words a few more times before I stood. It tore me apart to let go of my mom, but I had to see the monster. As much as I wanted to glance at my tía's body, I fought it. I knew one look would send me over the edge again. And I had to stay put together.

My mom was here, which meant her car was here. Which meant we were leaving.

I stepped away from the sound of cries and walked up to the elongated body. It was still and lifeless. It looked like it struggled the whole time. The way it lay there gave no sign of it giving up.

I felt something wrap around my arm and I jumped instinctively in fear. To my comfort, it was Carly. She didn't say anything, she just adjusted herself back around my arm and squeezed tight. I looked back at the monster, avoiding the scene where my mom and cousin were.

So much death, so much pain. Caused by this one abomination of nature.

I found myself thinking of all those I saw die at the hands of this thing. The police who came to our aid, Terry, and now Sofía, who constantly came to my rescue. I glanced at Lenny, who was now comforting Mateo. Lenny also saved my life many times. I could only hope to one day be as strong and as brave as him. Even having Carly there helped; her presence relieved a lot of the pain I currently felt.

Based off the monster's bulging eyes and twisted face, it died painfully. That fact alone made me feel the smallest hint of pity towards this thing. I felt a lot of things staring at the dead creature. But for the first time since I arrived here, I let out a large sigh of relief.

EPILOGUE

My eyes opened and I felt a smile form on my face. That smile turned into a grin when I stretched, letting out a long groan. I sat up letting the blanket fall from my body. I couldn't help but feel fucking great the mornings I woke up from the sleeps without nightmares. I began to take those nights without nightmares as good omens. A sign that the day would be a good one.

The smell of bacon and eggs invaded my nostrils, levitating me to the kitchen where my mom cooked breakfast. She spotted me, opening the fridge in search of orange juice. She said nothing as she opened a cabinet and took out three shiny, tall glasses.

"Did you brush your teeth?" she asked.

I looked at her and sarcastically smiled. "Good morning to you, too."

She gave me a look before saying, "Go brush."

"Please don't make me brush before I drink orange juice," I said, pouring the glasses.

She said nothing, only giving me a slight nod in agreement. She continued to prep the plates as I downed my first glass. When she turned back to me, she held out a plate for me. I noticed her eyes landed on something behind me.

I spun around, using the stool to face Mateo. His hair was messy and his eyes still heavy from his sleep.

"Good morning," Mom and I called to him.

He finished his yawn before returning the "Morning," with a smile.

I spun back to where my plate now steamed warmly in front of me. I wasted no time devouring my breakfast, drinking two more glasses of juice.

"So," my mom began, "what's the plan for today?"

Mateo swallowed a mouthful of scrambled eggs before answering, still with food in his mouth. "I'm visiting Mom."

My mom's face dropped, clearly filled with emotion. "Can I come?" she asked.

Mateo nodded enthusiastically, as if it were ridiculous for her to even have to ask. I felt like he would've said as much if he hadn't just shoved more food into his mouth.

My mom then faced me and asked, "How bout you?"

"I'm meeting up with Carly," I answered. "We have that appointment today."

She nodded as if reminded of the appointment. I'd mentioned it to her, but she didn't show much interest.

"Ok, well, be safe," Mom said. "And maybe come meet up with us when you're done."

"Of course," I said before drinking the last of my OJ.

My mom, spotting my empty plate, asked, "Do you want more?"

"Nah," I said quickly. "Thank you."

"Ok. Now go brush," Mom ordered.

While I was brushing my teeth, I felt my phone vibrating in my pocket. I pulled it out and it read, "I'm outside." A text from Carly.

She was never clear on when she'd show up to my house. I was very positive she did it on purpose, as the night before, we'd both agreed to meet at her apartment.

"Come on in," I texted back.

I spit out the white minty toothpaste and rushed the rest of getting ready. When I entered the living room, I found Carly and my mom talking. Or more like Carly talking. My mom sat on the sofa, reluctantly listening to Carly explain how much she hated living in the city.

When they noticed me, Carly sprang up and gave me a huge bear hug. I had to dodge her lips going for mine, as I wasn't quite ready for my mom to know I was dating this girl. Although the look she gave me as I glanced over Carly's shoulder made me question if my mom already knew of our relationship.

But she gave me no look of disapproval, only that of teasing.

After a hug and kiss goodbye, Carly and I found ourselves only a block away from our destination after about a forty-five-minute walk.

"Holy shit!" she said loudly. "I hate that I have to walk everywhere in the city! Now I know how the horses felt."

"Yeah, well, we're out of cars," I explained. "And I offered to take an Uber."

"You paid for dinner last week, I can't have you spend all your money on me."

"Don't think about it like that. I'm just trying to be a gentleman. And it's not like I'd prefer walking around in this summer heat."

Carly wasn't paying attention and almost bumped into an older couple walking opposite us. "Sorry!" she called to them before turning back to me and continuing. She looked down and emotionally stated, "I just feel bad."

I took her hand. "Don't," I comforted.

"As soon as I get a job," she said, springing back up, "I'll take YOU on a couple dates!"

I gave her hand a tight squeeze and said, "Don't worry about it."

Before long, we arrived at our destination. It was a church. Based on the architecture, it was a very old church. I looked at the sign which read, "Saint Anthony Church."

We entered, going through the huge doors. The outside of the church did nothing to show just how big this place was. There must've been hundreds of seats. There were a couple families sitting in those seats but for the most part, the place was empty.

"Wow!" Carly exclaimed before shutting her mouth and covering it with her hands. Her voice echoed through the giant room, causing the few people in there to turn and look. She shyly waved, turning red.

"Sorrryyyyyy," she apologized.

I would've laughed but something caught my eye. It was a door with a sign above it which read, "Office."

I took Carly's hand and led us both to the doors. I entered, and to my surprise it led to what seemed to be a whole other building. I woulda thought it was another building if it weren't for the same old architecture. There was a receptionist desk and hallways which led to what I assumed to be other parts of the church.

At the desk sat a young girl, typing away on a computer. At the sound of us entering, she looked up and smiled. "Can I help you?" she asked.

"Uh, yeah. We have an appointment."

She raised an eyebrow before asking excitedly, "Miguel? Miguel Esparza?"

She didn't check the computer, or any paper or clipboard on her desk.

"That's me," I answered.

"Ok, great. Can you give me a minute?" she asked.

I didn't have time to answer. She rushed away down the hallway and poked her head into a room. I heard her speaking to someone for a minute. She backed away from the door and someone followed her out.

The man who appeared was rather short. And old, very, very, old. However, the way he walked with such ease and grace made it hard to determine if he was actually as old as his face and hands made him look. He studied me and Carly from his room and after a second of awkward staring, at least from our side, he waved us over.

We walked over to the door and the old man met us inside. He held out a hand with a smile and I shook it. Once again, the firm handshake made me question if this guy was as old as he looked.

He shook Carly's hand and walked back to his desk. There were two chairs positioned to face the desk and the old man who sat there. It was like entering a principal's office. The door closed behind us, which prompted Carly and me to take our seats. I took a moment to study the office. There were a large number of religious statues and items. After some time, I also noticed items of football culture. Photos of Little League teams, and trophies accompanied the shelves.

"Hello," greeted the old man. His voice was raspy and he had a thick Spanish accent.

"Hi," I greeted.

"Hey," Carly followed.

"I'm Father Philippe," he said.

"My name is Miguel," I said. I found myself turning red as it dawned on me that he already knew, given the receptionist already did.

"Miguel, it's a pleasure to meet you," he smiled.

Suddenly he disappeared beneath his desk. From there he asked, "You two thirsty?" The both of us said yes, and he poked his head back up. "Is Coke ok?" he asked. We both nodded. He scrunched his face. "Is Diet Coke ok?"

We nodded our heads again. He smiled and brought out three cans of Diet Coke, holding two in each hand, using them to hold one in the middle. He placed the three cans on the desk and handed us a can each. Carly wasted no time popping hers open and taking a sip.

The Father did the same, taking a long sip before placing it on the desk and letting out a long, "Aaaahhhh…"

The can was cold and slippery. He had a fridge behind that desk. I opened mine and let the crispy drink bring delight to my tastebuds.

"So," Father Philippe started, "I assume there's something you two wanted to tell me. Or maybe you guys have questions."

"Both," I said. "But I don't know where to start."

Father Philippe leaned back in his chair and brushed his thick white beard. I sighed and figured that I should just come out with it.

"We encountered something supernatural," I explained. Father Philippe had no reaction. He just sat there and looked at me, taking sips of his coke.

After a long moment of no one saying anything, Philippe finally asked, "Like what? A ghost?"

"No," I said. "It wasn't a ghost, it was like a person?"

"A person?"

"I don't know how to explain it. It's hard to put into words."

The Father leaned forward in his chair and placed his Coke on the desk. He cleared his throat before he spoke. "Well, you say you had a supernatural encounter, but then you say it was a person? Are you trying to tell me there's some kind of possession?"

"No, it wasn't anything like that," I explained nervously. I could tell this man didn't believe me.

"Well, can you describe whatever it was you saw?" he asked.

I got goosebumps just thinking about the features and characteristics of the monster.

"It was tall and skinny," I described, "It was very tall, and very skinny," I repeated.

"Like Slender Man?" Philippe asked with a smirk.

"No!" I said loudly. "It was all bla—"

"Do you have a picture?" he asked, interrupting me.

"N-no," I stuttered.

"Really?" he said, frowning. "You kids, who are always tied to your phones, did not think to pull them out and take a picture of this very tall and very skinny person?"

"It turned our phones off," I said defensively.

Well, that wiped the smirk off his mouth. His eyes narrowed, and he sat still for a moment. He took the Coke back into his hands and took a few more sips. "Can you further describe this creature?" he asked.

His choice of words gave me hope. He said *creature*.

"It's skin was black, not like a person, it was literally the color black," I explained.

Philippe leaned forward, listening intently.

"It didn't have normal facial features. Its face was like a balloon, and its eyes, nose and mouth were—" I paused. "Its eyes glowed red. Like literally glowing, like lights."

The priest held his hand up, stopping me. He looked lost in thought. "Where did you guys find this creature?" he asked.

"I was visiting family, about a nine-hour drive," I told him.

He nodded. "Ok. Where?"

"They lived outside of town, in a rural area," I explained.

"Far from society?" he asked.

It was an overstatement, but not totally inaccurate. So I agreed.

"They lived on a farm. We were surrounded by cornfields, which it used to hide from us."

"It hid?" he asked.

"Yeah, until it didn't."

"Explain."

"When I first arrived, I couldn't help but feel like I was being watched. I brushed it off as I hadn't been there in so long, you know, I was somewhere I hadn't been in a while. I was uncomfortable. But at some point, it had killed one of our horses. When we found the body, it chased us." My body had a physical reaction just reliving the events of that night. "We hid in a house and called the cops. When he arrived, the monster was gone." I choked, mentioning Terry. But I pushed it down.

"Was that it?" the priest asked.

"No," Carly answered, her first time speaking in a while. Which surprised me. "It would continue to pop out randomly throughout the remaining time we spent there. It was violent each time."

"It tried to hurt you all?" he asked.

"It tried to kill us," Carly stated.

Father Philipe nodded taking in her words.

"What happened to the giant?" He asked.

"I killed it." I said coldly.

"And the body?"

I recalled to when the authorities finally arrived.

"Some people showed up alongside with the police." I explained. "They loaded it into a big ass truck and drove away." I paused for a moment before asking, "Was that you guys?"

The priest nodded and said nothing more.

He sat there for a moment. "How long had it been since you'd visited your family?" he asked.

I was shocked that he was able to guess that I had not seen my family or been to the farm in a long time. "It had been many years since I'd been there," I explained.

Father Philippe nodded thoughtfully. "I remember reading an article about you guys," said the priest. "The story is, there was a shooting."

"That's what we told them," Carly explained. "We told them a group of people tried to kill us."

"Why?" he asked. "Why not tell them the truth?"

"Because they wouldn't have believed us," Carly answered.

"And you think I will?" he asked.

"You do, though," I said. "Don't you?"

He faced me and slowly nodded, giving me a much-needed smile.

"What was that thing?" I asked.

Father Philippe leaned back in his chair and a loud leather fart noise filled the room. "Have you ever read the Bible?" he asked us.

I guiltily shook my head. Carly didn't answer.

He gave us a reassuring smile once again. "It's ok," he said, waving his hand. "But do read it soon, yes?"

I nodded.

"When the devils fell from the sky, some of them, well, some of them made love to humans. And what was born from those relations were giants. Those giants are known as the Nephilim." The Father took his Coke and took a few more sips before continuing. "These Nephilim were beings of unusual size and strength. They were all over the place, so was sin, and so was evil. So, the Lord flooded the Earth and wiped all sin and evil from the world. The Lord also wiped out the Nephilim."

"And the one that just so happened to survive the great flood just so happened to be in our cornfields." I scoffed.

"One of a few recorded in history," Philippe said.

His words filled me with so much dread, I would've cried if it weren't for Carly sitting next to me.

"There's more?" I asked dreadfully.

"Perhaps," he said. "For a time, we believed them to all be gone. The last we've known of them was encountered in a cave by a couple of soldiers somewhere in Afghanistan. We were sure we'd seen the last of the Nephilim." He looked at me. "We were wrong."

"Do you think there's more out there?" I asked again nervously.

"No," he answered nonchalantly. "The Church is a very powerful thing. People don't know just how powerful we are. So trust me when I tell you, there's no more of them out there. We are sure of it." He paused for a moment before saying, "We were wrong. But right enough that I can confidently tell you that what you have encountered is the last one. Although what happens now is not up to me, so I can't tell you. First, the Church will do everything in its power to prove you wrong."

"I thought you said you believed me," I said.

"I do," he said. "What you described is just too close to what is known of them. I can't help but believe you. Although I can't speak for the Church. We have to have irrefutable evidence of something in order for us to take action."

What he was saying angered me. Was the body not enough?

"What actions would you guys take?" Carly asked.

Father Phelippe looked at her and he frowned. "I don't know. But we'd do something." He looked down in thought, before looking back at us. "Everything you have told me fits perfectly into the possibility of it being a Nephilim. The creature must have been in those fields for years. But when you arrived after years, it must've shown itself due to the sudden change of the usual environment. Those creatures don't like change. It just makes sense."

"Ok, so what happens now?" I asked.

"Now," he began, "now I send word to my superiors. We'll go from there." He looked at us thoughtfully as if he was looking at old friends. "Listen. You look like good kids. And if it's the truth, then I'm sorry for what you all went through. I'll pray for you and ask others to pray for you. I'm sure others will want to speak with you, but until then, get reading your Bibles. Ok?"

"Ok," I said, frustrated. "Why the hell did God let this thing terrorize us? If the giant was some kind of demon, why didn't God help us?"

Father Philippe smiled and answered, "Did you ask for help?"

I opened my mouth, but nothing came out. I wasn't a very religious person. It never occurred to me. Even though I had nothing to say, I was still conflicted on his words.

"I'm sorry you feel the way you do," Father said. "I believe you will heal. And I believe you will find peace with the Lord."

I had nothing to say. I had many mixed emotions on his words. He asked a few more questions. But soon the meeting wrapped up.

We were walked out by Father Philippe, who gave us a few more encouraging words about getting to know God. He asked us to stay for the morning mass, but I declined. I explained that I wanted to go visit my tía, and that my mom and cousin were expecting me.

He understood and left us to it. When the doors closed behind Father Philippe, we didn't take five steps before I turned to Carly and said, "I'm not walking. I'm calling an Uber."

We sat in the back seat of this stranger's car in a rare moment of silence between us.

"Do you believe him?" she asked.

When I didn't answer she nudged me.

"I don't know." I sighed.

More silence followed. After some time, I felt her hand take mine.

"I'm not a believer," she said. "I never have been. But I remember going back and being held hostage in a place I never thought

I'd feel unsafe by something I never could've imagined. I remember thinking to myself how insane of a situation I was in. I don't know what you would call it, but I did call out to God. I asked Him, if He was real, to please do something, anything that could help us. Less than a minute later, you showed up."

I opened my mouth to speak but she stopped me with a hand to my mouth.

"You didn't ask for help," she said. "I did. And you were the answer to my prayer." She paused for a moment, gathering her thoughts and choosing her words. "I mean, if begging God for help in my head counts as a prayer, then I guess I was praying."

Carly let a moment of silence pass, she stared into my eyes smiling peacefully. "You being there saved my family and me." She said softly. She then sat back in her seat and sighed. "I believe him."

I said nothing. I didn't know what to say. Maybe, just maybe, there was truth to what Father Philippe was saying.

"I'm gonna visit Sofía," I said. "You wanna come?"

She looked at me and asked, "How is she?"

"I don't know," I answered, "the doctors haven't said anything."

"How's Mateo?" she asked.

"He's doing better. He visits the hospital every day. He's starting to act like himself again, he seems less worried."

"I can't imagine how hard it must be," Carly said. "Not knowing whether she'll be ok or not must be agony to Mateo."

"Yeah," I agreed.

She thought for a while before explaining that she'd rather go home and be with her family. When we arrived at her place, she invited me inside. I declined, wanting to get going to the hospital.

We exchanged a kiss and went our separate ways.

I walked for a few blocks, my thoughts heavy with the words of Father Philippe. And the words Carly had shared.

I decided to take another Uber to the hospital. I pulled out my phone and made the order. I'd have to wait a few minutes before they got here.

I took a seat on a bench and let out a large sigh. My phone buzzed in my hand. Upon checking it, I saw it was a missed call from Mateo. I also noticed a couple missed calls from my mom.

Before I could call either of them back, my phone buzzed with a text message popping up. The text message from Mateo read: "My mom's awake!"

www.ingramcontent.com/pod-product-compliance
Lightning Source LLC
Chambersburg PA
CBHW020134120726
47903CB00007B/2243